The Manuscript

Steven L. Wright

First published in 2025 by Blossom Spring Publishing
The Manuscript © 2025 Steven L Wright
ISBN 978-1-0684329-8-9
E: admin@blossomspringpublishing.com
W: www.blossomspringpublishing.com

Only by accepting the absurdity of life will we live completely.

Jacques de Cassis, 1523

For
Suzanne Lister Wright . . .
whose life rhythm has always been syncopated.

INTRODUCTION

"The phone, darling."

"*Whaaat?* What is it?"

"Phone's ringing. The phone."

"Okay ... okay, I'll get it. I'll get it. Please tell me why the hell we installed a landline?"

"You know the reason. Should be wondering why we're still in bed."

"You know *that* answer, Fiona. You didn't arrive home until early morning."

The unexpected phone call Peter Berners and Fiona Talbot received that mid-December morning was from Robert Atchison, proprietor of Atchison Rare & Vintage Books in Harrogate. Asked if they could see their way through to visit the shop soon. He had acquired a unique manuscript and thought they'd be interested. It concerned the period between the wars, roughly 1918–1940. An era that had fascinated Peter since secondary school. Government COVID restrictions, and the married couple's self-imposed isolation, had curtailed non-essential shopping for over nine months. Today they'd make an exception. They agreed to meet at noon.

Peter and Fiona had met at university and married a few years after graduating. The challenging trifecta of the 2007 banking collapse, followed by the lengthy economic crisis, Brexit and COVID had hindered both their academic and professional aspirations and dampened their marriage. That indescribable aura of innocent excitement surrounding newlyweds seemed absent. Although Peter hadn't lost his naiveté fault lines had begun to appear. He understood the inevitability of disappointment, of disillusionment, of breakage. But not today, not yet. Fiona, on the other hand, had been a habitual realist since adolescence. Pragmatism had served her well throughout her young life. She weighed the pros and cons, evaluated potential outcomes, and acted. She accepted how life was, not how it should be. Fiona's strong sense of self-possession enabled her to change her opinion, her circumstance and her surroundings with relative ease. She wouldn't be preoccupied or hemmed in by commitment or expectation. Once Fiona desired something—or somebody—she remained hell-bent. To family, friends and acquaintances alike, Peter and Fiona exemplified, better than most, the old adage, 'opposites attract'. They were made for each other.

Robert Atchison was an affable fellow. Soft-spoken, intelligent, with a hint of self-deprecation (used to conceal an otherwise privileged upbringing and a first-class education). Peter had been a customer for numerous years. While he rarely forked out the big money to purchase first editions, he'd occasionally indulge in purchasing affordable works of favourite authors. Robert wasn't bothered. He enjoyed the hunt for the elusive edition, relishing the look on the customer's face after acquiring a much-sought-after literary work.

Fiona and Peter arrived promptly at noon. After the customary small talk and the offer of coffee, Robert pulled a thick leather portfolio from the lower drawer of an antique mahogany desk. He handed it first to Fiona. She accepted the yellowed, unbound sheets and read the title aloud: "*The Universal Language Isn't Love or Music but Loneliness,* by William Travers, London, September 1940."

Fiona adjusted her rimless spectacles while simultaneously securing a dangly bit of her bobbed black hair behind her left ear. Thumbing through the manuscript, she paused on occasion, repeating aloud whatever had caught her attention: *Layers of life are occurring all the time only sometimes we know it. Most of the time we don't know it ... Imitation is the highest form of failure ... Women too old to be young, too young to be old ... Life is nothing but vanity ... I realise I'm not the first owner of your heart.*

Minutes passed before she handed it to Peter.

"Where did you ever find such an interesting document?"

"To be honest, it's from the Bolton-Leigh estate sale in Knaresborough I attended a few days ago. Neither I nor the auctioneer know anything about William Travers or how it ended up with the Bolton-Leigh family. Because it's a mystery, and Travers is unknown, it only cost £95.00. Could have acquired it a bit cheaper, I think—but the young lady who secretly works for the auctioneer kept bidding me up."

Peter, an intelligent, gregarious, and somewhat impulsive person who loved history, caressed the leather portfolio and opened it to the first page. He read a few sentences aloud:

Shouldn't have happened. On the morning of 11 November 1918, the commander of the 95th Aero Squadron—the Kicking Mule—asked for a volunteer. He wanted to ensure the enemy complied with the Armistice scheduled for 11:00, which was in about two hours. Had learned early in my army career never to volunteer for anything; however, today I scrapped that knowledge and replaced it with ego. Had to repay a debt. No combat. Just an easy, flight-school-like take-off in my Nieuport 28—The Queen City—from Rembercourt Aerodrome. I'd skirt the horizon toward Metz, south to Nancy, with a return flight over Verdun and Bar-le-Duc. After receiving clearance, I took off and climbed to 800 feet, remaining below an ever-descending ceiling. As I banked right toward Nancy, I received gunfire.

"That's incredibly bad luck. Poor fellow. Should have followed his instinct and not volunteered."

Fiona agreed. "It was so unnecessary. I wonder if he was wounded?"

"Well, I think the whole war was an unmitigated disaster. Should have been avoided."

Peter and Fiona didn't nibble Robert's bait. Discussions of that magnitude should occur in the late evening, energised by grain and grape. Peter thumbed through additional pages, trying to avoid the topic.

"The guy was connected somehow to the jazz scene in Paris. Listen to this."

At 10:15 we took the break we had negotiated earlier with Monsieur Lipp. The boys in the band got along together fine. We respected each other. We admired our collective musicianship. But when we drank, we wanted to drink alone, away from familiar faces.

"If that wasn't exciting enough, here's some more."

As she approached the empty chair beside me, I could see she displayed all the attributes of the current craze: flat chest, knee-length dress, bobbed hair, jewelled headband, a dangly pearl necklace, and kewpie-doll lips. After getting comfortable, she smiled and placed her left hand gently on my knee and started moving it toward my waist.

'You won't find what you want ... at least not now, Mam'selle. Monsieur Lipp doesn't take kindly to us jazzmen talking to customers, especially unattached

females. If he becomes privy, he'll throw me out onto Boulevard Saint-Germain followed by my saxophone, sans the case. Costs money, Doll'.

Fiona and Peter couldn't believe their luck.

"This is real, Robert. Not fiction."

Atchison beamed with pride. "Thought you'd appreciate it."

Eager to see how the manuscript ended, Peter sat on the leather sofa next to Fiona and jumped ahead to the epilogue. It totalled about five pages, so he handed them to his wife and asked if she'd begin reading. As Fiona read a page she passed it to him. She finished in about three minutes. Peter followed a minute or two later. As he shuffled the final page into its proper place and removed his steel-rimmed reading glasses, he looked at Fiona, who was trying to gauge his reaction.

"Can I tell you something for nothing? *That* was intense."

"My thoughts exactly."

They agreed to purchase it. Robert seemed happy, indulging in a bit of self-congratulations for understanding the passions of loyal customers. Out of some bizarre code of shared ethics, Fiona and Peter didn't negotiate. They wanted to give William Travers his due. To argue for a lower price would disrespect what they presumed to be Travers's nascent writing efforts. A philosophy Robert respected and from which he benefited. As a token of appreciation, Robert presented them with the first British printing of Hemingway's *Across the River and into The Trees* (1950).

"From what you read aloud I'm sure Mr Travers would appreciate being in the Papa's company. Maybe not the same pew, but certainly the same church."

"Thank you, Robert."

"What a lovely, thoughtful gift. Thank you."

The couple made their way through Harrogate to their sparsely furnished third-floor studio overlooking Valley Gardens, the town's manicured park. Peter, who prided himself on cocktail making, prepared two dry martinis as Fiona fluffed the sofa cushions, cleared the side table of newspapers, and removed the morning's coffee cups and cafetière. Both approached the coming afternoon with anticipation and agreed to the procedure established at Atchison's. They wouldn't answer mobiles, review emails, or do anything distracting until both had finished reading.

"Perhaps Travers's experience will offer ideas on making our lives …"

"Making our lives what?"

"Nothing. Nothing … doesn't matter. Not now, anyway. Perhaps when we're finished. Let's get reading."

'*The Universal Language Isn't Love or Music but Loneliness*'

By

William Travers

London, September 1940

PARIS

Chapter One

Shouldn't have happened. On the morning of 11 November 1918, the commander of the 95th Aero Squadron—the Kicking Mule—asked for a volunteer. He wanted to ensure the enemy complied with the Armistice scheduled for 11:00, which was in about two hours. Learned early in my army career never to volunteer for anything; however, today I scrapped that knowledge and replaced it with ego. Had to repay a debt. No combat. Just an easy, flight-school-like take off in my Nieuport 28— *The Queen City*—from Rembercourt Aerodrome. I'd skirt the horizon toward Metz, south to Nancy with a return flight over Verdun and Bar-le-Duc. After receiving clearance, I took off and climbed to 800 feet, remaining below an ever-descending ceiling. As I banked right toward Nancy, I received gunfire. I increased the throttle and made a gut-wrenching sharp turn when the fabric began separating from the left wing. Then the fuel line spurted petrol which, I knew, would lead inevitably to fire. I descended behind our lines. Saw a clearing on the left. Reduced power, stabilised the airframe the best I could and got it in trim. The aircraft began breaking apart as I touched ground. Felt a sudden surge of pain in my left ankle and upper leg. And that was it. Woke four days later in the main ward of the American Red Cross Military Hospital No-1 in Neuilly-sur-Seine located west of Paris.

The church-like tranquillity and smell of camphor and iodine couldn't deceive my senses. The ward resembled an oversized barracks housing the lame, the wounded and the disillusioned. The nurse checked my pulse.

"Is it over?"

"Armistice signed four days ago, Lieutenant. Even if it wasn't, your war's over."

"Bad?"

"Left ankle broken in two places. Dislocated patella and a broken femur. Your leg isn't suspended by a pulley for aesthetics, Lieutenant. It will be a lengthy recovery, but you'll survive. It's just, well, the left will be shorter than the right."

"So, running hurdles like I used to is out?"

"I'd say so. Your actions earned you the Distinguished Service Cross and the *Croix de Guerre*. An American general and a representative of the French government pinned them to the pillow days ago while you were sedated. Quite the honour, Lieutenant."

She handed me the medals that lay atop the nightstand. Their weightiness and newness betrayed how I looked and felt.

"Okay, enough gazing into the horizon, Lieutenant. Now get some rest. Please?"

She administered a dose of morphine, hoping I'd settle. It worked physically but not mentally. My mind remained at full throttle. I asked myself the same question repeatedly: Why had I volunteered? Why had I volunteered? Why had I volunteered? As I felt the ice-cold liquid travel through my arm and into my chest, it came to me. Guilt.

On 14 July 1918, I was one of several pilots assigned to conduct a major aerial engagement to open the curtain on the Second Battle of the Marne. During pre-flight I discovered *The Queen City* had a ruptured fuel line. Time was tight. None was left for a lengthy repair. So, Quentin

Roosevelt, the former president's son, volunteered in my place. During the mission that afternoon, after having taken out several enemy aircraft, he was shot down over the village of Chamery. I'll never know if it would have been me had *The Queen City* been operational. So, I guess, on 11 November at 09:00 hours, I needed to square it with my conscience. The fact that I was shot down made me think I would have met the same fate as Quentin that July day. The only difference between July and November—besides being separated by four months—was that I lived. I may never know the reason, but, if I find out, it had better be good.

Two additional surgeries caused me to lose another half-inch on my left leg. Seven months of rehabilitation seemed adequate enough for the doctors to send me on my way. My discharge date, effective 4 June 1919, had passed weeks earlier, so I visited the US Army out-processing annex located at the Elysee Palace Hotel on the corner of Rue de Bassono and the Champs Elysee. Thought it better be official. Didn't want Uncle Sam pursuing me for unauthorised procurement of government property. Received a belated promotion to captain along with my discharge papers. Seemed as if America, while in the throes of a victory celebration with the pending signing of the Versailles Treaty, had spread its benevolence and patriotic pity upon the wounded and permanently scarred. I didn't need it. I had life. That seemed enough.

I grabbed my kit bag and saxophone and walked from the hotel out onto Rue de Bassano. I had brought the instrument to France as a form of escape. Played on the edge of my bunk in the barracks. Entertained others in the officers' mess occasionally. It relaxed my fellow pilots' uneasiness about an approaching mission or one just completed.

Prior to leaving the hospital, I had asked my ward nurse—the sister to a million men—where I could obtain a cheap but clean bed and inexpensive but excellent meals.

"Enjoying a bit of Paris before returning home?"

"No, think I'll remain. After loafing a bit, might try something practical."

"But what about your parents, your sweetheart, don't you want to see them? Don't you want to return to the States? What could you possibly do in France?"

"Parents died in September. The influenza hit Cincinnati hard in early autumn. My sweetheart didn't think me sweet enough prior to joining the army and ended it. So, I've got no one and no reason to return. I'll play my sax on the street. You know, for tips. After I've grabbed enough of that grape, I may teach English in a French secondary school. Earned my degree in English Composition and Literature before joining the army. That's what I'm qualified for in the States, anyway. Perhaps France will take pity on a former pilot."

"You've thought it out, it seems."

"Had some downtime, you know. I'm going to embark on my own war now—the war to make the world safe for William Travers. I hope to be a busy, interesting man for several years. Knock 'em all for a loop. Now, about the restaurants and place to bunk?"

"Yes, sorry. You remaining in Paris took me aback. Let's see … well, my nurse friends and I thoroughly enjoyed a restaurant that opened only about four months ago, Lescure. It's on Rue de Mondovi—a small street off the Place-de-la-Concorde. It's small and intimate. A genuine French kitchen. Portions are ample. Saw the American ambassador dining there alone three times! And, let me think … the cheapest and, to my taste, the most dynamic and diverse places are on the Left Bank—Montparnasse and the Latin Quarter. You'll find everything there. Le Pré aux Clercs on Rue Bonaparte, off Rue Jacob, has wonderful food. Brasserie Lipp on Saint-Germain serves traditional French food, surrounded by a fabulous décor. Sorry to say, I don't know anywhere to stay. The girls and I always returned to the hospital after an evening out. Just boring, I guess."

"Never boring. Just too embarrassed to tell. That's fine. Thanks for the food tips. It's the Left Bank for me. *Au revoir and merci, Mam'selle.*"

"*Oh, là, là,* Lieutenant. *Bonne chance!*"

The leg played up so I got a cab. In my worst French possible, I asked the driver to drop me at or near the cheapest hotel he knew. Weeks later I learned how literally he had taken the request. On second thought, it could have been my horrible pronunciation. He deposited me outside Lapin hors du Chapeau—Rabbit Out of the Hat—located in the crevice of a back alley somewhere off Rue Saint-Sulpice.

I secured a room for a period of three weeks after an agonising negotiation: ten francs a week including *petit dejeuner*. The room was adequate. It fitted my needs: sink, stand-alone closet, small writing desk and chair, and a wrought iron-framed bed. The thin mattress had seen action. Passed its usefulness decades earlier. As I stretched out, my body plummeted toward the floor, while my head and feet remained elevated. The springs were shot. If I rolled over onto my stomach, I wouldn't be able to breathe. Still, it beat an open bay hospital bed.

I could regain some much sought-after privacy.

Unpacked my kit bag, carefully refolding the few civilian clothes I owned. Stripped my military tunic of any insignia and hung it in the closet alongside the silk aviator's scarf. At the bottom of the kit bag was a small wooden box, the 'last man' libation. A vintage bottle of what me and the boys called Scottish wine. Soon after earning our wings, we signed on to a rather macabre tradition: as each one of us was killed the bottle passed to the next in line—based on date of birth, from oldest to youngest. Obligated the last one alive to open the bottle and drink to the memory of the other four, whether the war was over or not.

My room was on a secluded corner so it got dark earlier in the afternoon than in the other rooms. A perfect ambience for remembering. I lit a candle, retrieved a glass and opened the whisky bottle—that golden elixir unique to those north of Hadrian's Wall. I poured half a glass and toasted Brian Waterstone. The Oregonian possessed such a maniacal laugh it earned him the nickname 'Wing Nut'. *Okay, laddie bucks,* he used to say, prior to lowering himself into the cockpit, *Let's go have some fun, shall we?* Whereupon he'd release his trademark laugh for all to hear. I raised the next glass to Robert Reed of Rhode Island. His innate self-confidence enabled him to never pre-flight an aircraft. Known as 'Dr Confidence', he cautioned that *Only God and the Germans decide who lives and who dies.* Of course, Antonio Cavilleri, known as 'Troubadour', whose poetry recitations from the Renaissance, physical swagger, and success with the ladies—from Parisian *femme fatales* to country milk-maidens—made us envious. He was a damn good pilot to boot! I thought it proper to pour a double to the memory of my friend from New York's East Harlem. Last, but not least, I toasted John Fitzgerald Termain of Nebraska. All of eighteen, he was known as 'The Kid'. On top of being full of piss and vinegar, he was innocently naïve but devilishly cocky. Had an innate ability to fly by the seat of his pants. Had he lived 'The Kid' would have been somebody. I selfishly raised a glass to myself with what remained. My idealism for the cause—to make the world safe for democracy—had earned me the name 'Woodrow' after the US president.

"I shouldn't be here, fellas. I didn't earn this. And it's not because I was a better pilot. All of you bested me. It was simple attrition. As 'Dr Confidence' always espoused, *Only God and the Germans decide who lives and who dies.* This time he was right. The Germans decided your fates, and God decided mine. I shall never forget."

I remained seated beside the table for hours, savouring each golden sip … and remembering. One thing about dying, I reflected, is the good people do it. Never known a shit that died. If I live long enough, maybe it'll happen.

Hours later, I awoke to a rhythmic banging against the wall where my bed was situated. Although bothersome, it lasted only a few minutes. I heard a bit of soft chatter afterwards—and then quiet. I returned to sleep. Walking down the hall toward the bathroom the next morning, I saw a middle-aged Frenchman leaving the room next door. We exchanged perfunctory greetings. The next night I experienced something similar: synchronised banging, soft chatter and then quiet. I started developing a theory but needed confirmation. The following morning, I heard the door of the neighbouring room open so I sprang from bed, wrapped a towel around me, and opened the door as if to go down the hall. Sure enough, a middle-aged Frenchman was leaving, attentively adjusting his necktie. After he walked down the stairs, I stood outside the room door to see what I could hear. There was a soft scurrying about but little else, except for the intense smell of women's perfume. My theory was taking shape, coming into its own. The exact scenario repeated itself the following three nights.

While paying the weekly rent a few days later, I casually asked the owner about my next-door neighbour. His face grew red as he cast his eyes toward the floor.

"I am sorry, my *États-Unis* friend, but ... but ... How do you say it ... ah, broth-*el*. *Oui, oui* ... brothel."

"I have rented a room in a brothel?"

"No, no, *Monsieur*. Not a brothel now. Used to be for many, many years. Thus, name for hotel: Lapin hors du Chapeau. I am pulling a rabbit from a hat. Making a surprise. Something new from something old. Florence is well, Florence is my *bon amie*. I told her she could stay longer than the others. Not too much longer, my *États-Unis* friend. Not long now. A little more. Perhaps you want to visit Florence? I arrange?"

"No, no, M*onsieur*. *Merci beaucoup*. I am fine. Perhaps after I'm healed and repaired."

With a week remaining on my lease, I took a risk and asked if he knew of an affordable apartment nearby. He took a sip of espresso, thought a moment and wrote on a piece of paper.

"My friend, *Madame* Rohrbeck, owns a building at 74 Rue du Cardinal Lemoine, fifth arrondissement—the Latin Quarter—near Panthéon and Jardin du Luxembourg. We talked a day or two ago, and she told me a room was available I call for you, my *États-Unis* friend?"

"Well … *Monsieur* is she … is she … does she rent apartments longer than one night?"

He belted out a hearty laugh.

"Oh, *Monsieur*, no, no. No brothel. Real apartments. *La liberté de conscience* is guaranteed."

"Then *oui*, please call and ask if we could meet late this morning."

I waited in the entrance lobby to prevent the impression of eavesdropping. He returned shortly. It was all arranged. I would meet *Madame* Rohrbeck at noon.

A detailed street map made finding 74 Rue du Cardinal Lemoine easy. I arrived early despite it taking twenty minutes. The area wasn't as posh and refined as Montparnasse but it exhibited what I imagined to be: a certain Gallic authenticity. *Madame* Rohrbeck arrived promptly at noon. She was an older woman, slightly frail and a bit hunched. Grey hair tied in a bun. Pince-nez glasses balanced on the end of her classically French-shaped nose. Her perfume reminded me of something my grandmother had enjoyed years earlier. Her flowery summer dress revealed she may also have cut a figure in her younger days—probably around the time Germany first invaded France.

After walking up a dark and narrow stairway, she showed me the fourth-floor apartment. A gilded mahogany bed occupied a large portion of the living-room-bedroom. A decrepit oak table with two chairs sat alongside the only window. Against the far wall was a medieval-like kitchen. On the opposite far wall was a dark mahogany mantelpiece. On its left stood a beautifully crafted armoire.

Before agreeing to a year's lease, I asked if I'd be

permitted to practise my saxophone in the morning, before noon. Would it be too disturbing? Would other tenants object?

"*Pas de soucis*. You play all day and into night. The building next to mine—the low, angular one, below—is our *Bal-musette*, a dance hall, with music and dancing and drinking and young women. Maybe if good enough, you play there over time. Maybe find a woman. Maybe need a woman, no?"

"Well, yes. Gives me a goal. Something to shoot for. *Merci beaucoup, Madame* Rohrbeck."

I gave her my first month's rent along with a security deposit. She said I could move in the end of next week, which seemed perfect. The last day of my contract at Lapin hors du Chapeau.

France held its Victory Celebration a few days before I moved, merging its annual 14 July Bastille Day with celebrations marking the end of the Great War. I arrived early, staking out a prime location on the Champs-Elysees near the Arc de Triomphe. I brought a baguette, a chunk of cheese and concealed a bottle of red wine in my sports coat. The noise increased as the crowd thickened. There was minimal pushing and shoving. No one misbehaved. Respect and decorum reigned. The parade started promptly at eight o'clock, with the solemn recognition of the maimed: the legless, the armless, those manoeuvring on crutches, and the blind, clutching the arm of a fellow soldier. An all-consuming hush gave way to vigorous clapping, followed by shouts of *Vive la France, Vive la France*. For the next two hours, small contingents of the armies allied with France paraded by. These included the Americans (led by General Pershing), the British (headed by General Haig) and a host of other nations, including Poland, Portugal, Greece, Italy, Belgium, the newly created nation of Czechoslovakia, and even Japan. The heavily native crowd saved its most boisterous cheering for Joffre, Foch, and, of course, Marshal Pétain.

When the celebration ended, and the crowd dispersed, a number of people patted my shoulder, followed by a hearty, *Merci*. Although I wasn't wearing any military attire, I suppose my obvious limp and silk aviator scarf identified my recent past. I made my way to an isolated park bench in a tree-lined area near the Invalides. I didn't know how to feel. I celebrated and welcomed the war's end. And the sweetness of victory remained intoxicating—but at what cost? Would peace endure or was this merely a temporary lull, an interregnum, feeding a needful sense of normalcy? I had no evidence, only a newly acquired cynical hunch. Perhaps it would have been better to have died during that happy period of non-disillusioned youth like 'Wing Nut', 'Dr Confidence', 'Troubadour' and 'The Kid'. They went out young, in a blaze of light rather than survive with a broken body and disillusioned mind.

I solidified another selfish thought while relaxing on that park bench: remaining in Paris. Having volunteered early for service, I considered myself amply patriotic. I was willing to die for America—and almost did. I just sure as hell didn't want to live in it. Not anymore. America, it seemed, represented an idea, not a place. One doesn't *live* in the States ... only exist. If I had thought deeper and longer about it, I would have realised these unflattering opinions weren't *caused* by the war, only nurtured by it. Paris offered hope. The opportunity to resurrect life.

Chapter Two

The move to Rue du Cardinal Lemoine proved uneventful. Owning only a kit bag and saxophone made the journey effortless. Sheet music brought from Cincinnati consisted of ragtime pieces played at university cotillions and a limited selection of highbrow waltzes and foxtrots that belonged to the house orchestra of the Sinton Hotel. The war had made comfortable, non-threatening songs from the past irrelevant. 'Over Here' and 'Pack Up Your Troubles in Your Old Kit Bag' were favourites among army pilots, but that was the only contemporary sheet music I owned. Times had changed. Music had become more daring. I needed current material, if available, especially the newest craze called jazz, or sometimes jass.

A casual walk around the shops bordering the Sorbonne yielded nothing. What music shops I visited sold only accordions, violins, violas, cellos, and grand pianos, and a limited range of brass instruments and woodwinds. Any sheet music consisted solely of classical music by French composers, with the occasional Italian mixed in for flavour. An attractive female clerk in the last shop I visited suggested the *bouquinistes*—the used-book stalls lining the Seine near Notre-Dame. She wasn't certain but thought some newer music might be mixed in amongst the antiquarian books. So, I headed north toward the river. The last hope of a desperate man pawning himself off as a musician.

Most stalls didn't stock sheet music. Some had a selection consisting only of classical music. I struck gold at the *bouquinistes* next to Pont Marie, the bridge across from Ile St Louis. The owner, a stooped, older

Frenchmen who sported a beret and a snub-nosed smoking pipe, told me he had purchased them a week or so after the Armistice from a soldier in the American army band. It seemed incredulous to me—a soldier playing in a US army band—but then I accepted my French was almost non-existent, so I tallied up my misinterpretation to poor language skills. Didn't matter *how* he got them, he had them—and that made all the difference. Best of all, the selection was damn current: 'Darktown Strutters' Ball', 'Oh Johnny, Oh Johnny, Oh', 'Someday Sweetheart', 'Oui, Oui, Marie', 'Chong (He Come From Hong Kong)', 'Poor Butterfly', and one so apropos for me: 'How Ya Gonna Keep 'Em Down on the Farm (After They've Seen Paree)'. As I wrapped the music in my cloth satchel, the owner extended his hand and softly uttered, *"Merci, America."* Not understanding whether he was thanking me for the purchase or for our nation's support in the last years of the war, I returned his handshake, replying, *"Vive la France."* He smiled, seeming to appreciate the gesture.

The following two weeks I dedicated myself to the sax, a task that occupied nine hours each day, even weekends. I needed excellence but expected perfection. The syncopation required in 'Tiger Rag' baffled me and confused my fingers. It required a great deal of additional practice. I understood early on that the reflective simplicity of 'Poor Butterfly' would be popular with couples at whatever street location I laid claim. And, once mastered, I expected 'How Ya Gonna Keep 'Em Down on the Farm (After They've Seen Paree)' to become a toe-tapping delight. Even thought someone might be bold and take to dancing on the pavement. On quick reflection, I chalked it up to post-adolescent hopefulness.

After ten days of regular practice, I developed a small following … outside my window. Paris is hot in August—muggy to—necessitating a window to always remain open. Late one afternoon someone shouted, *"Veuillex rejouer, Américain! Veuillex rejouer, Américain!"* Concerned something untoward had occurred on the street, I gazed from the window. Directly below was a young couple looking toward me.

"Veuillex rejouer, Américain!"

They gestured as if playing the saxophone. I had been practising 'Oui, Oui, Marie' so I assumed that's what they wanted to hear. I stood by the window and took it from the top. They immediately started dancing, arm in arm. At the appropriate point in the song, they stopped, knelt down, looked at each other face to face and loudly repeated the lyrics: *Oui oui, Marie, if you'll do zis for me, then I'll do zat for you. Oui, oui, Marie.* And then resumed dancing. When finished, they clapped their hands and shouted upwards toward me, *"Merci, Américain! Merci!"*

In my best, worst French, I smiled and shouted, *"Vous etes les bienvenus en tout temps."* [You are welcome, any time.]

They laughed and waved goodbye. *"Au revoir, Américain."*

Except for the foray to find sheet music, I had kept a low profile since my hospital release. Hadn't taken advantage of the restaurants recommended by the ward nurse. Stuck only to the basics, nothing fancy. Since the move to Rue du Cardinal Lemoine, I had consumed most, if not all, evening meals in the flat. Don't think what I ate could be called French. I also drank alone and enjoyed it.

Relished sitting by the window listening to the street noise, the conversations of couples walking by and hearing the gentle refrain of distant music. All this, and the hissing of a defensive cat against an encroaching dog, defined urban life five levels up.

My hesitancy in venturing out was due to being embarrassed by the three-inch difference between the left leg and the right. The limp was pronounced. I didn't want to draw sympathetic stares or inquiries into the past. Intelligent people could figure it for themselves—a twenty-four-year-old American, in Paris, alone, with minimal command of the French language, wearing a silk aviator's scarf and limping about—hell, he must be a former air ace. Whatever the reason for my self-imposed isolation, I needed a lateral adjustment from a known point. In other words, spruce up, look spiffy, exit the door and show Paris what I've got. Besides, when both legs were concealed underneath a table, or while sitting on a bar stool, how would a woman notice? Dealing with its hideousness would come later, when the lights dimmed.

I began exploring Parisian nightlife close to home— next door at the Bal au Printemps, the local *Bal-musette* recommended by *Madame* Rohrbeck. The darkened seediness of the smoked-filled room didn't obscure the pink walls or the red-coloured tables and chairs. The imposing wooden bar—with a well-used, zinc-lined counter and the soft but undeniable sound of an accordion in the far corner–suited me down to my shoestrings. Found a seat at the bar. The full-length mirror to my front, outlined with painted garlands, provided a panoramic view of the club. I ordered a double Scotch.

The barman was an Englishman from Brighton. Physically fat, black hair slicked straight back and minimal teeth in his head, he complemented an overall unkempt appearance. He introduced himself as Johnny, confessing he had left England a few days before the Archduke was assassinated.

"My woman pushed me to the street. Said I was a worthless git. Worse than her third husband. I still like her, though. Took care of me. Fed me good. A sweet lass. She worked in a small shop in The Lanes. Nothing for me in London, I thought—certainly not in Brighton. So, I left for Paris."

He assumed I had served in the American army and, luckily, didn't pursue my war experiences. Nor did he elaborate how he avoided serving in the army ... French or British. Never asked how I planned to make any seed to support myself either. Johnny only seemed interested in what I was going to do with myself recreationally.

"Those lovelies at the end of the bar, William— Carmen and Olga. Nice girls. Proper working types. Won't take advantage of their customer. Let me know when you want an introduction. Best of all, they don't drink. You get your hard-earned franc's worth. Let me know."

The mirror allowed me to glance secretively at the girls. Their dresses reflected what I presumed to be all the rage: loose-fitting cloth designed with low waists and revealing necklines; lips painted bright red; stockings rolled down to just above the knee. One girl attempted some mild sophistication by sporting a black cigarette holder containing an unlit cigarette. Perhaps waiting for a follow-through gesture from a prospective customer.

I thanked Johnny for his courtesies and concerns—but my gratitude was premature. He hadn't finished. Johnny wanted to offer additional advice. I ordered another

Scotch.

"Be aware, William, how an evening with a newly found lady could end in disaster. I'm only telling you this because, well, damn, I don't know you yet but I like the look of you. Do with it whatever you will, guv'nor. Here's their method: she approaches you; she looks damn nice; you're encouraged; she likes talking; she hangs on your every word and on your shoulder; caresses your cheek, then your lips; suggests she takes you to *her* place, not yours—that's the key; she opens the door; you walk in; you're feeling good—you're ready; an undergarment of hers drops to the floor; she's ready to bestow her favours, with great freedom and wild abandon."

I became a bit tense in anticipation, similar to how I felt on my first solo flight. Took a healthy sip of Scotch.

"Suddenly her 'husband'—actually her pimp—springs from inside the armoire. He threatens and demands full payment. You hand over the francs and return to your flat fleeced, frustrated and unfulfilled. I've heard about it … and experienced it a few times myself. Be ever so careful. There are sweet-smelling, attractive vipers out there. They'll suck you dry."

"Johnny, your advice has been catalogued. Appreciate your interest and concern. I'm impatient at certain times when in certain moods. The ending never serves me well. So, thank you."

I peered into the mirror to see the place was nearing capacity. Olga and Carmen had found success, busily entertaining two middle-aged men at an out-of-the-way corner table. The accordion player had moved to a more prominent position. Couples laughed. Couples danced. Couples hugged. And with Johnny shaking, stirring and pouring varieties of alcohol, I relaxed and enjoyed the atmosphere.

While paying the bill, I told Johnny I'd see him again soon. Appreciated the drink and the advice.

"Any time, guv'nor. Any time. Now go find a female dainty to occupy your mind so as to take it off the war. *À bientôt*."

"*À bientôt*, Johnny. *À bientôt*."

Before eating dinner, I walked around a bustling Montparnasse to scout out a centralised location to play my sax. The area bordering the sixth-century Abbey of Saint-Germain-des-Prés held instant appeal. Artists with easels were painting canvases but the area lacked musicians. Seemed perfect. It bordered Rue Jacob, Rue Bonaparte, Rue de Seine and the pedestrian filled Boulevard Saint-Germain. I could stand to one side on any of these streets and not trip-up passers-by or antagonise customers sitting outside Les Deux Magots or Café de Flore. Patrons of nearby Le Pre aux Clercs on Rue Bonaparte, the restaurant praised by my ward nurse, also could be entertained. The faint sound of a saxophone might entice them to drop random francs into my instrument case or at least not scurry away in the opposite direction. On a quieter night, hell, even outside diners at Brasserie Lipp on the opposite side of Boulevard Saint-Germain might find my interpretations rapturous.

I had formalised an 'operational code of conduct' prior to scouting a location: to not patronise bars or restaurants within my district prior to working or when on break. Too detrimental to cash flow. Why would someone toss coins into my case if only hours earlier they had seen me dining at Les Deux Magots, Café de Flore, or another nearby brasserie, devouring oysters on the half shell, nursing a neat Scotch, or enjoying a martini with toast points and *foie gras*? I wouldn't and neither would they. Street performers must possess a certain *je ne sais quoi,* an *élan*. If they lose it, all is lost. This morsel of discretion rings particularly true for musicians. It doesn't mean I'd have any reluctance to eating or to drinking thirty minutes or so before these institutions of culinary perfections closed. In fact, I'll put the record straight. I'd gladly accept if some oysters or the occasional lamb chop found their way unexpectedly to my plate, or that the barmen liquored me up in an affable manner. Double measures at the price of a single could work wonders for my malady. Incredibly medicinal.

Although I hadn't earned any seed since being discharged, I felt comfortable. Savings from army days and a small amount inherited from my parents kept the wolf outside the door. Not enough to impersonate a spendthrift—but I didn't have to mimic a Cistercian monk either. So, after assessing the district, and in recognition of my newly emerging life, I dined at the recently refurbished Brasserie Lipp. Glad I did.

The fare was delectably French: *soupe de poissons, confit de cuisse de canard* and *fromage blanc a la crème*. And, for dessert, something fresh for my virgin palate— *mille-feuille*. The entire feast was complemented by a fine Bourgogne wine from Beaune—an area I was familiar with but only from 800 feet. Served by lithe waiters wearing starched white coats, black trousers, highly polished shoes, and possessing faces with the requisite amount of seriousness as to not be mistreated by ill-mannered customers and pompous asses.

About to leave, I noticed a crumpled handbill laying on the ledge of the head waiter's station. It read, in part:

Commemorating one year since the Armistice, the Swaneeland Jazz Band will be performing three evenings a week at Brasserie Lipp. Limited seating. Reservations requested. Dinner dress required. At the bottom, in bold type, was written: *Profitez du jazz moderne à son meilleur et le plus chaud!* [Enjoy modern jazz at its best and hottest.] Although I knew somewhat less than nothing, there were two bits to which I'd stake a claim. First: I had two and one-half months to prepare. Second: I needed to be there. Somehow. Someway. Any way.

Wanting to mull over thoughts churning in my head, I found a quaint bar called Belle Époque on Rue de l'Odéon, just a short walk from the Odéon Théâtre. Since I was making my way to the apartment, in a roundabout kind of way, I thought I'd gave it a try. Why the hell not? I had learned early on that the smaller bars of Paris replaced the living room exceedingly well. Its Art Nouveau interior justified the name. Better yet, the intimate atmosphere encouraged reflection. Or so I thought. I had taken a few sips of Scotch when the woman sitting at the opposite end of the bar—there were four stools separating us—asked if I'd light her cigarette. While patting my pockets for the lighter, she stood up, faced me, and, sporting only a dressing grown, dropped it to the floor. Nothing but sheer nakedness. The ingénue's English was exceedingly better than my French.

"Oh, my. Oh, my. I am so careless. I forgot to get assembled before leaving this evening."

I lit the cigarette, reached into my back pocket and unfolded a white handkerchief.

"*Pardon, mam'selle*, wouldn't want you to catch the sniffles."

Not what she expected. She threw the handkerchief to

the floor, reassembled herself and left in a huff, muttering English and French profanities. I returned to my Scotch and reminisced. The outcome certainly would have been different if 'Troubadour' had been on site. An enlarged bravado for him, and another victory in 'spontaneity' for the naked ingénue.

As I made my way up to the fourth floor to my apartment, I encountered two fellow tenants: drunk, face down, hugging the contours of the curved stair steps. Sights like this would have concerned me before the war. Now, however, I couldn't be bothered. Paris is so beautiful, so alive, and so unique; it satisfies something that remained unfulfilled in the States. Only hoped the ol'boys would remember their memorable evening come morning.

My week-long preparations for serenading the public went reasonably well. Couldn't memorise the newest pieces, so the music stand accompanied me. Its presence added legitimacy, I thought. At least people would appreciate I read music and wasn't a two-franc grifter. Perhaps they'd accept that music and I had been together for some years. Personal appearance gained a sense of importance too. An air of vagrancy wouldn't work any more than one reflecting comfort. So, I decided it best to be genuine, to be true. Clean trousers, pressed white shirt, perfectly knotted tie, whisker-free face and slicked-back hair, brought together with my silk aviator's scarf emblazoned with the unit insignia of the Kicking Mule hanging from my neck. Whatever 'beauty' look I concocted would sink to irrelevancy minutes after playing. It was up to me whether I experienced a smooth assent or a turbulent one.

I chose Montparnasse mainly because its environment

offered the promise of complete escape. A home for the untried ideas about life; an incubator for differences. To nourish the impulses of unconventionality while simultaneously offering inspiration; to seek a living and pursue a craft; to conceive and to execute worthy things; and to be original without purposely trying to be original. I may fail, and fail many times over, but I'll never abandon the desire to keep trying. Plan to use whatever arrogance left over from the war as a defensive weapon against detractors. Believing in such theories enabled my foray into street performing to exceed any preconceived ideas about how good or how awful I'd be. The fact that women outnumbered men three to one worked in my favour. My burgeoning talents were rewarded. Coins landed in my case. Sometimes older women—presumably widows—or young lovelies—excited by newly acquired freedoms—contributed bills. Occasionally, kisses were blown. Oftentimes women approached and, whether I was playing or not, imprinted an outline of their brightly painted lips onto my cheeks. At the end of some evenings, I looked as if I had survived an explosion in a paint factory.

My efforts at unconventionality faded in comparison to others who called Montparnasse home. A Frenchman dressed as a Hindu regularly walked around the Abbey of Saint-Germain-des-Prés, where I had staked a claim, lecturing on ancient Asian philosophies. A young Hungarian, bedecked as an American Indian complete with feathered headdress and free-flowing leather loincloth, rode his bicycle up and down Boulevard Saint-Germain. A friend in tow, also pedalling a bicycle, was outfitted as a cowboy, wearing only chaps, pointy boots, a ten-gallon hat and red and white neckerchief. Diaphanous women wore transparent Grecian robes, gilded headbands and finely tooled leather sandals. One woman, in particular, fascinated me. Her interest in aviation was so keen that she wore a French aviation officer's uniform anytime she wandered through Montparnasse. Perhaps my silk scarf had sparked a memory of someone lost in the war. I never knew. She made her presence known to me not only while I played, but often sat at a nearby table of each brasserie where I ate dinner, or occupied a nearby stool at every bar where I nursed a drink. She never spoke. Weeks passed. Finally, she approached me one late evening.

"Please remember my lovely jazzman, that the universal language isn't love, but loneliness."

As I stood to introduce myself, she spurned my attempt at talking. She took my head gently into her hands and kissed me.

"*Au revoir*, my jazzman. *Je t'aime et adieu.*"

Never saw her again, nor did I understand how a sensitive soul had become so forlorn. Years later, I learned she had moved to London and married a prominent British writer.

All varieties of humankind ventured into Montparnasse. Many were there because they worked day and night and sacrificed for their art. They wanted to accomplish something. Something original. But there were also abundant wasters of time and talent, careless and worthless onlookers. Businessmen became artists. Upstanding churchgoers became degenerates. Inebriates became poets. I learned to accept that the area was one big theatre where a varying array of dramas were staged, exposing love trysts, dark intrigues, unbridled ambitions, laziness and greed. Intellectuals made themselves known, too. Powered by well and not-so-well thought out opinions, and supplemented by copious amounts of alcohol. Conversations lasted through the afternoon and into late evening. When neither party achieved anything approaching a conclusion, they departed. But the intention to find agreement had always been there.

Several weeks of good fortune necessitated a celebration: to drink at a classy bar. To mingle amongst people unlike myself. To touch elbows with the class whose interests we defended in the war. I decided upon the only grand hotel on the Left Bank: Hotel Lutetia. Named after what the Romans had called Paris, it mirrored the grandeur and sophistication of pre-1914 France. Equipped with an innate directional beacon, I found the main lounge bar without asking staff. Mahogany-framed chairs with overstuffed upholstery and bulbous-cushioned sofas complemented the honey-coloured herringbone parquet floor. A two-toned, glass-panelled ceiling provided the requisite amount of light for this distinctly intimate space. Strategically placed palms aided those desiring concealment or privacy. The whispers of guests were muffled further by a quartet playing waltzes and romantic pieces by French composers: Debussy, Saint-Saëns, Massenet and Satie. I slumped into a comfortable chair in an isolated corner.

I rejected my usual neat Scotch. Lutetia's exquisiteness necessitated something different. I opted for cognac and, with the sommelier's assistance, selected a glass of Bisquit Dubouché, vintage 1865. Its sheer splendidness was undeniable. But I became fond of the cognac a bit too quickly: it put me in a reflective mood— a place I didn't want to be.

A week before graduating from university and two weeks prior to leaving for army induction, Martha, whom I affectionately named the 'fragrant phantom', rejected all further advances. I was no longer her type. She needed something else. Two plus years of courting at university had been a mistake. Our romance, she said, had become "faded and grey". Though painful, my only option was to rationalise her rejection. She wasn't my dish, not my pigeon, no longer the cat's miaow—but lovely for what she was, what she represented to me at the time. I often wonder to this day if she ever found that something else?

My parents never concealed their disdain for the war. It was strictly a European affair, they argued. American meddling only would make it worse at home and abroad. Father could hide his contempt fairly easily from fellow musicians by getting lost in the music, but Mother couldn't conceal her dismay. Others decided my fate. Eighty-five percent of the men in the senior class volunteered for the army. Faced with few options, I fell in-step with the mob. Being a volunteer, combined with my aptitude, eased my way into being selected for the newly formed aero-squadrons. Thought it better to view trenches from high-up, instead of being mired knee-deep in them. And besides, flying was romantic. It was deadly. And it lent itself to arrogance—a characteristic necessary for survival. Something that my fellow pilots and I embraced without hesitation. Despite me leaving, or because of it, I never reconciled with my parents. They didn't see me off at Cincinnati's Pennsylvania Station. Never wrote during my training. Never congratulated me on earning aviator wings. Knew nothing of my war experiences. I learned of their deaths from influenza only because the Sinton Hotel house orchestra leader contacted the American Red Cross which, with Uncle Sam's assistance, informed me.

All of this, including the deaths of my fellow pilots,

now lay buried in the past. Couldn't return to the way life was, however it was. That existed only in my mind. I can't return. They won't return. So, I must move on. Find other things, something or somebody new.

As I waited for a third cognac, a well-dressed man appeared from nowhere.

"*Monsieur*, I've noticed you are alone and appear a bit melancholy. May I ask you to kindly join me at my table where I may offer you another drink?"

Dumbfounded, I didn't know what to think. Voice paralysis consumed me. I discerned quickly, however, that the wings of our aircrafts were cut from different bolts of cloth. I declined his offer, replying that I preferred to drink alone. As he returned to his table—on the opposite side of the room—I detected a daintiness in his step. As if holding a franc coin between his two cheeks.

Chapter Three

I visited the Musée du Luxembourg one October afternoon. Needed to view the Impressionist paintings. A newly opened temporary exhibition titled "Exposition D'Artistes de L'École Américaine" (Artists of the American School) also piqued some interest. Among the Impressionists, the work of Paul Cézanne inspired me the most. The minimal simplicity of his paintings remained with me long after leaving the museum. Although meant as an homage to Franco-American relations forged during the war, the American exhibit seemed too tame. Nothing 'modern,' nothing 'shocking' was displayed. At least it didn't appear so to my untrained eye. Uninspiring landscapes mostly but not all was lost. The tranquillity of Lowell Birge Harrison's *Moonlight on the River* compared favourably with the French Impressionists. And Oliver-Dennett Grover's *Mountain, Sea and Clouds* brought a bit of my hometown to Paris. Grover had been trained by Frank Duvaneck, a respected professor at the Art Academy of Cincinnati. When I was a young boy, I used to ride my bicycle around the cragged streets of Mount Adams that overlooked the city below, often pedalling by the Art Academy, curious to what was being created inside. I put all these memories aside when a dish-of-a-woman approached.

"*Bonjour, Monsieur*, you are American, no?"

"Is it *that* obvious?"

"You are tall, broad-shouldered and—"

"Open range and corn-fed?"

"No, no. It is wonderful to be tall and broad. Frenchmen tend towards the petit. I won't be rude or presumptuous any longer. Permit me to introduce myself.

I'm Véronique Vouvray, one of the curators at the Musée. I was struck—intrigued actually—at your level of concentration."

"*Enchanté*, Véronique. I'm William Travers … ex-army aviator and now, well … an expat who plays the sax in Montparnasse. I read music but have limited knowledge of fine art, I'm afraid. Need an education. That explains my intense look."

"Work is finished in about forty-five minutes. Could we meet for a drink outside in the garden café? A welcoming environment to begin your tutorial."

"Best offer I've had since demobilisation. Would it be presumptuous on this brisk October day if I ordered us a calvados?"

"*Merveilleux, Monsieur* Travers. *Merveilleux.*"

And, with that, she turned and walked into the adjoining room. I didn't know what to think. Why, of all people, would she engage me in conversation? Wasn't she taken aback by my gimpy leg? Maybe she didn't realise it. Her aptitude for English was of particular interest. Definitely a learned skill; not something picked up casually from reading the *Paris Herald*.

Leaving the museum, I walked through the gardens admiring the design and array of statues celebrating historical French artists, philosophers and writers. I came upon the café eventually. Few tables were occupied, but I selected one far removed from others. With only ten minutes before Véronique's anticipated arrival, I ordered the drinks. Wasn't bothered if she changed her mind. I'd enjoy two spirited 'drinks of Normandy' alone, in a peaceful setting.

She *didn't* change her mind—but I changed mine. Hadn't taken a full accounting when first introduced. Her demure knee-length woollen skirt and maroon-coloured wool sweater didn't conceal her figure—they accentuated it. And her black pumps, equipped with a wide buckle and two-inch heels, brought it together. Her face came into focus when she reached the table: shoulder-length black hair parted on the right; flawless, porcelain-white skin; and, the darkest blue eyes I've ever seen. Resembled a thunderstorm brewing on the far horizon of the Atlantic. Her gait oozed confidence. Her smile reflected sophisticated sensuality. I stood as she approached the table. We shook hands.

"Thank you for meeting me, William. I thought you may have judged my forwardness a bit scary and decided to leave."

"I've seen scary, Véronique, and it doesn't look like you."

"*Merci*. You're very kind. It's wonderful you remained in Paris, but why not return to the States?"

"Without becoming too detailed or philosophical, there wasn't anything or anybody in the States I cared enough about to return."

"Wouldn't cultural differences alone provide enough motivation to take the first available boat?"

"I learned during the war that if we understand ourselves and develop to a point where we can live with what we like and don't like about ourselves, Christ, we can have one corker of a time with what's left to us. I intend to do exactly that. Enough about me already— what about yourself, Véronique? Where did you learn to speak such flawless English?"

"It sounds irrational to many. My parents share different allegiances. Mother, having been born in Metz, is German while Father, a native of Nancy, is French.

Well before the war began—when I was young—Mother thought either England or Germany would control the world. So, to prepare, she insisted I learn English and German. Favouritism of one over the other wasn't permitted. In addition to French, of course, which was taught in school."

"So where are you from? To use an American saying, where's your hometown?"

"*Oh, là là,* I like that: 'hometown'. I must remember that. I was born and educated in Nancy. Taught German and English by university tutors four evenings a week—two nights German, two nights English. Excelled at school, enabling me to attend the Sorbonne. Earned my degree in June 1914, two weeks before the Archduke was assassinated. I faced a unique dilemma when war was declared. Mother fervently but quietly supported Germany, and Father ... obviously, France. Mother would disown me if I joined a French support organisation—whether a nursing contingent or a government ministry. Thought I should travel to Baden-Baden and work with relatives. Father, far more rational, recommended I stay in Paris and assist businesses short of male workers. So that's what I did. I even found time to attend art history classes at the Sorbonne."

"What kind of work?"

"Delivered coal. Chopped and delivered wood. Delivered the post. Worked as a typist at the Banque de France during the last two years of the war. Mother never knew about that. I thought it too aligned with the government to tell her. And last year, a week before the Armistice, I was offered two jobs: accessions clerk at the Bibliothèque nationale de France or assistant curator here at the Musée. A simple decision."

Listening to Véronique was melodically beautiful. She spoke with a faint but charming French lilt. Her hand, eye and mouth gestures enhanced her attractiveness. Never experienced a woman like this before. Far removed from any American *femme* I'd ever known.

"If too personal, please don't answer, but I noticed in the gallery—prior to us meeting—that walking may be onerous, perhaps painful? A war injury?"

"Ah, you noticed. But you came anyway. Thanks. Glad you hadn't discovered it now while we're enjoying the calvados. Could have been awkward. But to answer your question—yes, a war injury received during a morning reconnaissance flight on 11 November 1918."

"But ... but ... the last day of the war!"

"The Germans hoped for one less plane in the air and one more dead American pilot. It was prior to 11:00."

"And your injury?"

"Left leg three inches shorter than the right. And, with the corresponding muscle loss, the leg's width is narrower, too. What skin remains consists mainly of scar tissue. Walking puts unnatural pressures on the good leg and lower back. Have no idea what a Parisian winter will do."

"I'm sorry, so, so, sorry for you, William."

"Got off easy, Véronique. All my buddies—fellow pilots—bought it. Never got to experience what I'm enjoying now on this crisp October afternoon in the Luxembourg Gardens, in Paris ... with a lovely French woman."

"Are all American men this flattering or only you?"

"To be unromantic about it ... after the hell we've experienced ... I'm shocked to have survived. Right now, Véronique, I've got the world on a downhill drag, heartily embracing the smallest display of kindness. You offered; I accepted."

"Makes perfect, unromantic sense. Thank you. So, you lack the fundamentals for art appreciation but excel in music. How did that come about?"

"Father loved music. Played trumpet in the Sinton Hotel's house orchestra. One of the swankier hotels in Cincinnati, Ohio. On my eleventh birthday my parents presented me an alto saxophone. The same instrument that's with me now. Played in all the school bands. Don't know if it's innate but, for some reason, music came easily to me. At university I played in a pick-up band for cotillions and fraternity and sorority parties. Earned some decent seed doing that. At eighteen I was good enough to occupy a chair on weekends in the Hotel Sinton's orchestra. During the summers of 1913 to '16 I worked practically every evening. If America hadn't joined in the war, I'd still be there."

"What sort of music do you play?"

"Debussy, Satie, Richard Strauss, Mozart, Elgar, John Philip Sousa, even Wagner—well, before the war I did. At university we were neck-deep into ragtime. The kids loved it: 'Rusty Rags', 'St. Louis Rag', 'Maple Leaf Rag', 'Spaghetti Rag', and many more. I've become interested in jazz recently. It's eclectic, intoxicating and improvisational, at least to me. Bought some sheet music at a *bouquinistes* along the Seine. That's one of the styles I play in Montparnasse. I slip in a classical piece now and then for variety. People enjoy it and I get rewarded."

"Any chance of me hearing?"

"Come around the Abbey of Saint-Germain-des-Prés between three and midnight and you should see me. Of course, if embarrassed, you're permitted to turn away and fain ignorance. That's allowed. Depends on my playing, I suppose."

"I wouldn't do that … especially in Montparnasse, where anything goes. By chance do you play, 'Oui, Oui, Marie'? It's one of the few new songs I'm familiar with."

"You're in luck, Véronique. Happens to be one of the pieces of sheet music I purchased at the *bouquinistes*. It's a consistent crowd pleaser, almost an obligation. Couples are so enraptured they dance in front of me or off to one side. Humorous to watch."

"So, you live in Montparnasse?"

"No, no, a little outside. In the Latin Quarter on Rue du Cardinal Lemoine. Sparse, but adequate for my needs. The local *Bal-musette* is next door so excitement abounds. Whereabouts do you live?"

"Not too far from you but in the sixth arrondissement, on Rue Notre-Dame-des-Champs. It's a short walk to the Musée. Very convenient and, perhaps more importantly, close to a favourite café, La Closerie des Lilas. Perhaps we could share a drink there sometime if you're inclined."

"Sounds delightful and amply more sophisticated than my haunts. That said, one evening I did enjoy *too* many cognacs at Hotel Lutetia."

"Hotel Lutetia! *Très sophistiqué,* William. *Très sophistiqué.* I'm impressed."

"Celebrating a bit of good fortune and reflecting on what's come before. Sometimes I sink deep and remain there. Can be a bad scene."

We agreed to call it an afternoon when the wind picked-up and the sun disappeared over the rooftops. Véronique seemed tired after having what she termed, 'a confusing week'. And, if I wanted money, I needed to make music in Montparnasse.

"I appreciate your forwardness, Véronique. It's served me well. Our shared long-windedness has wreaked havoc with your original intentions."

"The tutorial was a ruse, William."

"An ulterior motive. Too weak-kneed and too short in the leg to have noticed, I guess."

We exited the park to go our separate ways. I extended my hand but she'd have none of it. Pulled me gently toward her and kissed both cheeks. Hadn't felt anything as sublime since my last days at university.

"Don't be surprised if Saturday evening you see me critiquing your performance."

My playing reached new heights Saturday evening. I guessed the mood of passers-by and those dining and drinking at nearby cafés correctly. A mix of styles suited everyone's wants and desires. Each time I played 'Poor Butterfly' a different couple performed a melancholy dance. The ever-increasing crowd showed their appreciation after each performance. After glancing at the tower of the church, bathed in ghostly white moonlight, I looked around but no sign of Véronique. Wasn't fussed. Just hungry, thirsty and curious as to what my waiter friend had found for me to eat. A few strokes before midnight, I continued the tradition of what I'd closed with since first performing in Montparnasse: 'How Ya Gonna Keep 'Em Down on the Farm (After They've Seen Paree)'. Afterward, as I packed my instrument, collapsed and folded the music stand, I heard a familiar voice.

"You can't 'keep 'em down on the farm' after they've met the assistant curator at the Musée du Luxembourg."

"So, you made it."

"Been sitting outside Les Deux Magots for the last

three hours. Didn't dare interfere with your playing. The waiter became a bit perturbed, I think, thought I drank Scotch too slowly."

"I'm on my way there now to devour whatever my friend Jacques has scavenged for me. Care for another?"

"I'll manage another very nicely, thank you."

After finding a table, Jacques rounded up a dozen Brittany oysters and a half bottle of Muscadet. Thought it a bit extravagant but he didn't worry. The manager had left him in charge. I welcomed the saltiness of the oysters and the freshness of the wine. A seafood—wine combination like no other. That they were *gratuit* enhanced their exquisiteness. Véronique nursed a neat double Scotch.

"No woman I've known drank Scotch. Impressed."

"How do you think I survived filling sacks of coal and chopping and delivering wood? It kept me warm; it kept me alive. And now … well, I'm fond of it."

"Bad hooch offers no pleasure at all; good hooch descends from God."

"What do you mean 'hooch'? That's not English."

"It's American slang for whisky. Stay close and your English dictionary will expand several pages."

"Don't be offended, but my tutors taught me British English. They believed it superior to American English. Mother wanted me to enunciate like the King."

"Heard that before. Makes sense. It's their language. They invented it. Americans are distant family, interlopers. Radicals. Revolutionaries."

"I enjoyed your playing, William. You're excellent. You've a way of expressing the mood. And I was impressed—taken aback, really—by the supportive crowd. Someone important is going to offer you a job."

"Who knows? If it *did* happen, don't know what I'd do. Would have to chew on it, you know, mull it over. Listen, it's late. I'm exhausted, and I'm sure you are too. Let's call it a night, but … maybe agree on a day to meet again."

"Tomorrow would be fine."

"Tomorrow? Rather soon, isn't it? Half-one now. Challenging, to say the least."

"Not if you accompany me …"

—She paused. I didn't want to appear surprised. Also didn't want to act if I expected it either.

"That would be … delightful, Véronique."

Rue Notre-Dame-des-Champs was deserted. Nobody about. You could hear leaves falling from the horse chestnut trees and landing on the pavement that bordered the Luxembourg Gardens. A cold, dense fog obscured visibility. After fifteen minutes, we reached the building. The subtle warmth of her cold flat was welcoming. Véronique lit a candle and added coal to a long-smouldering fire. After blowing the bellows a bit, it took. A blue-orange-yellow glow filled the room. Left on my coat as she showed me around. Neat and well considered, in comparison to my place. A narrow hallway led to a kitchen equipped with a stone sink and a two-ring gas cooker with small oven. The dining room contained a maple table and four chairs. A room on the left served as a sitting room: a small sofa, two comfortable chairs and a bookshelf cramped with books and papers. The bedroom held a potbelly stove and a double bed equipped with canopy. Véronique's femininity was on complete display.

"Noticed a photograph in the sitting room next to the dark leather chair. Your parents?"

"Yes. Taken in 1914, a few days after graduating from

the Sorbonne. I came home for a quick visit before returning to Paris."

"You have the sculptured cheeks and height of your mom, I see, and the dark hair and smile of your dad. The area looks impressive. Imposing, actually."

"It's Place Stanislas in Nancy. The city's central square. People say I'm a perfect composite of both. Personality-wise, I lean more towards Father. Mother can be Teutonic-like. And Father, being French, expects and receives nothing but enjoyment from life. A philosophy I share."

"How ironic. Was banking right toward Nancy the day I took fire."

"Being a few years older than you, William, I've learned in life that you never know who will and who won't matter. They descend. They fall. They rise. They leave and then return, often clinging to you for life. We met for a reason, a purpose. Of that I'm confident."

"To me, layers of life are occurring all the time, but only sometimes we know it. Most of the time we don't know it. Christ, how'd we become so philosophical so late at night? Must be the hooch."

"It *might* be the hooch. I don't know. What I *do* know is I want to undress, slip on a warm nightgown and find my bed. Give me a few minutes. Make yourself comfortable."

Didn't know what form of comfortable she expected. I was stoking the fire as she entered the living room.

"That should last until morning, William. Come join me in the bedroom."

The heat of our bodies partially minimised the damp chill of the cotton sheets until the warmth of the wool blankets kicked in.

"You soldiers went through hell during the war. The dead will remain dead. Can't bring them back. Their war's over. But it never will end for the lame, the wounded and the disillusioned. They'll always live with reminders. My heart aches for you."

"Wouldn't say it was hell, Véronique. Probably been overused since General Sherman pillaged the American South. But what I would say is there were at least six times when I would have preferred hell. My pain, and the suffering of thousands of others, will last our lifetimes. Can't escape the past. So, it's up to the governments and the politicians to ensure it won't happen again. Only that would legitimise my suffering—make it tolerable. Nothing else will do."

She removed her nightgown, dropped it on the floor and nestled her head tight against my chest. As she softly touched the length of my scarred and withered leg, I reconsidered the disquietude of my injury.

Haven't experienced such a deep sleep this side of the grave. Woke in the same position as when I dozed off. The room had warmed. The air smelled of coffee. Wrapped a blanket around me and entered the dining room. On the table sat bread fresh from the oven, apple preserves, Normandy butter, and coffee.

"Please don't tell me you baked bread this morning."

"A little flour, a pinch of yeast, some water and lots of patience until it rises. That's all, William. We French enjoy our bread fresh."

"Your energy is a wonderment. Looks stellar. Thank you."

"Look at you in that blanket, Willis. You should leave some clothes and other items here with me—if you want. Could make future visits more relaxing … less transient-like. That's if you want to return."

"Can't rationalise any reason to say no. Thank you. And, ahh, how'd 'Willis' come about?"

"Just rolled off the tongue. After last night, I thought 'William' too formal. I wanted something affectionate, personal—unique between us."

"Believe it or not, the only person to call me Willis was my mom. What do you think of that?"

"Unknowingly trying to fill some big shoes, I guess."

"I'm intrigued by the colourful glass vase on your bedroom dressing table."

"Isn't it beautiful? Daum glass from my—what's your term?—hometown: Nancy. The company was founded late last century. My vase depicts quinces. A gift of Grandmother's from about ten years ago. Its translucence depends on lighting. It's stunning on a nice day when the sun shines through the window."

"I like it. Haven't seen anything similar. Cincinnati is home to a unique studio too—Rookwood Pottery. Also founded late last century—and by a woman, no less. Its sheen—or glazing, I guess it's called—is unique. Easily identifiable, but not duplicable. My parents have a few items. Guess they've been boxed-up and stored by the neighbour who's awaiting my return. He'll be an old man, hunched over with white hair, sporting a long beard before I make my presence known."

"So, you really aren't returning?"

"Can't think of a reason. Which reminds me, to commemorate the first anniversary of the Armistice, the Swaneeland Jazz Band will be performing at Brasserie Lipp for three nights, beginning on Tuesday, 11 November. Seating is limited. Reservations are required, as is dinner dress. I know it's a weeknight; we could be out late. Care to join me? It's billed as 'modern jazz at its best and hottest'."

"Sounds fabulous. I'd love to. *Merci beaucoup*. And don't be concerned, I'm past worrying about late evenings. We couldn't have any during the war, so I eagerly embrace them now. Is the band from the States?"

"The handbill didn't specify. Believe they would be, but who knows? Could be five Sardinians who *think* they're playing jazz."

"American conceit—or jealousy?"

"Ahh, my Achilles' heel. *Très excellent*, Véronique. *Très excellent*. Jealousy."

I didn't work Montparnasse the next afternoon or evening. My lips needed a rest. Decided instead to visit Bal au Printemps and check in with Johnny. Actually, he had left a note asking if I'd stop by for a chat. Hadn't talked with him in weeks so I looked forward to it. When I arrived, Carmen and Olga had already found success, despite the early afternoon hour: two dapper men in pinstripes seemed intrigued, anxious to learn where their friendly conversation could lead. A well-dressed, middle-aged woman was sitting at the opposite end of the bar from where I plunked my sore body. I ordered my usual: a double neat Scotch. Told Johnny the playing was providing enough seed to cover the rent, and for me to enjoy life. Seemed pleased I'd met Véronique. Encouraged me to bring her by sometime soon. Despite their outward chic, he believed French women were proudly independent and undeniably confident; hard as petrified wood, actually. From the corner of my left eye, I could tell the woman was listening intently to our discussion. Johnny could, as well, so he introduced me.

"*Madame* Dominique Diguet, I introduce William

Travers, expat and saxophone player. A friend of Paris."

"*Enchanté, Madame* Diguet. Johnny is correct: I *am* a friend. Paris took pity and welcomed me in. I'll be forever grateful."

"I've seen you play in Montparnasse. That's why I'm here. I enlisted Johnny's assistance."

Her matter-of-fact manner indicated she wanted something. Johnny looked at the floor a bit sheepishly, concerned I might not take kindly to his strategic meddling.

"I founded and manage an exclusive entertainment club, where men can be men and women can be women. Music is played. Drinks are served. It's the highest calibre environment, possessing the utmost discretion. Lovely accommodations are available—and encouraged—if *un petit amour* is desired."

"And I fit into this, how?"

"By playing the saxophone, the way you do. It's sensual. It's mystical and … would relax the guests and please the girls."

"Thanks for the compliments, but I work Montparnasse from three until midnight. Then I eat dinner. Then I go to bed. Don't know when I could please your girls or your guests."

"Dominique's is open from three in the afternoon until five in the morning. Ample time for you. Say, between two and five in the morning a couple days a week? On rainy nights you could play from three until midnight, like you do when the weather isn't miserable in Montparnasse."

"And the compensation?"

"We're making progress. Good! I pay you twelve francs, in addition to two drinks from the bar. If you choose a girl, then you receive one drink and no francs."

"If forced to decide now, think I'd choose the twelve francs and two drinks. Sex would wreak havoc on my embouchure."

"Your desires will change after seeing the girls. Of that I'm confident."

"What is the address of Dominque's?"

"It's in the sixth arrondissement, 9 Rue de la Grande Chaumiere, near the Jardin du Luxembourg. It intersects Rue Notre-Dame-des-Champs."

"I'm familiar with the location, yes. And hope I don't offend, *Madame* Diguet, but would you mind terribly if I visited? Had a peek? As we say in the States, 'get a lay of the land'."

"*Oui, oui.* Not a problem. The girls and I will look forward to showing you the 'lay of the land' and anything else you might desire."

Whereupon she let out a belt of laughter, followed by violent coughing. She took a sip of wine and puffed her cigarette to calm herself.

"When can we expect you, *Monsieur* Travers?"

"Would early Sunday afternoon be convenient— before you open—say, two o'clock?"

"*Merveilleux. Parfait.*"

And with that we shook hands and she left. The off-putting mixture of perfume, body odour, cigarettes and wine seemed oddly welcoming.

"Sorry, guv'nor. Hope you're not angry. She'd been following you awhile. Discovered where you lived and, I guess, took a chance you'd drink here occasionally. Came in about a week ago. Asked if I'd arrange it."

"Johnny … how could I be upset? How many men you know play an instrument in the lounge of a whorehouse?"

"Thanks. And here, a 'double neat' *gratuit. Vive la*

France, guv'nor."

"*Vive la France*, Johnny. *Vive la France. Merci ... beaucoup.*"

I arrived Dominique's promptly at two o'clock. Didn't plan on spending too much time. Had arranged to meet Véronique at La Closerie des Lilas at three. Only wanted to scope out the environment—where I'd play, size of the lounge, dimness of the lighting. And, drawing from my Midwestern Methodist upbringing, I wanted to see if it fit any preconceived notions of seediness.

Shouldn't have worried. Dominique had described it perfectly: an environment of the highest calibre. A dark mahogany, curved bar fit tightly into a corner space. Behind, on the wall, was a varied selection of wines, liqueurs, Scotches, cognacs, even absinthe. The Bordeaux-coloured marble top complemented the dark velvet-cushioned furniture consisting of three two-seat sofas, four overstuffed single chairs, and a red leather chaise longue. A large mirror housed within a nickel-plated frame hung on the far wall, enabling the intimate space to appear a little larger. I learned later, however, that its real purpose was to provide male guests with a comprehensive and awe-inspiring view of the girls. The pink lighting softened whatever rough edges remained.

Madame was behind the bar as I entered. She greeted me warmly. Although the full contingent of girls hadn't arrived, *Madame* Diguet introduced me to the five or so girls who were straightening cushions, rearranging furniture and drying drink glasses. They were young. They were attractive. Wore the minimalist of clothing—sheer black or gold-coloured negligees with a couple strands of pearls dangling from their necks. Most had cropped hair, brightly painted lips, and alluring eyes reflecting what I would describe as a thousand-yard stare.

"Girls, may I introduce *Monsieur* William Travers. He will be increasing your enjoyment with guests by playing the saxophone, something he does so exceedingly well. He's agreed to three early mornings a week, but I hope it's only the beginning. By making him feel most welcomed he may consider playing more often. Questions, girls?

"Fabienne."

"Will you visit upstairs, *Monsieur* Travers, or are you the kind of man who doesn't enjoy women?"

"I admire and appreciate woman very much but, per my prior arrangement with *Madame* Diguet, I will be compensated by other means. But I'm quick to change my mind."

"*Oh, là là,* you are *Américain*, no?"

"*Oui, Américain* … and you are?"

"Salome, from Bordeaux."

"*Enchanté*, Salomé."

Whereupon all five girls started giggling, talking rapidly in French, gleefully and purposely keeping me uninformed.

"I am Juillet from Massiges, a small village in Champagne. I hear you play in Montparnasse. I enjoy it. Glad you will show your talents at Dominique's. I'm excited."

"I'm excited, too, Juillet. Should have a corking good time. And I hope you'll enjoy the music as much as in Montparnasse."

Again, a round of giggling and, rapid talking, with no effort to keep me informed. Thought I better quit while a bit ahead. Suppose they were nervous having a man around who wasn't asking anything in return … at least, not yet.

Madame Diguet and I talked some more; nailed down when I'd begin. She offered me a drink but I declined, telling her I was meeting a close friend at La Closerie des Lilas.

"Ah, des Lilas … wonderful. If Gaston is behind the bar, tell him you're a friend. He was my first customer twenty years ago."

"I shall, *Madame* Diguet. *Merci.* Until next week."

I made my way up Boulevard du Montparnasse, tipped my hat to the statue of Marshal Ney, the hero of the Revolution and Napoleonic Wars, and sauntered—the best I could—into the dark, relaxed comfort of the bar. Always prompt, in the far right-hand-side corner and facing the mirrored wall, sat Véronique. I leaned down and kissed her cheek.

"*Enchanté, Mam'selle.* The seat across from you, is it free?"

"I'm expecting an American friend, but, until he arrives, you're welcome to share a drink."

After laughing, she stood up and hugged and kissed me.

"Been too long, Willis. Much too long. I've missed you."

"Missed you too, Véronique. Time lost we won't recoup. Can't happen again."

"Promise?"

"Promise. But I have exciting news. Remember what you said after hearing me in Montparnasse—at Les Deux Magots? *Someone important is going to offer you a job.* Well, it's happened. I've been offered a gig three mornings a week at a brothel on Rue de la Grande Chaumiere. A short walk from your flat."

"A brothel, during the slumbering hours of morning? *Non, allez, tu es folle*?"

"Don't understand."

"Put simply—no. Come on, are you crazy?"

"No, I'm not. The money's good, plus two free drinks. And who knows about the customers? Could make important connections. One never knows. Not foregoing Montparnasse, don't worry. This is in addition. And please don't be concerned about me exploring upstairs."

"I'm not concerned about perceived immoralities. Such activity intrigues Frenchmen. My disappointment is you won't be joining me until four or five o'clock in the morning … especially if it's a Saturday or Sunday. I'll be alone and blue. Not know what to do."

Her piercing blue eyes looked sad. Her lower lip protruded over the upper one. She bowed her head downward toward her Scotch glass. I was at a loss for words for several seconds, staring at the swirling intricacies of the mosaic floor.

"Come. Come. I'll stop if it becomes too distracting and too unsettling. Promise. It's just, well, somebody important is going to hear me some early morning and offer me a proper job, with proper hours, with a proper salary. Don't want to miss it."

A long pause. I hadn't ordered a drink yet, so I took a sip of her Scotch. As I placed the glass in front of her, she took my hand and kissed it.

"*Merci*, Willis. *Je vous adore. Désolé.*

"I adore you too. No need to apologise. And, I promise, I'll leave if it becomes disruptive."

I approached the bar and ordered two double Scotches. The name embroidered on the barman's white tunic was Gaston. I was in luck. After introducing myself, I told him *Madame* Diguet sent her kind regards and fond memories of a friendship forged decades ago.

"Ah, Dominique. *Oui. Oui.* A special woman."

Gaston brought our drinks minutes later. He leaned in close, turned his head away so Véronique couldn't hear or read his lips, and softly said—

"A friend of Dominique's remains a friend of mine. No charge for drinks now, or any time I'm working the bar. *Voilà.*"

Véronique doesn't suffer hearing loss. She overheard everything. After Gaston returned to the bar, she looked up and smiled.

"I didn't know Dominique Diguet snagged you. You're fortunate, Willis. She's well connected to the influential and the wealthy. The *Madame* of all *Madames*. I know the building. Never been inside though, despite delivering coal to the girls throughout the war. Who knows, Dominique's may be the job that gets you the proper job you want. Until that happens, we'll be able to enjoy Scotch—*gratuit*—whenever Gaston is pouring."

"Don't think Gaston understands our weakness for Scotch."

"Definitely not. But tell me, how is it you receive meals and drinks, and God knows what else, for free? Every time I'm with you something delicious arrives at no charge."

"Funny, isn't it? Like to say it's my innate charm—but I don't have any. Perhaps it because I'm a foreigner, an American—except there're other Yanks about. Then I think maybe pity. My gimp leg draws on emotion—but there are thousands of injured *poilus*, your own countrymen, hobbling around Paris, who deserve equal if not better treatment. So, yeah, I've noticed ... but can't rationalise why. This city's generosity is humbling."

"Well, it's impressive. No Frenchman I know receives anything similar. It's your *élan*. That's how I got drawn in."

"Stop. It's embarrassing. What about Tuesday evening, excited?"

"Very much looking forward to a wonderful evening filled with jazz, drink and whatever enters our minds. I bought a dress at an exclusive atelier. First new clothes I've purchased since spring 1914. So, I feel quite special … and so should you."

"Always feel special with you around, Véronique. Had to purchase a dinner suit. Nothing posh like yours, though. My waiter friend, Jacques, at Les Deux Magots, put me in touch with an Annamite tailor who crafts top quality but affordable men's clothes in the back of his flat. Took my measurements late one evening after I'd finished working Montparnasse. The guy could compete with Henry Ford on production output. Finished the job in four days. It's immaculate. Fits better than anything from Brooks Brothers in New York. Cheaper too."

"Surprised he didn't tailor it for free."

"You'll never know because I'll never tell. Anyway, about Tuesday. How about if I drop off my dinner suit early afternoon while you're at the Musée? I'll come by late Monday evening, immediately after work. We'll enjoy a leisurely morning, a relaxing afternoon, and hit Brasserie Lipp around seven. The jazzmen begin playing at nine. Probably won't return to your place until late."

"Sounds fine. I'll try to stay awake if you're not too late."

"If I am, I'll do my best not to wake you. I'll just slide in."

"I don't know. I might fancy a wake-up . . ."

We spent the remainder of our day walking through the *Jardin,* discussing Impressionist and Post-Impressionist art. Actually, Véronique talked; I listened. Her encyclopaedic knowledge was exceptional. Helped me understand and appreciate fine art more, a subject largely ignored in American schools. We said our goodbyes as evening approached. She desperately wanted me to spend the night, but I couldn't. I'd been away from the horn two days and needed to practise. I thought she understood.

Earned a haul of seed Monday evening. Found the perfect opportunity to try a piece of music I'd brought from the States. A lovely lady, dressed as an Egyptian courtesan, approached late in the evening. Her alluring looks and diaphanous gowns spurred me on at moment's notice. I found the music and began playing 'Méditation' from Massenet's opera *Thaïs*. Shouldn't have been surprised, in retrospect. Comfortable and familiar with the music, she staged a most erotic dance. Crowds gathered. Their eyes transfixed on her sinewy figure, her free-flowing arm movements and her copulating-like leg gestures. As the piece neared conclusion, I heard shouts of, *rejouer, rejouer, rejouer*. I looked at my 'associate' and shrugged my shoulders. I raised my eyebrows and tilted my head—a physical gesture asking if she'd perform again.

"Oui, oui, saxman."

The longer and louder the crowd clapped, the more people from nearby cafes and passers-by gathered. Must have been seventy-five people gathered in a semi-circle when we'd finished the second time. A memorable moment indeed, etched deep in my reverie. As handfuls of francs, and even more notes, made their way into my case, I presented the courtesan with half the earnings. She was entitled. My takings had increased solely because of her hypnotic performance.

When I arrived at Véronique's flat, it was dark and cold and she was asleep. Despite her desire to be awakened, I couldn't do it. Simply undressed, slithered underneath the blankets and lay on my back. She moaned a contented sigh, moved her head close to my ear and softly said, "My jazzman is home."

We woke late. Looked at my watch: 09:45.

"A year ago, I was unconscious and being transported from the crudely equipped field hospital near Rembercourt Aerodrome to the American Red Cross Hospital in Paris."

"And I had signed a lease on this flat a week after beginning at the Musée. No thoughts of what life could be. No thoughts about Americans. Certainly, no thoughts of a male relationship."

"Know what won't leave my head? Sounds selfish—and certainly unimportant—but if I *had* bought it, who would have taken ownership of the 'last man' libation? Whoever found it, would they have raised a glass? Would they have reflected on our lives? Why and how we died?"

"You lived aptly, honouring your fellow pilots. And you're here with me now, to love and to enjoy for however long. That's what's important."

"Yeah, I guess. And there's no doubt you're helpful, Véronique. Just wish I could live untroubled, impervious to what's come before but …"

"You're too damn intelligent, Willis. It's rare in people. But everyone I know who possesses it has a bad time with it. They become bitter, antagonistic, maudlin—not much use to themselves or anyone else. I hope your soul fattens with me at your side. While our pasts never will disappear, they will diminish in importance. They must. They simply must."

"Here we are, in bed, not having drank any hooch and, yet again, our cups overflow with droplets of philosophical nonsense."

"Then I suggest you start the fire and make coffee. I'll bake beignets using my French great-great-grandmother's recipe. A tightly held secret within the family since before the revolution."

A leisurely late morning gave way to an equally relaxing afternoon. Nothing of great import, just a comfortable walk near the Panthéon and down alongside the Seine. Véronique recommended that instead of viewing Notre-Dame from the front we see it from Ile Saint-Louis. Glad she suggested it. An impressive perspective, dominated by the cathedral's flying buttresses, a view not captured by picture postcards. We returned to the apartment after a token lunch in the Latin Quarter that included a fine bottle of wine. Sitting by her fireplace, we talked about our expectations of the post-war world.

"I recalled reading in the *Paris Herald* a few days ago, Véronique, that next week—around the nineteenth, I think—the US Senate votes on the Treaty of Versailles, including membership in the League of Nations. Even if the margin is as thin as a gnat's ass, this passage will demonstrate that, despite all the death and destruction, there's a new world a-comin'. My buddies died for something. Their deaths brought change, a new era. It was a different war ... so the world must develop a different way of governing itself."

"Agreed, but please remember, France and Britain

went through over four years of hell and privation. That doesn't diminish the American contribution—we may have lost without it—but the US experienced only nineteen months or so of war. We want a peace that lasts too—something respectful for the million-plus of my countrymen who perished."

"I've never told anyone this, Véronique, but I didn't join the army in 1917 because of any love of gold-braided glory and heroism. I signed-up only because I knew I wouldn't be able to face anyone who been it after the damn thing was over. But, having served and nearly died, I believe America has an obligation, having offered its youth. Hope it doesn't renege on the promise."

"Another topic where a French woman and an American man find agreement. I hope America doesn't, either."

We prepared for our evening at Brasserie Lipp a little past five. Véronique asked if I minded getting dressed in the sitting room. She couldn't surprise me if we got fancied-up together in the bedroom. I was glad to do it, anxious to see the results.

I was sitting on the dark leather chair when she sauntered in … stunningly beautiful. She wore a slightly below-the-knee emerald green satin dress with shiny silver beadwork that bordered a low neckline. Similar beadwork was repeated around the high upper sleeves. Black satiny pumps with a green buckle sealed the look. The right-side of her hair was pinned slightly upward with a silver hair clip, highlighting her sculpted cheeks and deep blue eyes. I caught a whiff of perfume as she twirled around, modelling the whole megillah.

"I can only think 'beautiful,' Véronique. Beautiful. You'll be the talk of Montparnasse."

"I'm glad you like it. Feel fresh wearing it."

"Speaking of fresh, the perfume or scented oil you're wearing is unlike anything I've ever smelled. So classically French."

"Surprisingly, Willis, it's not French. It's Shem-El-Nessim, an exotic offering from a family-owned London perfumery. That's between you and me. My friends would be horrified if they knew it was British."

We took a cab to Lipp. Couldn't jeopardise Véronique's 'put together' look. There was a spattering of men wearing black dinner jackets and an equal number of ladies displaying refined couture dining on the ground floor. A sure giveaway we'd encounter these fine people again on the first floor. The place was abuzz. Waiters carrying crowded food trays double-timed around the floor. Corks popping and the glasses clanging drowned out any hoped-for conversation between tables. Luscious smells from a variety of foods permeated the air. The overstuffed cornucopia of Paris, I thought. Véronique beamed with pride, anticipating what lay ahead.

Our exquisite meal—something to which I had become accustomed at Brasserie Lipp—was surpassed only by the wine Véronique chose: a 1901 bottle of Chateau de Pommard from Beaune, that region I recognised only from higher altitude. My unit had used the uniquely coloured roof tiles of the Hospice de Beaune as a navigational landmark whenever the ceiling descended. The oversized glasses the sommelier brought, although customary and expected by French oenophiles, were a revelation. I took it in my stride, trying carefully not to convey American ignorance to the wine steward or to Véronique. I failed.

"It's wide, Willis, so you can swirl it, sniff it and, by

tilting to one side, see if it has legs."

"Didn't want you to think I'd just ridden in from the countryside and fell off the turnip cart. Thanks for the education."

"He didn't know, don't worry. Recognised your facial expression. Sensed your bewilderment. I crossed my fingers and a couple of toes you wouldn't ask *him* questions. They can be snobby and rude. I admire how you kept silent."

"A skill I acquired in the army, I suppose."

Twenty minutes before nine the head waiter approached those holding performance tickets. Made our way upstairs and located our respective tables and seats. Everything accomplished without fuss, fanfare or trouble. We looked around after establishing ourselves and getting comfortable. What a sight to behold. Each of the thirty tables had a lighted candle covered by an amber-coloured lampshade with tiny beads dangling downward toward the table top. An ice bucket, bottle of champagne and two crystal coupe glasses adorned each table. Waiters served a medium-sized bowl of caviar with the requisite amount of toast points. To our immediate front was a slightly elevated stage. No music stands. No instruments other than a piano and the drum/cymbals ensemble. The house lights dimmed. A noisy room became silent. The hush of anticipation filled the room.

Monsieur Lipp, the proprietor of the brasserie, approached the stage. I wasn't bothered that his introduction was in French. I picked out the important bits—especially the home-grown purity of the jazz. None were Sardinians, thank God. Four of five jazzmen had served in the American Army's 'Hellfighters Band' led by Lieutenant James Reese Europe. During the height of

US involvement, the band regularly performed the new music called 'jazz' to British and French audiences alike. While most of the regiment's band members returned to the States, four remained. A kindred spirit, found 'wandering aimlessly through France,' was recruited to beat the drums and keep the beat. After a few self-promoting words about the brasserie, *Monsieur* Lipp left the stage. Seconds later, the five band members entered the room to loud applause.

Not a word was spoken. The members launched immediately into an introductory number. After finishing, and when clapping stopped, the pianist and band leader, James 'Skeeter' Walker, introduced the others: Pete 'Sticks' Calhoun beat the drums; Louie 'Pearl Keys' Watkins played alto saxophone; Randolph Jackson blew the trumpet; and, 'Sliding Jack' Beauregard heated-up the trombone. Walker's introduction was warm and inviting and in English. This time, I reaped the rewards. No one minded though. Almost expected it. To this day I remember Walker's description of jazz.

"Please prepare yourselves, 'kind' ladies and 'gentle' men of Paris. Toes will tap. Bodies will sway. Limbs will loosen. Restraints will lift. Inhibitions will disappear. By letting go, you will be consumed by passionate truth, overtaken with physical emotion. Me and the boys of Swaneeland take personal responsibility if, at the end of the evening, you're not experiencing a swaggering Yankee buzz."

And for the next ninety-minutes we heard what I'd swear was the hottest jazz this side of the Atlantic. 'The Memphis Blue', 'St Louis Blues' and 'Beale Street Blues', all composed by WC Handy, went over well. I noticed with 'Darktown Strutter's Ball'—a piece I perform regularly in Montparnasse—at least one foot underneath every table was tapping. The melancholy and reflective 'Baby, Won't You Please Come Home' slowed things down a bit. Some may have reminisced about a soldier lost in the war or recalled a poorly ended love affair. Walker introduced 'Tiger Rag' as the song sweeping through America faster than winds from a spring tornado. Once the band started, a woman, whom we hadn't recognised earlier, approached the stage and began dancing in a most peculiar manner. Movement wasn't her sole uniqueness. Appearance played an equal if not greater part in everyone's fascination. She had what I only can describe as a 'Joan of Arc' hairstyle or, if pressed for another description, an artistic twist on a German infantryman's helmet: bangs cropped short on the forehead; angular cut alongside the cheeks to the mouth; back cut straight across, well above the neck and shoulders. No curls at all—every follicle—ramrod straight. She looked modern. She looked like fun. Her short sleeveless dress hung low on the hips. There was little delineation of a feminine figure. Any natural curves appeared absent. She wore a silver headband and three, almost waist-length pearl necklaces. Each strand comprised different-sized pearls. Band members weren't offended. They shared in her enjoyment, too. She continued her 'ballroom strutting' in the next number, 'Royal Garden Blues'. Seemed the sought-after 'swaggering Yankee buzz' had taken hold of this young thing earlier than expected. She returned to her seat when the band slowed the pace and darkened the mood with a personal favourite of mine, 'Poor Butterfly'. Ever the gracious gentleman, James Walker congratulated the young thing for being the first to capture the Yankee buzz. Prior to leaving the stage she faced the band and curtsied. The audience clapped.

Swaneeland's final number was a gasser. Took me, Véronique and, I'm sure, everyone else by complete and utter surprise—a jazz version of 'La Marseillaise'. At first, we weren't certain we were hearing the national anthem. Ten bars in, it dawned on the crowd what it was. The room stood up immediately, their faces smiling in disbelief. At the rousing conclusion the crowd chanted *Vive la France, Vive la France. Monsieur* Lipp ran from the back cheering, *États-Unis, États-Unis.* The crowd took the hint and began chanting, *États-Unis, États-Unis.* A jazz concert had morphed into a patriotic rally of battlefield allies. Bands members smiled, clapped toward the audience, waved, and left through a side door.

"That's what I call hot jazz for a cool evening, Véronique. Hope you enjoyed it."

"Thoroughly, thoroughly relished every number. Every number. How talented. So different. So incredibly unique. If they heard you, think they'd ask you to join?"

"They wouldn't permit me to shine their instruments, let alone play alongside them. And besides, kinda think Pearl Keys owns the sax. His cork is fresh and well-greased. His leather keypads are soft and new. He isn't going anywhere."

"Anything can happen, Willis. It's Montparnasse."

The loveliness of the evening and the cool temperatures served as our invitation to walk home. Didn't discuss events from a year ago. Those reminiscences had been sealed earlier in the day. Couldn't add anything. We'd arrive at the same conclusion. Once home we shared a neat Scotch by the freshly made roaring fire. Couldn't believe that, at such a late hour, Véronique still looked stunning. Nature never messes with perfection.

"A special evening together I'll long remember."

"So will I. Thanks again for inviting me."

"Wouldn't have been the same without you nearby. But I've reached the point now, I think, where I'm looking forward to some solid rack time. Been an emotionally reflective day."

"Might we follow through on what I expected last night?"

Chapter Four

At half one I made my way to Dominique Diguet's club after a lucrative evening in Montparnasse. First evening at the brothel. No idea what to expect. Would guests consider me a bothersome intruder or a meddlesome voyeur? And, artistically speaking, would they enjoy my playing?

Madame greeted me warmly and escorted me to the performance corner. I heard soft chatter in the adjoining room. Saw one of *Madame's* girls in the distance escorting a guest by the hand up the narrow set of stairs. After reaching the landing, another couple descended, having completed the evening's transaction. I recognised the girl—Salomé from Bordeaux. The customer seemed flushed and a bit peeved at her friendly greeting.

"Oh, là là, fantastique, mon Américain."

To appease the guest's insecurity, told him I was the evening's entertainment, pointing to my sax case and music stand. His fragile male ego repaired, he nodded and took a seat at the bar. Salomé, seemingly oblivious to male territorial issues, retreated to the chaise longue where she twirled her lengthy pearl necklace repeatedly around her finger.

Three men were enjoying the company of women when I began playing. Wanting to avoid competing with what appeared to be semi-intimate conversation, I kept it soft, slow and classical: Jacques Offenbach's 'Barcarolle', Satie's 'Gymnopédie No.1' as well as his 'Gnossienne No. 3' and Debussy's 'Clair de lune'. Even threw in a bit of America—Stephen Foster's 'Beautiful Dreamer', a piece apropos for the temporary fulfilment of elusive desires. Whether because of or in spite of the music, the couples adjourned upstairs within minutes of each other. The room was empty except for me and three girls.

In addition to Salomé, there was Juillet from Massiges, whom I had met earlier, and Gabrielle, whom I learned hailed from a farm village outside Nîmes. Since there weren't customers, I wondered if this might be a convenient time to enjoy one of my two drinks. The girls interpreted my question as a request. Gabrielle went behind the bar, poured a Scotch, handed it to me and then sat close by, absorbing my every gesture.

Conversing with the girls revealed a lot … sadness, mostly. All had arrived in Paris due to circumstances over which they had minimal control. Salomé was from the small village of Mussidan in Bordeaux, the site of a temporary American army field hospital. She fell in love with a young army doctor who promised to marry her in Paris as soon as the war ended. She arrived a few days before the wedding—excited, anxiously anticipating an exotic life in America. The doctor didn't come. She never received a reason. Weeks passed. But still, no word. Alone, scared, little money and with minimal prospects, she began working the streets. Months passed. *Madame* Diguet found her in a terrible state and took her in. The same profession, of course—but in a safer, cleaner environment.

Juillet's story proved equally dismal. The village in which her family lived, Massiges in Champagne, served as the frontline of fighting after September 1915. She arrived from school one afternoon to find her parents and younger sister dead. Their ancient farmhouse had been reduced to rubble with bits of animals—sheep, cows, chickens, and horses—strewn everywhere. She had never seen such carnage. Juillet packed what clothes she could find. Didn't matter if the items were her mother's or father's. She'd wear them regardless. Feeling the capital was the safest place to live, she departed Massiges on foot the following morning. A week later, she arrived in Paris in good spirits due to the kindness of strangers encountered along the way. They provided her a comfortable bed, a hot meal and a warm bath. One older lady washed her soiled clothes and mended any torn items. She landed on *Madame* Diguet's step only because a high-ranking government official—a regular customer of Dominique's—found her sitting alone on a street kerb one evening and took pity.

Whether it was Gabrielle's training, young age or sheer excitement of having a foreigner around, she talked longer and in more precise detail than the others. Fortunately, her English surpassed my French any number of ways. After learning her father had been killed at the First Battle of the Marne, Gabrielle's mother escorted the young girl to Paris in autumn 1914, telling her they'd live out the duration with relatives. They became separated in the train station immediately after arriving. Gabrielle thought, initially, it was an accident. Decided later it had been intentional. Without names or contact information for the supposed relatives, Gabrielle wandered the city's streets for weeks, surviving on discarded food from cafés and brasseries. Even stole bread from unsuspecting customers sitting at outside café tables. Her mother had, at least, some decency—packed her bag with warm clothes so she didn't suffer too badly from the cold and damp. One sunny afternoon, the fourteen-year-old stretched out on a remote bench in Jardin du Luxembourg and fell asleep. When she woke,

Madame Diguet was sitting beside her. Initially startled by *Madame's* persistent questioning, she soon warmed to her and accepted the proposal.

"You certainly weren't presented as one of her girls at age fourteen?"

"No, no. *Madame* offered me a room on the top floor—away from everything. She insisted I attend the nearby Lycée. I had chores in the house, of course, cleaning rooms and fireplaces, keeping the kitchen neat— but, no, never friendliness or conversations with guests. That was forbidden."

"But you are one of her girls *now*, correct?"

"I decided when I completed school and turned eighteen. Sounds different, I suppose, to you, but I felt an obligation. *Madame* more or less raised me—took me off the street, fed me, clothed me, protected me and oversaw my education. I owe her. I owe her much. Another girl, Madeleine, arrived not long after me. We were treated the same but she left immediately after completing school. She had other plans, I suppose."

"Your loyalty is admirable, but did you think of possibly pursuing another type job so you could compensate her more directly for her kindness and support?"

"I did. Worked in a perfumery shop on Rue Jacob for nearly a year. But I missed Dominique. I missed the girls who had taken a keen interest in me. They're my family. All I had. I liked the security. Comforted by the familiar."

Didn't know exactly how to react. Respected Dominique's intentions. A cynic would see them as self-serving but Gabrielle had survived and thrived because of her. In a small way she had become Dominique's adopted daughter. Made sure she received an education, thereby guaranteeing other opportunities and different options could become available. But Gabrielle had decided to remain, finding security in familiar surroundings. Whatever preconceived opinion I held in the States, prior to 1917, toward 'working' women and the men who used them had been supplanted by the immorality of war and the complicity of governments that supported wholesale slaughter. Any sane person could identify, without hesitation, which activity reeked of inhumanity and immorality. Gabrielle looked at me as I finished my drink, accurately condensing thoughts and feelings I'd been unable to articulate for over a year.

"The war was a thief, *Monsieur* Travers. It robbed us all. And all are here because of it, even you."

Three couples arrived downstairs within minutes of each other. Made me think each room was equipped with a wind-up metronome. Sessions ended when the pendulum stopped pulsating. So ... I offered some jazz for their entertainment. Thought 'Oh Johnny, Oh Johnny, Oh!' particularly appropriate, as was 'Oui, Oui, Marie'. 'Darktown Strutter's Ball' and 'Chong (He Come from Hong Kong)' rounded out the set. Two men said their goodbyes. The third man took a seat at the bar. For the final hour, I reprised my Montparnasse act, with one exception: my last song was a Dvorak symphony, 'From the New World', specifically the lyrical segment known popularly as 'Going Home'. And with that I packed the instrument, organised the music and collapsed the stand. To my—and the man at the bar's—utter surprise, each girl came over and kissed me goodbye—including the three girls I didn't know.

"*À bientôt, mon Américain. À bientôt.*"

It had been a fine evening, a worthwhile gig. Any performance is a beneficial one if the audience enjoys it. I knew the girls did. And I received some indication their guests did, too. Prior to leaving, the guy at the bar handed me some francs. So, I felt good. Sensed a wholeness. Music and Véronique and Paris were doing their best to repair me in the broken places. Seemed to be going well.

Véronique and I had agreed that on weekdays I'd return to my flat after working at *Madame's*. No use waking her. Too damn early in the morning. She'd be useless at work. It also provided me six or seven hopeful hours of uninterrupted sleep. This arrangement worked fine. Oftentimes, she'd join me after work for drinks at Bal au Printemps. She liked Johnny, especially his decidedly uncharacteristic British manner. He told you how he felt. Inference, for which the British are well-known, didn't exist with Johnny. He inferred nothing. Told you how he felt and what he believed. And Johnny certainly relished her. I remember his comment after first being introduced: *I can think of no finer tonic than you, Mam'selle Vouvray, to soothe this sorry arse American.*

One evening, while waiting for Véronique, the place seemed unusually crowded. Johnny had time only for a cursory greeting. Too busy to chew even the smallest gristle and fat. The place hummed with noisy American tourists and self-conscious British transplants. An enclave of aristocratic Russians was discussing the revolution, including plans for a clandestine return. Their supposed pedigree, however, seemed dubious, giving credence to the old adage: *Scratch a Russian and you'll always find a peasant underneath.* There also were two overly painted girls introducing themselves to any unaccompanied man possessing two legs and a bulging wallet, as well as an impeccably dressed conman in the corner, peddling questionable deals to unsuspecting customers. All three were pursuing their craft, making a living off the desires of others. In some ways, I thought, that's what we all do. Just too dishonest with ourselves to acknowledge it.

My contentedness turned to displeasure after reading a week-old *Paris Herald* I found sitting atop the bar. The United States Senate had voted against ratifying the Treaty of Versailles, which also meant, of course, rejecting membership in the League. Seemed President Wilson had instructed Democrats not to vote for the Treaty with the reservations Republicans had attached, specifically those penned by Henry Cabot Lodge, the cantankerous and isolationist senator from Massachusetts. While Democrats held out hope for another vote—and victory—early next year, I didn't. Deep in thought, I didn't realise Véronique had arrived and sitting on the stool next to me.

"A franc for your thoughts."

"Oh, God, sorry. I do apologise. Been there long?"

"Three minutes. You had that thousand-metre stare."

I handed her the newspaper and pointed to the article.

"It's justified."

She put down the paper after finishing. Didn't look at me face to face but through the full-length mirror on the wall over the bar. I glanced at the mirror. Her face reflected a frustration that words couldn't describe.

"Johnny, two double neats for Willis and me, please."

Always admired a woman who could order drinks for a man. Rare as vintage Scotch.

"The destruction. The horror. The deaths. Similar laments will be heard within nations for decades, by allies and former foes alike. The waste. The lies. The betrayal of the young who fought by the old who made the peace."

"So, I'm guessing the promise of a new world a-comin' isn't happening."

"Gone in a year."

"It's all going to occur again, you know."

"My buddies' death proved the worthlessness of modern man, of politicians, of nations. Lies, bitterness and greed, that's all that remains in life."

My disillusion only increased on a sunny afternoon in late March 1920. Véronique and I found ourselves sitting on the same stools at Bal au Printemps when Johnny handed us a British newspaper. The US Senate fell seven votes short of the two-thirds majority required to pass the treaty, and with it the nation's membership in the League of Nations.

"That's it, Véronique—America's turned its back to the world. Going to isolate itself. Lick its wounds. Pout. Ignore its obligation to the dead, the wounded, the scarred, not to mention future generations."

"Idealists always get crushed, you know that. You're alive; I'm alive; we can't squander life. To do so would make those who died—your flying comrades—worthless martyrs."

"Here, a bottle on the house. Drink till it no longer hurts."

"Got twenty years' worth, Johnny?"

"*Merci*, Johnny."

"America turned its back on me, so I'll reciprocate. Never returning. Dumping the Stars and Stripes, the land of the free, 'In God We Trust' and the other hokum it peddles. It's unadulterated horseshit. *Fini et au revoir*."

"Then let's not hold back. Do everything, anything, and ignore the consequences. Convention be damned. *N'est-ce pas?*"

"*Oui, Mam'selle, Oui*."

I didn't know if it was my dead buddies intervening so my life would count for something or what, but a month or so after Véronique encouraged us 'not to hold back', I got a feeling somebody, somewhere, wanted me to succeed. I fell, neck-deep, into some seriously good luck.

One evening, while performing in Montparnasse a tall, lanky man deposited several francs in my case. Catching my eye, he asked when finished if I'd join him for a drink at Les Deux Magots. The natty dresser looked familiar and spoke with an American accent, but I couldn't place him. Told him I'd be over after midnight. Encouraged him to ask for Jacques.

"He'll give a generous pour at a good price."

I arrived fifteen minutes after midnight. The gentleman had told Jacques I'd be over soon so, true to form, Jacques had a double neat waiting for me. The gentlemen stood up as I approached. We shook hands. He, too, was nursing a double neat.

"Thanks for agreeing to meet. I'm Louie Watkins, but you can call me Pearl Keys. That's what the boys of Swaneeland call me."

"Damn! I knew you looked familiar. Just couldn't place it. My girl and I attended the Armistice anniversary gig at Brasserie Lipp. I tell you, the band was something else. Hot. Smooth. Pure class. Loved the evening."

"In a roundabout kind of way, that's why I approached you. You see, I've been watching you play for over two months now. You're good. Real good. Have a way of bringing in the audience—even if they're only walking by. They stop. They listen. They continue to listen. They drop coins in your case. And continue to listen."

"Kinda lucky, I guess. More out of pity probably than ability. Amazing what a gimp leg and aviator scarf does."

"Well, let me say that James Skeeter Walker—the band's leader—doesn't believe in luck. He believes in ability. He believes in talent. He believes in skill. Thinks you've got it."

"Nice to know I'm appreciated."

"I'll get to the point: Ever consider joining Swaneeland?"

"The band needs another saxophone?"

"No. I gotta leave. Returning to the States. Don't know how much you've heard about what's going on back there, but ..."

"Know the politicians fucked us by not ratifying the Treaty. Keeping us out of the League. I know that much!"

"There's a lot of bad stuff going on. My wife's a marked woman. She worked as a copy editor for *The Masses*—a progressive magazine you may have heard of—until 1917, when the government labelled it subversive and shut it down. She luckily found work as a secretary at the AFL (American Federation of Labour). Hell, now the Attorney General of the US, one A. Mitchell Palmer, is rounding up supposed radicals throughout the country and charging them with sedition—not for overt actions but only for political and organisational memberships. And the AFL, well, hell, it's high on their list of undesirables. Some are being deported."

"Your wife's being deported?"

"No, not yet, and hopefully won't be. But I'm pretty sure with her interests and memberships, she's on a list of supposed radicals somewhere. I'm worried if she comes to join the tour, when it's over and we want to return, the government won't let us. Even worse, they'd let us in and then lock us up."

"Afraid you'd be locked-up if you went back now?"

"Well ... that's a risk I'm willing to take. I want to be with the woman. She's stood by and with me for years—

through all kinds of crap, not least of which was the war. Won't let her down now when she needs me."

"Admirable. I respect that. Truly."

"It's only fair to tell you that there is another guy we're considering. Our trombonist, Sliding Jack Beauregard, has visited a whorehouse a couple times and told James about a sax player who—get this—serenades the girls and their guests, pumps them up so they're all excited, I guess, before and after the transaction. Beauregard says the guy plays eclectic sets—classical, jazz, ragtime ... hell, even heard a couple pre-Civil War Stephen Foster tunes one night. The guy plays three nights a week, apparently, so tonight Beauregard's going to ask the *Madame* when she next expects him."

"It isn't by chance on Rue de la Grande Chaumiere, somewhat close to the Jardin du Luxembourg?"

"Yeah, might be. My French isn't good, non-existent actually. Sounds fairly close though. The *Madame* is Domino Doo-get. Something like that."

"Could it possibly be Dominique Diguet?"

"Ahh, you've visited a few times then, too, huh?"

"Oh, I've visited all right. I'm the sax player Sliding Jack's looking for. Been working that gig for months, three days a week from two to five in the morning."

"Well, I'm damned. Hell, pretty much settles it then, I guess. Provided you're interested."

"I'm interested. Damn sure about that."

"Good. Can't wait to tell Skeeter and Sliding Jack. They're going to be shocked. The band's playing a private club in Montmartre from one until four all this week, so I better get hustling. Promise to think long and hard over it, will you?"

"I excel at the long and hard."

"Hell, you'll fit right in from the get-go. Damn nice."

I wrote down my address as well as Véronique's. Said Mr Walker would be in touch soon. Probably early morning … half five or six. In that case, I asked Pearl Keys to pass along that if Walker visited on a weekday, try the Rue du Cardinal Lemoine address first. Couldn't predict the reaction he'd receive from the beautiful but unsuspecting woman who'd answer the door at such an ungodly hour.

Meeting James Walker became as improvisational as jazz. Every band member eagerly offered their opinions on music, on jazz, on the band and on the future. I remain impressed, to this day, by their collective ability to ferret out my locations to speak with me or to leave notes through the door of my or Véronique's apartment. Each band member, from drummer Sticks Calhoun and trumpeter Randolph Jackson to trombonist Sliding Jack (met me one early morning at Dominque's) or Pearl Keys, whom I had met first, contributed their perspective prior to handing me off to Skeeter. Should have expected, of course, the hand-off would be as unique as sight-reading music.

Walker visited Véronique's early one Saturday morning, confident I'd be there. He had remembered my request not to come around on a weekday and, to be fair, Saturday morning is the weekend. So, he wasn't bothered and neither was I. He was correct on another score. Véronique and I were nestled tight as intertwined banjo strings, oblivious to any knocking. What finally woke us, ironically, was Walker's loud but perfectly in-tune humming of 'Tiger Rag'. Thought initially it was a passing street vendor making his way to the Saturday market. But the humming grew steadily louder. Finally awake, I stumbled to open the door. And there stood Walker—all smiles, dressed in an immaculate dinner jacket with an undone tie.

"*Bonjour, Monsieur* Travers. Got any Scotch?"

"Damn, as I live and breathe. We finally meet. Please, come in, Mr Walker."

"James, please or Skeeter, if you prefer."

"Okay … James. Let me say two things. First, a bottle of Scotch is guaranteed to be hiding in the apartment. Second, that's the best sounding reveille I've heard. Puts the army's rendition to shame."

While I poured the Scotch, Véronique assembled herself and welcomed our guest.

"If I were in bed with a woman as pretty as you, ma'am, no way would I have answered the door."

"You're very kind. But please remember, Mr Walker, I've experienced over a year of American flattery. The deserved and undeserved kind. Now, if you'll excuse me, I'll prepare some Saturday morning beignets."

"Scotch and beignets and a pretty woman on a Saturday morning. Only in France."

We sat in the living room near the fire. He possessed a sophisticated confidence, easily enhanced by his handsome looks and pleasant demeanour. Had a smoothness of speech Shakespearian actors would envy. I drank water while he enjoyed a Scotch. Unbeknownst to me, I learned he was the first band member to hear me in Montparnasse, not Pearl Keys. After the other boys had seen my gig, they became keen, too. Asked when I could start. Wanted to slide me in gently so Watkins could leave without interruption. I'd practice with the band during the day, but Pearl Keys would perform at gigs until the boys felt comfortable with me and me with them. Once accepted, we'd play three nights a week at a private club in Montmartre. Occasionally, he said, the muckety-muck Americans in their oversized homes on the Right Bank, hire the band for dinner parties. I learned also that arrangements had been made for summer gigs in Provins, Reims, Dijon, Limoges, Bordeaux, Avignon, Aix-en-Provence, Lyon and Troyes. Everything sounded jake. Even the workload.

"Although our Right Bank clientele wear stiff collars, they feed us well. The bar's open to us when the gig's finished. Sometimes, when only the hosts remain, they ask if we'd play through the night. A concert for two, I suppose. Hell, a few times they've even gone to bed. We kept playing and … the bar remained open."

"Sounds as if I'll be able to keep the gig at *Madame* Diguet's, then. Might have to rearrange some days, depending on the schedule, of course, but …"

"Is that the whorehouse? Sure, keep it—your playing might increase sales. Some connected people 'shop' there, you know?"

"Seen them. Heard them. They seem a bit embarrassed, I think, with me being a foreigner and all. Thinking I'd pursue a blackmail trick or something. Of course … not interested. Least of my concerns is discovering that a high-ranking minister, a titan of post-war finance or an elected politician is upstairs shootin' his wad."

No sooner had I finished when Véronique came in with a tray of fresh beignets, blackberry preserves and black coffee.

"Shootin' his wad … is that similar to hooch?"

James looked at me, puzzled and concerned, wondering how I'd explain it.

"Exactly, Véronique. American English."

James started laughing. Véronique offered her characteristic *I'll let it go ... for now* look."

"If not a problem, ma'am, could I trouble you for another Scotch and forgo the coffee?"

"What about you, then, Willis—Scotch?"

All three of us started to laugh.

"Why not? It's bad manners for a jazzman to drink alone."

"Won't have any man labelling me a teetotaller. I'll find two more glasses."

The buttery richness of Véronique's beignets and the silkiness of the Scotch—aided and abetted, of course, by the tartness of the preserves—enlivened the conversation. Learned James became the rightful owner of the nickname Skeeter when just a small boy. Obviously, a piano prodigy: parents said his fingers bounced over the black and white keys 'faster than a buzzing skeeter' (American slang for mosquito). After war was declared, he finagled his way into New York's 369th Regiment's 'Hellfighters Band' under the direction of Lieutenant James Reese Europe. Returning to America a few months after the Armistice, Skeeter decided Europe offered him more freedom, more respect, more security, and more independence, both musically and personally, than the States. He convinced others to join him, arriving Paris a few weeks before the Treaty was signed. About the same time, I was discharged from the hospital. He holds no regrets.

For some reason—caused either by the Scotch or Walker's infectious personality—Véronique divulged an aspect of *her* war that she never had told anyone, including me.

"Our family farmhouse bordered the area where the

Battle of Grand Couronné was fought in early September 1914. One morning, while my mother was gathering breakfast eggs, she found a wounded German soldier sitting upright alongside the chicken coop. Not worried in the least of any danger, she approached him and, conversed a little in German—her birth language—and analysed the injured leg. After some quick thinking, she brought him into the house, attended the wound and cooked him a hearty meal. My father, who returned several hours later from working a distant field, wasn't pleased. He wanted to alert the army and have him transported to a prisoner camp. Mother would have none of it. So, guess what? The soldier—a sworn enemy of France—remained holed-up inside *our* house for over a year. Worked as a servant mostly. Cleaned, cooked, mended things. Finally, had enough—or saw an opportunity, I guess—and left one evening while my parents slept. He wrote Mother a kind letter. Left it on the table, thanking her for her Christian humanity. Never knew any of this, of course, until Father's funeral a few months before the Armistice."

"No one found out? Wasn't somebody, somewhere, suspicious?"

"There wasn't anyone nearby. The farmhouse was isolated. That's probably why the soldier chose to hide there. And besides, a war was being fought. Other issues, other concerns. If someone had found out … I'm sure my parents would have been convicted of 'providing aid and comfort to the enemy' and summarily executed. To this day I think the experience brought about Father's premature death. He died aged forty-four. Mother returned to Germany after he was buried. Haven't seen, heard or written to her since."

"What happened to the soldier?"

"Probably lived to fight again. Killing my countrymen or Tommies, maybe even Doughboys."

"Could have been the guy who shot down one of my buddies or delivered the shots that brought my aircraft down."

"Look at us in this room—one American went home, found it unappealing and returned; another American never left; and a French woman lost her father and stopped communicating with her mother. Are we a unique but sorry lot, or are others out there like us?"

Véronique's analysis seemed spot on. She not only spoke in English; she thought in English. Such a reflective but unanswerable query could only be asked by someone damaged by the war—not physically, perhaps—but emotionally. A person who understood that what existed before couldn't exist after. A new world was a-comin', just not the one she and thousands of others expected.

"Let me freshen your Scotch, Véronique."

"Please … thank you. Wonder if this glass will help me utter more uplifting thoughts."

Laughter filled the room and the mood was lightened. Each took another healthy sip.

Skeeter confirmed I'd begin immediately. Rehearsal times ran from noon until four. The schedule allowed me to continue at Dominique's from six until nine three times a week. It also enabled me, if the mood struck and the weather cooperated, to perform a few hours in Montparnasse. The band's current gig was at Brin de Quelque Chose (Wisp of Something), a private club in Montmartre on Rue Pigalle. A bit off Boulevard de Clichy, not too far from Sacré-Coeur but far enough to be inconvenient to tourists. I wouldn't play. I'd listen to the band and watch the customers' reactions. Soaking up the atmosphere and the learning.

Skeeter stood up and shook my hand, welcoming me to the band. After drinking what little remained of his Scotch, he put down the glass and offered me a not-too-subtle challenge.

"Pearl Keys is a great sax man. You've got dulcet tones and quick fingerings to live up to, William. But you'll blend in, despite the way you appear this morning. I believe in you. Véronique's charm and beignets have made it so."

Whereupon he belted out what I learned only later was his characteristic yelp.

"To paraphrase the wonderful WC Handy, *Ashes to ashes, and dust to dust. If my laughing don't get you, my jazzin' must. Bonjour, au revoir* and *merci* for the Scotch."

Closing the door, Véronique turned, walked over, and hugged me.

"Happy for you, sad for me. I'll see much less of my American, I think."

"Only initially, until I get comfortable. Probably drop Montparnasse once I jive with the band."

"But your evenings—our evenings together—will be fewer and fewer. In your apartment more than mine. In your bed more than mine."

"I need you. And you want me. We've experienced too much pain and loss the last six years for this to dampen affections. My absence will intensify the days and evenings when we are together. I promise."

"Allow me to use the key you gave me."

"Be nice to think so."

Chapter Five

I arrived at Brin de Quelque Chose a little before noon. Wasn't late but I *was* the last one. Lesson learned. Wouldn't happen again. Felt odd being back in a band. Hadn't experienced a joint musical effort since early 1917—my last night playing with the Sinton Hotel's house orchestra. The world's churned and flipped around a few times since then, I thought. But the boys were welcoming. Felt sorry for Pearl Keys. Could tell he wanted to meet up with his wife, but I also knew he'd never experience the camaraderie of something like Swaneeland again.

Walker handed out the sheet music he had acquired recently in the mail. All purported to be the most popular numbers in the speakeasy clubs in the States: 'Whispering', 'Wang Blues', 'Avalon', 'The Japanese Sandman', 'Irene', 'Crazy Blues', and—my personal favourite—'Hold Me', containing a luscious sax lead. Pearl Keys and I handled it well together. Damn powerful noise with both playing.

We took a break after ninety minutes. The respectful professionalism shared amongst bandsmen gave way to what in the army, we called 'grab-assing'. Insulting, playful banter filled the room. I was too new to give or to receive, so I observed. All the guys honed in on Sliding Jack Beauregard's frequent visits to various whorehouses. The drummer, Pete Sticks Calhoun, thought the visits bordered on the medicinal.

"Hell, fellas, don't chastise him. All that activity with females probably eases the overuse of his right hand and arm. Keeps it from being longer than his left."

Randolph Jackson, the trumpeter, disagreed.

"Well, shit, if he laid off the women a bit his embouchure might improve and he'd hit the correct notes more often."

Beauregard stood his ground. Embarrassment wouldn't be his.

"Let me tell you something, Calhoun. At least I'm spending the money I earn enjoying myself. You're so tight no one could shove a piece of birdseed up your ass with a cold chisel. And, Jackson, just remember—if I thought seriously of putting the screws to you, you'd fold like a cheap suit."

Everybody laughed. Couple of boys clapped hands. Learned later that Calhoun was incredibly cheap. Disliked spending money. Occupied his spare time visiting museums and historical buildings and reading books while sitting in various Paris gardens. And he'd only drink if it were offered for free. Jackson, it seemed, liked sparring, but when the heat intensified he'd leave the scene faster than a lit match.

Grab-assing over, we returned to practising. Skeeter surprised us with a sight-reading exercise. An intense jazz number where each instrument performed a lengthy solo, with the band coming together for a rip-roaring, foot-tapping and body-swaying completion. Damn, it was good.

"Gentlemen, that's my own composition. Been nurturing it awhile. Finalised it last week. Named it this weekend."

"Hell, Skeeter, what you calling it then?"

"Calm yourself, Sticks—no need to dent a cymbal. It's called 'Scotch, Beignets on Saturday Mornings'."

Looked at me, nodded his head and smiled.

"Was introduced to a lovely, inspirational French lady last weekend. It's dedicated to her."

"Been holding out on us, Skeeter?"

"Not at all, Pearl Keys, not at all. Hope you have the

good fortune one day to meet Travers's girl. A refined lady for our times."

Embarrassed, I graciously thanked Skeeter for the dedication and kind words.

"Don't think I'll look at Véronique's beignets the same way ever again."

"Hey, Travers ... do you *parlez-vous* or just stare longingly into her eyes each evening without uttering a word?"

"Sorry to disappoint, Sticks. She rewards me for each word I speak in French."

"What do you mean, 'reward'?"

"If you used all the imagination skills God gave you, well, you'd be halfway toward the answer."

"Damn, Pearl Keys said you'd fit in. You certainly do!"

That evening's performance was a revelation. British, Americans, French and Russians dressed in their finest fine. Never seen such gorgeous women. Not stuffy at all, only loose and free. Must be the jazz, I thought. Flaunts individual freedom and craves independence at the expense of societal convention. Not a lot of people, but a lot of the people I like. And the booze, hell, flowed quicker than the Ohio River during a spring flood.

I accomplished what I set out to do. Watched. Watched the crowd's reaction to the music. Watched the band's performance. Skeeter asked me to critique with an eye toward improving the gig visually. Difficult to mess with near perfection, I thought, but I tried my best. Going so far as to write comments in a small pad I had stuck in my rear trouser pocket. While standing in a far corner scribbling a few thoughts, a woman approached.

"I see you're alone. Stuck in this corner by yourself.

Care to join me and my husband for a drink?"

Her accent defined her as an American but a different kind of American. A woman of society. A woman of money. And she looked it. Hourglass figure. Fashionable clothes. Long, single strand of pearls. Neck length, auburn-coloured hair. Owned a captivating smile that seemed genuine. She reminded me of the famed 'Gibson Girl' from earlier in the century.

"That's kind, very kind indeed, ma'am, but I'm charged with reviewing the band's performance and the crowd's reaction, so I better maintain my post."

"Ah, an American. Whereabouts in the States?"

"Cincinnati … a little town beside the Ohio River."

"Oh my—so am I, surprisingly. Born and raised in Clifton, near the university. The family maintains our home on Senator Place, but I haven't been there in well over eight years. I'm Sara, Sara Wiborg Murphy. My husband's Gerald."

"I know exactly where you lived, Mrs Murphy. I'm William Travers."

After shaking hands, I was struck by the smoothness of her palms, the petiteness of her fingers. Could tell that, unlike Véronique, this woman never had done a lick of hard work in her life. Would have been surprised if she had even pulled a dandelion.

"Grew up in Clifton myself, a small house on Telford Street. Graduated from the university right before shipping off to the army. If memory serves, isn't there a small footbridge to Senator Place off Clifton Avenue?"

"There certainly is or was. Suppose it's still there."

"I haven't been back since 1917. And have no real need to return. And let's see, Wiborg: as in the printing ink company, Ault and Wiborg?"

"Yes, exactly. Father's company. Still doing well, as far as we know. You live in Paris and, I guess, play—or hope to play with the band?"

"Yes, ma'am. Play alto sax. Scheduled to replace Pearl Keys—I mean, Louie Watkins—when he returns to the States."

"My husband and I are in London for the season. Only visiting Paris for a few weeks. Have decided already to return next autumn for a longer visit—hopefully a couple years."

"I'm sure we mingle with different crowds, ma'am, and you didn't ask my opinion but you both should enjoy it. I certainly have. There's a freedom here that I never experienced in the States. But, then again, after the war any place would be fine so as long as it's got plenty of booze and jazz. America has got one—but not the other."

"Interesting perspective. I feel something unique, too. Something new. Something exciting. Something modern is happening here."

"Absent the puritanical side of America. Thankfully."

I feared I had overstepped as soon as the words left my tongue.

"We've all had too much fire and brimstone of late, I'm afraid. We're both discontented with America right now. A fraudulent morality seems to have prevailed. But, since we're here and not there, now's the time to enjoy. Now's the time to let go. Now's the time to experiment. Gerald and I are ready. We want to participate, not simply watch from afar. Beg your pardon, but I should return otherwise my husband will think we're planning a clandestine adventure. Nice to meet you, William."

"Always a pleasure, Mrs Murphy. That you're a fellow Cincinnatian makes it special."

"You're very kind. And please, call me Sara."

I watched as she returned to her husband. Her step had a slight lift to it, as if she were keeping time to the music. I liked her casualness. But, on second thought, the rich can afford to be casual wherever they are and to whomever they're speaking and then turn on a franc to become assholes.

Talking and listening had made me thirsty. I surveyed the crowd while standing at the bar, waiting for a double neat. They tapped their feet. Those who remained seated swayed their bodies. All seemed attentive, excited by each number. The music also unleashed a sexual amorousness, not amongst men necessarily, but amongst women toward their men. What my mother would have referred to as 'forwardness'. Heads on shoulders. Hands on torsos. Bottoms on laps. Legs around legs. Lips on lips. Constraints lifted. Energy released.

Skeeter approached during a brief interlude. Told me the fellas didn't socialise with one other at break time. That would come later. All they wanted now was to drink alone. Rework the music in their heads. Talk to a few guests, if so inclined. And while Skeeter usually adhered to these rules, he broke them tonight to hear my thoughts.

"Think it's self-evident the crowd loves the band and the jazz. The band's camaraderie is on full display. It's obvious. The members like each other. They like the music. And … the crowd likes you, Skeeter, is of paramount importance if people are going to enjoy themselves."

"Okay, Travers, fine. Give me something to gnaw on. To swallow. To digest for a couple of days."

"Well … visually, how about if each member had a maroon or yellow coloured handkerchief dangling from their left breast pocket? Help accentuate the band a bit, I think. Instead of a stream of black dinner jackets and black ties against starched white shirts, there'd be a hint of moving colour. Also … except for the twelve-inch-by-twelve-inch sign in the lobby, there's no other reference to the band. With all the booze they're swilling, no one will remember in the morning who the hell they jazzed with the prior evening. Perhaps we should paint Swaneeland Jazz Band inside and around the bass drum. Have it done professionally, of course, not by some third-rate proletarian. My final suggestion … when one instrument is carrying the melody, soloing, more or less, they should stand up, be highlighted—except for Sticks, obviously. But hell, the way he beats the skin and throws the sticks, everyone will appreciate it's him. And, as we know all too well, he loves calling attention to himself."

"Damn, Travers. Your brain's a wonderment. No wonder Uncle Sam had you flying those death contraptions. And for landing and frolicking with a classy French woman … now I get it. Thanks. Great ideas. Sounds good. Looks good. Go enjoy yourself."

Did what I was told. Ordered another double neat and savoured the music. Sara approached me again toward the end of the evening. After offering her visiting card, she asked if the band performed at private functions. I accepted her card and, out of courtesy, gave her mine. Told her the band could perform and probably would, but recommended she broach the subject with James Walker, the band's manager. And, sure enough, after the band played its highly anticipated encore performance of 'La Marseillaise', Mrs Murphy approached Skeeter and introduced herself. They chatted a few minutes and exchanged cards. Had no idea where Mr Murphy was but

Mrs Murphy seemed capable of forging ahead on her own. After shaking hands, and before she turned away, Skeeter offered a semi-deferential bow.

"No need for that, Mr Walker."

"Sorry, ma'am. Just my way of showing respect to those who respect jazz."

"Well then, I accept with gracious appreciation and much anticipation for what's to come."

Skeeter called me over after Mrs Murphy left the room.

"Travers, to hell with your playing. Think I'm gonna have you stroll through the room and chat up people at every gig."

"I want to play—not talk."

"Kidding, Travers, just kidding. That Mrs Murphy you talked to—the shapely woman from your hometown— well, damn, we're booked in for a few nights next autumn after they get settled into their new home. She'll provide me details in the coming months."

"Fantastic. Wonderful news. Although I kinda think it had more to do with the music than sharing a hometown."

"Perhaps, but you've got a—ah, what the hell do the French say?—*je ne sais quoi*. Women like you. Strangers like you. Hell, even I like you. And, along with your playing, both are good for business."

After he'd finished, he let out that familiar yelp.

"You ready to booze with me and boys?"

"Love to, Skeeter, but I promised *Madame* Diguet a few hours this morning. Can't disappoint her."

"I understand. I understand. That's good. Honouring commitments. Next time, then?"

"Next time, for sure."

After congratulating the boys on a fine-sounding gig,

Sliding Jack seemed surprised I was shunning the grain and grape.

"Knocking it back with the boys just isn't where it's at. Gotta get home to Ver-on-neek, huh?"

To be honest, in a couple hours (when the brothel gig's over), I'll be soaking up some grape with three *femme fatales* wearing nice little nothings. So, I guess what I'm saying, Sliding Jack, is that I know where it's at. It's with them. And I know where it ain't. And that's with your sorry ass."

All the boys laughed. Sliding Jack joined in once he realised I was joshing.

"Just envious, Travers. I know those ladies, some more and better than others. Fine women, they are. Fine women. Everyone here would do the same thing if given the opportunity. What's the French term ... *bonne chance*?"

Madame Diguet's place was quiet but fully occupied. Three girls were upstairs. Juillet was cleaning and reorganising the bar. Since no customers were around, I asked if she had any special requests. Surprisingly, she chose Satie and Debussy.

"I want your jazz usually, but tonight ... difficult time. Want something quiet and *songeur*. Think you English would say, 'pensive,' no?"

"Yes, yes ... pensive."

After pouring herself a drink she reclined on the red leather chaise longue, covering herself with a small crocheted throw. I started with Satie's 'Gnossienne No. 1', followed by 'Gymnopédie No. 1'. I could tell she was listening but also preoccupied. Something was amiss. About ten measures into Debussy's 'Clair de lune' we heard furious shouting, followed by a slamming door. On the landing stood Gabrielle and a half-dressed customer.

"I cannot *do* that. You didn't pay for that. I can't, and I won't!"

"What do you mean, 'I didn't pay for that'? We gave our lives for you snail-eaters. Started paying in 1914 with our lads, then my friends, then my brother. We've paid. Now deliver!"

He slapped her across the face. She began crying and ran down the stairs. Retrieving his clothes, he pursued her down the steps. Sometime in that brief interim I put down my sax and repositioned myself at the bottom of the stairs, prepared for confrontation. The ruckus had brought customers out of their rooms and onto the landing. Awakened by the commotion, *Madame* Diguet appeared from the back room located behind the bar. After the man made his way down the stairs he didn't look left, right or at me. He simply sucker-punched me in the gut. Then he pushed *Madame* Diguet to the floor. She landed hard. I got up, caught my breath and made my way to the bar where he was pouring a drink. Thought I caught a glimpse of him eyeing my instrument.

"Ready for another round, gimp?"

"The war ruined us all. Pay for the drink and leave."

"Didn't know Yanks were so goddamned philosophical."

"Didn't realise Brits only thought with their cocks."

Before he could react, I took the neck of a bottle of *eau de vie*, broke it over the edge of the bar and began slashing the air, moving ever closer toward him.

"Bloody hell, gimp's gone doolally."

My mad adrenaline rush worked. He cleared out so fast his money clip dropped to the floor. *Madame* Diguet picked it up and counted it. Said she'd take what was needed for repairs and divide the rest amongst the girls.

"He deserves nothing. I never want to see him."

"Have to agree with you on this one, *Madame* Diguet."

"Mr Travers, thank you for your action. I don't know what would have happened if you weren't here."

"Sorry it happened. Sounds selfish, but I don't know what I would have done if he'd broken my instrument. She's my mistress, you know. Couldn't exist without her."

"A man with *la passion*. I knew that. I like that. No more playing tonight. Help yourself to anything behind the bar."

After pouring a double neat, I found a seat next to Gabrielle. She appeared anxious and frightened. Rightfully so, I thought. After I sat down, she inched herself over, placing her head on my shoulder. She didn't speak. Only nestled closer. I had intended to talk but followed her lead instead. I extended my left arm along the length of the sofa, enabling her head to rest more comfortably on my chest. She placed her right arm alongside my gimp leg. Nothing was said. After a few minutes all I heard was the soft sounds of her in a deep sleep.

An hour later I wiggled free of Gabrielle's sleepy embrace, I packed my saxophone and offered my regards to *Madame* Diguet. She thanked me again for putting myself forward to protect them.

"I have no right to say this, perhaps, but Gabrielle believes you're special. She'll be drawn closer after tonight. Find you even more endearing, I'm afraid. She's special, but she's also broken."

"Like us all, *Madame* Diguet. Like us all."

What a day, I thought. The band, Mrs Murphy, the

brothel. Three 'at bats' and three 'home runs'. Damn good, I reflected. Damn good. I made my way back to the apartment. As I climbed what by now felt like an endless flight of stairs, all I could think of was the promise of the big sleep in a comfortable bed. As I turned the key and opened the door, I caught a whiff of what smelled eerily similar to Véronique's perfume. Christ, I thought, haven't seen the girl for so long, I'm … Couldn't complete the thought. On the edge of the bed, wearing a loosely fitted slip, sat Véronique. Hair tousled. Legs crossed. Eyes hardly open.

"My saxman is home."

"I am and you're not. A fabulous first. God, I'm four for four today."

"What do you mean, 'four for four'? More American English?"

"No, well yes, baseball talk. I had four chances to deliver the goods and I came through four times. Doesn't matter. I'll explain later. You're here. That's what's important."

"American English is too complicated."

"Your French lilt makes it more beautiful and less complicated."

"Come, Willis, lay next to me. Tell me everything."

Chapter Six

One evening the owner of Brin de Quelque Chose asked if the band would cut the gig short by an hour. We were disappointed but took it in our stride. Gave us an opportunity to see what Montmartre had to offer. Must have been a sight for locals. Except for Sticks, who concealed his drumsticks in a nondescript leather portfolio and Skeeter, who was carrying a suitcase full of our music, everyone else was schlepping instrument cases. Suppose we resembled door-to-door peddlers wearing dinner suits, trying to impress potential customers. Somewhere on Rue des Saules near the Sacré Coeur Basilica, we heard singing and guitar and accordion playing. The air smelled of wine. Those irresistible combinations propelled us onward, across the threshold and into Au Lapin Agile. Didn't take long to appreciate that we had stumbled into a unique cabaret club. It also didn't take long to realise our fellow guests consisted of artists and intellectuals, know-nothing anarchists, prostitutes, local down-and-outs, poets, and the curiosity-seeking rich who broke free from their Right Bank mansions.

We were greeted warmly despite our obvious foreignness and formal attire. I approached the bar to order five bottles of French red. A classic-looking, well-dressed man, whom I learned was the proprietor, Aristide Bruant, asked if we were musicians. I filled him in using the best French possible. He became frustrated. Pleaded I speak in English. Would be easier than listening to me butcher French.

"The singer finishes soon. She's followed by a poet. When he's completed the recitation—supposed to be excellent; highly accomplished—would you perform for us the jazz you play so well?"

"That's kind. Very kind, *Monsieur*. Recommend you ask the man at the far end of the table. The one with the undone tie. He's the leader. I'm certain whatever he says will be fine with us boys."

Knew Skeeter would jump at the opportunity. He'd consider the nightspot the perfect venue for spreading the gospel. Twenty minutes passed before Swaneeland reassembled itself and took control of the slightly elevated stage. Skeeter could use the house piano but, since there were no drums, Sticks had to improvise: tin buckets of various sizes, a large empty water vase and a thick oak tabletop that sounded surprisingly similar to his base. Although not perfect, it would have to do. Skeeter cautioned Pearl Keys and me not to overpower the others. Make two sound as if one.

Skeeter decided it best to begin with what we didn't get to play earlier at Brin de Quelque Chose. Numbers included 'Whispering', 'Avalon', 'Crazy Blues' and 'The Japanese Sandman'. The audience adored it. Many assumed a trance-like state of disbelief before succumbing to the rhythms of the music. It wasn't long before *Monsieur* Bruant begged us to continue. Long lines had formed outside. The inside, already crowded when we first arrived, had become packed as tight as a tin of sardines.

"When finished, I open the bar to you. Anything you want. As much as you want."

That type of payment settled in nicely with us. No squawking. No complaining. For the sake of variety and pure professionalism, we started from the top: those toe-tappers the band had played since first arriving in Paris. 'Darktown Strutters' Ball' and 'That's a Plenty' hit a responsive chord with everyone, inside and outside. We closed our impromptu gig in typical Swaneeland fashion: 'La Marseillaise'. It stunned the audience. Many joined in and sang, others pounded on tables, some stood atop stools and repeatedly shouted *Vive la France.* Customers surrounded us after we'd finished. Patted our shoulders. Shook our hands. Must have been kissed by at least nine women—all ages, all sizes and shapes, in various stages of undress. One girl, in particular, fancied Sliding Jack. I could see where it was leading but I bided my time. Didn't want to ruin his buzz.

As the crowd thinned, I noticed a framed photograph on the wall at the far end of the bar. The faded, handwritten label identified the two men standing in front of a large oil painting as Fréderic Gérard and Pablo Picasso, 1906. The painting focused on a sad, reflective couple standing at the bar inside Au Lapin Agile. Neither smiled. Both stared into the distance, ignoring each other and the guitarist playing in the background.

"*Monsieur* Gérard was the prior owner. I bought it from him. And Picasso, well, he's a genius. Everyone knows him now. He was poor then. No money. No fame. Gérard took pity and commissioned a painting. To remain inside the cabaret and hang on the wall. Instead of money, Picasso asked for food and drinks. And *voilà.*"

I didn't have to conceal any ignorance about Picasso—thanks to Véronique's tutorial, I was well informed.

"What happened to it? In your home?"

"No, no, *Monsieur.* Afraid, no. Gérard sold it in 1912 to a collector. Surprisingly, a German. Don't know where it is. Destroyed in the war probably. Picasso visits occasionally. Asked him if he'd paint another. 'No'. He doesn't need food and drink, and I can't afford his work. A date and time now gone forever, I'm afraid."

Just then Sliding Jack approached. Said he and a new love interest were going elsewhere. Thanked me for a fabulous evening.

"She isn't by chance taking you to *her* place, is she?"

"Come on, Travers, what hotel would give us a room at this hour? And that's if we could find one open. They'll all *fermé*. You know that."

"Be careful. She's liable to fleece you. If not her, then her pimp. She's not one of Dominique's girls, you know. You'll be walking home poorer and frustrated."

"Travers … with all the crap I've seen and experienced, think I can handle it. But appreciate the 'mother hen' concern. *Merci*."

He slapped my shoulder and left. His new love stood outside waiting. I imagined her pimp had left earlier. Whispered, 'Good luck'. Doubt he heard.

A few days later Swaneeland hosted a party for Pearl Keys upstairs in Brasserie Lipp. My comfort with the boys, and their confidence in me, enabled it to happen. Of paramount importance, however, was for Pearl Keys to return to the States. His wife had faced constant intimidation and now feared for her physical safety. She hadn't left their ramshackle house in weeks, relying on neighbours to drop off food parcels late at night.

A variety of toasts were made: some funny; some serious. And Pearl Keys relished them all. Skeeter presented him a framed copy of the sheet music to 'La Marseillaise', offset by our signatures around the border. Each member gave him a bottle of Scotch that would have to be consumed on the boat. The last thing he needed re-entering America was to be arrested for trafficking booze. He didn't seem to mind.

"I know it's a hell of thing to drink before noon, but some things have to be done … to protect the guilty."

Being the guy attempting to replace him, I presented Pearl Keys with what I thought a special gift: something only an alto sax man would appreciate and nurture. Something to consume over time: box of reeds—twenty in total—from a collection once owned by Adolphe Sax. The inventor of the instrument had died in Paris twenty-six years earlier. Véronique, who knew the collection curator (and executor of Sax's estate), purchased them. Weren't expensive—but they weren't cheap either.

"Damn, Travers, every time I stick a reed in my mouth, I'll think of you."

"I'm flattered, Pearl Keys. Genuinely flattered but, to appease my conscience, is it too big a request for you to think of Véronique instead?"

He looked at me inquisitively. The others started snickering. Skeeter belted out his trademark laugh. The implication finally dawned on him.

"When I'm boozing, I can't think deeply. You're just too educated for your own britches, Travers. But, hell, I knew that from the beginning. That's why you fit so damn well with Swaneeland. I'll happily think of Véronique. She looks better and she damn well smells better. No problem. No problem at all."

I went over and gave him a firm handshake and an encouraging slap on the shoulder. Wished him well. Hoped his wife would be out of harm's way soon.

As the party began to wind down, I noticed Sliding Jack was too pensive for his and the band's own good. Damn quiet, actually. So, I went over, poured a double neat, handed it to him and asked if he was alright.

"Travers, keep this under your hat. I'm embarrassed. You were right about that Au Lapin Agile dame. Damn sure should have listened. Got back to her place, right. She's naked in a damn jiffy. My shoes, trousers and shorts … off, okay? Only wearing my shirt, jacket and tie. She's slowly undoing my tie. Unbuttoning my shirt. Real close to sliding off my dinner jacket when this guy—well, her pimp—jumps out from the armoire, grabs my trousers, which have my shorts rolled up within the legs, and runs out. She screams, slaps me in the face, steals my shoes and runs after him. I had a dickens of a time walking to Montparnasse."

"They got everything, then?"

"As you know, our trousers don't have pockets. All my money was inside the dinner jacket. Except for ruining my dinner suit ensemble, they got nothing. Wounded my pride. Made me the fool. That's all."

"Your pride will heal and the experience has made you wiser. Curious, though—how they hell did you get back?"

"Shit, Travers, had to walk. You think a cab will pick up a guy with no shoes, no britches? Probably thinks I don't have any money, either. The only thing covering my front was the long tail of the white shirt. When walking down hill I used our colourful handkerchief a few times, you know, keeping everything together. And for my ass, well, the jacket did its job. You should have seen the looks on peoples' faces. Stunned doesn't begin to describe it, Travers. Not in the least."

Couldn't contain my laughter. Played out exactly how Johnny described.

"Laughing provides little comfort."

"Sorry. Sometimes dark humour gets us through rough patches. Be glad you weren't gifted a swollen lip. Skeeter wouldn't have taken too kindly to that misfortune. Stick with Dominique's girls. Won't lose from the familiar.

In August the band boarded the train at Gare de l'Est. Destination: Provins, the first stop on our eagerly awaited summer tour. We were filled with great anticipation, with only a smidgen of trepidation. This 'smidgen' soon snowballed into a huge issue. First, our agent, Jérôme Basset, failed to meet us outside the station. Struggling a bit with transportation logistics, we found our way—eventually—to the brasserie Bouillon Julien, the sponsor of our first gig. Skeeter introduced us to the proprietor. If it's possible for a man to look concerned, act confused, and seem bewildered, he did. Had never heard of us. Had never spoken to or known a 'Jérôme Basset'. And had never signed a contract obligating to pay us one sweet franc. But he allowed Skeeter to make a trunk call to Basset's office. The conversation was brief.

"Fellow jazzmen, Swaneeland's been played and fleeced. It seems our dear Mr Basset hasn't worked with this agency for over a year. Fired for 'not showing up for work and inappropriate use of company funds'. An office acquaintance said he last saw Basset in June. Bragged about all the money he was making off an American jazz band. Left in mid-July for Sanremo, Italy. His friend has no idea where he's staying. In fact, he doubts Basset even went to Sanremo."

"That means Reims, Dijon, Limoges, Bordeaux, Avignon, Aix-en-Provence, Lyon and Troyes … is all bullshit? Not gonna happen?"

"Afraid so, Sliding Jack. Gave our loot to that fleecing carnival barker. And now we've got no work. No work at all. No gigs scheduled in Montmartre until autumn. I see it now, in hindsight. He had grifting eyes and if a man owns grifting eyes—well, shit, not difficult to accept the bastard's a grifter."

"Not your fault, Skeeter. There are more horses' asses than horses. Just need to improve your knowledge of the equine. That's all."

"Where the hell do you pull this stuff from, Travers? And don't tell me your ass. I might believe you!"

The proprietor—a chubby, bald man sporting an enormous handlebar moustache whose name was Jacques Callot—sensed our frustration and disgust. He brought over a bottle of cognac and five glasses to soften the blow.

"*Je suis vraiment désolé. Je suis vraiment désolé.*"

"*Merci, Monsieur* Callot. *Merci.* It is not your fault. Not your fault, at all."

He seemed to understand. Bowed graciously and left.

The band huddled together, deciding when to leave for Paris. It was split. Three wanted to remain in Provins, see what the town had to offer and return in the morning. The other two wanted on the first available train. As each faction argued their position, *Monsieur* Callot approached the table with five bowls of *moules mariniére*, five French *baguettes* and three bottles of white burgundy.

"Please enjoy. *Gratuit. Gratuit.* You eat. I make arrangements. Perhaps."

In the midst of devouring an exquisite lunch, our misfortunes turned upward. *Monsieur* Callot had contacted individuals of position and influence and arranged for Swaneeland to perform the gig outside—at the base of Caesar's Tower, the imposing twelfth-century watchtower once used to defend the town. He couldn't guarantee a crowd. And, also, couldn't pay us—that would be up to the villagers who attended and passed around a jar. In July the French government had passed a law imposing heavy taxes on all entertainment offerings held in restaurants, brasseries, clubs and cafés. Required the proprietor to pay upwards of fifty percent of gross receipts, something unsustainable over the long-term. *Monsieur* Callot apologised. He wasn't a wealthy man and couldn't afford to host inside Bouillon Julien.

"No matter how many people. No matter what we charge. Half my money … gone … disappears."

Skeeter tried to allay *Monsieur's* troubling concerns.

"*Monsieur* Callot, you have been amply generous. We look forward to jazzin' outside. Don't worry yourself, okay? Jazz will bring the world together and make it modern. Years from now Provins will remember and be proud of your contributions. One thing, though: any thoughts on where the band could hole up for the night? Ah, a hotel?"

Without hesitation, Callot explained that his sister operated an adorable *auberge* located nearby. He'd check availability. Reappeared minutes later. Everything was set. One glitch: only four rooms. Two would have to share a room. Since I had the least seniority, I volunteered first. Sticks, the second-'newest' member, agreed to share.

"Looking forward to it, Travers. Want to hear how you snagged Véronique. Might offer me pointers on how to land a French *femme*."

"Be prepared to take copious notes."

Monsieur Callot gave directions to the *auberge*. And it truly was close. Around the corner and down the street a hundred or so yards. Although old as dirt, it looked charming. One of those mud and half-timbered numbers. Callot's sister greeted us warmly. Considerably younger than her brother, and much prettier, she had an air of self-confidence and no-nonsense about her. Possessed all the street smarts and wherewithal of a city woman. Because of the day's precariousness, Skeeter recommended we nap for a couple hours and then reassemble to discuss the evening's gig. All agreed. It had been a difficult day. We needed to be refreshed. To give the citizens of Provins a jazz concert they'd remember. And provide the band with much-needed seed.

The medieval setting would never be surpassed in my lifetime. An ancient fortress playing host to modern music. The well-heeled, in refined dress and smelling of perfume, mingled with farmers with dirt under their nails, who smelled of having worked all day. The demand for wine was great but easily fulfilled. The town's mayor made a few opening remarks followed by *Monsieur* Callot, who described how events had unfolded. Not certain, but I think he embellished his role a bit. Made it more about him as the noble Frenchman, and less about the ignoble Frenchman who swindled us. Then it was our turn: Swaneeland took control.

Couldn't believe my eyes as we left the tower and walked single file to the open area on our left. The audience started clapping as soon as they saw us, continuing until we sat down to await Skeeter's direction. Didn't know the population of Provins but it appeared a majority had resettled for the evening within the ancient fortress. We played with unequalled fervour; a passion I had never experienced before or ever would again. The audience understood our appreciation of how they came together to assist us in our day of need. For certain songs, everyone remained seated, tapping their feet and swaying their bodies. For other songs—like 'Whispering', 'Crazy Blues' and 'Avalon'—couples walked off to one side and danced, not caring what others thought. And it wasn't only the young. I was struck how one farmer held his wife tender and close, placing her hand low at his side, almost behind him while holding her right hand high in the air with his left. Even the young couldn't match their physical agility. If ever there was a crowd that genuinely appreciated Swaneeland's rendition of 'La Marseillaise', this was it. They were so ebullient, so enthused, we were forced to repeat it three times.

The gig finished, *Monsieur* Callot approached as we wiped down and packed away our instruments. He was carrying a wooden wine box and grinning so widely that his only detectable feature was that damn handlebar moustache. It dominated his face, extending at least two inches beyond each cheek. He had totalled the money— 5,500 francs. And, with the current exchange rate of eleven francs to the dollar, the band had netted $500 dollars. Almost double what we earn at Brin de Quelque Chose and triple what he would have earned with the carnival barker.

The return to Paris the next morning proved uneventful. Skeeter had ideas for making some seed but wanted to think it over, work out the details and explore the unknowns. All agreed to meet at Brasserie Lipp the next evening.

Looked forward to surprising Véronique. We had planned to meet in Aix near the end of the tour. She'd be shocked and saddened simultaneously that I was home early. Didn't use my key. Didn't want to scare Véronique out of her skin. So, I knocked. After a slight delay the door opened.

"Collecting alms for a depressed and downtrodden saxophonist. Spare any francs, *Mam'selle*?"

"Willis!"

She opened the door wide and jumped into my arms. She smelled good. She felt good. And ... she was barely wearing her loose-fitting nightgown.

"Why are you home? Tell me you didn't get fired? Tell me someone offered you a new job?"

"If a multiple-choice test, is 'none of the above' an option?"

"American English does me no good, Willis. Just tell me, please! I'm so excited."

I told her our tale of woe. But, also, how marvellous the citizens of Provins were—with food, drink, lodging and, of course, their generous financial contribution.

"But ... but ... what are you going to do?"

"Well, the band's meeting tomorrow evening at Brasserie Lipp. Skeeter has some ideas. We'll mull them around. See what happens. Grateful I'm still in Dominique's good graces. Her money will come in handy, no doubt. And, who knows, maybe one of her clients will be the big cannon that shoots me ever upward to the top."

As I made myself comfortable, I was struck by Véronique's unmade bed. In fact, it was a mess. Pillows on the floor. Sheets spread far and wide. An unfamiliar perfume scented the air. An opened bottle of hooch atop her dressing table. Christ, it was noon on Saturday.

"Damn, Véronique, we last saw each other two days ago. Hardly had time to miss me. Even changed your perfume. What's happened?"

"I'm embarrassed. I did miss you. Terribly. Knew it would be a month before we'd see each other. I was lonely and availed myself of too much hooch, I think. Don't remember, to be honest. Am I bad?"

"Hardly think you're 'bad'. Emotional? Wouldn't be

you without it. Romantic? Unquestionably. Sentimental? Always."

"Stop it. I know I was bad. Awfully bad. Sorry. Now join me in this unmade, wonderful mess of a bed. Will you? Please?"

Entering the brasserie the next evening, *Monsieur* Lipp directed me to a room downstairs. Said Skeeter had been there a long time but didn't seem himself. Lacked his characteristic *joie de vie*. I supposed his hoped-for plans hadn't materialised. So, in preparation for what probably would be the end of Swaneeland, I asked *Monsieur* Lipp to send down three bottles of Scotch— requesting each bottle be a minimum of twelve years old. Skeeter didn't raise his head as I entered the room. Didn't acknowledge my presence. Minutes later the other three came in and sat down. Sensing something wrong, all remained quiet. Not a word was spoken. Didn't even greet each other.

After taking a few sips of his double neat, Skeeter reached inside his sport coat and unfolded a two-or three-page typewritten letter.

"Gentlemen, I hate to tell you this. Tragic, really. Simply unbelievable. Disgusting. A few weeks after Pearl Keys arrived home, his wife, Ethel, was dragged from their ramshackle home and beaten and raped in the front yard. Accused of being a 'Red'. In trying to defend her, four vigilante thugs overpowered Pearl Keys, held him to the ground and broke all his fingers and both thumbs. Feeling their hate and intimidation too tame, they then torched the house. Burned it to the ground. In a dictated letter, Pearl Keys states that while Ethel is mending physically, he fears the psychological damage may be permanent. As for himself … difficult to do much of anything right now, but the doctor thinks after three or four months the hand casts will be removed and he'll begin the arduous task of learning to use his fingers again."

"Did his instrument go up in flames?"

"Thank goodness, no, Travers. Pearl Keys had been practising in a faraway barn and simply forgot to bring it into the house that evening. Both the sax and his music survived. He did write that while breaking his fingers they tried desperately to find out where he kept it. Before he passed out, he remembered one guy continually asking: *Where's that god-damn horn that fills everybody's ears with your infernal communist music?*"

"Who the hell did this? What, in God's name, is going on in our country?"

"Not sure exactly, Sliding Jack. From what I've learned, it seems the US Attorney General had uncovered evidence that a bunch of communists planned to overthrow the government on May first—you know, May Day. State militias and police forces were mobilised but nothing happened. Former members of the defunct American Protective League got involved with some extralegal action. Decided amongst themselves to intimidate, to harass, to punish and to ruin lives of people they didn't like."

"What the hell is this American Protective League?"

"When we were over here killing Germans, 'upright and outstanding citizens' organised what became known as the APL. Its job, I guess, was to ferret out German supporters and sympathisers amongst our own people. Pretty brutal. Pretty unfair. And not too judicious, I imagine. Of course, after victory was achieved, they decided to go after others whose politics they didn't like."

"Didn't we fight to make the world safe for democracy? Hell, can't even be safe in our own country amongst our own countrymen. That's the shits."

"Feel horribly for Pearl Keys. I'm certain he'll regain use of his fingers but I wonder if he'll ever, ever regain that flawless fingering I so admire. His fingers worked that saxophone like no one I'd seen or probably will see again. Made the mechanics of that instrument do things I didn't think possible, elevating the tonal dynamics to a refined artistry."

We learned also that Pearl Keys and Ethel, with no place to live, moved in with her sister in the next county, about fifty miles away. Safer but not out of danger. Our trumpeter, Randolph Jackson, who usually avoided extending his neck into other people's business, made a helpful suggestion.

"We can't send Pearl Keys clothes—customs duty would be more than the cost of the clothes. But what if, after we start making some seed, we siphon off the cream from our takings? After a month or so, we could wire him some serious money. I know him, all too well, and he'd refuse if we asked. If we just did it ... hell, he'd take it, appreciate it and always remember how the boys of Swaneeland stuck by him and his wife."

"Good thinkin', Jackson, but what about the transaction fee and exchange rate?"

"It's not bad. Not bad at all. Transaction fee equals a couple of dollars. And hell, the exchange rate right now is what, eleven francs to the dollar? Cakewalk money. We can handle it. Can't we?"

"Yeah, we could handle it if we worked. Can't print it. Got to earn it. And that's not happening any time soon."

"Loosen the attitude, Sliding Jack. We're meeting here

for a reason, remember? Damn unfortunate that letter from Pearl Keys was waiting for me when I returned from Provins. Wanted to deal with the bad news first … then the good stuff."

Everyone refilled their glasses. Skeeter had our undivided attention. All of it.

"Fellas, had a long discussion yesterday evening and this morning with *Monsieur* Lipp. He's going to take us on now and well into autumn. The arrangement will be different from what we're used to, but I told him we're resilient. We're flexible. We're jazzmen, for Christ's sake. We thrive on improvisation."

"What's he gonna have us do—bus tables?"

"Damn, Sliding Jack, you need a serious attitude adjustment."

"Sorry. I'm sorry. Just keyed-up, I guess. Frustrated."

"Visit Dominque's, then."

"Here's the straight dope. Because of the levy placed on musical venues, there can't be specific gigs that feature or highlight Swaneeland. Instead, we will perform upstairs—you know, the place where we performed on the first anniversary of the Armistice—as background music for those dining on the ground floor. No guests will see us. No one will be seated separately to enjoy our jazzin'. No one will be permitted on the first floor."

"How do we earn any seed then?"

"*Monsieur* Lipp will tag extra francs to every bottle of wine consumed, every cocktail served and to the daily specials. Should be a good haul, he thinks. Makes most of his money on booze anyway. So, unless I'm getting set-up to be rolled again, sounds good to me. How you guys feel?"

Typical of Swaneeland, there was consensus. All were

sad that it wasn't a formal, advertised gig as such but understood why. The problem would be the same wherever we performed. The owners couldn't afford it. And the guests wouldn't pay the difference. We get to work; we make money. And we remain together. It fulfilled our immediate need.

"One more titbit I think you're gonna like. We're allocated two breaks and three drinks. Can sit at the bar but fraternisation with unattached females is forbidden—especially younger ones. He'll throw us out if he catches anyone casting a glimmer or a catching a glimpse—the perpetrator *and* the rest of us. Got it?"

We nodded in agreement, like adolescent schoolboys being told how to behave in a co-ed classroom. It helped that, if we failed, we already knew the punishment. I excused myself from the big drink Skeeter had planned, celebrating Swaneeland's survival. Had to meet Véronique at La Closerie des Lilas. I certainly hoped Gaston was working. Relished a couple free double neats.

The evening was warm—sweltering for Paris, actually. As I arrived most guests were dining outside amongst the leafy barricade that provided respite from the heat and the gawking of passers-by. But Véronique and I always desired the privacy and intimacy of the bar. Entered and turned left. Our table was free. The bar entertained only one other.

She was usually the first to arrive. Not this time. And I was in luck. The gregarious and efficient Gaston was working the bar. I had barely sat down at the corner table when he served me a double neat.

"No need to rush, Gaston, but Véronique will be arriving soon, so …"

"I'll bring a bottle. Have to manage an author's private

reception upstairs, so … I'll close out the tab. My replacement, Jérôme, will assume the bottle's been paid already. Stay as long as you desire, *Monsieur* Travers. Enjoy."

"*Merci*, Gaston. What the hell would Véronique and I do without your generosity?"

"Have fewer francs."

I took his smart-ass reply as a sign that he felt comfortable with me. Didn't take me too seriously. I liked that. Gaston was genuine. So was his hooch. Véronique arrived as I was pouring a glass. She seemed a bit dishevelled while inquisitively looking for me, suspecting I hadn't arrived. She wore her untidiness well. Conveyed a sense of purpose far beyond her innate attractiveness. Saw me as soon as I stood up.

"With hardly anyone inside, I wondered who that charming man was in the corner … and then realised it was my Willis."

"French flattery will get *you* everything."

"Promise?"

"Promise."

"Then continue pouring, please. I have some news."

"So do I. You first."

"I'll be travelling to Montpellier, Avignon, Marseille and Collioure to survey several paintings of artists from the Fauves movement."

"Ah, the 'Wild Beasts' much in vogue from what, 1905 to about '10 or '12? Learned this from my attractive French tutor."

"May I add, 'exceedingly well'. Good retention, Willis. Proud of my teaching abilities. Anyway, I must discuss with the owners the possibility of acquiring the works or negotiating a temporary loan. It's a coup for me,

Willis. A real professional honour. To these people—rich people, I might add—of the south, I am the Musée. Most of them probably haven't visited Paris in over a decade or more."

"Sounds exciting. Truly. Happy for you. How long you gone?"

"Two weeks. Maybe longer if I discover other paintings in other cities. Things like this evolve. Take on a life of their own. Rich owners know other rich owners."

"Amazing, isn't it, if the tour hadn't gone bust, we would have had corker of a time down there? Pretty certain Avignon was on the list."

"Don't be disappointed. We'll add another line to the definition of 'reunion' when I return. What's your news?"

I told her. She echoed what all thought: luck, this time, was on Swaneeland's side. She laughed when I told her about Lipp's fraternisation rules. Thought I'd have a difficult time adhering.

"It's not *your* manoeuvring and posturing—it's the women's. Don't you understand, Willis? They're a moth; you're the light."

"Then I'll lessen the wattage. Maybe I'll slur my words and drool. Can't lose this gig, no matter how untraditional."

"Then bring a handkerchief."

Told her also what happened to Pearl Keys and his wife. Had a look of tragic disbelief.

"Don't understand how they'd be perceived as pro-German during the war and then, after peace was assured, be labelled communists or socialists. That kind of twisted logic happens during civil wars, not when a nation is whole."

"I'm seeing, you're seeing, the whole god-damn world's seeing that America isn't whole."

"Perhaps it's not as tolerant as it purports. Perhaps the ideals inscribed on the Statue of Liberty—a gift from France—is a canard."

"America has loved peddling shit about itself that doesn't pass inspection for decades."

"When a nation announces its ideals to the world—by actually writing them down—it *will* be held to a higher standard."

"Damn, you amaze me with your ability to analyse complexities and explain them so they make sense and in a foreign language! You possess an intellect superior to mine."

"I'm thinking now that American flattery will get *you* everything. Care to inspect my cleaned and straightened bedroom?"

"To only mess it up?"

"Why not?"

Finished our hooch and left.

The strangeness of the band's first evening at Brasserie Lipp cannot be exaggerated. Not seeing the audience but hearing their appreciative applause seemed odd. Any facial expressions, gyrating bodies or tapping toes had to be imagined. Segregation shrouded us in a veil of mystery. During our break, as walked down to the bar and dining area, I felt like the angel of jazz, descending from on high to proselytise to the heathen.

At 10:15 we took the break we had negotiated earlier with *Monsieur* Lipp. The boys in the band got along together fine. We respected each other. We admired our collective musicianship. But, when we drank, we wanted to drink alone, away from familiar faces. We went our separate ways, to out-of-the way tables, to remote stools or to outside café tables. I sat at the bar.

As she approached the empty chair beside me, I could see she displayed all the attributes of the current craze: flat chest, knee-length dress, bobbed hair, jewelled headband, a dangly pearl necklace, and kewpie-doll lips. After getting comfortable, she smiled and placed her left hand gently on my knee and started moving it toward my waist.

"You won't find what you want … at least not now, *Mam'selle. Monsieur* Lipp doesn't take kindly to us jazzmen talking to customers, especially unattached females. If he becomes privy, he'll throw me out onto Boulevard Saint-Germain, followed by my saxophone, sans the case. Costs money, Doll."

Although her strong accent lacked the sophisticated lilt of Véronique's, her coquettish demeanour appealed to me. Thought anything and everything would be possible at another time and another place.

"Jazzman not like woman? I change your mind."

"I like women, for sure, Doll. Right now, though, I prefer my instrument and employment. Nothing personal."

She drew closer. I knew a subtle kiss wasn't far behind. In fact, it was looking directly at me. I turned and left. She became unbalanced, fell over and hit the floor. Cocktail glass followed along with her satin clutch. The last thing I saw prior to ascending the stairs was her on the floor, legs akimbo, laughing. *Monsieur* Lipp ran to assist. When asked what happened she blamed the drink … and the slippery floor. Embarrassed *Monsieur* Lipp knelt down to feel the floor. Bone dry. He looked at her. She raised her painted eyebrows, shrugged her shoulders, giggled and asked the barman for another Bee's Knees.

Prior to beginning the second set, Skeeter came over, concerned beads of sweat dotted his forehead.

"Travers, goddamn, what is it with you and French women?"

"She didn't say a thing."

"That's what I mean. How'd you make her so loyal so quickly?"

Wanted to keep that mystery a secret. Didn't reply because I didn't know. Simply tuned my horn and started playing the chromatic scale.

When the gig ended, I packed my instrument and said goodnight to the boys. No post-gig boozing for me. Tiredness had grabbed hold. I wanted undisturbed sleep. As I walked down the stairs to the ground floor, the brasserie was practically empty. The coquettish vixen who seemed intent on befriending me was nowhere. As I walked out the door and turned right, I saw her, enraptured by another. Ah, I thought, the fickleness of desire—how temporary, how fleeting. We caught one another's eye briefly. She smiled; I returned the gesture. She then rose from the lap of her conquering hero and, using her right hand, invited me and anyone else watching to follow its journey downward as she outlined the contours of her body. When finished, she giggled and returned to the lap of her bemused suitor. I bowed my head in deference. The remaining male customers stood and applauded. They had made her night. As I lowered my hat and turned my coat collar upward to brace myself against a sudden downpour, I wondered if she would make *his* night.

One evening at Dominique's a few days later a customer remained seated at the bar for a long time. The entire time I played, as a matter of fact. I assumed his visit upstairs had been gratifying. Unlike most visitors, he remained, nursing any number of drinks, engaging in meaningless talk with whichever girl was working the bar. Well-dressed, well-mannered—the epitome of a gentleman—he spoke with a soft English accent, something I hadn't heard since the war. A prerequisite, I always had thought, for promotion into the senior ranks of the British Army. His slicked-back hair, straight nose and attentive eyes fit his smallish frame, convincing me he was someone of importance—or had been in the past and was trying to recapture what he had lost or perhaps squandered.

He left a little bit before I closed the set. While packing my instrument and reorganising the music, Gabrielle came over. Handed me thirty francs.

"That well-dressed man who sat at the bar all evening left this for you. Said he didn't want to interrupt. Hoped I'd ensure you'd get it."

"Thank you, Gabrielle. Did he say anything else? Leave his name?"

"No, nothing. Talked about London a lot. Music. Jazz. The war. That's about it. Liked his Scotch."

"Then he can't be too awful a man. Can he?"

She laughed.

Speaking of which …"

"It's poured already, *Monsieur* Travers. Sitting atop the bar."

"Gabrielle, you're a wonderment of efficiency and beauty. But you knew that already. *Merci*."

I returned to my apartment to find a letter from Véronique. Her trip to the south was going smoothly. So successful, in fact, she had approval to stay another week. Travelling a bit further afield than planned. *Don't be sad,*

Willis. Reunions after long absences are always the best. I'll show you ... ever so soon. Love, V. I wasn't bothered. I wasn't concerned. Could earn more money at Dominique's after working Lipp. We both were working for selfish causes.

Véronique *did* show me the joys of reunion when she returned. Arriving at my apartment from Brasserie Lipp, I found her propped up comfortably in bed, sipping hooch. It was late, and we were tired. None of that mattered.

The next evening, we ventured over the river to the Right Bank, an area I had experienced only rarely. Heard about a bar called Le Gaya, where a band called Les Six played. Consisted of six musicians who composed and performed a unique French version of jazz. Paying homage to older French musical traditions while incorporating rhythmic elements and harmonies of jazz. Was told Les Six infused ragtime, foxtrots even classical pieces into their Saturday night gigs.

That experience was for later. First, we needed food and drink. I deferred to a long-ago recommendation from my ward nurse—Lescure, tucked tightly in a corner on Rue de Mondovi behind Place de Concorde. I remembered her giddiness at seeing the American ambassador dining there three times. If I had known who the ambassador was then, I sure as hell didn't know now. Didn't give a damn, either. He neither prepared the food nor uncorked the bottles. He only ate and drank like everyone else.

My ward nurse had been correct. With or without the ambassador, the place reflected everything an inexperienced novice like myself would expect from a restaurant smack-dab in the French countryside. Thick, honey-coloured wooden beams hugged the ceiling.

Twelve highly polished wooden tables occupied the dining area. Starched white napkins, centred alongside the white china table settings, adorned at the top with 'Lescure' hand-painted in forest-green. Solid silver cutlery glistened by the light of a single candle atop each table. The zinc-covered bar wasn't for leaners. Waiters picked up their customers' meals, piping hot, from a tiny kitchen in the rear. Bottles of wine, including magnums and jeroboams, covered the surface of a well-maintained antique buffet table against the far wall. My ability to decipher smells—especially food—remains pitiful. 'Superlative' best describes my wonderment. There was the herb, or herb and spice mixture, that defied words. A smell I'd recognise again anywhere, even on my death bed.

At Véronique's urging, I tasted duck *foie gras* for the first time. Spread like creamy butter. Tasted of wild game. A flute of champagne made it exquisite. Being the true French woman, Véronique devoured a plate of snails. She tried desperately to get me to try one. I did. Then excused myself for the toilet. Our shared enjoyment of fowl was made evident by my ordering hen in a stuffed pot—à la Henri IV—for the main course, with Véronique selecting baked chicken in a Basques sauce. Complemented with two bottles of Pouilly-Fuissé made for a memorable meal. But then, day-old army chow would taste good if Véronique sat across from me. After delighting in a crème caramel each, we nursed two glasses of a vintage cognac.

"Appreciate now why artists love the south. The blue skies and warming sun were revelations."

"Your alabaster skin has adopted a peach-coloured glow."

"It's only my face and arms and lower legs, Willis.

You've seen all of me."

"Perhaps we could visit together."

"The light cast itself so differently. The smell of lavender permeates the air. The soil, a rich pinkish-red-like colour. And the night air cool and hypnotic."

"Perhaps we could visit together."

"And the food …"

"Perhaps we could visit together … or not?"

"… Of course we could. But you shouldn't come if I'm here for work."

"I'd keep my own counsel. Except at night, of course."

"Too difficult. Too many receptions. Too many meetings. Too many dinners with potential donors."

"I can cope."

"You'd feel abandoned."

"Okay. Point made. Shall we find Le Gaya?"

Rue Duphot was close-by, practically around the corner. Arrived ten minutes after leaving Lescure. True to what I'd been told, the place was small and crowded. The air was thick with varieties of tobacco smoke. And filled with an abundance of smells: human sweat poorly concealed by a cheap, fragrant water; men reeking of garlic and cognac; women—tarts and those from 'polite' company—wearing the newest fragrance so heavily, I wondered if they received remuneration from the perfumery. Despite its pungency, the crowd was eclectic. Unkempt labourers wearing ripped and soiled trousers sat next to men outfitted in dinner jackets. Women with bruised eyes and dirty faces mixed with women adorned in modern couture. Poets talked with the illiterate. Artists discussed poverty with the unemployed. The ugly and the beautiful, the fortunate and the damned—whatever their station in life—had come to hear French jazz. No

Americans. No English tourists. This audience comprised of live people.

We leaned against a wall for a long time and pounced when a table became free. Small and uncomfortable, for sure, but close to the musicians, with no obstructions. Ordered two cognacs and settled in for what, in hindsight, was a unique performance. More diverse and more radical than anything I'd heard up to that time. The band took a break after ninety-minutes of uninterrupted playing, unless you count the numerous gaps caused by crowd's enthusiastic clapping.

"Guessing Les Six will resurrect French music. Increase its vitality. Its relevance. These boys have fused jazz syncopations and styles from America within a French milieu. Might be easier for your countrymen to accept, to understand. Seems these guys have acclimated it to fit in France. It may no longer be perceived as so foreign."

"You're always complimenting me on understanding difficult subjects. That explanation of French jazz—if that's what *this* is—was, was *magnifique*. *Trés bon*, Willis. *Trés bon*."

Just then an attractive woman, making her way through the crowd and toward the door, touched Véronique on the shoulder, bent down toward her and whispered loudly enough for me to hear.

"*C'est different pour toi, Véronique*."

Even with her peach-coloured glow Véronique turned red.

"Certainly attractive. Who is she?"

"Madeline Dupont ... a girl ... a woman I worked with at the bank during the war."

"Christ, with you two working the window I'd be

consistently overdrawn."

"We worked in the back office with managers. Away from customers. You never would have seen us."

"What did she mean, '*This is different for you, Véronique?*'"

"Your translation is improving."

"Not difficult. Damn easy, in fact. So, what'd she mean?"

"Well, I … it's just … I always told her the Left Bank was more alive. More French, if that's possible, than the Right Bank. She preferred the Right. Wealthier. Cleaner. More *bourgeoisie*. Constantly argued about it. She's surprised to see me enjoying myself over here, I suppose."

"*I'm* surprised she was alone."

"Follow after her then. Hurry. *Vite! Vite!*"

I'd hit a nerve. Hadn't experienced this before. Seemed out of character. *Not* the Véronique I had come to know, to admire and to love.

"That was callous and arrogant. I'm sorry. You didn't deserve that."

"Perhaps I do."

"What do you mean?"

"Is she gone?"

"Yes."

"Sorry, I got irritated."

"Don't be. You're justified."

"I'm too complicated."

"That's why we met, Véronique. I'll uncomplicate you."

The musicians stopped around half three. We were one of the last to leave. A damp, foggy night meant autumn was approaching. The late hour allowed for a peaceful meander to her apartment. Across the Place de Concorde, through the Tuileries and down Rue de Rivoli alongside the Musée de Louvre until we reached Pont Neuf. To our front was the Seine, like a sheet of glass reflecting the surroundings. Except for the yellowish glow around the street lanterns, Véronique thought the scene resembled a black-and-white impressionist painting.

"We waste a lot of time, not to mention francs, keeping two apartments. Ever think of consolidating?"

"Who would give up their apartment?"

"Yours is bigger, nicer, quieter ... so mine, I'd imagine."

"Look, Willis, a coal delivery. Remember it well. Cold, dank, quiet and alone. And sad. So, so sad. Terrible memories."

"All memories from the war are terrible. Those deliveries were damn hard physical work, Véronique. Hell, with my bum leg and knee, I can't lift much beyond the weight of my own damn foot."

"Apartments are difficult to come by. Extremely difficult. We're fortunate to each have our own. If something happened ... you no longer cared for me, I think it would be challenging for you to find something. Especially something nestled near Montparnasse and so close to Dominique's."

"I'll never stop caring. But if *you* stopped, well, perhaps Madeline will take pity."

Didn't know how she'd take my comment, so I smiled while uttering it. She understood I was kidding.

"I assure you, she's *not* your type and you're certainly *not* hers."

"How can you be so sure? And besides, nothing sad or bad will happen. We've experienced enough pain and disappointment. We're on the uptick. Loneliness never will find a home with either of us. I assure you."

While fumbling for her key outside the apartment, I turned Véronique toward me and kissed her lips. Tears fell gently down her cheekbones.

"You're too good for me, Willis. Too damn good for me. But please, please … do it again. Please … do it again. Please … do it again. And again. And again."

Chapter Seven

The band continued performing at Brasserie Lipp throughout autumn and into the bleakness of winter. By spring 1921, the large influx of visitors—those with and without money—offset the cost of the tax levied a year earlier on entertainment venues. This reality reopened the door for Swaneeland to return a few nights a week to Brin de Quelque Chose.

By then, however, our music had changed. We had refreshed it. Made it new. Made it improvisational. Made it personal. Varied both the melody and the intonation. No longer tied to notes on a page. No longer did the song sound the same each time it was played. The music oozed such passion that detractors thought it bordered on libellous sensuality. What had been warm, we made hot. What had been romantic, we made provocative. Years later 'Hot Jazz' would become a moniker known the world over.

I continued also playing at Dominique's three nights a week. The environment relaxed me. Immune from the intense pressure indicative of performing with Swaneeland. Best of all, the girls remained welcoming. Months passed before I realised that they'd concocted a game to see who would serve me Scotch. Unsurprisingly, Gabrielle passed the post first.

Something else occurred during these halcyon days. About five or six times in a four-month period a guest rewarded me with overly generous tips. Unaware that Dominique's contract supplied me with two drinks, he asked the girls my 'drink of choice' and, after paying, requested they 'have it poured in the breech' after he had left the premises and prior to me packing my instrument.

Twice he covered the cost of an entire bottle. I asked whichever girl waited on him to describe his appearance and demeanour. Always the same: a well-dressed, well-mannered gentleman with a soft English accent. Because I encountered so many well-dressed people of various nationalities at Lipp and Brin de Quelque Chose, the description didn't resonate. Perhaps he attended those venues; perhaps he didn't. His other consistency: he never ventured up the circuitous steps with any girl. He limited his conversation to the war, to music, to jazz and to London—while consuming copious amounts of Scotch. And to make it more frustrating, and, because the girls waited on so many different men at various times of the day, it seemed none had encountered him more than once. All of this, of course, begged the question, since he was English, why in the hell didn't he approach me or leave contact details?

A breakthrough occurred in mid-August. Toward the end of my gig Gabrielle came over, sheepishly asking a question.

"*Monsieur* Travers, can you explain what 'fornicate like a badger' means?"

"Why, in God's name, ask me that?"

"Because the man at the bar—I think, but not certain, he's visited once before—asked me. He said: *The French women I knew in the late war fornicated like badgers. You act similarly?* When I replied I did not understand, he recommended I *broach the subject with*—how did he say?—*that splendid saxophonist in the far corner. He'll explain.*"

Didn't know what to think. A proper, well-dressed man asking if a women fornicated like a badger. Certainly rude. Undoubtedly perverse. Hoping to forgo another incident with an unruly Englishman, I approached the bar and sat carefully at the stool next to him.

"Excuse me, sir, but the young lady was confused by your question as am I, to be honest. May I assist with something in particular?"

"I wanted your attention and I got it. Splendid. Thank you for coming over."

"Ah, now I'm more confused ... if that's possible."

"The generous tips didn't work, nor the drink, nor the bottles of Scotch. I want to discuss a matter—an opportunity—with you but, regardless of how I approached it, nothing garnered a response. My mistake. Faulty strategy overall, I'm afraid. Sorry about that, old man."

"So, you're the mystery guest. I understand now. Nice to meet you finally. Your past generosities were appreciated—but why not tell one of the girls you wanted to chat? Easier, and less perverse, than the option you chose."

"I didn't want to interrupt the playing or ruin the mood. Each time I visited, I thought the girl would remember me from before and take the requisite action. Weeks passed before I realised that I'd never talked to the same girl twice. They all look alike to me now, I'm afraid. A deadline is approaching, tying my hands, forcing me to act. Unsavoury, yes. But here we are, talking. Success at last. Let me introduce myself: I'm WF Dabney, Entertainment director, The Savoy Hotel—on the Strand, London."

His unabashed introduction gave way to absolute professionalism. A business proposition, it seemed, was about to be extended or, at a minimum, discussed.

"I've seen you perform at Lipp's, as well as the club in Montmartre. You're good. Excellent, actually. I want to entice you to London."

"Swaneeland, travelling to London?"

"Sorry, again I've made myself unclear. Not the band, only you."

"Leave Swaneeland?"

"I have seen the band perform repeatedly. Truly excellent jazz. Somehow, I learned you soloed here at Dominique's occasionally. Perhaps someone at Lipp's told me; I don't recall. It took some effort. It took some time. But I persevered. And the quality of your playing here, of all places, surpasses anything I've heard from any alto sax player. The passion; the rapport; the style. On constant display, confirming my intuitions. The girls, I know, appreciate it. The lads, unfortunately, seem preoccupied. Damn shame really. They're missing out. But there you are."

"What exactly are you proposing, sir?"

"Please, please, call me WF. The hotel is forming a new band—to be called The Savoy Havana Band. All positions have been filled except the alto sax. I scurried all over England, even ventured north to Scotland. Dreadful place. Nothing. Too stodgy. Too treacle-like. So, not accepting defeat, I travelled to Paris. I've been visiting for, I don't know, the last eight or nine months, hoping for success. My search is finally over."

"I'm flattered, WF, but I'm content with …"

"Sorry to interrupt, old man, but I need to dedicate some time to describe what's in the offing. And you, I'm certain, eagerly await a good night's rest. So … could we meet for dinner one evening next week, perhaps? The choice of the establishment is yours."

"Well, I, I … let's see … would Thursday at Les Deux Magots, say half past seven, be convenient?"

"Yes, fine, excellent. I'm surprised you didn't recommend Lipp's."

"Oh, no, *Monsieur* Lipp, not only does he resemble one, but he also possesses the eyes and ears of a sparrowhawk. Magots is across the street, down a bit toward Rue Bonaparte."

"I'm familiar with it. Fine choice. Until Thursday then, Mr Travers."

After leaving Dominque's and walking to the apartment, my head became stuffed with possibilities. Bit of room remained for disparate scenarios to ricochet, to collide, to merge and to dissolve ultimately into insignificance. Was I that good or was WF blowing smoke, funnelling it up my ass without any obstruction? He had a deadline but didn't seem to be acting irrationally. Couldn't deny his persistence in locating *only* me. And, regardless how unorthodox and perverse his strategy, it worked: I'm dining with him at Les Deux Magots.

Arrived early. Seeing me made my waiter friend, Jacques, a bit concerned. He apologised that he couldn't possibly find enough food and drink *gratuit* at such an hour. Told him not to worry.

"I'm the guest of an Englishman from London. He's paying the bill … at least I hope he is. So, by God, I'm going to select the most expensive items on the menu, including the finest wine. Depending on what transpires, may order a vintage cognac."

"Ah, *Monsieur* Travers, we have a fine selection. The best in Paris. If opportunity becomes present, I suggest, ah, Bisquit Dubouché, 1865. *Perfection absolu.*"

"*Merci,* Jacques. *Merci.* We'll see how the evening progresses."

Didn't have the heart to tell him that I had enjoyed the

same cognac—too much, in fact—at Hotel Lutetia. Why deflate him? He had been repeatedly kind to me during my sojourn in Montparnasse.

Mimicking the precision of a military operation, WF appeared outside Magots at half seven. He returned his watch to a vest pocket upon seeing me. His 'Englishness' became fully apparent as he approached: dark pinstriped suit, starched white shirt, silver-coloured necktie, a miniature regimental insignia pinned to his left lapel, and, of course, the quintessential bowler hat. Only lacked spats and a walking stick.

Our drink and culinary tastes matched perfectly. We both ordered a double neat to relax, followed by duck *foie gras* and six *Gillardeau* oysters. Before selecting the main dish, WF emphasised that I was the guest of The Savoy, whereupon he unabashedly ordered the most expensive entrée on the menu: pan-seared Normandy-style rib steak with thick pepper sauce. Sensing the 'coop had been opened and the chickens let out,' I did the same. Recognising I wouldn't be paying the cheque Jacques recommended a fine Bordeaux—Saint-Estéphe, Château Calon-Ségur, 1900. WF thought it a 'splendid choice. Simply splendid.'

His first discussion point wasn't about jazz or the potential offer.

"Your gammy leg ... the war?"

I repeated the oft-heard rendition of how the whole damn thing began and ended.

"Nasty, wasn't it? I served in the Royal Field Artillery myself. I wanted to be 'in it', so to speak, not 'above it'. Schooled and trained at Larkhill in Wiltshire—close to Stonehenge, of which you certainly have heard. Then to France. I participated in the week-long bombardment of the Somme in late June 1916, in preparation for the infantry's attack. Fired 1.5 million shells in seven days. Half didn't detonate. Damn shame, actually. Wasteful. At the end of day over 19,000 Tommies were killed and 57,000 wounded."

"Let's see ... June 1916 ... my last summer playing with the Sinton Hotel's house orchestra. I was enjoying myself, and you were knee-deep in hell. Five years later, we're devouring Paris. Scarred but living. Broken but strong."

"Correct, old man. Correct. The surface appears mended for all to see. But, but ... when the weather's right and the wind blows in a certain direction, and the Scotch is of excellent quality, I can descend deep. Damn deep, actually. It's not pretty; I'm not proud of it. But there you are. I only divulge these revelations to those who served. If one didn't experience it, it's, well ... pointless to explain."

"My parents didn't support the war, so I never would have served probably except that eighty-five percent of the senior class had volunteered. Faced with few options, I stood in formation, raised my right hand and saluted the flag. Too cowardly, I expect, to face what would have come my way had I not donned a uniform."

"You did your bit, as did I. But, oddly, it seems another man's life to me now."

"Well stated, WF—I heartily agree."

He smiled with satisfaction after taking two healthy sips and returning the wine glass to the table. After pausing briefly to admire a lovely woman sauntering nearby, he began discussing the opportunity in detail.

"Management wants a band to capture the modern sound that also will appeal to a certain kind of

Englishman. It wasn't forthcoming with specifics, so I took it upon myself to decide who that 'kind' would be. I concluded it would consist of aristocrats, the titled, the wealthy, the country gentlemen, and yes, royalty. Edward, Prince of Wales, has developed an enormous liking for the place. I hope that fondness continues. And, of course, one cannot neglect rich American tourists—common clay, mostly, but I dare say all have oversized pockets bulging with money. Amazing what financing the war has brought to your country."

"Why, then, would you want a 'common clay' sax playing jazzman in the band? Seems hypocritical."

"That's what I've always respected about Americans: no subtlety. Why dilly-dally? One has to admire that."

"But do *you*, then?"

"Persistent, too—well done! Why? Because, at an Englishman's core, he respects ability and talent—whether innate or acquired. Watching you these past months, I've determined you have both. And you possess personal style and exhibit exquisite manners. Exactly what The Savoy desires and, I dare say, expects."

"Can you elaborate then, on what 'capturing the modern sound' means, specifically?"

"We're striving for a balanced, less noisy, less wild kind of jazz. Softening it. Making it more danceable, more digestible. The improvisation that you and Swaneeland perform so exquisitely will be toned down, become more orchestrated."

"Aren't you afraid of it becoming boring and predictable?"

"I see you point, and it's a good one. There *is* that possibility; however, we feel that by leaving out the guesswork and keeping the music and the sound balanced, the band will develop its own unique sound—its moniker, so to speak. The musicians' ability to elevate the purity of their instruments will transcend what's been heard any time prior. If you pardon my language, it promises to be bloody marvellous."

"So, jazz for the soft set—those who can't handle the pseudo-chaos of the real thing?"

"Precisely, old man. Precisely. But don't be put off. In addition to playing in the Thames Foyer for afternoon teas, the band will perform nightly in the main ball room from 8:00 pm until 12:30 am. I don't know how familiar you are, if at all, with the social season but it begins in earnest in March and runs through July. August is dead, so the entire band is on holiday. It picks up again in mid-September and runs through December. New Year's Eve is our swan-song event for the year. The band will practise four days a week during the January—February period. Break out new music, new arrangements, keeping it fresh, you know. A small contingent will continue playing for afternoon teas."

"Can't underestimate the draw of continuity and regularity, that's for sure. Doesn't exist with Swaneeland."

"There's a bit more, something I'm sure you'll like. The band is under contract—or will be, I should emphasise, beginning in 1922 with Columbia Records. Pressings will be made regularly, increasing the notoriety of the band as well as increasing the popularity of certain band members—mainly the flamboyant type—much like yourself, I imagine."

"Sounds sweet. Too good to be true."

"I know what you're pondering but are too well-mannered to ask ... money. I'll put you at ease. We're not going to discuss it tonight, for two reasons. One, I must protect The Savoy, so cannot have salaries bandied about the sullied streets of Paris. That's how rumours begin and inflate to a level of ridiculousness. Two, you need to think about what we've discussed. Ponder it. Ponder it deeply. Don't discuss with anyone. Mull it over until you're content with your decision. And please, Mr Travers, take … your … time. When you've made a decision, call. I'm at Hôtel de Crillon until the third week of September. About a month from now."

"If I haven't decided by the time you return to London …?"

"Here's my card with contact details. Send a wire and, if positive, I'll return to Paris and discuss finances and other various issues. Does that address your concerns?"

"Yes, completely. Thank you."

"I must get the cheque. A most appealing woman is waiting anxiously for me in the American bar at de Crillon. I must not keep her waiting any longer. I look forward to hearing your decision, Mr Travers. Enjoy your evening."

Immediately after WF departed, Jacques sauntered over, cleared the table and asked if I wanted anything.

"Fine evening, Jacques, but not worth pouring a glass of Bisquit Dubouché. But if you can muster up a double neat …"

"*Tout de suite, Monsieur* Travers. *Tout de suite.*"

Always respected Jacques. A man of few words who always brought happiness.

I still had not decided by the third week of September. A week remained before WF returned to London. When talking to myself, I thought he'd be more than a little disappointed that I hadn't made a decision. Yes, he said I could take time. And, yes, if I decided in The Savoy's favour after he'd left, he'd return to Paris. Deep down, however, I doubted he'd follow through. No musician, no matter how good, was worth kowtowing to. I wasn't an employee of The Savoy and was already costing it money.

After a particularly difficult and lengthy day practising a slew of new pieces, Skeeter made an announcement. Thought initially it was a harbinger, but I put that unfortunate thought out of my mind after he'd finished his first sentence.

"If you boys remember last year when working at Brin de Quelque Chose, long before Pearl Keys left, our ol' buddy Travers befriended a woman—a shapely woman— from his hometown, Cincinnati. He put her in contact with me and, well, to make a boring story shorter, she's asked us to play at a private dinner party at their house on Rue Greuze on the Right Bank. Bordered by the Seine on one side and Bois de Boulogne on the other. You know who I'm talking about, don't you, Travers?"

"The wealthy woman with the healthy figure—Sara Wiborg Murphy, of course."

"Correct. The event is scheduled for 3 October. The pay is damn excellent. Food and, to quote her, 'the requisite amount of drink for our times' will be available *after* the gig."

"Is she gonna provide us a place to bed down for the night, too?"

"Afraid not, Sliding Jack. The good news ... I'm kinda guessing Mrs Murphy isn't the type to invite whores, so ... your trousers will be safe."

"Damn, Travers, I thought you said you'd never say anything."

"Honest, I ..."

"He didn't utter a word. I have myriad ways of keeping tabs on you fellas. I've got the band's reputation, as well as my own, to protect. Let that be a lesson. You're not as slick as you think you are, Sliding Jack."

Poor old Sliding Jack held his head low, more out of embarrassment than anything else. Everyone started laughing. He came around eventually. Even joined in. That's what was so damn fine about Swaneeland: no one was more important than the other. The group succeeded because we failed at being individuals. That's when I began wondering if something even remotely similar could be possible at The Savoy.

Naturally, we arrived early. It was a stately building, solidly constructed and, being near the Trocadéro metro, close enough to walk. Looked around as we waited for someone to answer the door. So, this is where money lives, I thought. Clean, quiet streets. Spotlessly maintained buildings. Oversized windows with drawn curtains to keep gawking voyeurs at bay. The doors opened. The doorman didn't ask questions. Didn't raise an eyebrow. Our look of naïve enthralment gave us away. He welcomed us inside the decorous sanctum almost immediately. After checking our overcoats, hats and scarves the butler requested we follow him up the spiralling staircase to the second floor. I spotted Mrs Murphy as soon as we entered the refined dining room. She made a few inquiries to staff on her way to greet us. Although I perceived that she and her husband were masters in the art of living, she didn't own pretension—at least none that was visible. She shook hands with each of us, trying desperately to match our name with our instrument and commit both to memory.

"I'm familiar with my sax-playing neighbour from

138

Clifton in Cincinnati already. Memorise the rest and I can relax and enjoy myself this evening. Thank you for coming. Looking forward very much to our dinner guests experiencing the jazzin' of Swaneeland."

The guests comprised of three couples, four if counting the Murphy's. Per prior arrangement, we agreed to play soft music—tangos, foxtrots, waltzes, even some classical pieces—during the reception, silence while dinner was served, and our own rip-roaring jazz after everyone had enjoyed dessert.

Gerald Murphy, who had remained an enigma prior to this evening, approached as we assembled our instruments and prepared the music. An outward friendliness didn't conceal his spare, whippet-like physique. Here was a man, I thought, a slightly balding, soft, rich man who couldn't possibly possess a goddamn care in the world. He had the time. He coined in the money. And lived comfortably in one of the world's great cities with an equally rich, attractive and unconventional woman.

Murphy seemed in awe of my flying exploits. Asked numerous questions. Intrigued about any thoughts I had after being shot down. How did I control the aircraft? How great was the pain in my left leg as I descended? Was I worried the aircraft might catch fire prior to landing? Did I remember meeting the ground? His pestering queries soon made sense.

"I received basic flight training at Kelly Field in Texas—like yourself, I suppose—and then transferred to Roosevelt Field on Long Island for further instruction. In early November I received orders to the Handley-Paige flight training unit in England. Unfortunately—well, fortunately, I suppose, in hindsight—the Armistice was declared the day I was scheduled to sail. So, I never went.

Never flew. Received my discharge a few weeks later. My attempt to make a contribution to 'saving democracy' was over. As you can tell from the questioning, disappointment barely describes how I felt. But that was then, certainly not now."

"Too early to tell if I'd do it again, Mr Murphy. But since America's politicians lack any semblance of a spine, I kinda think it can be judged a terrible waste. A colossal mistake."

"Please, call me Gerald. And, yes, I agree. However bad the world before the war, the war has made it worse. All will experience it again, I'm afraid. Probably in fifteen, twenty years."

"That's why I'm jazzin', drinking and enjoying. There's no guaranteeing our futures."

"I'll make a deal with you this evening. You provide the jazz. I'll provide my signature drink when you've finished."

"Second-best offer since demobilisation. Thank you."

"Curious: what was the first?"

"An affectionate French woman—the precursor to the cat's miaow volunteered to tutor me in art history."

"Definitely better, I agree. I'll leave you now, then. Enjoyed the conversation. Looking forward to the music."

We played well. Excellent, actually. While no one danced to the tangos or foxtrots, the music set the mood. Created the sophisticated atmosphere that sophisticates expected and what Mrs Murphy desired. Being well-mannered guests, they showed their appreciation after each number while imbibing in God's own amount of booze.

As the cocktail reception transitioned to dinner,

Skeeter told us to leave our instruments and adjourn quietly to the kitchen. Mrs Murphy had shown him earlier the easiest way to proceed. Exit through two ceiling-high oak doors, walk along a black-and-white marble tiled hallway to a narrow set of stairs. After negotiating three flights we found ourselves in the kitchen. And greeted by a table, set with fine china and silver utensils on a starched white tablecloth. A leaded crystal vase containing fresh flowers adorned the middle.

"Damn, fellas, only items missing are five bottles of wine and five wine glasses."

"Come on, Sticks, do you think Mrs Murphy trusts our ability to limit the intake? Remember, the most important part of the gig—our jazzin'—hasn't happened yet. And it's got to be perfect. I know your cheapness leans toward downing free booze but damn, don't worry. She assured me the bar will remain open long after the jazzin' is over."

"I know, Skeeter—it's just, well, I play more intensely when I'm sweating out the liquor."

"Your so-called 'intensity' may be a bit much for this crowd. Keep it calm so we receive another invitation."

Two hours later we received word: time to occupy the room. We didn't disappoint. In addition to our normal litany, we added the hot numbers fresh from the States that we'd been practising so intently: 'April Showers', 'Ain't We Got Fun', 'I'm Just Wild About Harry', 'Jazz Me Blues', 'The Sheik of Araby', and 'Bandana Days'. The genuine crowd-pleaser, however, was 'Kitten on the Keys'. The piece accentuated Skeeter's nimble fingers and confirmed his nickname. The number's dance-ability brought everyone to the floor. Mrs Murphy and an attractive woman, who oozed wealth, took hold of each other, turned sideways as if joined at the hip, leaned their heads slightly toward the other so each touched the other's cheek, outstretched their arms, and danced in a straight line across the floor. At the appropriate time and in strict adherence to the music's rhythm, they turned around and danced to the other side of the room. Appraising the 'competition,' the other guests left the floor, seeking refuge against the wall to watch. The ladies repeated their trot across the floor probably about six times, causing us to play the piece three times in succession. Skeeter didn't mind. We sure as hell didn't mind. He kept a watchful eye on the ladies and, when he thought they'd had enough, brought it to a conclusion. We stood up, raised our hands, extended our arms and applauded the ladies. The other guests began laughing when the newly crowned jazzin' queens bowed in semi-bashful acknowledgement. And with that, the gig ended.

As we cleaned our instruments to put them in their cases, a short man possessing dark, wide eyes and slicked-back black hair approached Skeeter. He introduced himself as Cole Porter, a friend of Gerald's since their languid days at Yale a decade earlier, and husband of Linda, the woman who had danced with Sara Murphy. Songwriter by profession, he admitted, sadly, that he'd yet to land the big hit. Asked if the band would be offended if he tried a few of his compositions on the piano.

"I'd certainly enjoy it if the boys joined in. Contribute some unique rhythms wherever they perceived an opening."

Skeeter turned to us, posed the question and, despite our overwhelming desire for booze, couldn't bypass the opportunity. What transpired was inspirational and indescribable. Don't think any of us ever had experienced such improvisational playing. Everyone enjoyed it. Porter provided the initial melody, enabling us to enhance it, add to it or take it far and bring it back to the beginning. We were careful never to overpower his weak, timid voice. Didn't want anyone questioning who the main performer was. The result: twenty minutes of bliss, absolute and total bliss.

"If not too presumptuous, would you gentlemen be available for me to take advantage of sometime in the future?"

Didn't know if he was serious or joshing. Skeeter interpreted it as a serious query.

"Of course we would. Cross over to the Left Bank sometime, Mr Porter. Anything is possible because in Montparnasse ... anything goes."

"Might just do that, Mr Walker. May prove inspirational."

While putting away my instrument I glanced at the bar to see Gerald shaking a mixture, which I presumed was his signature Manhattan. He had dismissed the professional bartender earlier to assume sole responsibility for getting everyone drunk. And he was relishing it.

"There you have it, Mr Skeeter: my creation. Enjoy. Care for another, Mr Sliding Jack? I say, where's that sax man, Travers?"

Overhearing the folderol, I spoke up and approached the bar. Saw Skeeter, drink in hand, performing a soft-shoe number slightly left of the bar.

"Try and hold it together, Skeeter. Don't want to ruin having another go with the Murphys?"

"Travers ... this is sublime. The ultimate elixir. Will set you free."

"No need to worry about Sara and my opinions of

Swaneeland, Mr Travers. Neither can recall when we've had such an enjoyable evening. Swaneeland is the top."

"Thank you, Gerald. Thank you very much. Now … about that Manhattan."

I watched carefully as he mixed the concoction, anticipating that if it went down without a fuss, as evidenced by Skeeter, I'd want to replicate it. My mixology virginity played havoc, but I discerned that it consisted of two-thirds whisky, one-third Italian vermouth, two dashes of Angostura, and an olive with a lemon twist.

"I'll be curious what you think, Mr Travers. Seems your fellow band members are having one hell of an enjoyable time."

Looked to my right to see what Gerald was referring to: Sticks had joined Skeeter in another soft-shoe number. As I accepted the Manhattan I shook my head in disbelief.

"Not a dancing man, Gerald, so don't worry. Won't be joining in. Prefer thinking when drinking."

Admired the colour. Absorbed the aroma. Took a sip. Swallowed slowly. Tasted deliberately. Waited for a kick. Pondered the aftertaste. Ridiculously good. Second sip exceeded the first. My earlier 'ridiculously good' description transitioned into 'simply exquisite'. Skeeter was correct: a drink that set one free. Free from the past. Free from the present. Enabled me to ponder only the future, my future.

Found a small marble table in a far corner and got comfortable. Had taken my third sip when Sara approached. Reflecting the epitome of manners, asked if she could join me … in her own house, at her own table. Could I refuse?

"The boys and I certainly enjoy Gerald's Manhattans, Sara. One or all of us will be on the roof if not careful."

"Not worried in the least. The band deserves a little *joie de vivre* after such a performance. And Gerald ... he loves being a conduit to people's pleasure. Helping them retreat into their private world."

"Appears you've retreated into your private world successfully."

"We have. We have. The invented part of our lives has sensuous beauty. Elevated happiness. Life will blunder in one day, I'm sure. Scarring, disappointing and destroying what we'd known. But that's me. Gerald doesn't think so, but then he's an optimist."

"You didn't ask, but I must agree with you. My problem is idealism—my flying buddies nicknamed me 'Woodrow', after the president—and it brews nothing but trouble and creates disappointment. Maybe disillusionment, I don't know. It damn sure hurts."

"And I'm sure the war and its aftermath has only exacerbated your disquietude."

"Sounds harsh, Sara, perhaps even crude—but war is about killing. Life is about survival. One's easier than the other."

"I recommend you find a smart, fun-loving woman, William, have a child or two and imbue Europe with your jazz."

"Fine with the 'woman' and the 'jazz' part, Sara. Don't think much of the child idea, though."

"Children give one purpose, a reason beyond themselves. Now, if you'll excuse me, I believe Linda needs me. I've philosophised enough for one night, I think."

Took another long-desired sip of Gerald's Manhattan.

Hell, no. Never thought of children. Never entered my mind. As intimate as Véronique and I've been, had never discussed it.

Chapter Eight

Returning to Véronique's apartment one brisk October afternoon, I found a note attached to the door: *Meet me at half four in the garden café, Musée du Luxembourg. Order two glasses of calvados. Don't be late, please. Tout de suite. Love, V.* Looked at my watch. Had twenty minutes. Needed to hustle. Owning an ungainly walk, I *might* make it in time. But barely.

Luck was with me. Found an out-of-the-way table and ordered the drinks. Within minutes I caught a glimpse of Véronique, walking toward me smiling. As she came closer, I saw she was carrying a beautifully wrapped package. Placed it on the table, sat on my lap, ran her hand through my hair and kissed me.

"It's a special day, today. For you and for me."

"It is?"

"Don't you remember? 25 October 1919—two years ago this very day. You visited the 'Exposition D'Artistes de L'École Américaine'."

"Vaguely. So much has happened since the Armistice. Difficult to separate what's happened in which months and in what years."

She lovingly tapped my face as she got up.

"I remember if you don't. It's when we met. When I cavalierly approached and …"

"The whole damn thing started!"

"So, you *do* remember."

"Etched permanently within me."

"Oh, Willis, I wish I didn't love you so much."

"Kinda glad you do, to be perfectly honest."

"I have something that commemorates our relationship, our love. Something to remember me by."

"You're not planning on going somewhere, are you?"

"No … no … no. It's … it's … Here: what love I have remaining, it's yours, Willis. All yours."

I unwrapped the gift slowly. I removed the lid, folded back the tissue paper. Encased in a silver frame was a black-and-white photograph of Véronique. Her image was captivating, stunning actually. A work of exquisite artistry. She was wearing the emerald-green dress she wore when Swaneeland performed at Brasserie Lipp. This time, however, there was more *décolletage*—a lot more. The chair she was sitting on was obscured by a white cloth, making her appear as if she were floating. Her legs were crossed, head tilted slightly downward and a bit to the left. Her figure and cheekbones were highlighted, somehow, by soft background light. Her entire image was reflected behind her in a blurred, charcoal-like manner. Hauntingly mysterious. Almost as if she were a mirage, not real, a figment of her lover's imagination.

"It's taken by an American who arrived a few months ago. He opened a studio on Rue Campagne-Premiére, near my apartment, other side of Boulevard Montparnasse in an imposing, artistic-looking building. Wonderful studio. Heard about him from the president of Musée. So … I visited."

"Certainly unique. What's his name?"

"Calls himself Man Ray. Don't think that's his actual name, though. He certainly liked me. *Let me move your leg here. Let me place your head there. Now, if I may, let me accentuate your chest.* Got too comfortable too quickly. Held my breath and bit my lip."

"Have to say, despite your nervousness, takes one hell of an artistic photograph. You happy with it?"

"Overjoyed. It appears as if I'm hiding something—a

secret, perhaps."

"Makes two of us."

I reached inside my blazer and placed a small red leather box on the table. Sipped calvados and sat back.

"Willis, you remembered. Really remembered. Oh, my. And from Cartier. Willis, you shouldn't. You couldn't. Too costly for my saxman of Montparnasse and Swaneeland. It's ..."

"Wanted to do it. Needed to do it. For our sakes."

As she opened the lid, her oceanic eyes sparkled with excitement. She looked at the necklace and then looked at me. Repeated the gesture three times in quick secession.

"Oh, Willis. I'm touched."

"Try it on and read the inscription."

It was a necklace suspending a gold saxophone. A diamond—of what quality, I had no idea—affixed as the mouthpiece. Attached separately behind the sax was a small gold plate with an inscription. Véronique read it, first to herself and then quietly out loud.

"Véronique—who's never sharp or flat and always in tune. Love, Willis, 251019 - 251021."

It was my time to go over and kiss her. The smell of her perfume, the whisper of calvados on her lips, the warmth of her body ... damn intoxicating.

"Je t'aime, Willis. *Merci beaucoup."*

"Je t'aime, Véronique. *Je t'aime."*

Possessing some angst and subtle indecisiveness, I finally sent WF a wire in mid-October, a couple days after the Murphy's party and a week prior to meeting Véronique in the Luxembourg gardens. It read, in part: *I'm interested. Want the gig. Can we meet to discuss specifics?* Although difficult, I never uttered a word or even hinted about it to Véronique. If the money was good and the logistics well-planned, I'd be leaving Paris with more than myself.

WF replied. Meet him at Hôtel de Crillon around half eight on Sunday, 20 November. Anticipating that the de Crillon would be *très chic*, I wore a dinner jacket. Didn't want to offend WF or embarrass myself. Arrived early. Couldn't leave anything to chance. For some strange reason, I brought my instrument. Maybe I thought I'd work Montparnasse later in the evening, either to drown my sorrows or to celebrate with wild abandon. The bar was quaint: panelled in wood throughout, complete with a small but imposing bar that dwarfed the height of the barman. Dim lighting and a mosaic floor of concentric circles outlined with green laurel wreaths created a welcoming environment for business discussions and intimate conversations. WF had chosen wisely.

Similar to our meeting at Les Deux Magots, WF arrived on time, wearing the exact attire he'd worn at our first meeting. Made me feel overdressed. If he thought similarly, he didn't comment. We shook hands, whereupon he ordered two double neats from the barman with whom he was on a first-name basis. After settling in, we shared some inconsequential small talk. And then, without mincing words, he pulled a page of notes from an inside suit pocket.

"The Savoy will pay you £25 per week for six days' work, Tuesday–Sunday. The band performs regularly from March–July. You will be free the month of August, which means, of course, no remuneration. The band reconvenes from September–December. New Year's Eve, as I stated earlier, is the band's final performance of the year. While I cannot definitely say 'everything is in place', I expect to receive contracts soon, committing the band to special performances at the London Coliseum, the Queen's Hall, and Covent Garden—which conveniently is near the hotel. And, as I alluded to earlier at Margots, in all likelihood the band will be pressing several records on the Columbia label in the coming year. Band members will be compensated accordingly."

"During August, will I be permitted to engage in work at private clubs, dinner dances and ..."

"... Of course, old man. The Savoy doesn't want to see you in September looking gaunt, or appearing scruffy and smelling unkempt. By no means, however, is *any* member permitted to play at clubs or other nightspots during the season, while engaged at The Savoy. Even after the 12:30 am closing time. No one can play at Soho clubs or elsewhere—jazz or otherwise—that remain open later or, God forbid, those that never shut. Not permitted. If I, or management, find you in violation, you shall be sacked. No questions. No excuses. We must protect the integrity of The Savoy. Understand?"

"Certainly. I can appreciate that. Continuity is important and absolutely necessary."

"Well then, if you're amenable, I'd like you to arrive in London no later than 15 December. You'll practise with the boys for a week or two, making your debut on New Year's Eve. May I expect you then?"

"Yes, sir, very much so. One question. Until I find an apartment, will The Savoy provide a room or offer a similar accommodation?

"No, absolutely not. We lose money on that kind of proposition, old man. Rooms are for guests, not jazzmen. The hotel has an arrangement, however, for affordable accommodation with two establishments in Bloomsbury on Gower Street, close to the university. If you'd like, I'll make an inquiry and book a room under your name. I'll forward the particulars via post in the coming week."

"That should be fine. I'm not particular, so it won't be too challenging for me finding an apartment. You should see where I've lived for the past two-and-a-half years. On second thought … you shouldn't. Might retract the offer."

"If you have no further questions, Mr Travers, please review this document. It outlines, in writing, what we've discussed and what I've promised. If accurate, and you have no concerns, please date and sign."

Everything was detailed exactly how WF had explained. I reached inside my pocket for my fountain pen. As I unscrewed the cap, memories of Skeeter, Pearl Keys, Sliding Jack, the girls at Dominique's, Brasserie Lipp, even Johnny, fell heavily upon me. I paused. Reflected on the past; thought of the future. While the first downward movement of the 'W' was wobbly, I finished with determined confidence.

"Congratulations, Mr Travers. You are the newest and final member of the soon-to-be eponymous Savoy Havana Band. I look forward to a successful association."

"I do as well, WF. Hope not to disappoint you and The Savoy."

"Nonsense. You're the right colour and possess the right disposition. I'm expecting wonderful things from you. Now, if you'll excuse me. I have reservations at Maxim's with that charming lady I met earlier this summer. Captivating woman. Truly captivating—and very generous."

We stood and shook hands. Perhaps as a demonstration of support he patted me on the shoulder. And with that he departed. I remained still and quiet, contemplating and absorbing the momentousness of my decision. Barman George approached and placed a double neat on the table.

"As he left, *Monsieur* Dabney asked me to serve a double neat on the house. Another is available, if desired. It will be also on the house.

"*Merci*, George. *Merci beaucoup*."

My immediate thought, after receiving the drink, was whether I'd garner free drinks and food in England? Serious thoughts occupied me about halfway through the second one. Put aside all remaining doubts and embraced my decision. *I'll earn more. Make better connections. No telling how lucrative records could be.* And who knows, I thought, after a couple years with The Savoy, might be bull-headed and cock-eyed enough to form my own band.

Then there was the personal side of life—probably the most important outcome of surviving the war. Couldn't wait to tell Véronique. Would she follow me to London? Of course she would. Why wouldn't she? Walking toward her apartment I decided to ask her to marry me. Now was the time. I was ready. I'm certain she was. We'd celebrate and put the seal on it prior to leaving. Everything tied tightly. No loose ends. I also knew her well enough that, although midnight, she wouldn't mind being woken up. She'd be excited. Happy for us. And say *yes*.

As I opened the door, shadows from a candle flickered in another room. Heard soft whispering. As I placed my instrument on the floor the handle hit the case, making a slight noise. Silence. I walked into the bedroom. Except for the half-unbuttoned tunic of a German aviator, an otherwise naked woman was sitting atop Véronique. The 'aviator' looked at me, left the bed and gathered bits of her uniform from the floor. She walked past and uttered, *Désolé, Monsieur, je ne savais pas*. I recognised her perfume. Had first smelled it a year earlier after returning early from Provins. I said nothing. Simply stared at Véronique lying in bed. She remained still. Eyes closed.

The rage I should have felt was absent. Another by-product of the war, I thought. Found a full bottle of hooch and sunk into the chair by a smouldering fire. Don't know why I stayed. Did I expect an explanation? Did the truth matter? Not really. That it was another betrayal seemed adequate. And yet, I remained. Five, ten, maybe twenty minutes passed. No idea of time. Half the bottle was gone. She walked in eventually. Sat in the chair opposite as my eyes started to glaze over. Despite the awful circumstances, she looked beautiful.

"Willis …"

"Don't call me Willis. You've lost that privilege."

"William … things happened during the war that I've neglected to tell you. 'Neglected' is the wrong word. 'Never' told you … purposely."

"Could be interesting, maybe artistic. Perhaps Skeeter will put it to music."

"This will be difficult for you to hear, let alone understand: I love women. It's natural with me. It's pure. And there's something else. Something I've never mentioned to anyone. One dark, bitter morning while delivering coal during the war a man attacked me. That incident, that violent, horrible act turned me decidedly against ever trusting men. Any hope, any desire I once had for a family was destroyed that morning. Taken from me forever. Remember your surprise at me liking hooch? I told you it had kept me alive. It did that but, more importantly, it masked pain. Enabled me to temporarily forget. To cover. To conceal. To hide. And, yes, to lie to myself and to others."

"Why didn't you tell me after we became close? After

154

we started giving a damn about each other?"

"My dislike of men is great ... not all of them, of course, and ... not always. I befriended you, I suppose, because you're an American. Regardless of you bragging about not returning to the States, I somehow rationalised that you'd return eventually. You wouldn't stay. I'd remain in Paris. And my secret would stay a secret. I never thought you'd last. But you didn't leave. You stayed and got deeper and deeper into me. You treated me with such respect. Plans percolated in your head. What you hoped for with me. Despite everything ... it felt strangely comforting. But soon I became scared, fearful of my past, the choices I'd made. My wants and desires. Hoped everything we shared—romance and love—would be temporary. But you kept offering the opposite."

"That worked for a few months. How the hell do you rationalise two years?"

"You've got to understand: my love for Fortunée will endure. It must last. One day I'll need her ... her companionship, her love, her being, more than ever. Especially after you've gone—have found someone new. Haven't you ever thought it odd that I took you to *my* bed in *my* apartment so soon after our first meeting? No fear. No precautions."

"Your quickness for passion and lack of caution? I believed it genuine. Thought we meshed."

"Don't you understand, can't you comprehend? That attack prevented me from nurturing life. Ever. Something you will want is something I can't provide."

"We discussed us. Nothing more."

"Few men will admit it's probably the biggest thing— the only thing—that gives them credence. If not now, if not tomorrow, someday you will wish it. If we could have been together, you'd resent me and leave. I know you would. I know how you think. You feel cheated by the war. You couldn't tolerate being cheated a second time."

"You're wrong. I've been cheated a second time. Just earlier than you imagined. Hoped for honesty and faithfulness. Attributes, I realise now, you don't possess. About the German aviator ... your Fortunée ... is she the only one or were there others? Or aren't you the kind that tell?"

"There've been others through the years—even before you and I pledged to ignore convention. Something I'd been doing for some time. You embracing it simmered my angst. The woman who whispered to me at Le Gaya, Madeline Dupont—she was the first. I figured one day you'd come by the apartment to surprise me. In some wishful but bizarre way, I hoped you'd see me, be angry enough to storm out and that would end it."

"Feel sad for the indignity you went through during the war. Experiencing such hell alone makes it unbearable. Your anger and distrust toward men ... justified. I get it. And if I thought long and hard in a non-drunken state, probably wouldn't have issues with your female infatuations. Reflects the goddamn times we live in, I suppose."

"You may want to think it's 'fashionable' or an 'infatuation,' William—it isn't. I can't give her up. I won't throw her aside. I can't change who I am or what I want or what I need."

"If I accept that, and I'm not saying I do, then we still have the problem of lying, Véronique. The lying. Can't live with deceit. So, you win. You've ended it."

"You're hard, William. Too hard."

"Life's hard."

"I've destroyed everything. Everything good. Everything, haven't I?"

"That you have, *Mam'selle*. Our life together has unravelled, been blown to hell. Only thing one can expect a good life to do, I suppose."

She curled up her lower legs and feet onto the chair and began crying. No, it wasn't crying. It was sobbing. Tears streamed down her face as she looked up at me. I patted her right shoulder before retrieving my instrument. Had it inside me to see her again someday.

Battling an emotionally fractured skull and owning an ungracious walk, I looked the misfit to anyone watching as I made my way sloppily to Rue du Cardinal Lemoine. Halfway there it dawned me: I hadn't told Véronique about The Savoy. Unless one sought out the other, she wouldn't know I'd left Paris, nor where I'd gone. A bit cruel, I thought, but liked it nonetheless. I owed her nothing. Saw with my own eyes that we didn't have what I thought we had. What I wanted. What I needed. Proved as fake and fraudulent as everything else this century. Nothing and no one are fully accountable anymore. Excuses abound. Nothing can be trusted. No one can be believed. All the good times we had shared … shit, like the few other decent things in life, now belonged to the past too. And this meant only one thing: the future will become darker and lonelier.

Struggled to reach the fourth floor. My spirits were lifted, however, once I remembered plenty of hooch awaited me. I'd be able to fly high for several hours before crashing. The flight would be memorable. The crash, hell, no one ever remembers those.

I woke with a hatchet in my head and to a persistent

knock at the door. Slowly worked my way over to open it to find Skeeter looking concerned but smiling nonetheless.

"Where in the dickens have you been, Travers? Everyone became worried, believe it or not. Went to Véronique's, no answer. Paraded up, down and around Montparnasse, nothing. Hell, Sliding Jack even visited Dominique's place. Girls said that hadn't seen you in a couple days."

"What day of the week is it?"

"Day of the week? Hell . . . Wednesday."

"Wednesday? Christ, been out for two days."

"Shit, Travers, why the hell do you think I'm here? You've missed two days of practice. The boys and I find it difficult jazzin' without a sax! Ever tried it? Ain't easy."

"Oh, God, I... am... sorry, Skeeter. Saw something I didn't want to see."

"Christ, with a face resembling thirteen miles of bad country road, that can mean only one thing. Found Véronique with someone else, huh?"

"Someone like herself."

"What do you mean, 'like herself'?"

"Another woman, for God's sake, dressed as a German aviator."

Skeeter looked as if someone had torched his piano. His smile became a frown. His smooth forehead became wrinkled. His wide eyes narrowed.

"Why, I'll be goddamned, Travers. Never would have thought that. Didn't seem into experimenting."

Didn't tell him everything. Some things, I thought, should remain personal. Wasn't out to soil her reputation, her character or her livelihood. Women, in general—and

Véronique, in particular—didn't deserve having their sexual preferences bandied about in brasseries and clubs. And she certainly deserved better than what befell her on that dark street.

"Yeah, it's a gasser, for sure. Guess I drank hell's own amount of hooch the last two days. Experienced a bad low. Developed a genuine case of the black ass. Really sorry about missing practices."

"I understand the reason now but ... well, gotta rise above it, Travers. Shake it off. Can't let down Swaneeland. And besides, all kinds of women adore jazzmen. Those who will introduce you to their mother and those who won't."

"Got a bit more. Before all this occurred, I was about to ask Véronique to marry me and ... well, accompany me to London."

"London? We don't have a gig in London."

"I do—with The Savoy Havana Band ... on New Year's Eve. The manager of the hotel's orchestra, WF Dabney, visited Dominique's place a couple times. More than a couple, actually. About six times or so, to be exact. Heard me playing. Caught us at Lipp's a few times, too. He certainly was persistent. Finally gave in. Was going to tell you Monday but depression and drink overwhelmed me, I guess."

"Damn, Travers. Damn. What can I say? How can I change your mind?"

"Any persuasion tactics may have worked if I hadn't seen the German aviator atop Véronique. I know Paris is big, and there are lots of nooks and crannies this side of the river, but there are also lots of memories. I'd be surrounded by ghosts. Besides, too many Americans arriving, trying their hand at being something they're not.

These 'Eiffel Towerists' are beginning to bore me. Nothing but gawkers and sycophants."

"So, you're leaving Paris because of the influx of Americans and going to England to be surrounded by stuffy, opinionated and overly tight Brits?"

"Better that than American bumpkins."

"So, when's the departure date? Can you help the band honour its commitments through Christmas?

"Leaving in a little more than three weeks. Ten days before Christmas."

"God almighty. That's slimmer than a single sheet of shit paper. Damn."

"I've got to find an apartment. Work myself into the band quickly. The Savoy needs me for New Year's Eve."

"Hell, won't they put you up in a room for a few weeks?"

"Stuffy, up tight Brits lodging a bloody Yank in one of London's swankiest hotels? I know I'm hungover, but it sure as hell sounds like you're the one nursing delusions."

"Okay, I get it. You're leaving. And leaving us with a goddamn rotten peach of a mess."

"Sorry, Skeeter. I'm truly sorry. I sure will continue playing our gigs at Lipp's and Brin de Quelque Chose until the tenth or so."

"You will, will you?"

"Of course."

"Tell you what, Travers, why don't you pucker up and put a few well-placed, wet kisses right smack-dab in the middle of my moist sphincter muscle!"

He turned and left, slamming the door on his way out. Profane muttering echoed down the stairwell. The rant continued as he exited and made his way across the street. Don't believe a respectful, professional friendship ever had died so abruptly. I sat at the table and poured a double neat. Seemed eerily similar to two-and-a-half years earlier when I sat in my room at Lapin hors du Chapeau. Back then I drank to the memory of my dead buddies. Now I was drinking to forget, to simply forget.

Although rightly or wrongly shunned from jazzin' with Swaneeland, I kept my commitment to Dominique. Couldn't let down the 'Grand Dame' of Montparnasse. I also reclaimed my preferred spot outside Abbey of Saint-Germain-des-Prés in Montparnasse. Since it began there, thought it might as well as end there.

Things had changed in the eighteen months or so since I last played the pavement. Although I'd updated my repertoire to include numbers that I had performed earlier with the band, such as 'I Ain't Got Nobody', 'St Louis Blues', 'I'm Just Wild About Harry', 'Avalon', and—my personal favourite—'Ain't We Get Fun?', everything seemed askew. Different crowd. Less genuine. Noisier. Richer. All watched and commented as if attending a zoological exhibit of exotic animals or a post-mortem inquest.

"Booze is spelled with a capital *B* and art with a small *a* here on Boulevard Montparnasse. Wouldn't experience this on North Pearl Street in Albany, would we, Margaret?"

"Mommy and Daddy would love hearing this little Frenchman playing his saxophone. Would never hear anything like it in Altoona. Look how he sways, taps his crippled foot and so politely acknowledges people throwing francs into his case. Poor thing."

"You realise, don't you, Josephine, your mother never would permit such a song being played on the phonograph? She'd be horrified if fellow parishioners at Wichita's Epworth Methodist Church found out."

"Do you think, Herbert, if I asked him something in English he'd reply in French?"

"Why wouldn't he? Give it the old college try, Charmaine. If I'd taken French instead of Latin in school, I'd be able to converse with ol' Jacques."

I continued playing with bewildered amusement as Charmaine built up the nerve to ask her question—loudly and slowly, as if talking to a deaf two-year-old.

"You … are … very … good … Really … Excellent. Where … did … you … learn … to … play?"

Thought about how to respond. As a native using grammatically flawed French or as a Frenchman who speaks in elegant American English. The other option, the truthful option, was to be the American expat. Pure, simple, and with some condescension thrown in for flavour. Gave Herbert and Charmaine all the dope on my instrument playing, including my fascination with Montparnasse, Paris and French culture.

"It certainly isn't America, is it? So different. No one works. Idleness abounds. And the food … we'll never understand the food. So, when are you returning to God's country and leaving this oddity behind?"

"Hopefully never. In fact, ma'am, to my way of thinking there's too much 'God' in America. He's taken to telling everyone they can't drink. Even Christ drank wine with twelve of his closest buddies—well, only eleven, actually—at a long, wooden table in an emotionally charged setting!"

"What a horrible thing to say. For being over here, you certainly don't represent the best of America."

"No, suppose I don't, and for that I apologise. I grieve

over my poor manners every evening. But if you're looking for the best of America, they're buried throughout France in what will become well-manicured cemeteries one day soon, I imagine. Recommend you pay them *all* a visit."

They turned beetroot-red. Stumbling through thoughts they'd never utter. Herbert reached down into my case and retrieved the four francs or so he'd deposited earlier. I didn't say anything. I didn't care. As they walked away, I overheard Charmaine's exasperated reaction:

"So ill-mannered, Herbert. So rude. Obviously not from Ohio. Wait till I tell 'em back home."

Met *Madame* Rohrbeck one morning and told her my plans. I'd vacate the apartment early on the fifteenth and wouldn't expect a partial rent refund.

"I wouldn't give it if you did—but you were a reliable tenant. *Agréable.* You understand, *oui*?"

"*Oui, oui, Madame Rohrbeck.* You, too, were most *agréable. Merci.* I am sorry, disappointed actually, to be leaving Rue du Cardinal Lemoine and Paris. Hope you find another tenant quickly."

"*Pas de problèm, Monsieur* Travers. A new tenant arrives early January. Americans, again. A young man and his wife. From a town near Chicago."

"Hope they enjoy the apartment and the *Bal-musette* as much as I did. Pray he's not a musician. Don't think the area could cope."

"Never know what tenants work at until they arrive. And with Americans, it's even more of a—how does one say?—*jeu de devinettes.* Anyway, *bonne chance, Monsieur* Travers. *Bonne chance.*"

Next stop: Johnny at the *Bal-musette*. Hadn't seen him in weeks, which meant, of course, he wasn't privy to my recent travails. The place appeared empty, making it easy to lay claim to my favourite stool. And, per custom, didn't have to ask for a drink. Johnny had seen me enter and poured a double neat already, placed it on the bar and sat a full, uncapped bottle next to the glass.

"Damn, guv'nor, would never have guessed she enjoyed riding two horses with one arse."

Cast my eyes to the floor. Lower back hurt. Withered leg tightened. Righthand shook. Mouth parched. Christ, it's out.

"Crude, but appreciate the sentiment. How the hell did you find out, anyway?"

"She came by weeks ago searching for you. Told her to check the apartment but she declined. Said something like, *He doesn't like to be interrupted when practising.* Knew then it smelled. Know you well enough that you'd happily be disturbed by a fine specimen of French womanhood like Véronique. She realised immediately I wasn't buying it. Being the self-anointed 'King of Liars,' I can sniff a lie before it's even left the mouth. So, she filled me in."

"I've consumed a lot to drown the memory. To cauterise her from my mind. Burning it with plenty of hooch."

"Hasn't worked. You look like shit."

"Keep seeing that woman atop her, dressed in a German tunic."

"Didn't know about the Boche fetish. Christ. No wonder you look like shit."

"Thanks."

"Suggest you employ Carmen and Olga."

"Whom do you prefer?"

"You're not listening. It's not one over the other. It's

both simultaneously."

"Thanks, Johnny, but I'll pass. If I desired a gymnastics act, I'd ask Dominique's girls. I know their stories and respect them."

"Well then, guv'nor, you've found your answer. But since I've got you here and, being this bottle has lost its cap, be a damn shame to waste it."

"You'll never make money, Johnny, if you give away your hooch."

"Never entertained a customer so worthy of losing what few francs I make on a bottle of Scotch."

"Johnny, if your brethren in London are as friendly, I might do okay. Kinda think, though, you're a rare British breed. A one-off. Not reflective of the general populous."

"You'll fit in eventually. Will take time, maybe years. The Brits you'll encounter will be friendly, decorous and appear interested in your story. That you fought in the war and are a damn fine jazz musician will hold instant appeal. Just be aware, all outward admiration is insincere. They'll criticise you to hell and back—from stem to stern—after you've left. You'll only know you've been accepted when you're invited to their home. Whether for cocktails or dinner, either venue will indicate you're worthy of their graciousness. But, more importantly for them, your presence offers something unique and entertaining for their guests."

"Well, shit—I'm not an organ grinder, *sans* the monkey, Johnny. I perform only if I get paid."

"Not the point, guv'nor, not the point. You see, they're not interested in *you*. They're showing friends *their* ability at attracting unusual people. Someone different. Someone unlike themselves. Someone not of their class. Someone whom most in their circle couldn't possibly meet or befriend. In the end it's about them, not you."

"Christ, then I'll stick with longshoremen, prostitutes and cockneys."

"I know nothing about English prostitutes, but dockworkers and the typical cockney won't understand jazz music or a jazz musician. They'll think you're either a homosexual, a communist or a rich American with nothing better to do. Worst case, they'll think you're all three!"

"Sounds God-awful. Bleak. Lonely."

"Not necessarily, guv'nor. You'll find an attractive British lass wrapped around your arm and inside your pocket in no time. Remember how quickly things happened with Véronique ..."

"Bad salesmanship, Johnny. Bad salesmanship. There's a reason it happened so quickly. Not explaining. Ever."

No one could accuse Johnny of being unperceptive. Suppose that's why he stood behind the bar. After pouring another double neat he feigned work in a far corner. Knew I needed to be alone, to nurse a drink and to repair severed emotions.

Consuming upwards of three-quarters of the bottle enabled me to understand a bit more precisely where I'd been and where I was headed. Soon after our first meeting, I recalled Véronique saying something to the effect: *We never know who will and who won't matter. They come and they leave, but oftentimes return, clinging to you for life.* She believed—almost deterministically— that we had met for a reason. I thought, initially, her hooch consumption had elevated the conversation to a lofty sense of amorousness, but now, after everything, I thought differently.

Idealism had taken hold of me years earlier and, if honest with myself, long before I had entered university. Pragmatism held little appeal. Doing right, thinking morally and acting ethically had dominated my life. Controlled it. Never settle. Never compromise. Always search and stretch for the higher ideal. We're never told, however, something or somebody eventually will come along in life with a heavy enough force that crushes most, if not all, vestiges of idealism. The war, especially the self-centred aftermath pursued by the US, destroyed any remnants of political beliefs I held prior to 1917. And, sadly, I think Véronique's dishonesty—using me for *her* ends—was the real reason we met. Her selfishness will wreak havoc for a long, long time.

The bottle empty, I searched for Johnny to wish him well and to say goodbye. Found him cleaning up the mess left by any unruly customer. A boisterous scuffle had become physical, apparently, but I never heard a thing. Had travelled deep and remained there for some time, I suppose.

"When we met two-plus years ago, Johnny, you were merely an acquaintance. But now, as London beckons, I consider you a prized friend. The rarest among men. Thank you … and I haven't even discussed the damn fine hooch you pour."

"Inspirational phrases aren't my specialty, guv'nor. Can't string the right words together in the right order. But there *is* a guy I'm familiar with; you may be, as well … William Shakespeare. *Good company, good wine, good welcome, can make good people.* Think it's from his play, *Henry VIII*. It's what we shared. I'll always be grateful. *Au revoir*, guv'nor."

"*Au revoir*, Johnny. *Au revoir.* Wish you only the

best."

A day or so after telling Johnny farewell, I received a written invitation from *Madame* Diguet. She requested I visit.

I realise 6 am is early but, as you know, it's when the club is closed. The girls are arranging a petite fête prior to your departure in two days and didn't want to deal with the hassle of customers prowling about. Hope you will not disappoint.

Kind regards, DD

Flattered by the girls' kindness, I responded immediately.

Gale-force winds continued blowing from the east the morning of the party, guaranteeing the city soon would be covered in snow. The only benefit to the miserably cold wind was it cleared my head. After entering the club, however, I thought differently. Had the wind affected my vision? Were my eyes deceiving me? The girls had exchanged their diaphanous, everyday work clothes for, what I took as, *haute couture* finery. Crass as it sounds, none resembled women in the profession. I was taken aback. Genuinely shocked. Sitting on the bar was a silver bowl filled with caviar, side plates of toast points and numerous bottles of champagne. The girls were milling about, relaxing and enjoying themselves, commenting on one another's dresses, excited about the festivity.

Madame Diguet took the floor, making several respectful comments about my playing, my professionalism and my manhood (which I didn't fully understand). She regaled everyone, yet again, with how I fought off the insufferable Brit, slashing the air with a broken bottle of *eau de vie*. She wished me luck and hoped I wouldn't encounter many like him in London.

"If you 'befriend' British toughs, *Monsieur* Travers, I beg you to do Parisians a favour—keep them over there!"

"I'll try my damnedest, *Madame* Diguet, but they're bulldogs at heart, you know. Difficult to rein in."

"*Oui, oui,* but, of course, that's exactly what France needed during the war, wasn't it?"

"It certainly was, *Madame* Diguet. It certainly was."

"Now rich Americans are arriving in droves. Wish you would remain, *Monsieur* Travers. Help me with them. Just days ago, an American wanted his wife to watch him with a girl. I said, *No. No.* He then asked if two girls could come into the room and make a sexual *tableau* for them. What could I say? Thought quickly and doubled the price. More *la bizarrerie* will follow, I am certain."

Almost as if rehearsed—knowing Dominique as well as I did, I'm certain it was—Gabrielle inched herself from behind the bar holding a beautifully wrapped package. She walked forward and, while handing me the package, kissed my lips.

"That's from me. This is something to remember *all* of us by."

I put down my champagne glass and unwrapped the package: a solid silver frame containing a professionally taken group photograph of the girls wearing 'working' attire. An inscription at the bottom summarised my experience perfectly: *À l'homme qui n'admirait que de loin* [To the Man Who Only Admired from Afar]. On the reverse, an attached sheet of paper with their signatures.

Recognising both Gabrielle's feelings toward me and her command of English, Dominique asked her to make the concluding remarks.

"We decided to post the names, *Monsieur* Travers,

because we hope you will remember the times we shared at Dominque's. When you become frail and feeble and alone, you can reflect on what was but could never be again. Memories of a life well led ... part of which included us. *Jamais au revoir* [Never goodbye]."

A week before departing Paris I ventured to the Right Bank, an area I largely had neglected. Wanted to stroll through the Tuileries, study Charles Garnier's Opera House as well as visit La Madeleine. Also thought, if I happened upon an affordable brasserie, I'd celebrate my failure with a fine dinner. It started pouring rain immediately after arriving. Believing it would be only a brief, but powerful, deluge, I sought shelter under the arched colonnade on Rue de Rivoli, near the entrance to Hôtel Le Meurice. While watching the rain bounce upward from the pavement, I heard an American-accented voice questioningly call my name.

"Sara ... and Gerald, how wonderful to see you. Surprised you recognised me with two weeks' beard growth and not wearing dinner clothes. How are you both?"

"We're fine, William. Excellent, actually. Disappointed to have learned you're no longer playing with Swaneeland."

"That news travelled quickly. Haven't even departed the country yet."

"We're engaging the band for our New Year's Day *fête*. I mentioned you to Mr Walker and, well ... he told us the unfortunate news. The whole affair remains openly raw for him, I believe."

"Raw for me, too. End of an era, I suppose, but I was presented an opportunity I thought beneficial for professional and, well, now personal reasons."

"It's The Savoy, isn't it?"

"Yes, a new orchestra's being formed, The Savoy

Havana Band. Leans toward orchestrated jazz, not improvisational like Swaneeland. The manager hopes it will appeal to—what was his term?—'a certain kind of Englishman'. The work promises to be steady and the money—though impolite to discuss—will enable me to drink and eat regularly."

"We've never visited The Savoy. We found the Langham to our liking years ago, so, consequently, we've never looked elsewhere."

"Perhaps a drink at the Langham's bar then. Been told already that band members cannot, under any circumstances, patronise The Savoy's bar—whether with the band or when alone."

"Please do visit the Langham. They mix the most marvellous martini."

"As good as your Manhattan, Gerald?"

"Because he won't tell the truth, I'll answer for him: a close second."

"I've heard Brits have immense respect for the also-rans, so that's quite the compliment."

"Which reminds me: last summer, before Gerald and I visited Paris, we met a lovely young lady at the Langham. Owner of a sad, tragic story but continues on the best that she's able. Her tenaciousness astounds me. Remember Gerald?

"Helena Bolton-Leigh? Yes, beautiful girl. A choice bit of calico, for sure. Resembles a pre-Raphaelite painting, William. Tall, spirited lady with long, flowing red hair, green eyes ..."

"Gerald, please, enough. Perhaps you could tell William her shoe size. Do you, by chance, remember it?"

I'd fallen into the beginnings of a row; I wanted to leave. I didn't. Both began laughing, enabling me to join in.

"Unfortunately, she doesn't live in London, William, but up north. The area that's famous for stone walls and sheep. What's it called, Sara?"

"Yorkshire Dales."

"Yes, yes, the Yorkshire Dales. Her father died a month before Britain declared war. Her two older brothers were killed on the Western Front. So, since about 1916 or '17, she's been trying to manage sprawling amounts of land and, I suppose, the requisite number of sheep. Her mother remains withdrawn, too distraught to care about much of anything. It's all on Helena's shoulders. Poor girl."

"Sounds difficult. A sad story indeed. I doubt, however, I'll be venturing away from London anytime soon."

"She travels often to London. The member of a government agency, committee or some-sort organisation analysing the post-war wool industry. I don't want to appear forward but, if you'd like, I'll pass along your details. If interested, she may contact you. She's a lovely, lovely woman. Might enjoy each other's occasional company. Perhaps a cocktail or two some afternoon."

"That's kind, Sara. Very kind. I can provide only a calling card with my name. Don't have an address yet. Must find an apartment as soon as I arrive. From the way you described her, I can't think of any possible reason why she'd find me interesting, but if she's wants to contact me whenever next in London, let's see … may be easiest for her to leave a message at The Savoy's front desk."

"Splendid idea, William. Simply splendid. You may be surprised. Helena doesn't strike me as desiring sympathy or accepting pity. You may find comfort in each other, however fleeting."

"Perhaps, but please tell her I'm a jazzman. Many are offended by the music and its acolytes. Wouldn't want to surprise her. Best never to have met than meet only to be rejected."

"I'll make sure Helena knows. She seemed attuned to everything modern when we met. Have a feeling she holds the 'old order' responsible for the loss of her brothers, so she may embrace the new ... including the music."

"We're meeting Linda and Cole for drinks. Care to join?"

"Gerald, please, don't embarrass the man. He's not dressed appropriately."

"Exactly, Sara. My thoughts exactly. Too scruffy. Too untidy. Couldn't embarrass the Porters. When I left today, I had little imaginings of drinking at Le Meurice. But thanks for asking."

"We wish you only the best, William. And if we ever cross the Channel, we'll certainly visit The Savoy."

"Please do. I'd enjoy seeing familiar faces. Until then ... *au revoir*."

"*Au revoir*, William. *Bonne chance*. And as Brits say, 'Happy Christmas'."

"I'm not in Britain yet, so I'll continue with the American greeting and wish you both a Merry Christmas."

I remained outside, sheltering from the rain, a bit longer. Glad I did. Was entertained by something that could happen only in Paris. Saw a sleek black cat emerge from underneath a tree in the Tuileries. He slipped through a narrow space in the cast-iron fence, shook off his wetness, crossed Rue de Rivoli and sat outside the hotel, waiting patiently for the doorman.

"Bonjour Monet, bienvenu à la maison."

Certainly, I thought, this couldn't be true. The 'resident cat' of an exceedingly swanky hotel waiting to be let inside? It was true. After 'Monet' entered, and prior to the door closing, I heard a respectable but boisterous 'miaow' from inside. An obliging 'thank you,' I surmised, for the doorman.

I began analysing my years in Paris as I made my way down Rue Royale toward La Madeleine. The city had offered, gave it without my asking, an ambiguity, the chance to dispose of who I was prior to the war, including responsibilities and expectations inherited from the past. And—most importantly, perhaps—it released personal ambitions and secret desires supressed long ago. And yet, the morality of my recent experience could be measured only by its naiveté. Any charm, any virtue that emerged did so because of the sheer novelty of the whole goddamn thing. I needed to find my life.

A week later, as the train pulled out of Gare du Nord for the cross-Channel ferry and then onwards to London's Victoria Station, I reflected on comments from those who had meant something to me during my sojourn: Véronique: *You're hard, William. Too hard.* Skeeter: *All kinds of women adore jazzmen. Those who will introduce you to their mother and those who won't.* Gabrielle: *Memories of a life well led.* It was Gabrielle's words that resonated the longest. *Memories of a life well led.* I repeated them as if responding to a Bible reading.

INTERMISSION

Peter and Fiona abandoned their earlier agreement to read without interruption. They had decided Travers's predicament invited, almost necessitated, discussion. Peter refreshed the martinis. He had only got comfortable when Fiona sprang up and began pacing the room.

"God, Fiona, you're wound up as tight as when you were preparing for finals at university."

"I just can't get my head around Véronique's duplicity. The sordidness ... unspeakable. And I'm not talking about the sex aspect. She and Travers had been through a lot. Shared so much. Cared for one another. Why wasn't she honest from the beginning? Which begs the question: if she preferred women and disliked men, why'd she pursue him in the first place?"

"Yeah, I agree. Travers seemed fragile when we first met him. No one left in America gave a damn. Buddies from the war were dead. He was alone. He had invested in Véronique—emotionally and physically. She gave him purpose. She patched the holes. She repaired the broken parts. I got the impression—wrongly, it turns out—that he had done something similar for her. But, obviously, she couldn't alter her preferences. She was who she was and knew what she wanted. She also couldn't escape what happened. Too horrific. Too many reminders. What's the term used today ... compartmentalise. A life-altering event like that couldn't be locked away. And, of course, that raises another question. Tragic as her circumstance genuinely was, why did she assume Travers wanted children?"

After pacing from one end of the room to the other, Fiona stopped briefly and stared out the window. She ran a hand through her short hair and adjusted her glasses. As Fiona turned, Peter realised not only had she finished her drink but she seemed preoccupied.

"Record time, Fiona. Impressive. If a double neat, you'd be giving ol'Travers some competition. Are you worried or concerned about something?"

No, nothing. Really. I'm sorry."

"Want another?"

"Suppose I would. Yes. Thanks. I can't understand Véronique's cruelty. That she thought in 'some wishful but bizarre way,' he'd wander into the apartment only to see her in bed with a woman. That's stooping low, awfully low, to shock a partner. To drive him away. To end a relationship. I thought she was a caring person. And, with Travers's war baggage, her callousness could have unhinged him. Caused him to pack it in."

Peter handed her the martini. A double this time, in a glass pulled fresh from the freezer.

"Yeah, something like that could have happened, but he'd experienced far worse during the war. Fortunately, London and The Savoy beckoned. A fresh opportunity. A new start. A place to leave the past behind."

"I could forgive a dalliance, if a one-off. But her …"

"What would be the point, Fiona? If you forgave, could you forget? Don't … think … I … could. No … I know I couldn't. I thought Travers handled the shock of seeing it play out in front of him fairly well. What devastated him more than her bisexuality, or inability to have children, was her lying. That's at the crux of why he walked out. Got to admire his apparent calmness. Of course, Travers wrote it, didn't he? So, we're only reading his take almost twenty years later."

Peter took a self-congratulatory sip of his martini for

the roundabout kind of way he had announced unquestioned fidelity towards his wife.

"We're also discussing Paris in the 1920s. Her behaviour wasn't *that* outlandish. Probably accepted. Many sought the unconventional. Certainly, it intrigued others. Literature from the period is riddled with experimentation."

"You've got a point. Although she insisted her love of women wasn't an 'infatuation' or a nod to 'fashion,' some of it certainly reflected the era. Would like to find out more about her personal life. How she ended up. And another point: despite Travers's war experience and participating in the uniqueness of Montparnasse, I think he remained fairly naïve. His flying buddies nicknamed him 'Woodrow' for a reason, for God's sake. I doubt he'd ever heard of lesbianism or bisexuality growing up in Ohio. Not certain exactly where that state's located. Pretty much a backwater, isn't it?"

"I'm not familiar with America's geography … if at all. Just the coasts. Anyway, I think Véronique respected his naïveté. Relished in it, actually. It may have been the reason she dominated the physical and emotional aspects of the relationship. Little doubt, to my mind, she loved and cared for him. He wasn't like other men with whom she'd been acquainted—the indifferent and the bad."

"Well, he definitely drew sustenance from her. It may not have been her intention but, I think, she gave Travers back his life. So, in that sense, she was good for him, he benefitted. Received something in return—however fleeting. If he reflected on the whole damn experience years later, he might recall a kernel or two of happiness from an otherwise loathsome tale. It was her selfishness, her exploitation that destroyed the relationship. Became impossible. Simply untenable afterwards. Call me a cynical idealist, Fiona, but I thought Travers's comment about the first twenty years of the twentieth century described the next hundred perfectly: *Nothing and no one are fully accountable anymore. Excuses abound. Nothing can be trusted. No one can be believed."*

"No, I can't accept that. It may apply to governments, to corporations and to multi-nationals—but not individuals, not relationships. My God, Peter, there's got to be some accounting for a nurturing love between two humans."

"Are you saying her exploitation and lying were nurturing?"

"Of course not. No. But, I think, somewhere deep within she loved him. Had no desire to hurt him. She honestly didn't think he'd remain in Paris. Her hope of being found out reflected desperation. An ill-devised strategy to force the issue. To bring it to the fore. She thought he'd be so appalled he'd leave, enabling her to continue unencumbered. To be herself, fully and completely. And, as you said, continue to be who she truly was."

"You may have won this one, Fiona. Perhaps my idealistic cynicism got the better of me this time."

"This time? I've never known a time when you *weren't* shrouded in idealistic pessimism."

"It's not a competition, but you win. I'll give you the victory. And I'll also change the subject. Know what surprised me? It appears Travers and Swaneeland led the vanguard of expats. The personalities we're familiar with—you know—Pound, Fitzgerald, Hemingway, Joyce, Beach, Boyle, HD, Aldington, Cowley, Dos Passos, even the Murphys—arrived in 1921, '22, and '23. Travers lived and played in Montparnasse in 1919.

Swaneeland performed in 1919,'20 and '21. So, I'm thinking what the French call *Les Annéss Folles* and what Brits and Americans refer to as The Roaring Twenties started earlier."

"While you were mansplaining, I googled Travers, Swaneeland Jazz Band and its members. Nothing. Zero results."

"So, unless they're referenced in an unread document in a folder of an obscure archives, no one's ever heard of them. Makes me want to research more."

"If you don't find anything, it means we've got a historical document. Not worth much financially, perhaps, but certainly revelatory. Should be donated to the appropriate archives."

"It certainly should. I always hoped my scavenging would yield something important someday."

"Living in the past for its own merits may finally have paid off for you, Peter."

"Always thought it a joint venture, Fiona. Something we both enjoyed. You share in a bit in my work since I can't share in yours."

"Yeah, maybe. But, I'm sorry, this is definitely you. I lose interest after a while. Can't be bothered with boring details. It all lacks purpose and meaning to me. You enjoy being sequestered like a monk, contemplating, making sense of the past. I don't."

Peter hid his disappointment. He'd heard Fiona's lament often.

"Listen … I know we agreed to no breaks, but would you mind awfully if I took a walk around the gardens? I want to clear my head. Prepare me for what's coming."

"Sure. No problem. I'll straighten up a bit and prepare two fresh martinis. Enjoy yourself."

*****

"Some walk. You were gone longer than I thought. Damn. Had to drink both martinis myself. Glad I've built up some tolerance."

"Sorry, Peter. I bumped into Dorothy Smithfield. We sat on a bench near the monument—keeping our distance, of course—and chatted about everything and nothing. Only realised we'd been talking so long when the outside lights came on."

"Funny, I thought they'd moved."

"Ah, well … no … no … I talked to her, so obviously they didn't."

"Great news. Glad they're still in Harrogate. I always liked David. Must ring him."

"Said he's constantly travelling, despite all the restrictions. Rarely home these days."

"Anyway, I had time to think some more while you were out. Most men probably wouldn't give a damn, but I'm curious if Travers meets or hears from Véronique again. He admitted, a bit cryptically, when leaving her apartment that he had it inside him to see her again."

"And I thought of something, too. Véronique never knew he was going to ask her to marry him. She didn't know his intentions. Sad really, isn't it? Those who love each other best hurt each other most. And, again, I apologise awfully for being late."

"Don't worry. It's fine. At least your head's clear. Now that you mentioned the proposal never happening, isn't it interesting that when Travers was returning to his apartment, he only recalled he hadn't told her about The Savoy? Never reflected about not asking her to marry."

"Perhaps he felt some things, especially personal ones,

180

should remain secret. Or, maybe it was at that moment when he began to think women weren't as essential to life as *they* imagined themselves to be."

"In the state he was in, I suppose anything was possible. Who knows, we may have uncovered the beginning of Travers's journey towards underserved loneliness."

"If correct, that's sad. Very sad."

"Got a deal for you."

"What this time?"

"If you make a fire, I'll prepare another round. And let's get back to reading!"

"I'm in. All in, darling."

LONDON

Chapter Nine

I disembarked from the train, walked through Victoria Station and joined a lengthy queue for a cab. Unlike America, and certainly uncharacteristic of Paris, the line was organised, no one cut in. Everyone remained fairly quiet. Any detectable conversation occurred at a whisper level. Apart from language and accent, the sights and signs of not being in Paris soon became obvious. A dark, ethereal-like mist and fog filled the horizon. The distinctive smell of coal permeated the air. And, from my vantage point, the surrounding buildings hugged tightly to every twist and turn of narrow streets. To my immediate front lay what appeared to be three well-maintained pubs: Bag of Nails, The Prince of Wales and The Lord Nelson. Those names signified, more than anything else, that I had journeyed across the English Channel to launch myself into the throes of a fresh beginning. Another chance to be, as Charles Dickens wrote, *recalled to life.*

"Where to, guv'nor?"

"Ah, me?"

"See anyone else?"

"No, no. It's just … doesn't matter. Gower Street, numbers 65—67. The Avalon."

Hoped he'd take a route so I could gaze at Parliament, London Bridge, and the Tower of London. Realised weeks later such a wish was impossible. Not only were they nowhere near each other, but all were a fair distance from Bloomsbury. After ten minutes or so he began talking.

"You a student, maybe a teacher?"

"No. No."

"'Cause where you're going is across from the university and in Bloomsbury ... home to some of those Bright Young Things. That's why I thought ..."

"No, I'm a musician. Saxophone. Play at The Savoy."

"Blimey, can't see any point to music. Not nowadays."

"Has that effect on people."

Seemed crusty so I kept to myself. I failed.

"Noticed a limp. War injury?"

"Yes. Lost three inches. Last day of the war."

"Lost my son at Loos in 1915. Two months later me wife, poor lass, took it upon herself to drown in the Thames. That was *my* last day of the war."

"Sad to hear, sir. Sad indeed. Tragic."

"Only a Yank would call a bloke like me 'sir'. Don't let anyone else hear you address my lot with it. Especially one of those tall gents, in pinstripes and a bowler. Wouldn't take kindly to that."

"As a foreigner, I can make mistakes and get away with it. Worked wonderfully well in Paris. Should work here. Counting on it."

"There you are, guv'nor: The Avalon."

Grabbed my suitcases and instrument case. Standing alongside the car, I fumbled while finding the correct change—shillings, pounds, pennies, half-crowns—and couldn't distinguish one from the other, either by weight or shape. He soon had enough and told me not to worry. But I wasn't content. Couldn't accept him driving me for free. So, I handed him what I later discovered amounted to a little over five pounds.

"Generous, guv'nor. With all this coin, might see you at The Savoy!"

"Well then, we'll look forward to meeting again."

As I grabbed my luggage an open-topped car drove by, crowded with three men in dinner jackets and sporting white silk scarves, along with three women outfitted in their 'nearly-not-wearing-a-thing' finery. Each had a champagne bottle in one hand and a glass in the other.

"Welcome to England! Welcome to London! Welcome to Life!"

I watched as they passed by, celebrating the recklessness of their moneyed and disillusioned youth. My driver wasn't amused.

"That's what me boy died for. Be careful with these Bright Young Things, Yank. You'll find some are nothing but trollops living in the East End. Might develop a dose."

Half smiling, I thanked him again for the sage advice.

A shy university student working the graveyard shift registered me as a guest, 'courtesy of The Savoy'. Didn't mean I received anything free, only a small discount from the normal extended-stay rate. The youngster handed me an incongruous piece of unpolished brass with the room key attached, provided me a schematic of how to find the room and location of the toilet, as well as informing me where and when the innkeeper served breakfast. He wished me a pleasant stay prior to uncapping a fountain pen and returning to his notes.

I woke to the pungent smell of toast, fried eggs and burning meat. The odour intensified as I walked down the hallway toward the toilet. Damn, I thought. Army mess halls smelled, but they were feeding hundreds of fellas. Made myself presentable and walked down three flights of stairs to the basement. Opened the door to find ten tables, nine of which were occupied. I was the last remaining guest. A thin, ruddy-faced man with unruly white hair greeted me and pointed me toward the empty table.

"You must be Mr Travers. Welcome to The Avalon. I do hope you had a sound sleep. May I bring you our English breakfast?"

Although the gentleman had fired three questions in quick succession, I got the feeling he only expected me to answer the last one.

"Afraid I'm not familiar with what an 'English breakfast' consists of, exactly."

"Bacon, eggs, sausage, black pudding, baked beans, grilled tomato, fried bread, and toast with marmalade. Served with either tea or coffee."

"That is quite, ah ... more substantial than beignets and coffee ..."

"You're in England, not France. We do things differently. Even differently than America, I presume."

"I'm sure you do. Well, then, that's settled. English breakfast, sir."

"'Sir,' I *could* get used to that ... best I don't."

Never seen so much breakfast food on a plate. It sparkled with colour and oozed grease. Discovered later that the dark, silver dollar-sized pieces were black pudding: a concoction derived from beef blood, pork fat and oatmeal. I tried but couldn't finish it. Worse still, I left over half the food. Contented myself with toast and marmalade and black coffee that, unfortunately, was weaker than rat piss. Not wishing to offend or be confronted, I waited until the proprietor returned to kitchen before leaving.

My introduction to the band wasn't until the next day so I thought I get a lay of the land, so to speak, try and find an available flat, locate exactly where The Savoy was, as well as the building on John Adam Street where the band practised. As I passed by reception the proprietor, whose name I learned was Charles Cordwainer, popped up from behind the desk.

"Only dry toast and marmalade tomorrow, Mr Travers. Can't waste food, no matter how unwanted."

"I apologise, Mr Cordwainer. Wasn't to my liking. Toast, marmalade and coffee will be fine. And I agree, food shouldn't be wasted. Especially when it was so difficult to come by during the war."

Leaving the building and walking along Gower Street, I reflected that my introduction to England, and London in particular, wasn't going smoothly. In less than twenty-four hours I had frustrated a cab driver and offended an innkeeper. I apologetically wondered to myself whom I'd irritate today. Perhaps I should have remained in Paris. The French, it seemed, understood me—or at least acted like they did. But then again, it may only have been pity.

Walked through Bloomsbury, from the British Museum on one end to the university on the other. Eager students crowded the pavements, while those riding bicycles presented taxis with stiff competition. Regardless of where or how far I walked, didn't see any 'To Let' signs. Found myself in Fitzrovia eventually. It seemed seedier and less youthful than Bloomsbury, so I thought lady luck might prevail. It didn't. Not a sign to be had. After admiring John Nash's beautifully designed All Souls Church at the intersection of Regent Street and Langham Place, I hailed a cab to The Savoy. My leg and lower back were giving me an untold amount of pain and, not knowing exactly how far away the hotel was, thought it best to let the driver do the navigating.

I arrived in ten minutes. It was exciting to glance at Piccadilly Circus and Trafalgar Square while en route. Also caught a glimpse of St Martin-in-the-Fields. After a minute or two on the Strand, I found myself standing outside the building of my employer. Although band members weren't permitted to use the hotel's front door, I decided that, since I hadn't checked in officially and because no one knew me, I'd take the initiative. Felt mighty good breaking some rules.

The interior reflected refined luxury wrapped tightly around hushed civility. A marble frieze dating from earlier in the century filled the upper walls just below the ceiling. Described as 'An Idyll of a Golden Age' it invoked an era of innocence and peace, a time with no relevance to today, I thought. Its pastoral simplicity, nonetheless, gave me pause. Walking between highly polished columns of reddish-brown marble, I eavesdropped on conversations, studied the demeanour of guests and wondered if they'd embrace our orchestrated version of jazz. Wouldn't these people with wealth and position believe it nothing but insolent noise? Would they sway, smile and tap their feet like so many others? Could the stiff-necked and the entrenched become, if only temporarily, relaxed and free—or would centuries of inveterate behaviour stifle enjoyment? I pondered these questions as I walked through a foyer richly outfitted with marble support columns, floor-to-ceiling mirrors and an exquisite skylight that dominated the centre room. A small staircase to the left led directly from the foyer to my new place of business—the downstairs ballroom. I learned later that guests who dined at the restaurant or enjoyed drinks in the foyer could take the stairs to dance and enjoy our mild form of jazzin'. The room *was* grand.

Considerably different from The Sinton in Cincinnati. Designed to reflect class and taste and money from another era. The lightly coloured blue walls accentuated the musically themed plaster filigrees comprised of a violin, a trumpet, a director's baton and loose sheets of music. The ornate ceiling supported six crystal chandeliers. The focal point of the room, however, was the elevated clamshell-shaped bandstand. Heavy satin curtains softened the stage's curved edges, removing any doubt as to where guests should focus their eyes. A curved door to the right of the stage was the band's point of entry and exit. A uniquely designed parquet floor assured our jazzin' would ricochet off the ceiling and the floors and the mirrors and land at our guest's feet. That was my fervent hope, anyway.

After leaving The Savoy, I decided to walk to Gower Street. Needed to determine the distance on foot because I sure as hell knew I couldn't afford a cab each day. Learned a quicker route eventually, but right then I suffered too much pain to investigate, so I repeated the taxi's journey but in reverse. Along the Strand to Trafalgar Square, up Charing Cross a bit where I cut through to an open area that I learned later was Leicester Square. Sauntered through Piccadilly and then along the length of Regent Street, gawking at the luscious shop windows and exquisite restaurants. The Café Royal appeared expensive and, I presumed, frequented by all the Bright Young Things. Used the spire of All Souls Church as my beacon. Walking along Langham Street toward Fitzrovia, the pain in my lower back forced me to take a break. I decided this, not too coincidently, while standing outside a quaint pub called the Yorkshire Grey.

The distinct smell of a coal-burning fire filled the air.

The brown and orange mosaic-tiled floor, accented with white lines swirling like a dervish, made the small space appear larger. Not wanting to be taken as a tourist, I stood behind a beautifully carved oak bar and ordered a double neat immediately. Unlike Johnny in Paris, the bartender wasn't the talkative type. Made my way to the rear, to a small round table to the right of the fireplace. Sat my sore body on a red, tufted leather sofa secured to the wall, stretched out my left leg and let the fire's warmth rid me of London's chill.

I nursed the British hooch for over an hour. Went to the bar and ordered another. The staff had changed. The new bartender was a tall, well-dressed fellow wearing tortoiseshell glasses and owner of a pleasing smile. Little did I realise how my personal fortunes also would change.

"Haven't seen you around before. Visiting?"

"No, no. Arrived yesterday. Out and about trying to find an apartment. No luck so far."

"Basic or posh?"

"Wallet dictates basic."

"She doesn't use 'To Let' signs, but if you turn round, the top rear unit—a garret, I'm guessing—is available. At least it was last evening. She visits regularly, always complaining about not letting the place but, hell, she won't put out a sign."

I turned to see a freshly painted, white, four-storey building. If looking at the right unit, it had two windows. One looked out over the pub and Regent Street and the other toward Fitzrovia. Plenty of natural light, I thought. Would help cut electricity costs and enable me to practise without disturbing anyone nearby.

"There's no lift. You'd have to walk up a few flights."

"I'm injured, not crippled."

"Sorry. Didn't mean anything. Just noticed as you approached the bar that …"

"No, I apologise. Out of order."

"I'm Johnny, and you are …?"

"Christ, what is about barmen being named 'Johnny'?"

"Excuse me?"

"Sorry, sorry. I'm William Travers."

"American?"

"Rightly or wrongly, A-mer-i-can."

Johnny smiled and encouraged me to go over and inquire. Felt certain she'd be there.

"Tell you what, I'll put your drink behind the bar. Go see her, look around and see if the flat suits. Then come back. Your Famous Grouse will be waiting."

"Don't think she'll mind?"

"Naw. By the way, her name is Mrs Joy, Beatrice Joy."

So that's exactly what I did. Her surname may have been Joy, but happiness wasn't hers. All I saw was a depressed, buxom cockney in her rapidly fading forties. A half-smoked fag dangled from an oversized lower lip. And, despite what Johnny said, I got the impression I'd inconvenienced her. Said she didn't like Americans. A bit startled, my reply nonetheless won her over. *Don't care much for them these days, either.* She looked at me in partial disbelief. *Well then, Yank, sounds like we'll get along lovely.* Whereupon she asked me to follow her up the steps as she showed me the flat. Sparse and small, it fit my needs perfectly. She didn't mind if I practised. Being practically deaf, said she didn't give two figs what other tenants thought. How did she phrase it? *If I can't hear it, love, can't be bothered now, can I?* To make the math easier, I delayed moving in until 1 January. The rent wasn't expensive enabling me to keep a little on the side. At the landing I extended my hand in gratitude.

"Your limp, love. The war?"

"Yes. Nailed the last day."

"You came back, didn't yeah? None my boys did— Albert's in some French village and Jimmy ... nothing to bury."

She lowered her head, turned, entered the flat and closed the door. Like the cab driver, the price of *her* war had been costly. As I walked the few steps and returned to the Yorkshire Grey I thought about the folly of the *Great War*. The dead remain dead, but the living ... the living endure the suffering waste for the rest of their lives, descending eventually into the well of emptiness. It was at this point when I realised, perhaps for the first time in my life, that if one let themselves be coerced into thinking they were responsible and could do something for the world, well, that's surely the first sign of madness taking seed.

Johnny placed the double neat on the bench as soon as I entered.

"Shall be forever grateful, Johnny. Thank you. I'm set. Move in New Year's Day. Might become a regular at the Yorkshire Grey, so long as you keep pouring this ... ah ... Famous Grouse."

"Pleased for you and Mrs Joy and the pub. And don't worry, my friend—the Grey never runs dry of The Grouse. By the way, Mr Travers, with the place crowding up, I took the liberty and placed a reserved sign on the table you'd been sitting at, if you still want it."

"Johnny, you're the consummate gentleman. Hell of a

bartender, too. Thank you. And please, call me William."

Chapter Ten

My first day at The Savoy went well. Quiet and uneventful. Didn't call attention to myself or attempt to ingratiate myself to the other eight. Kept my counsel and opinions to myself. All were British and quiet and well-mannered and polite. No kick-ass banter, no smart-ass remarks—which, of course, reigned supreme with Swaneeland, practically a prerequisite for survival. Our leader, Bill Ralton, also played clarinet; Thomas Marcus slid the trombone; Clifford Evans managed the bass; Cyril Scott worked as the occasional vocalist; John Freeman handled the piano; Daniel Wallace picked the banjo; Eddie Transwell nailed the trumpet; and, rightly or wrongly, James McCabe beat the drums.

During a lull in the practice room at midday, WF Dabney stopped by to see how I was managing. He displayed confidence in me, and himself, with characteristic aplomb. Retold the story to the boys of how and where he found me. Whatever doubts they held earlier about my playing skills melted into insignificance after learning about my brothel background. If I were a penny stock at 9 a.m., by 1 p.m. my market value would have become unattainable to most. WF also possessed a cat's sixth sense that the boys might have problems with a Yank infiltrating their ranks. So, he put them on edge, which put me at ease.

"As well known to you gentlemen, I'm the Entertainment director here at The Savoy, as well as the Berkeley and Claridges, and can vouch for each of your musical abilities. I recruited you personally to form this exquisite band. Of that, I'm immensely proud. I cannot emphasise enough, however, that if disenchantment with someone or something ever consumes you, don't conceal it: bring it forward and, if possible, I'll transfer you to one of the other hotel bands. I trust this won't happen, but egos and accents can corrupt an otherwise splendid relationship. So, there you have it. The house is full on New Year's Eve. Best of luck. Play out your hearts. Make our guests feel the jazz to such a level that the only thing they desire is more."

Spoken like a true army officer, I thought, and an artilleryman at that. The sum is greater than its parts.

With only nine days before the New Year's celebration the band practised continually, often ten hours a day. Being the outsider, I placed additional pressure on myself to perform the best I could. Developed a regular routine that, I hoped, would merit success. Returned to the flat around seven, shovelled in a bit of food and practised until half nine. Then took a few long strides to a bar stool in the Yorkshire Grey and nursed a couple double neats of the Famous Grouse. Mrs Joy was correct about her hearing or rather her lack of hearing. Never uttered a word. Never even slipped a note under the door.

While warming up in the practice room late in the afternoon on New Year's Eve, I started playing the jazz version of 'La Marseillaise' made famous by Swaneeland. Didn't think much about it. Just wanted to loosen my fingers. It was a piece I'd practised often during warmups while alone but never played during those early days at The Savoy. The boys stopped whatever they were doing and stared. Gradually made their way and surrounded me. Feeling self-conscious, I stopped. The leader, Bill Ralton, begged me to continue.

"Travers, don't stop on our account. It's rather … rather sublime. Bloody sublime. Wouldn't have dreamed a national anthem could be jazzed."

While familiar with British history, I wasn't knowledgeable about the nation's patriotic anthems. I knew only one.

"I think 'Rule, Britannia' could be the cat's nuts, don't you?"

Whereupon I laid into a few bars composed on the spot in real time. Got a couple notes wrong, but the boys got the gist.

"If we developed the arrangement exclusively for us and played it one evening unannounced, wonder where it'd take us?"

"Unemployment! WF would never permit something like that at his beloved Savoy. His own job would be in jeopardy too, I imagine."

Fortunately, Ralton thought quickly on his feet.

"Marcus, Freeman, you're both correct. Even if we had the time to prepare and perform it tonight, on New Year's, I wouldn't. It would cause WF to keel over. Hell of a way to start 1922, I'd say. But that doesn't discount the possibility, when we reassemble in March, that we shouldn't take the risk. Some evening, when the crowd is quiet and small ... we'll shake the chandeliers."

Everyone agreed. I felt a tinge of acceptance. We'd never be as tight as Swaneeland, who were all Americans, with similar backgrounds, similar war experiences. That a Brit gave my idea any credence at all was, hell, an unexpected pleasure. Got me thinking how else Britain might surprise me.

The evening went off without a hitch. Even a bit boring for my taste. Didn't play anything remotely 'hot' for fear of upsetting the guests' digestions. Overheard one of the older set utter to her even-older friend: *Each song is so pretty, Mildred, don't you think*? That summed up the evening. In addition to Christmas tunes, we serenaded the audience with a couple numbers we planned to record in early 1922. These included 'All I Need Is You', 'Dancing Time', 'Jazz Band Partout', and 'Whose Baby Are You?'. The numbers would never have been in Swaneeland's repertoire, but The Savoy's management liked them and their guests liked them, so we were forced to play them. What I *did* enjoy was the money they brought. Made enough to open a bank account. Also took time to observe the demeanour of the ladies and their requisite fashions. The scent of money filled the air. Formal Edwardian evening clothes dominated amongst the older set, who remained doused with the face powder of stuffiness. But the younger women—ah, the younger women—similar to those in Paris, whose bodies were overexposed and underdeveloped, wholeheartedly embraced the latest styles and attitudes, filled with devilment and fervency. They looked nice. They talked nice. They smelled nice. Were fine dancers and excellent drinkers. Far removed from the dewy-eyed girls of my hometown.

After practice one late February afternoon, Thomas Marcus, the trombone player, approached me, sensing I needed a certain something—or, rather, was lacking a certain something.

"Travers, with the way you blow that horn coupled with your New World accent, have you found a woman yet in old London town?"

"I don't find them. They find me."

"Damn, you're either lucky or cocky, Travers. Don't know you well enough to decide which applies."

"Whatever my attributes, Marcus, cockiness isn't

among them."

"You're damn honest. I'll give you that."

"Yeah ... well, honesty's never done me any favours. So why do you ask?"

"The boys and I feel ... well, you're incomplete. Lacking the soft touch of a woman while, you know, listening to her questionable and uninformed opinions on things."

I endured Marcus's soft-voice philosophy a bit longer. In a self-deprecating, British kind of way, he finally made his point: encouraged me to visit his favourite 'Mayfair Honey Pot'—a brothel located in Shepherd Market.

On a particularly nasty evening, a week or so later, I followed his advice. The building's exterior and interior hallway were seedier than *Madame* Diguet's, which gave me pause—but, sensing I had nothing to lose, I knocked on No. 4's door anyway. Heard a faint and breathy, *It's unlocked*. Walked into a small room, consisting of an iron bed stand, a ratted-out cushioned chair and a corner sink. The interior, for the most part, was weathered but neat and tidy. Soft-green-coloured walls, accented with pale yellow trim, made the place seem far removed from its purpose. Dainty linen curtains concealed two large windows. Four cathedral candles provided the light. My all-absorbing gaze wasn't appreciated. Hadn't even noticed the woman on the bed.

"Let's go, love. Don't got all evening. Have to earn a living, y'know?"

"Sorry, sorry. It's only ... "

I took off a few items of clothing and placed them neatly on the back of the chair. She honed in immediately on my leg despite the minimal light.

"Another ex-soldier, I see. Gettin' a lot nowadays.

More than during the war."

I must have appeared a bit forlorn sitting on the edge of the bed. She was young, sported a short bob of smooth black hair, bright red lips and an ample figure. The scent of perfume filled the air.

"Look all you want, love, but if you have any desire to see what I can do …"

"Thanks … really … it's just … I just …"

"So, you here for what then, darlin'?"

"Revenging my past … perhaps? No, no … talk, I guess. Just talk."

"Fancy that, a philosopher. Blimey, never had one of your lot before. Still want payment, though. My advice ain't free."

She got out of bed, put on her dressing gown and, after rummaging for a cigarette, returned gracefully and somewhat alluringly to bed. Once comfortable, she looked at me.

"So, love, what'd you want to talk about?"

"May seem a bit unorthodox, but mind telling me about yourself?"

After removing an annoying piece of tobacco from her lip, she looked at me and smiled. The kind of smile reserved for apologies.

"Don't know what 'unorthodox' is or isn't, but … haven't always been a working type, if that's what you mean. This kind of work, anyway."

"Wait, wait, not so fast. What's your name?"

"You're gettin' personal, aren't you? Most lads don't want to know. And I don't want to know about them. You're certainly a different one. Anyway, I'm Saffron, Saffron Bartlett. Parents both dead. Died when I was fourteen. Married a few weeks before he joined the army.

And damn, if the bloke wasn't killed three weeks after arriving France. His mother never took to me and, when she learned her son was dead, kicked me to the street. No qualifications, no anything really. Didn't know what to do. Then it came to me. Thought I'd take advantage of the soldiers leaving for France. You know? Do something patriotic. Some had never been with a woman. So, I taught 'em. Taught 'em everything I knew. Even learned few things myself. Now I'm trapped, I think. Don't matter none though. Make good money and been working steady as of late, so no worries. One day I'm hoping someone will offer me a better job. Not with the government, though. A lot of them types visit regular—you know, MPs—but I can't type or write quickly or anything, so probably don't think anything will come of it. Can hope, though, can't I?"

"Be nice to think so."

Then it was my turn. She asked a little about America, my sax playing and why I was in London. Seemed curious about my war experiences, especially the flying bit. She'd never met an aviator before. But mostly I talked about Véronique. The why and the how it disintegrated. Must have babbled on for twenty minutes.

"Always thought there was more between us than the delicate friction of our skin, but even that proved false in the end."

"One learns as one lives, love. The harder you live, the more you learn. That doesn't mean it don't hurt. Hurts plenty but you recover, somehow … anyhow. I did. Got a feeling, though, that if a woman's involved, thinking men suffer the longest. And after hearing you talk, afraid it's gonna be harder for someone like you. Some don't ever recover. Can't tell you how many men been lying next to me in this bed, spinning a woeful tale. Can't determine yet if you're one of those who won't recover. Hope you will. Hope you move on. Find something or someone good. You seem like a nice boy."

Although her words weren't profound, they were comforting nonetheless. Their simplicity awakened me to my task ahead. It was my life to either live or to waste. I had been through everything. Learned a lot and didn't owe anyone—expect my dead flying buddies—a damn thing. As I placed the money on the bed, she rose to her knees, pulled me closer, wrapped her arms loosely around my neck and kissed my cheek.

"Travers, next time you come for a chat I won't charge you nothing."

I stood up to see her smiling, a smile that expressed contentment.

"Thanks, Saffron. May surprise you on some wet, dreary night."

"This time of year, love, every night's wet and dreary in London."

"So it is. So it is."

Walked along a narrow alley toward Regent Street and caught a cab to the flat. Poured a double neat and sat with the night.

Chapter Eleven

Arriving at The Savoy one Saturday afternoon in early March, I checked my pigeonhole for any post. Never received anything, usually. Performed the ritual more out of habit than getting any hoped-for letters from Paris. Today was different. A light-blue-coloured envelope occupied the slot. Addressed simply:

Mr William Travers, The Savoy Havana Band

It lacked a stamp, which meant it had been hand-delivered by the concierge. The handwriting was so beautiful my initial reaction was to wonder who the hell I knew in London that could write so perfectly precise. After reading the first line it dawned on me. My past had infiltrated my present.

Dear Mr Travers-

As you are aware, Sara and Gerald Murphy are keen on us meeting one another. I visited The Savoy last evening with friends. We found your music most enjoyable and, thanks to Sara's description as well as the band having only one saxophonist, had little difficulty identifying you.

If convenient, could we meet late afternoon Monday, say, around four o'clock? While I found The Savoy lovely, fresh and well-appointed, when in London I adhere to tradition and take rooms at the Langham.

I'll be at a reserved table in the Palm Court Lounge. If you face difficulty, the concierge knows me well and will direct you. If this appeals to you, please leave a message at the Langham's front desk confirming the appointment. I look forward to what promises to be a pleasant introduction.

Until Monday, I remain,

Helena Bolton-Leigh

Well, damn, the Murphy's had followed through. It seemed the hometown connection proved more important to Sara than wealth or class or upbringing. But then, it could also be jazz and Sara's wish, as mentioned at her dinner party, of encouraging me to find a smart, fun-loving woman and retreat into our own private world.

Although my flat was on Langham Street, and I'd often seen the neo-Gothic designed building when approaching Regent Street, I hadn't visited. Meeting Helena provided the perfect excuse. The place was buzzing as I entered. Pageboys were outfitted in crimson-coloured uniforms, complete with stiff collars, epaulettes with brass buttons lining the length of their tunics. Atop their adolescent heads sat a crimson pillbox hat embroidered with 'The Langham' in gold. To my mind, they resembled Napoleonic era 'cannon cockers' in His Majesty's Royal Artillery from a hundred years earlier. Only their questioning calls interrupted the soft, hushed conversation of well-appointed guests.

After entering the hotel and climbing the five or six marble steps onto the foyer, the Palm Court Lounge lay directly to my front. The geometrically designed glass skylight gave way to an intricately plastered cove ceiling. Three chandeliers adorned with several gold-coloured lampshades illuminated the room. Inlaid mirrors recessed into several walls made the room appear larger than it was. Cushioned chairs and sofas of dark green mohair with the random gold cushion melded perfectly with the white rattan lounge chairs that dotted the area. A gold-coloured wool rug filled the middle portion of the room, while two smaller, similarly designed rugs dominated either side. The richness of the wooden tables matched the tone of the exposed dark oak floor. A well-concealed bar stood on the far-left side. And it was from there, I imagined, where some of the newest creations of the 'cocktail epoch' were formulated. Refined ladies, accompanied by a spattering of well-dressed men, dominated the room, making my task of identifying Helena impossible without assistance.

The maître d' greeted me. Told him a friend was expecting me. He interjected before I could finish.

"Miss Bolton-Leigh … of course, sir."

She was sitting at a table on the concealed side of a support column. Learned later that the location was chosen purposefully. As the maître d' and I approached, she rose from her chair, extended her hand in a manner that made it clear it wasn't to be shaken but merely held for a few seconds.

A tall woman with an appealing feminine figure looked me squarely in the eye. I absorbed as much of her as I could before speaking. Long, red hair, coiled and held from behind with numerous pins. Emerald eyes glistened like spring raindrops. Flawless porcelain skin, accentuated by a faint line of freckles, relaxed on chiselled cheekbones. A dark blue tunic dress rode low on her hips, while a loosely tied belt accentuated her curves. Sleeves, outlined with white piping, extended slightly below the elbow. A square-shaped platinum watch, worn on the right wrist, was her sole piece of jewellery.

As we took our seats, I didn't know exactly how to

start the conversation, so I sought common ground.

"Gerald said you resembled the woman in Rossetti's pre-Raphaelite paintings. And I happily agree. If you hadn't been behind this column, fairly confident I could have found you on my own."

"Oh, Gerald: he's always fawning. And this column enables private conversations to remain private. British love a good gossip."

"Being a foreigner, I stick close to myself. The boys at The Savoy are fine fellows, but … I can't become too close, too early. Only been with them a little over two months. Never know *exactly* how they feel about a Yank in *their* band. The British excel at masking their true intentions, so …"

"Am I masking my intentions, Mr Travers?"

"Oh, please don't be offended. I apologise. And call me William. It's just …"

Giggling softly, she ran her index finger slowly around the rim of her cocktail glass and looked up.

"Sara said you had the sensibility and morality of a true Midwesterner."

"Well, to be frank, if you believe that then I'm afraid you're in for disappointment. I've become insensitive and immoral since the war and, as you experienced, a bit ill-mannered."

"Then all the better. More modern, less Edwardian."

Her confidence and self-assurance surprised me. Couldn't determine if it was genuine, or was she masking insecurity? It certainly was unique. Was about to say something profound when the waiter approached to take our drinks order. She reordered champagne, while I settled for the old reliable double neat.

"I couldn't help noticing what I presume is a painful

war injury. Earned while fighting for my country?"

"No, for mine."

"That's what I mean. You see, William, I'm half American."

"Half American? Didn't know anybody could be half anything nowadays."

"On Mummy's side. Her family owns a woollen mill company in Massachusetts. Been in the family since 1810. She met Father when he was on business to the States in about 1890 or so. A casual acquaintance blossomed over the next year into a romance, and hence, Mummy's move to England. Her only brother, my Uncle Ned, operates the business now. Fallen on difficult times recently—not as challenging as the wool business here but difficult nonetheless."

"Hope I'm not betraying any confidences, but Sara said your father died a month or so before the war and both brothers were killed in France, leaving you and your mother to manage the business. Did I understand that right?"

"Except or one, perhaps insignificant, detail. George was killed at the Somme during the big push in 1916, but Edward—whom I admired very much and was close to— died on the Asiago Plateau in northern Italy, summer of 1918."

"I agree . . . 'insignificant'. Didn't matter where one died in the war, did it? The government sent us, we fought, and millions died. Only those alive give a damn about specifics."

"A bit cynical, are we?"

"Yeah, sorry. It's only that ..."

"Don't be. They had me, too. Remained front and centre until November 1918, when I realised, entirely too late, of course, that at its crux the war was a battle between three cousins—the doddery monarch of Austria, with the Sick Man of Europe thrown in for diversity. Most of us thought if there was going to be fighting in the summer of 1914 it would have occurred in Ireland."

"Ironic, isn't it? America was busy with Mexico in 1914. Invaded the country a year or so later. And then in 1917 we declared war on Germany. Europe wasn't on anyone's mind."

"Seems Europe caused both nations to become distracted, if that's the right word. On second thoughts, though, 'distracted' isn't correct, is it? The lure of power and profits seems more accurate."

"Now who's the cynic? Make a deal with you: Why don't we jettison this seriousness and lighten the airframe, so to speak? If you're half American, Helena, how or why do you speak with such a gorgeous English accent?"

"My accent and pronunciation came about because Mummy insisted on me 'becoming' British. She had suffered through too many social indignities because of her Yankee accent and determined something similar wouldn't happen to me. So, from age eleven to eighteen I attended Cheltenham Ladies' College in Gloucestershire. The institution prides itself on developing young girls into proper British ladies, who simultaneously earn a first-class education."

"I've experienced only the 'improper' kind, so I'm a bit shocked someone owning such a pedigree would consent to meet, let alone share a drink at the Langham."

"I hope you're kidding—but, if not, don't be daft. I've been democratised. Mingled a lot with the common man. You see, Mummy wanted me to experience what

America could offer, hoping I'd attend an all-female, liberal arts university like herself. She went to Mount Holyoke in Massachusetts. I could have gone there too, but didn't want to be watched over, if you will, by my American grandparents and older cousins. So, I chose Bryn Mawr College outside Philadelphia. The choice caused a family fracas, but I held my ground and won in the end."

"Hate to disabuse you, but I don't think you rubbed elbows with many a 'common man' at Bryn Mawr."

"Just consider it my dismal attempt at humour. But honestly, I experienced a lot during my two years there. Learned about myself and more about Britain. One learns a lot about their country when living away from it, don't you think? It certainly tempered my admiration for the Empire. But, besides all of that, I made some wonderful friends. Many of the boys I met at Penn volunteered later for the army, only to be killed. I won't take anything I have, or done, or hope to do, for granted. It was Father's death, sadly, that made me return home in summer of 1914. Britain hadn't declared war yet. So, even if Father hadn't died, I probably would have been forced home once it began. Wasn't meant to earn a degree, I suppose."

"Seems the certainty of uncertainty was something we shared during those years. Oftentimes I think I'm still in it. You know, not grounded. Definitely not settled. No idea what the past means or little thought of what tomorrow might bring."

Feeling she had all but monopolised the conversation, Helena asked about me. Wanted to hear it all. I didn't hold anything back, except, of course, my troubles in Paris.

"Swaneeland and I submerged Paris in jazz. And had a

gasser of a time doing it. Everywhere we preformed, people drank, people danced unashamedly and as publicly as possible. In the early days, naysayers and detractors bloviated that jazz was the mindless energy of the masses. We proved them wrong. All of 'em."

"How original ... *submerged Paris in jazz*."

"Didn't invent that, Helena. Sorry. Read it in a travel magazine a few months ago. Thought I'd borrow it from time to time. It's not trademarked."

"Forthright and honest. I'm impressed. That Midwestern ethic coming out again. Unfortunately, Mummy doesn't like your music. In fact, she believes calling it music is a misnomer. Does nothing but disrespect the audience. How does she describe it? *Insolent noise, discordantly savage and unseemly in its ugliness.* Believes it *overexcites the senses.* Compares it to putting cocoa in a wine glass, mixing it up and calling it brandy. Afraid you'll have to act like a minister proselytising to the heathen if you want to change her opinion. Will be a difficult slog."

"As the leader of Swaneeland used to say, *all kinds of women adore jazzmen. Those who will introduce you to their mother and those who won't.* So, if I have the honour of ever meeting your mother, then I accept the challenge. Been successful turning non-believers into ardent followers of the jazz gospel."

"Bit sacrilegious, don't you think?"

"Told you I was immoral and ill-mannered. But putting that aside—and more importantly—how do you react to jazz? Well enough, so I *might* be introduced to your mother other someday?"

"I heard it once at the Palladium. Called themselves the Original Dixie Jazz Band or Dixieland Jazz Quintet, something like that. There were five band members, no saxophone though. It was after the Armistice, probably spring 1919. In London for a post-war wool industry meeting, so I gave it a try. My ... that's almost three years ago."

"Spring 1919 ... hell, I hadn't been discharged from the hospital yet. So much has transpired ... so much has gone ..."

"You see, Mummy despises jazz because it's unrecognisable. It doesn't provide comfort or conjure any sense of shared memories for her. Her pre-war world seemed so wonderfully secure. Realises now that the past, her life and most of the people in it before 1914, are gone. And, because she prefers the past over the present, jazz can't be a part of that. I enjoy it precisely for the opposite reason. It enables me to forget the past, especially the world that made 1914 to '18 happen. Jazz is new, fresh, invigorating, intoxicating and yeah, it may be discordant, as Mummy believes, but I think it reflects the world we live in today. How could we return to foxtrots and waltzes when we've all been cut and torn asunder? Our world was broken in two."

I told her the music she heard at The Savoy the other evening was a toned-down, orchestrated version of the hot jazz me and the boys played in Paris. She seemed confused at first. Even a bit disappointed.

"So how, William, how do you describe your kind of jazz?"

"It's primitive. It's noisy. It's rhythmic. And always can be played and heard differently. No two nights will be the same. While mass culture thrives at obliterating the individual, jazz embraces the individual, permitting the musician to go out, to explore, to experiment and then

209

return to the fold, so to speak, and rejoin society. And, following along the lines of your thought that jazz reflects current times, I believe it does. It challenges moral codes and stifles Edwardian stuffiness. May sound strange, Helena, but it can change your outlook on life. It did mine."

I asked her to think back to the band she heard in 1919 and whether it was anything like what she heard at the hotel? Said she remained too numb from the war's ending and couldn't remember exactly what the band sounded like.

"I looked at the stage and heard the music, but my mind was elsewhere … wondering, I suppose, about the graves of my brothers. How much, if anything, was left of them to have been buried."

I remained silent as she looked away to gather her composure. Minutes later she turned toward me, smiled and apologised.

"That's not like me at all. Sorry to have put you in such a position, William."

"No need, Helena. I'd be more worried if you hadn't reacted that way."

She took the handkerchief I offered.

"Thank you. And please … please continue."

"Well, The Savoy Band is aimed at a different audience, Helena. A more sophisticated one in many aspects—except one: musical palette. Theirs remains undeveloped, utterly confused by the sounds, the syncopations and the rhythms. So, we've created a kind of jazz masquerade. Cynically, I suppose, The Savoy is pandering to the whims of the marketplace."

"Is there somewhere in London where I can hear this 'hot' jazz you played?"

"Haven't been yet but I overheard the boys talking about a place in Soho called The Forty-Three Club. It's small and intimate, opens late and remains so until almost dawn—illegally, I suppose. Anyway, I'll give it a look-see and ..."

"I'm back in London in three weeks. Mind awfully taking me ... *Mr Travers*?"

After asking the question, Helena lowered her head toward the table then turned her eyes upward to me, as if already knowing my reaction. If she were a cat I would have prepared for a playful head-butt. A tactic, I imagined, she had used successfully numerous times in the past had worked yet again. I was smitten. Made the pain in my left leg subside a bit.

"It would be a pleasure, *Miss Bolton-Leigh*. I'd enjoy that very much. Very much indeed."

"Good. One evening's taken care of, then. How exciting."

I had passed initial inspection. An evening at The Forty-Three Club with a 'proper' British woman holding gently onto my arm. I guess ol' Johnny from the *Balmusette* was correct: *You'll find an attractive British lass wrapped around your arm and inside your pocket in no time.* Why, I wondered, are bartenders—British bartenders, in particular—so damn perceptive?

"As usual, I'll be at the Langham, not too far from your flat, I hope. Especially since I imagine it will be a late evening."

"Actually, Helena, my apartment or flat, if you prefer, is more a garret, actually—is close by, on Langham Street. The spire of All Souls Church practically fills my window. And, while you may wish for a *late* evening, best prepare for an *early* morning. Newsagents will be extending their shop awnings as you return to the hotel."

"Haven't done anything naughty like that since Bryn Mawr days. Staying up late in the Yorkshire Dales and retreating into your own private world doesn't have near the same level of naughtiness, does it?"

"Oh, I don't know. Seem to recall several evenings alone in my Paris apartment, drinking, thinking mischievous thoughts—looking forward to some future happiness. Appreciating all along, of course, that if I hadn't found it by a certain age, I'd be forced to reflect wistfully about the past. And that, Helena, is something I don't want to let happen."

"I hadn't thought of it that way, but since you've said it … I suppose in those hours of solitude after Mummy has retired, I ponder things I thought I had dealt with and forgotten long ago but are still present. Mine more bitter than yours—far, far removed from wistful."

"Then that's something else we *almost* share in, huh?"

"Suppose it is, William. I suppose it is."

Helena appeared in no hurry to leave the Palm Court after we'd finalised plans for The Forty-Three Club. Still wanted to know more about me. Even seemed concerned about my welfare. Thought it ironic that after escaping death I found myself again playing in a hotel band—granted, it was on the other side of the Atlantic and in a swankier establishment, performing an entirely different style of music—but the same profession nonetheless. I deflected answering questions on past romances, particularly those after university graduation. That she seemed content answering it out loud to herself was fine with me. Less factual but more romantic. On a sombre note, she believed the melancholia I still experience from the loss of my flying comrades seemed eerily similar to how she feels about her brothers: *We both need to make the lives that were saved worth saving.* She expressed sadness that I didn't have any family members back in the States.

"That being said, I don't derive happiness or receive support from Mummy, sadly. The loss of her three men—so close together—has become insurmountable. Try as I might, I come up empty most of the time. I can't even mention my brothers' names in her presence. She went as far as wrapping all their photos into storage boxes. She's kept the rooms exactly as they were when both boys left. Nothing is allowed to change. Edward always kept a glass of water by the bed. The water's evaporated, but the glass remains. I'm sure Mummy would try to communicate with them through a credible medium if she could find one. Any pleasurable conversation we have during late-afternoon cocktails is in proportion to her alcohol intake. Up to two drinks, she resembles the modern-day flapper we read about, fun and exciting. Anything beyond it, maudlin and depressing."

She paused, embarrassed she had revealed too much.

"I do apologise. You needn't hear me wittering about Mummy. She's fine, really. And I'm fine being with her. Honestly."

"No need, Helena. I understand. Really, I do. Her grief will end someday, but pity … your pity, I'm sorry to say, may last forever."

"We learn as we live then, don't we? Means I'll be doing a lot more of both. But now, unfortunately, I must get along, for I have an engagement with a friend from Cheltenham. We're dining at Kettner's."

"That should be enjoyable. Here's my card. Please, contact me when you finalise the trip to London. On second thought, drop me a line anytime. Would love hearing from you."

"Why don't you join us? You'll enjoy Margaret. She's an absolute scream."

"No, no. Too much conversation would be spent on introductions and backgrounds—and that, Helena, would spoil both your evenings."

"How perceptive. You are beginning to understand the British. Here's my card. Write me a letter. No, no, not *a* letter—please, write many letters. I would enjoy hearing what you're up to. Don't know how, but when we meet next, I hope to understand more about your jazz music."

I intended to stand and say goodbye but she insisted I remain seated. She came over and leaned her card against my Scotch glass.

"A thoroughly enjoyable time, William. One of the best afternoons ever at the Palm Court. I must write Sara and Gerald to thank them."

She lowered her head slightly and kissed my cheek.

"Now you appreciate why I chose a table hidden by this column."

And with that quip, Helena departed. As she was about to leave the room she turned, smiled and offered a timid wave goodbye. Taking a sip of Scotch I read the card: Miss Helena Bolton-Leigh, Ure Manor House, Askrigg under Scar, North Riding, Yorkshire. Tel. Askrigg 221. Contentment, it seemed, had become mine.

Chapter Twelve

We corresponded regularly throughout the month. Supplied her with stories about the music and the fellas in the band, as well as antics of the highfalutin but fun-loving guests. She reciprocated, describing tasks associated with managing a thousand acres of pasture and meadowland, hundreds of grazing sheep and the few local men who ensure the operation functions properly.

Edwardian stuffiness reigned supreme at The Savoy but, on certain evenings, there'd be two or three couples who rejected conventional decorum. Dancing atop tables ruffled the feathers of a few Edwardians. Others looked aghast as coupe glasses were stacked, resembling a pyramid. The top glass would be filled by an initially sober, well-attired man, who continued pouring from a jeroboam while champagne trickled downward into each glass until all had been filled. Then, little by little, sip by sip, guests deconstructed the modernist edifice. When evening ended, all that remained were forty to fifty glasses scattered over three or four dishevelled tables.

Also told her about the faces of several female stalwarts who became progressively perplexed when a man, dancing with a woman, began undressing in perfect rhythm to the music—which always tended toward a tango. With each perfectly choreographed turn, he discarded items of clothing: first a tie, then the studs and links, followed by the jacket, the shirt and finally the trousers to reveal that 'he' was a beautiful woman wearing an ultra-sheer, flesh-coloured dress. The women hugged, then kissed, and continued dancing, ignoring the vocal snorts of the old who had congregated, seeking moral support.

The final escapade I described paralleled what I'd read recently about how American university students were occupying their ample free time: flagpole sitting. Bright Young Things at The Savoy's ballroom would sit on the shoulders of their dates, who remained anchored to their seats at the table. The svelte lovelies weren't discussing Kant or reciting Herodotus from on high—oh no, no, they were equipped with a bottle of champagne and a coupe glass each. And it was from these 'dizzying' heights where they chatted to one other while watching fellow guests twirl around the floor. The game was over when the bottles were emptied. Their farce proved how few regretted the change from elegant talk to inelegant nonsense.

There was no doubt Helena's work was infinitely more challenging than mine. Her responsibilities never ended. She had returned from London only days before lambing season began. Anxious days and cold, wet nights became the norm as she and several employees launched into the time-honoured birthing regimen. They had to intervene frequently to save a ewe's life or the life of a newborn. When a ewe died giving birth, it was on Helena's shoulders to find a surrogate—either to wet adopt or dry adopt the new lamb; to trick the ewe into accepting the orphaned lamb as her own. A week or so later, Helena wrote, commenting on the successful season: *Wonderful result, William: 937 lambs added to the flock with a loss of only twenty-eight ewes.* If only imagining the birth of nine hundred-plus lambs didn't exhaust me, Helena offered more gristle to chew on: *I don't believe a city boy from Ohio would know about the ins-and-outs of sheep farming so here's an overview.*

No doubt, lambing was *the* indispensable part of farm

life; however, it was Helena's responsibility to ensure the operation turned a profit. Lambing was finished in April or early May. In July the tups and ewes were clipped, the wool bundled and sent to market. This was followed in August with haymaking; silage for the harsh winter months was stored in barns scattered throughout the one thousand acres the family owned in Wensleydale and a neighbouring dale. Harvesting was dependent on the weather. A dry spring delayed the process, while a welcomed mix of rain and sun permitted early collection and efficient storage. Dipping—the process of immersing sheep in water doused with fungicides for protection against external parasites—happened in August and September. Muck spreading occurred in early winter so the cold and frost could break it down more easily. The physical challenge of breeding (or tupping, as it's known in Yorkshire) started in November. Tups—rams—were integrated with receptive ewes for the sole purpose of conceiving. Five months later, the cycle repeated itself.

A couple loyal farmers who had advised Helena's father accompanied her to three sheep fairs held annually in Hawes, a market town seven or so miles from her home. She'd sell several from her flock in exchange for top-notch Swaledales and Wensleydales, hoping to raise the generational quality of her own. All this and more had to be accounted for in the books for which she was solely responsible.

Our letter exchanges eased any anxiousness that might have developed before her visit. There was something, however, I wasn't expecting. Something I never anticipated. Something I couldn't have imagined. Didn't recognise her. She'd been transformed. She embodied the modern. Her long, once pinned-up, lovely ginger hair had been stylised into a bob that extended only slightly below the ears. The back wasn't cut straight across but layered at an upward angle, accentuating the longer bits flowing freely toward the front. And, for whatever reason, the hair's shortness intensified its reddishness. While her mother and close friends probably lamented the loss of the tasselled locks, Helena didn't. She capitalised on it. Chiselled cheekbones and crystalline emerald eyes set her apart from any woman I'd known. She dominated the room. What made Helena's presence more special was how oblivious she was to the envious stares of others. As she sauntered over, I remembered her promise during our first meeting: *We learn as we live then, don't we? Means I'll be doing a lot more of both.* Unlike most, Helena had listened to herself.

I rose when she approached, sneakily kissing a cheek as I gestured her toward a chair. Also caught a scent of her perfume, Shem-El-Nessim. Recognised the smell— Véronique's perfume of choice.

So transfixed by her physical transformation, I hadn't noticed her dress or any accoutrements until she sat down. The exquisiteness of her knee-length vermilion dress that hung low on her hips would have been wasted on other women. The dull sheen of her black suede shoes highlighted the narrowness of her ankle. I had no idea if wearing a single earring was the newest trend. If it was … fine. If it wasn't … then Helena invented it. My first indication of how she thrived on defying expectations. If suddenly it became the rage, splendid, I'd know where it started. What impressed me more than its singularity was the earring itself—a miniature saxophone suspended a few inches above her left shoulder.

"It would be inadequate to call you beautiful, too

flippant to say you're the cat's miaow. So, I'll leave it at this: too beautiful for words. And believe me, Helena, that's not an easy confession for an English Lit graduate to admit."

"I've been admired by both fashionable and unfashionable lips, William. And though we barely know one another, for some peculiar reason I value your opinion the most. Thank you so much. Now, stop embarrassing me and order a glass of champagne, please. I'm parched."

"When and why did you adopt the modern look?"

She took a sip of champagne and, what I learned overtime to be a characteristic of hers, rubbed her index finger slowly around the rim of the glass.

"Only a few days ago. I made a special trip to Harrogate. Mummy didn't even know. Why did I do it? I'm too young to hold onto the past, onto something that will never return."

"I must say, your long locks were elegant but this short bob makes you fun-lovingly beautiful. A bit naughty and amply coquettish."

"So, you approve?"

"Only a fool wouldn't."

"Mummy didn't. Not one bit. Also didn't like the dress. Couldn't understand why having almost nothing on could be called progress. Said women shouldn't sacrifice their health to adhere to some flippant, exaggerated idea created by a fashion house that women lack curves."

I laughed. Helena tried to suppress a giggle but couldn't. Showed me she didn't take 'Mummy's' criticism seriously. Took a sip of Scotch while gently touching her nearby knee.

"So glad you're here, Helena. Each letter I read made

me more excited to see you. Been looking forward to this evening for so long, with so much anticipation."

"Thank you, William. I was bursting, simply bursting as I boarded the train. It couldn't travel fast enough."

"I must say one thing though, Helena, your obligations and responsibilities make mine appear ... well, horribly hedonistic and second rate."

"Dalespeople have their own peccadilloes, William. Believe me. Just doesn't involve women dressing as men or alcohol-induced-virility romps. In the Dales, it's pure. It's unabashed. It's ... it's, oh, my ... what can I compare it to? How about a landmine that's remained buried for years and suddenly explodes? Too many episodes to include in a letter so thought I'd wait until we met."

"Fire away, then. Need a hearty laugh."

"Some years back, before the war, the Methodist vicar of Askrigg under Scar seduced the wife of the parish vicar. Could have been the other way around, no one knows for certain. Gossip had been spewing around them for months. Had reached a fever pitch by early autumn. People recalled seeing them at social gatherings throughout the year. Never together but always, always leaving together. Anyway, on Christmas Eve the village was in an uproar, not by the sordidness of it all, but because midnight services had to be cancelled. The Methodists lacked a vicar, and the parish vicar had become intoxicated. Found solace, not in the Bible as many hoped, but in drink. Lots and lots of drink. Uncorked bottles of vintage Scotch parishioners had presented to him as gifts through the years."

"The cause was good. Dame shame to waste quality hooch at one setting."

"There's more William, much more. This kind of

behaviour is ecumenical. It isn't prone to prejudice nor does it court favouritism. A highly respected elder of the Friends' Meeting House in a nearby village ran off with young parishioner who had turned eighteen only a week earlier. Bet the worshipers didn't gather in silence that Sunday morning."

"Ever know what happened?"

"No, no. One can easily leave the Dales as long as the distance exceeds eighty miles or so. Villagers where they settled may gossip but would never broach the topic directly."

"How ... incredibly ... odd."

"Of course, there's Thomas Warricke. Puts your 'drinking nymphs sitting on high' to shame. Warricke's the product—the human equivalent—of what sheep farmers in the Dales avoid: *Breed rubbish, you get rubbish.* Known simply as 'Little T'—suppose his father was 'Big T' whom, I'm proud to say, I never met. A caustic, mean-spirited person from what I've heard. Few liked him. 'Little T' was mollycoddled as a boy and, when he came of age, he overindulged in alcohol. An addiction to laudanum soon followed. How he missed serving in the war ... I'll never understand. He's clearly a toerag. Wanders his fields and along the riverbank, barking at the moon, cursing at people, stumbling about in the light of day without trousers or pants. Fell over drunk once and lost his front teeth. A surly, smelly and most unpleasant person, whom locals never hold to account.

"Why not?"

"Family connections, I suppose. Dalespeople are keen to set newcomers right but won't do it with their own. The 'my family was here first' mentality holds weight, lots of weight."

"Sounds medieval."

"Probably right. But no one's clamouring for change. That's for certain. The Dales also support an eccentric artist who lives in one of the few remaining forested areas in Wensleydale. Name's Peter Lightfoot, studied in Paris before the war. Nothing modern, landscapes mostly. Had two or three showings in London where he was lauded over by the rich and well-born. Those connections, I imagine, hastened his appointment as an official war artist. Peter returned to Wensleydale after the war and, if it's possible, became a partial recluse. During the Peace Day Celebration in July 1919 in the market square, he announced from that day forward he was painting only nudes. He asked for volunteers—women of all ages—whom he thought epitomised the Yorkshire Dales."

"No farmer's wife has admitted to modelling, but there are ample reports that a gallery on the Left Bank in Paris sells his work. Can't keep them on wall."

"Believe this or not, Helena, I seem to recall passing a gallery on Rue Jacob and seeing a painting showcased in the window. Depicted a bodacious woman, white as a full moon, laying suggestively atop ferns in a forest. Seem to recall a waterfall in the background that complemented the woman's skin colour perfectly. Believe it was titled, 'The Beauty of England,' something like that. Don't know if it's your friend's work … certainly wasn't cubist. Everything in its proper place."

"He's *not* my friend. Just another character in the Dales."

"How many times has he asked you to model?"

"Bit presumptuous."

"You're a woman of the Dales, aren't you?"

"I've lost count. His suggestiveness puts me off. Always asks if I'm a natural redhead."

"If not for that …"

"Perhaps … couldn't cope modelling for someone I know."

"Neglected to ask about your government work. What do you do exactly?"

"I don't work for the government, William. I serve on a committee with others in the wool trade to discuss current conditions. We meet quarterly or so with an official from the Ministry of Agriculture and Fisheries."

"That's pretty damn important. Shouldn't minimise it."

"I don't minimise it. Not at all. I think I was appointed because of Father's reputation and … it sounds cynical, but it's probably true. Other committee members—all well-positioned men, of course—keep sniffing about, curious about Mummy's and my long-term intentions. They're anxious to be 'first past the post' when the Bolton-Leigh business comes on the market."

"Your hunch is probably correct. From what you've told me it would put the proverbial feather in the cap of whomever acquired it. Provided it's for sale, of course."

"They'll have to wait a long, long time, I'm afraid. The fact that I assumed Father's membership in the British Wool Confederation should signify my intention to remain actively involved."

"So, the business is performing well."

"The sheep and wool business prospered wonderfully well prior to the war. The value of wool, cloth and exports had almost doubled since 1900. And Father took advantage of it. That's how we were able to assist Uncle Ned in America. But everything changed after the war.

Shipments overseas were lost and although domestic consumption was strong, it paled in comparison to what it had been. I've already told you how Mummy doesn't like today's fashions. Interestingly enough, the popularity of shorter skirts, lighter dresses and shorter coats means less wool cloth is required. The *la garçonne* look has reduced what's required for a woman's outfit from twenty yards to ten yards. What appears to be only a minor annoyance has huge implications."

"Fashion changes."

"That example was for easy digestion. There are more serious issues than that, William. About one-fourth of weaving looms in the country have stopped production; spinning capacity also has declined. And the government fellow we work with doesn't anticipate it becoming any better, only worse. What's more disconcerting is the increased competition from Europe's wool producers, especially Italy of all places!"

"Never liked Italians."

"Oh, don't be silly. I love Italy and Italians. Rome is gorgeous, one of my favourite cities. Surrounded by all that history makes one realise—makes *me* realise, anyway—how insignificant one's own life is."

"Funny, that. Had a similar feeling when the Germans were shooting my aircraft full of holes."

"Okay, okay. If it's a competition, you win."

After finishing our drinks, we decided to skip dinner. Helena had eaten on the train. I wasn't hungry. The Forty-Three beckoned. It was a pleasant evening, so we walked. The Club's location on Gerrard Street in Soho made for a short stroll. Had heard titbits about the place from The Savoy boys but arguably didn't know what to expect. It had been opened a little over two years. Only knew it was one of the nightclubs that WF had warned me about during contract discussions. Would be sacked if he learned I'd played at such a place during the season. Could only play a gig at a jazz or nightclub in August. That was it.

Felt excited immediately upon entering. Ladies dressed in all their finery, drinking martinis, gossiping, and hanging on to their men for love or for stability—perhaps both. Local toughs were present, too. Strutting about, flashing overstuffed money clips, bragging about real or imagined conquests. Most importantly for me was the sound of jazz—real jazz—emanating from the basement. The owner, Kate Meyrick, was managing the front office. She seemed a welcoming, if somewhat frail, middle-aged, slightly bowlegged, untidy Irish redhead, who I could tell, wouldn't accept guff from guests or employees. We weren't exempt. Seemed an amalgam of schoolteacher and brothel manager.

"I entertain all kinds here at The Forty-Three—from poets and potentates to jazzmen, lawbreakers and rich Americans. All our silver utensils, small change trays, candlesticks and cocktail stirrers are hallmarked and accounted for, so I'm hoping none will fall into your pockets."

"Rest assured, Mrs Meyrick, I do not lean toward stealing or breaking the law. To be honest, I fall over if I lean too far."

"Not insinuating you do. You seem like a good lad, a gentleman. War veteran, I'm guessing."

After paying the ten shillings per person entry fee she encouraged us to dance, to drink and to enjoy the music. All the time, while talking, she still seemed to be sizing us up, determining whether we'd invite trouble or be good for settling the tab. I saw a small bar on the far left-hand side but decided we'd go downstairs, hopefully find a table and order a bottle of champagne.

After descending the steep, narrow steps we entered an intimate area about 150 feet long and 50 feet wide crammed with over eighty revellers. The atmosphere was first-rate: dark wooden floor, lush blue walls trimmed with gold-coloured paint and enhanced by a scattering of oak panels and mirrors, recessed ceiling lights and about twenty circular wood tables covered in white tablecloths and a single candle. To our immediate front was a slightly elevated bandstand. Any remaining space was dedicated to dancing. Two small alcoves behind the dance floor had bench-like seats with silk cushions where, I imagined, couples could go for private conversation or to sit out a dance number.

We took the only unoccupied table. While ordering a bottle of champagne the band, called The Lamplighter Jazz Band, started playing 'Kitten on the Keys'. Returned me to the gig at Sara and Gerald Murphy's Right Bank mansion. Where she showcased her *tour de force* routine with Cole Porter's wife and, of course, Skeeter's exquisite piano playing. Those were some days, I thought. Golden days indeed.

"This is wonderful, William. There's movement everywhere. Drinking, dancing, talking, jazzin' … even intense arguing at the table on the right side of the band."

"Hope it's kept under control, or we'll be up to our neck in it."

"Sounds silly, I suppose, but there's a seedy spiffiness to the place and the people. It's different. It's unique. And it's certainly *not* Yorkshire. I'm liking it."

"Jazz attracts all kinds, Helena. Probably the most

democratic music ever created. Welcomes anyone and everyone. Those with vices, those without. Those with money, those without. Those with a title, those without. Only one prerequisite: you've got to have the palate."

As the band started playing 'Jazzin' Baby Blues' the Club's taxi dancers descended upon any unaccompanied man, encouraging them to dance for a small fee. In less than twenty seconds the floor was packed. This was followed by 'I Want a Jazzy Kiss'. By the time the band started playing 'Toot, Toot, Tootsie (Goo' Bye!)', Helena and I were the only ones seated.

"Impolite to ask, perhaps, but would you care to dance?"

"If pre-11 November 1918, I would, Helena. Gladly. It's simply, well, too painful and, I imagine, could be embarrassing for you. I'd resemble the opening act in a travelling circus freak show. You know, right before the bearded woman performs. Think I'd upset the other guests. Mrs Meyrick could throw us out. And besides, looks like the floor is crowded to the point of suffocation."

"Oh, William, that's ridiculous. I wouldn't be ashamed ... ever. But if it's painful, don't bother. I understand. I love listening and adore watching how excited you are by it all."

She declined my suggestion to ask another man if they'd be kind enough to dance with her. I pulled closer and kissed her cheek.

"Then let's share another bottle, shall we?"

While trying to catch the girl's attention, someone mentioned my name in a voice I only vaguely recognised.

"Travers, how are you? Long time since you've visited."

"Ah …"

Tried desperately to recall the time and place I'd met this captivating female. Strung it out as long as I could so as to not make it awkward.

"This is my—or, should I say, *our*—first time."

"Not here, my place."

Blood rushed to my head. Sweat dotted my forehead. Pain rose up my left leg. Then it all came back.

"Hello, Saffron. You've landed on your feet."

"Ain't Saffron here, Travers. I'm one of Meyrick's Merry Maids. She forces us to use our real names. So, it's Winifred Cobblesmith. Horrible, isn't it?"

"Saffron rolled over the tongue more easily."

"Enjoy the work more, so worth it, I suppose. Make almost eighty quid a week. A lot of Merry Maids have experiences similar to mine. Kate said she hired us on appearance and for our manners. If we did good and carved out a new life then all the better for it. I think she's a swell gal."

"Aren't you going to introduce me, William?"

"Yes, yes. I'm sorry. I'm sorry. Winifred, this is Helena Bolton-Leigh from North Riding."

"Nice to make your acquaintance, Miss Bolton-Leigh. Your Travers is a nice boy. Deep thinker, kind of a philosopher, if I remember. In my old job you only remember the really mean or the really polite. Your Travers belongs in the last category."

"Thank you, Miss Cobblesmith. That's kind. Very kind."

"No need for formalities. Just call me 'Cobbie'. That goes for both of you. Now, if you'll excuse me. The fat man in the corner table wants champagne. Hope he don't want me to join him in a dance. Be wonderful to see you again at The Forty-Three. And, so you know, after eleven champagne is served in teacups. It's a way Kate dodges the law prohibiting alcohol after hours in case the police from Bow Street visit. Price goes up to thirty shillings a bottle. But even if you're late and tell me after eleven, I'll only charge twenty-two. Don't tell no one, though. Promise?"

"We promise. And that's very kind. Thank you."

Cobbie sauntered over in a proud and confident manner to her fat, sweaty customer. Was glad for her, but she deposited a smelly problem on my lap. I looked at Helena, whose eyes were piercing through me already.

"Well, I'm certainly relieved 'my' Travers was polite. Would have been something terrible had you been mean. What *would* I think?"

"Helena … Helena, you must believe me. I never followed through. Nothing happened. Visited because I wanted to talk. And that's what we did: talk. You heard her say I was a thinker. She thought it strange initially but, in hindsight, seems we both wanted to talk about our lives, what needed changing. I needed to dump any remaining thoughts and feelings about Paris. If you don't want to believe me or trust me, fine. We'll leave and I'll understand. Never see or hear from me again. I'm a lot of things, a hell of a lot of things—but one thing I'm *not* is dishonest."

Her slight giggle transitioned into a hearty laugh.

"That's such a preposterous excuse. You couldn't possibly have thought it up just now, at this moment. Impossible. Of *course* I believe you, William. The best liar and most accomplished storyteller on this fair island couldn't have been as smooth and said it with so little hesitation as you did. Marvellous."

"Thanks, I guess, for the backhanded compliment."

"Look at it another way, darling: knowing Cobbie will save us eight shillings when we order another bottle."

Couple of hours later, around half three, while the band stopped for a brief pause, Mrs Meyrick took it upon herself to chat with each guest. Asked if they were enjoying themselves and how they liked the music. She also asked whether having light food available after 3 am–eggs, kippers, toast, marmalade and the like—would be welcomed or not. Meyrick didn't ask Helena and me any of those questions.

"Talked briefly to Cobbie earlier this evening. Understand you're an excellent sax player at The Savoy?"

"Oh, Cobbie … always singing my undeserved praises. Currently, I am, yes. Arrived from Paris last year, where I played in a five-member hot jazz band comprised of Americans."

"Notice you emphasised 'currently'. Any chance you'd consider anywhere else, anytime soon? Tuesday and Thursday evenings are available if you'd like them, beginning at 1 am."

"I'm sorry, but if my manager learned about it, I'd be fired. No questions. No excuses. Besides, Mrs Meyrick, there'd be only me—rather boring, don't you think? At a minimum I'd need a pianist, and perhaps a drummer."

"No, I understand. It's just that those days, at those hours, demand something different. Tends to be quiet, reflective clientele. I'll find you a good pianist and a drummer—no problem."

"Come to think of it, Mrs Meyrick, I *am* permitted to work through the entire month of August at any club that'll have me. Think an arrangement could be worked out along those lines?"

"Really need someone through the year. A jazzman that develops a following. The expectation of certainty creates customer loyalty. It's good for you and essential for The Forty-Three. Sure, you understand?"

"Absolutely, absolutely."

"Nice to meet you, then. Think it over, Mr Travers. Here's my card if you reconsider. And please … continue enjoying the evening."

"Don't find that level of interaction in many places do you, Helena?"

"Certainly not. So, think you might follow through, then?"

"Oh, yeah, sure, and if WF took a sniff I'd be kicked out onto the Strand. Wish I could persuade her about August. That'd boost my spirits and keep my playing fresh."

"She's extended the offer, William. It's up to you to make it work, don't you think?"

"Suppose it is. Suppose it is."

"Think The Lamplighters' sax player might go elsewhere?"

"Oh, no. Travelled down that road in Paris. The Lamplighters' jazzin' is fine. I like the combination of piano, saxophone, trumpet, guitar and drums. It's tight. And to me, personally, their kind of jazzin' is the underground music of our time. Wouldn't hear it anywhere else but at a club like this. The boys know it. I can tell. They're enjoying themselves. That sax man is going nowhere fast."

"Give it time, William. Everyone's on the move since the war ended."

"If we came back tomorrow, Helena, and they played

the same numbers, it would sound different from tonight. Guaranteed. If we played anything akin to this, it would compromise The Savoy's reputation for taste and fine entertainment. Their guests couldn't abide. The hotel would lose money. So, we're forced to comply with want management wants: the same damn number, the same damn way, every damn night. Calling it trite only half explains it."

"Oh, dear."

We called it an evening as night became morning. While walking through Soho I learned that the melodic lilt of Helena's soft Yorkshire voice reverted to a flawless American accent when she became tired or slightly tipsy. Seemed The Forty-Three experience had transported her across the Atlantic. Anyone walking past and hearing us would have guessed we were American tourists out on a jolly. Otherwise, the only time Helena would, as she admitted, 'speak like a true red, white and blue American' was to prove naysayers wrong.

After walking a short distance on Oxford Street, we turned right onto Regent Street. The spire of All Souls Church lay directly in front, the Langham directly across from it. As we got closer, Helena slowed her pace to a stop. Leaned forward and kissed my cheek.

"I'd love to see your flat."

"Your room at the Langham's far fancier than my garret, I assure you. And besides, can't remember how I left it. Could be a shambles."

"Couldn't have lost your military discipline for tidiness that quickly."

"Okay, you win. But don't be concerned if we encounter the landlord, Mrs Joy. She's harmless—and a lovely lady, at heart—but it's just, well, she's prickly at times. Lost both her boys in the war. Doesn't have much to live for, I imagine."

"It's almost five in the morning Couldn't possibly be up this early, could she?"

"She enjoys a tipple, or two or three, most times of the day—so anything's possible."

As we made our way up the stairs, I became concerned about the state of my room. How it looked and the comforts it lacked. What would she think? Bet her bedroom in Yorkshire was larger than my entire unit. I quickly rationalised she was too kind a person to be rude. She's half British, after all. She indulged in The Forty-Three Club. Had a grand time. Enjoys jazz, so why worry? Hell, she can even speak with an American accent. After I took her coat, she removed her shoes and walked around the place.

"Why, William ... it's quaint ... and so tidy. You're very neat."

She gently, and I thought, a bit suggestively, ran her fingers up the length of my saxophone that was resting on its stand, pausing at the mouthpiece. Sauntered over to the fireplace and gazed at the framed photo that took pride of place on the mantel.

"My buddies, as you probably guessed. Just weeks before they began getting picked off, one by one, little by little until there was only me. Yep, that's me in the cockpit of *The Queen City*. Full of arrogance and attitude."

"Tell me the names of the other boys, please. And where they're from."

"The tall, lanky guy on the far left is Brian Waterstone from Oregon. What a character. His nickname was 'Wing Nut'. Had the most maniacal laugh that he'd belt out each time prior to taking off. Next to him, looking self-assured and cocky, is Robert Reed from Rhode Island. The son-of-a-bitch never pre-flighted his aircraft. Can you believe it? Said it was unnecessary. Believed God and the Germans decided who'd live and who'd die. His self-assurance earned him the name 'Dr Confidence'. Kneeling next to him is 'The Kid', John Fitzgerald Termain from Nebraska. My God, he was young and impressionable—but one hell of a pilot. He'd make that airframe do things I wouldn't have thought possible. And last, but certainly not least, is Antonio Cavilleri—the 'Troubadour'—who'd conquer and then break the heart of every woman he'd meet. Was from East Harlem, New York City. His skill at reciting Renaissance poetry from memory was unmatched. But that skill didn't excuse him from extruding more shit than a Thanksgiving turkey. Didn't seem to matter. Women swooned over him."

Helena stared at the photo after I'd finished. Maybe she was remembering friends from Bryn Mawr or perhaps her brothers. I didn't interrupt.

"What about you, William, what was your nickname?"

"'Woodrow', after the president. My idealism and naiveté got the best of me, I'm afraid. Owner of a beautiful dream, that's for sure. But it turned sour, didn't it? Went horribly wrong. And, although it didn't come true, rather thrilling to have dreamed it, don't you think? At least once."

She turned around, put her arms on my shoulders, pulled herself close and kissed me. Long and slow and wonderfully.

"Perhaps you should shut out the world's nonsense, William. Retreat into your own private world."

"The outside intrudes eventually."

"Perhaps, but until then we'll have had a lovely time. Can be alone, against the others. Left to ourselves. No rules. No intrusions."

"We?"

"You need someone to love, don't you?"

Chapter Thirteen

We woke a little past one. Gave Helena a woollen jumper to wear. It was far from fashionable, but she wasn't bothered. Kept the cold and damp at bay. I prepared coffee. She enjoyed hers black, or at least that's what she said after learning I didn't have milk. Her British accent also made a rapturous return.

"The Langham's maid will have one less room to clean and tidy this afternoon."

"Maybe you should run over, Helena, you know, tighten down loose talk."

"Let them talk. Let them gossip. Not bothered in the least what frumpy Mrs Mukerheide says or rotund Lady Octavia Tempest insinuates. I'd enjoy hearing their thoughts, either directly or second-hand. Could be wonderfully salacious! I think I'd enjoy listening, actually. And besides, the rooms are freshened up around eleven. I'm late already."

"So, no more hiding behind columns to sneak a kiss?"

"That was for your benefit, darling, not mine! Didn't want people rudely commenting about The Savoy's newest saxophonist."

"Overwhelmed by your consideration. Thank you."

"Okay, enough. Since you mussed me about early this morning, what do you plan to do with me this afternoon?"

"Anything. Up for anything, really. Haven't ventured out except to work and next door to the Yorkshire Grey for a couple drinks. Holed up in my garret to practise, with whatever spare time I have."

"Don't you practise enough during the week with the boys?"

"No, no—the kind of practising I'm doing is the hot jazz I played in Montparnasse, not the diluted renditions *à la* The Savoy."

"Tell you what, grab my arm and let's walk a bit. Want to show you a few things and hear your thoughts."

Wasn't permitted to ask where we were going or what we were going to see or how far away it was. I persevered the best I could before complaining. By the time we approached the National Gallery, the leg and lower back pain had become too intense. Asked if we could take a taxi the rest of the way.

"We're close, very close—but I understand, William. You've been marvellous, but I see you're in discomfort.

The ride was short. In the middle of the street, surrounded by an array of government buildings, stood a tall, solitary monument made of stone.

"It's the nation's war memorial, William, dedicated to the fallen."

The base of the Cenotaph remained laden with poppy wreaths from the November remembrance service. I thought it austere, modern ... almost abstract, certainly not celebratory. No angels clutching a dead solider ascending to heaven. No soldier in a heroic pose, repelling an advancing enemy. Its only inscription: 'The Glorious Dead'. We stood nearby, gazing at the edifice. I noticed that, as men walked by on the pavement, they took off their hats in a sign of respect. Needing little coaxing, I repeated the gesture. Helena asked whether I could walk a tad further, down Parliament Street, across Great George Street to Westminster Abbey. Not wanting to give in easily, I said I'd try my best.

Helena directed me toward the grave of the Unknown Warrior upon entering the Abbey. Despite the obvious grandeur of the cathedral's interior, my eyes were drawn to the deep blackness of the marble stone covering the crypt. I found the last sentence of the inscription especially telling: *They Buried Him Among the Kings Because He Had Done Good Toward God and Toward His House.*

After leaving the cathedral, we found a nearby bench in St James's Park to give my leg a rest and to relish the beautiful apricot light so unique to a late-afternoon winter sky.

"What's your impression, William? Did they bring feelings to the surface?"

I realised if I told her the truth—my well-thought-out feelings—she'd find them offensive. If I wasn't truthful, then the foundation of this new relationship would be based on a lie. Been through one of those already. Didn't want another.

"It's ironic, isn't it, when a government can't acknowledge guilt, they erect a monument? A kind of emotional doping of the public."

"How can you be so, so ..."

"Well, the Unknown Warrior is emotional, isn't it? Has to be. A former newsagent or sheep farmer or coal miner or bank clerk could be lying in that crypt. He's there because the government said he was needed. But he also could be one of the entitled classes, couldn't he? A lord's son or an aristocrat or an Oxford graduate. Someone who embraced a duty thrust upon him because of position or for some bizarre sense of ancestral obligation. Those remains—however much there is, whoever it is—represent *all* of Britain."

"You certainly couldn't have rattled these thoughts off the cuff just now."

"No, no, you're right ... I didn't. Been festering for some time, actually. America interred, what it calls, the

Tomb of the Unknown Soldier at Arlington Cemetery in Washington, DC, this past November. Learned about it in the *Paris Herald* a month or so before leaving for London. I guess that's when my cynicism began, if that's what this is. Never heard of the Cenotaph or Unknown Warrior until you showed me."

"I attended the unveiling of the monument where over a million mourners filed past. Also left my flower contribution that, by the time I walked by, had reached over two metres deep. Then joined thousands of others outside Westminster Abbey as the casket arrived on a gun carriage. The King and other members of the Royal Family walked mournfully behind it. It was touching, William. Very respectful. Very emotional."

"Seems the need for that sort of acknowledgment is even greater in Britain. The war brought an end to three European monarchies, didn't it? So, George V or some keen advisor skilfully sought a democratic handshake among equals, a public display—an important, emotional, public display—acknowledging the sacrifice of the common man. Without him, the soldier in the crypt, and the hundreds of thousands who died, the British monarchy would have passed into history, too."

"I can't share your disrespect. No, not disrespect—what you asserted earlier … cynicism. It's exactly what I needed, and hundreds of thousands of sisters, brothers, spouses, mothers—even grandparents—needed. Perhaps it is all 'hokum', as you believe, but for this country it serves as a balm—a much-needed, soothing balm—that, I'm sure, will be reapplied each eleventh day in November for decades, if not centuries, to come."

"I'm sorry. Forgive me. Have no right really to criticise the manner in which another nation's government pays homage to a mistake. I'm glad it offers you and others solace. Truly, I am. It's just, well, I'd rather be drinking and raising hell with my fellow aviators than remembering them by staring at a stone monument or the grave of an unknown. I'll admit one thing though: the Cenotaph and the crypt work together well, especially for those who haven't experienced war."

"Is this our first argument?"

"Come on, it's a disagreement, not an argument. We're permitted, aren't we? British society can't frown upon that, can it? I mean, for better or for worse, you're half American."

"No, of course not. And yes, we are permitted to disagree. In case you're unaware, we're not ruled by Cromwell anymore. But it's important to remember, William, life consists of tiny things that slowly and over time become important enough to ruin your entire life. We shouldn't let this—whatever *this* is—come between us."

"You're probably right. Wise philosophy. Can think of times from the past when I should have ignored things instead of dwelling on them. Rightly or wrongly, I got rid of 'em by drinking. That usually leads to forgetting but forgetting, forgetting is so long and so damn difficult."

"Drinking to forget isn't the answer either, William."

"But you know what? I never forget people I'm fond of. Never seem dead to me. Someone I cared about in Paris once told me I was *too hard*. Maybe I am, maybe I am, but looking at a monument or a crypt simply doesn't offer peace or reconciliation or resurrect fond memories. Borders on being a hateful reminder. Only when I'm alone, in my solitude, are my buddies artfully alive— harassing me, enjoying my sax music and discussing what we're going do after the damn thing's over. None of them got the opportunity, did they? Their futures were left to me."

"Then make their deaths mean something. Stand for something. Do something with the life that was saved. As I said this morning, shut out the world's nonsense and retreat into your own private world."

"How will retreating into my own private world bring meaning to their deaths?"

"Because you won't abide by rules. You'll ignore intrusions. You'll ignore conventions and, most importantly, you'll ignore the consequences. I'm ready to ignore the conventions of Britain, the conventions of Yorkshire, the conventions of the Bolton-Leigh family. And I'm guessing you'll easily ignore however little's left of your American conventions and expectations."

"You know, it's odd, even strange. A friend in Paris offered similar advice. Proffered the identical mantra. Also wanted to participate."

"The same woman who said you were *too hard?*"

"You think it was a woman?"

"Men always remember what mothers and former lovers said."

"I'll tell you someday, if you remain interested, but right now …"

"You're still aching?"

"Christ, no! Cauterised her on the strength of two magnums. What I want to say is I'm hungry and betting you are too. Know an intimate place for dinner?"

"Let me think. Remember when we met at the Palm Court and you declined to join Margaret and me at Kettner's? One of numerous topics she talked about was a wonderful restaurant that, if I remember correctly, is in

Fitzrovia."

"Ah, I declined so you'd have a more enjoyable time. Wasn't being difficult."

"Oh, I know, I know. All part of developing a 'British mindset'. And I loved you for it."

We continued through the park, crossed the Mall and walked past the Palace of St James. We stopped when reaching Fortnum & Mason on Piccadilly. I kept quiet, captivated by her concentration. Eyes focused straight ahead. Left index finger tugging gently on her bottom lip, pausing occasionally to take stock and arrive at an answer.

"I remember now. It's only come to me: Restaurant de la Tour Eiffel in Fitzrovia. Not certain, but I think Margaret said it's on the corner of Percy and Charlotte streets, near your flat, ironically."

"Let's go for a wander until we find it, shall we? Think you'll manage?"

"I'll give it a go. Throw me over your shoulder if I falter."

"My weight limit is a lamb. Sorry."

"Then push on. Where you lead, I'll try my best to follow."

"Supposed to serve genuine French cuisine, William. It could be special, so your efforts will be rewarded. May find this even humorous. Couldn't believe it when Margaret told me. Since about 1908 or so it's been owned by an Austrian chef who began working as a kitchen boy for Franz Joseph in Vienna before moving on to Monte Carlo, Egypt and finally Paris. Don't know *how* he survived the war in London. Remember reading in the *Daily Mail,* which advised guests should refuse to be served by Austrian and German waiters. Anyway, I'm sure by now you've had your fill of boiled beef, overcooked vegetables and greasy potatoes—so hopefully his food and wine will reignite memories of Paris."

Helena had chosen wisely. Tour Eiffel was intimate. Modern cubist-like art adorned forest-green walls. Twenty or so small, dark wooden tables were outfitted with a magnum wine bottle and topped with a narrow candle. The place smelled of garlic and rosemary and truffles and lavender and, as Helena thought, returned me to Paris. The owner, whose named we learned was Rudolph Stulik, bore a striking resemblance to the deceased Austrian Emperor, especially the grey moustache that practically concealed his entire mouth. His English pronunciation bordered on the romantic, a composite of all the countries in which he had worked and lived.

Helena's culinary likes mirrored mine. We both ordered the *petit saumon bouilli* with Hollandaise as a starter and the *poulet de graine casserole paysanne* for the main course. And the *bombe glacée pralinée* capped an exquisite meal or, as Helena exclaimed, *Put the tin hat on it*. For some unknown reason, Chef Stulik appreciated our presence so much that he poured two brandies in glasses that could have sustained three goldfish for weeks. More importantly than the food, however, was Helena's personal revelation.

"I think I'm still engaged."

"What do you mean? How can you put 'think' and 'engaged' together in the same sentence? You either are or you're not!"

"Well, I may be. Mummy believes I am. So do his parents."

"When, or how the hell, did that happen? Whose parents? And if you're engaged, why in Sam Hill's name are you ... are you ... with me?"

"Calm down, calm down, and I'll explain. At least try to. It's complicated. His name is Robert Chesterfield, but everyone calls him Robbie. Our parents were good friends and had known each other for years. Enjoyed picnics, Christmas luncheons and other social events throughout the year together. Sometimes they'd visit us in Wensleydale; other times we'd make the trek to Richmond to see them. Robbie and I played together all the time as children. Had wonderful fun, creating plenty of made-up adventure stories that somehow always included Richmond Castle. Robbie's father was the modern history teacher and occasional temporary headmaster at Richmond School, making education mightily important to the Chesterfields. When I attended Cheltenham, Robbie attended Uppingham School, a public school in the county of Rutland. Fortunately, or unfortunately, he joined the OTC—Officer Training Corps—where he excelled, catching the eye of well-positioned adults who took notice of his innate leadership skills. Fate, it seemed, had destined us not to see one another for several years. We went our separate ways in 1912. I left for America; he studied at Cambridge. And, as you know, I returned to Yorkshire in July 1914 after Daddy passed way. The Chesterfields, along with Robbie, attended the funeral. So, as terrible and disrespectful as it may sound, the funeral reunited us. But we weren't children anymore, were we? We were adults possessing an innocent level of maturity which, of course, enabled .... Anyway, we enjoyed a few wonderful, carefree weeks together before war was declared. He volunteered the first week, expecting to be sent to France immediately—but that never happened. Because of his OTC background and experience, the army decided it best if he remained in England to train and indoctrinate new recruits. Although he was disappointed, I was ecstatic."

"Would have been killed in the first months if he'd gone over early."

"Fortunately, he was selected as the chief training officer of the newly formed 7th Battalion of the Yorkshire Regiment, known as the Green Howards, garrisoned at Richmond. We couldn't believe our luck. Didn't last, of course. The unit departed soon—to Dorset and Hampshire, for additional training before being sent to France. Robbie was wounded at the Battle of Albert in 1916 and sent home to convalesce. This proved more serious than originally thought, so it took longer to heal."

"Acquainted with dubious timelines to repair a broken body."

"And that's when he asked me to marry him. Sounds cruel, I know, but I put him on hold. Made an excuse. Encouraged him to wait. I didn't tell him, but I'll tell you. If he were killed, I didn't want to be known as a war widow, not at twenty-one years old. Selfish? Yes. Cold? Perhaps. But look around, William, look at all the superfluous women in mourning. And we will … I mean, *they* will carry that label until they die. Women too old to be young, too young to be old."

"The war burdened us all, didn't it? Weighted down by emotions for a long, long time. Permanently, I'm guessing. Sorry to keep interrupting. Go ahead."

"He returned to France and participated in several terrible, horrible battles. Don't know how but he miraculously survived them all. Came home in early October for what I thought at the time was a specially granted leave to become engaged."

"So that's when you became engaged."

"I accepted his offer because … well, by October there were constant reports of the Germans being routed. The war would soon be over. Not immediately but soon. Thanks largely, I guess, to you Yanks. So, I agreed. I wouldn't have to worry about becoming a superfluous woman. Six days after the Armistice—17 November—I received a telegram. I'll never forget it. I was stunned. Simply stunned. Robbie had transferred to the 13th Battalion of the Green Howards to participate in the North Russia campaign against the Bolsheviks. Sent to bolster the White Russians opposing the revolution. Didn't know it then but the army was headquartered in Archangel in Siberia by the White Sea, not far south of the Arctic Circle. His so-called 'leave' in October was partly a ruse, I suppose, enabling him to coordinate and finalise logistics for the expedition."

"I remember reading a little about that. The Americans were involved in this colossal mistake too, somehow. Could be wrong but I thought the troops returned in autumn 1919 or so.

"They did—but Robbie didn't."

"He was killed?"

"Don't know what happened. No one does. Never found his body. No abandoned kit. No … anything. He simply vanished. Since we weren't married yet, the army notified his parents first and then they told me. It is awful. Truly awful. Robbie's their only child."

"Think he deserted? Men act strangely in war. Can't ignore the possibility."

"Now you understand, William, why I said I *might* be engaged. And, if we ever find out what happened and it's the worst, then I become one of those superfluous women. But you know what? I'd rather be a superfluous woman than a woman in persistent limbo, the way I am now. I've been cast aside and pitied by everyone for nearly three years. I don't *want* pity. I want life. I want love. Locals believe that since, I pledged myself to Robbie, I can't possibly entertain anyone else until I learn whether he's alive or dead. Until then I'm a marked woman. A marked, lonesome, pathetic woman, aren't I?"

Helena's recounting of events finally had taken its toll. She began crying and shaking, unconcerned what others may have thought. I got up, grabbed my chair and placed it next to her. She leaned over and buried her head in my shoulder. She regained her composure after several minutes. I offered my handkerchief. She wiped her eyes, took hold of my left hand and looked at me with tears still trickling down her cheek.

"Don't know why this has happened … of course I do, stupid of me. Sorry, William, I'm so very, very sorry."

"Don't apologise, Helena. Been bottled up, suppressed for a long time. You needed to tell someone. Glad it was me."

"I'm embarrassing myself and you."

"Don't be silly. The way I look, walking and strutting about, how the hell could I possibly be embarrassed witnessing a strong cry from a beautiful woman?"

Caught the glimpse of a smile and a slight giggle.

"You're good to me and for me, William. Love you . . . and thank you."

When calm returned, Mr Stulik poured us two more brandies. He smiled, patted my shoulder and retreated to the kitchen. What a marvellous way to endear himself to customers, I thought.

"Knowing your awkward situation, wonder why Sara Murphy encouraged you to contact me."

"She didn't know. I never told her."

"So, no one in Yorkshire knows anything about us?"

"Nobody. Not even Mummy. Can only imagine what'll be said if they do."

"Then we have a serious problem, Helena. Should we continue? Not certain we can. No use ruining your life. Could restrict ourselves to London and the southeast. I'd never visit Yorkshire, obviously. And please be honest: if, by some chance, anyone from Wensleydale *did* see us, what would they think? Would there be repercussions?"

"They'd probably consider me a few pegs above a shameless hussy. A lot of gossiping, a lot of pettiness, a lot of staring and looking the other way. But they'd never confront me. To make matters worse, Mummy's convinced herself I display such an intense air of determined virginity that I've spent my adult life masquerading as a part-time nun. So, I'd have to deal with that too."

"You're engaged, not married. Is there a statute of limitations on engagements? Why couldn't you be involved with someone else? I mean, hell, it's not a crime. Of course, that being said, I'm guessing societal convention dictates ..."

"There's no limit—it's ... it's the emotional commitment others have placed on me and ... well, the loyalty I'm expected to have toward Robbie, I suppose."

"You could move to London or somewhere else in the south. Brighton's nice."

"I wouldn't leave Mummy alone in the house with all

the land and the business. She couldn't possibly cope, especially the sheep end of things. It would be different if one of my brothers had survived. And I can't leave it to God and good neighbours. So, it's up to me. On my shoulders."

"Then we'll just have to be content with London, Helena. I can handle it. I'm willing to wait until the others—and perhaps you—feel it's time to begin your life again."

Didn't know if I sounded convincing. I sure as shit wasn't buying what I was peddling. Seemed complete 'bull feathers' to me. Couldn't give two hoots in hell what others thought about her and me or what's right or what's inappropriate. Soldiers were told they were right to volunteer, right to fight, and right to defeat Germany— and then, after the carnage ended, the grey men came out and imposed *their* peace. The tally of 'rights' was ignored in favour of a huge wrong. I didn't give two figs, to use the British term, whether or how our relationship could offend others. How Helena would be treated was another issue, my only concern.

She glanced toward another table, deep in thought. Minutes ticked by. I said nothing. She turned toward me, took a sip of brandy, placed the glass to one side and touched my outstretched hand laying on the white tablecloth.

"I admonished you earlier today, William, about abiding by rules and ignoring conventions, didn't I? Bragged that I was prepared to ignore everything expected by my country, by the people in Yorkshire, even by my family. If now isn't that time, then when ... age fifty?"

"Yes, yes, but, but ... the outcome could be brutal.

Absolutely horrendous for you."

"Let me finish. It's important to let me finish."

Kept quiet and looked straight into her determined green eyes.

"When you think you've found something in your life that makes up for everything that's happened before, but are forced to abide by an earlier decision—an almost whimsical decision—that entails losing you, I'm not willing to do that. Ever. Do you understand?"

I was stunned. Stupefied. Was she genuinely prepared to forego perhaps everything for a man of uncertain means, a jazzman who desired nothing but to shun conformity?

We returned to my garret but strangely never discussed how our relationship would proceed. Helena stayed until morning. After a cursory breakfast, I walked her to King's Cross station to catch the return train to Yorkshire. As the last call was announced, Helena pulled me close and kissed me.

"I could see in your eyes when I first met you, William, that you were determined to cut an enormous slice—the most luscious, scrumptious piece—from the cake of life. Please don't surrender what we've found. I'll make it work. We'll make it work."

Unlike me to put aside doubt and believe her but at the time, in that instance, I did. Completely and without reservation.

"No matter how our being in love sorts itself, Helena, it sure as hell will be worth it while it's going on. Won't let it wither and die. I promise."

She boarded the train, found her seat and lowered the window. Steam filled the air as the train pulled slowly from the station.

"My world is beginning to make sense now, William. Thank you."

And, with those parting words, she was gone. Waited until the train turned the bend and disappeared. I collected my thoughts while walking to my apartment. After twenty-seven years of uncommon wanderings and frequent mistakes, it seemed a real life, a real relationship and a real love, had found me. What a triumph our lives will be, I thought. For the first time in a long time, I believed in something, something true and something pure and something complete.

Chapter Fourteen

For several weeks the band rehearsed the numbers selected for pressing into records. The session was scheduled for early April, so there wasn't much time. One afternoon, before we broke for dinner and prepared for the evening's gig, I received a message to visit WF Dabney's office. Had something he wanted to ask me. If it was about music, why didn't the band's leader, Bill Ralton, ask me? Suddenly became concerned about what he wanted. Perhaps another band member or a waiter had filed a complaint. Maybe a female customer thought me too flirtatious. The pain in my left leg intensified, something I noticed recently that occurred when I was worried or concerned about my personal well-being. Nonetheless—keeping the proverbial British stiff upper lip of an expat—I knocked on his door at half five.

"Come in, Travers. Come in. Please sit yourself down. Get comfortable. Can I pour a double neat?"

"Well, WF, ah … we've got …"

"Of course not. Sorry. Forgot you're performing tonight. Setting a bad example, aren't I?"

"I'd be happy to partake if it wasn't a work night."

"Of course, of course. Certainly. Travers … I have a request. Comes from the top. Would you be willing to take on another instrument? The tenor sax, to be specific."

"And stop playing the alto?"

"Good God, no, man. In *addition* to your alto. In addition. You see, the higher-ups, they love your playing—love it. But they want more deepness, more mellowness. Moodiness, I guess, is the best way to describe it. Basically, you'd be alternating between the two depending on what the music calls for. You'll look spiffy up there with one sax on a stand and another in your mouth. It'll impress our female guests. Ralton's all in favour. Only need you to accept the challenge. Your compensation will be adjusted, of course."

"I'll certainly accept, WF but … well, a new instrument is costly. Don't think I have enough to cover it right now."

"Don't be silly, Travers. The Savoy will provide the instrument. In fact, the owner has a friend who owns one of the originals designed by the inventor … ah, Rudolph or Edward or …"

"Adolphe Sax."

"Yes, yes, precisely. Adolphe Sax. A gorgeous piece of kit. Not brass, but silver. Almost eighty years old but it looks brand new. And he's entrusting you with it. Quite the honour, I'd say."

"I'm humbled, WF. Truly humbled and honoured. The tone's deeper but the fingering's the same. So, I guess what I'm saying is, shouldn't be any delay. Embouchure will be different, bigger mouthpiece, longer reed. Mouth will just have to adjust. No issues."

"Spoken like a true jazzman and an air ace. Excellent my man. Well then, enough faffing."

Whereupon WF walked to a closet, pulled out a slightly soiled red leather instrument case and placed it on my lap. I unclasped the hinges and opened the lid. Cocooned in dark crushed velvet lay the shiny silver tenor saxophone. Not a smudge or dent on it. Sax's signature was emblazoned on the bell. Underneath the thumb rest was the number: *2 of 7, Adolphe Sax, 1846.* Christ, I thought, this needed to be in a museum, not in my grubby hands!

"There it is, Travers. It's yours. Well, it's The Savoy's, of course, but you're the caretaker. The responsible party."

"Thanks for entrusting me, WF. First thing tomorrow morning, I'll visit a favourite music shop on Denmark Street and order some reeds. Should have this beaut operational by the middle of next week. No problem."

"Have no doubts about you, Travers. You'll be smashing. Just one reminder: the instrument belongs to the hotel owner's friend and has been in his family for generations. He only consented because I vouched for you. I told him if the US Army trusted you with an expensive aircraft, then, well, hell, The Savoy should do likewise. Treat it as tenderly as you treated your aircraft. What'd you say its name was?"

"*The Queen City*, WF."

"Yes, yes, of course, *The Queen City*. Fascinating name. Quite romantic. Blow the hell out of the horn, Travers, but never treat it rough. Always put it to bed nicely."

Didn't know whether WF intended his comment to serve as a metaphor about women but, because of Helena and being in a certain romantic frame of mind, I took it as such.

"Don't worry, sir. Would never mistreat or abuse anything I truly loved."

"Jolly good, Travers. Jolly good. Now go and give our customers a fine performance. And thank you."

Didn't ask why or how but the music shop, fortunately, had a couple boxes of tenor sax reeds in stock. Also had some sheet music. Not jazz but tunes that made me hone and develop needed technical skills. The embouchure required was definitely different. Kept squeaking on both the high and low register 'D', as well as the occasional 'G'. After several frustrating hours I learned that if I loosened my lips on the mouthpiece—directly opposite of the tight embouchure required on an alto—deep, smooth, dulcet tones emanated from this almost eighty-year-old instrument. Delighted, I couldn't wait to meld with the band. But I also became concerned how they'd view it: an uppity Yank who bootlicked senior management or maybe, just maybe, as a talented sax player helping make a good band great.

The British boys were fine with it. The trumpet player, Eddie Transwell, who never had warmed to me for some reason, pulled me aside, shook my hand and congratulated me in the typical British, roundabout kind-of-way.

"Glad it's not me, Travers. Couldn't accept the responsibility for someone else's instrument. But I must say, one of the originals of Adolphe Sax ... now that *is* something. Hell, knowing myself, I'd get pissed and forget where I left it. Can't tell you the number of army issue compasses I lost in the trenches."

"In fairness, a compass is easier to lose, don't you think? Conditions weren't too favourable either, were they?"

"I suppose you're correct on that score. I've always found too much pudding causes indigestion."

"Don't worry, Transwell, I'll be careful—if not for myself, for the sake of the band."

The leader and clarinettist, Bill Ralton, looked forward to finding arrangements emphasising the tenor.

"It's good to have more than one string to your bow, Travers. Helps secure the job, as long as you don't get your nose out of joint. Congratulations."

Told him not to worry, emphasising that only women cause my nose to become disjointed. He thought it a wise philosophy, one he shared. Found this surprising, as I never heard him speak about a woman or comment on the scantily clad Bright Young Things that shimmied so near him on the dance floor.

My first evening playing the tenor went well. For what it's worth, thought the guests were impressed that I had two horns by my feet. No one said anything, but I could tell. I … could … tell. Whatever self-serving ego boost I perceived from the guests was replaced in due time by the 'performance' of a young female. Immediately after playing 'All I Need Is You'—a pleasant little foxtrot number—a 'young lovely' stood on a chair and announced she was going for a swim in the Thames. She assured everyone it would be n*othing short of the cat's whiskers.* Even encouraged others to join her. No one accepted. And that was that or so I and everyone else thought.

About halfway through playing 'Hugs and Kisses', the young beauty re-entered the room sopping wet and shoeless. Eye makeup and lipstick had run. Hair had dropped. And a soaked dress left little need for imagination. She spurned the dinner jacket offered by an attentive waiter, opting instead to stand on her chair and dance in place. It wasn't dancing, exactly, more like the indiscriminate flailing of arms with the occasional sideways lift of a leg. It was something to watch but being professionals we continued playing without interruption. Despite overhearing a few older women gasping in unbridled shock, and male Edwardians mumbling to their wives that the girl was obviously a *shameless tart*, most continued enjoying themselves.

Three weeks or so after 'Aquatic Alice's' spontaneous performance, I received a shock. While putting away my instrument after the evening's performance, Clifford Evans, the bass player, approached me.

"Hey, Travers, there's a dish of a woman in the hallway asking for you. No worries if you're too busy. Think she fancies me. Think I could be in there, you know."

"I'll have to cry bullshit on that. Even if she *did* fancy you, Evans, you wouldn't know what to do after she said *Hello*. You'd stutter, you'd go wobbly, you'd wet yourself and then faint. After ensuring you had recovered, she'd apologise for causing such distress. Could hear her now: *It's best perhaps if I get along and don't see you again*. And that'd be it, Evans. Your chance of experiencing the purring perfection of a genuine woman … poof, gone forever."

"Rather harsh, isn't it, Travers."

"Surely you realise by now that, unlike Brits, Americans have never earned medals for subtlety?"

Closed the instrument case and opened the door.

"Hello, William, it's me."

There stood Helena, looking ravishing.

"Why I'm damned. From Evans's description I thought it was Cobbie from The Forty-Three."

She looked stunned. He lips opened slightly, and she cast her head downward and to the side.

"Kidding, Helena. Only kidding. Wonderful to see you. Damn sure fantastic!"

"You're awful, simply awful."

Kissed her cheek after we had finished laughing.

"That's all you've got?"

She pulled me close.

"There … much better."

"Agree. Much, much better."

"I planned this little adventure some time ago. Dying to surprise you. Arrived only a few hours ago. Dropped my suitcase, changed out of my travel clothes and came here directly. I thought about hiding in the back of the ballroom but feared you'd catch a glance. So, I had a few drinks in the American Bar. You know the bartender's a woman? Ada 'Coley' Coleman. She shakes and stirs and still manages to keep things hopping."

"Know all about her. Unfortunately, employees can't enjoy anything the hotel offers. Strictly forbidden. Everything at the Langham to your liking? Were they glad to see their most favoured customer?"

"Don't know. Not staying there."

"Not staying at the Langham? Sacrilege! Can't believe you broke the long-held tradition of the Bolton-Leigh clan."

"Found a wonderful little room on a top floor on Langham Street. It's quaint, rather romantic, with wonderful views of All Souls Church."

"That's my garret! How'd you arrange that? I'm beyond impressed, my dear."

"Mrs Joy seemed suspicious initially. Once she understood how much I knew—where you're from, what you did in the war and how you play saxophone at The Savoy—she let me in. Apologised while opening the door to your flat. She was actually cute, William. Honestly. *Well, I'm damned,* she said. *Sorry I was suspicious, love. Thought you a floozy from Soho. Them lot parade around here, you know. Now you take care of young William, hear? He's a fine, well-mannered lad. He's going places.* After relighting the half-smoked cigarette that had been dangling from her lower lip the entire time, she gave a suggestive wink. *Enjoy him, love. 'Cause if I was a few years younger, I know I would.* Promised I would and that no harm would come to you."

"Ah, good ol' Beatrice. Prickly as a porcupine initially, but she's come around. Even shared a few Famous Grouse double neats together in the Yorkshire Grey. Johnny, the bartender, takes fine care of us. You should hear her stories as a youngster growing up in Hurstpierpoint, Sussex. What a firecracker. Often wonder what her two boys were like. Sure she thinks about them all the time. And if they hadn't been killed, what would they be doing today?"

"I feel similarly about my brothers. They'd have a life, and mine would be different from what it is—so would Mummy's. Anyway, since you thought I was Cobbie, can we visit The Forty-Three, you know, check how she's doing? I want a night on the tiles."

"Certainly. I was on my way there now. Been visiting regularly after work, to be honest. Infinitely better with you along, though. Have become such a regular Mrs Meyrick insists I call her 'Evie'—short for Evelyn, her middle name. Can you imagine?"

"Of course I can … easily. You won over Mrs Joy and now Mrs Meyrick. Hope you have similar success with Mummy."

"So, you've decided to tell her?"

"Already did."

"And …"

"This hallway is too quiet, William. Can we discuss it at The Forty-Three?"

"Certainly can. Curious about her reaction."

I had written Helena about the tenor sax and she

seemed excited to see it. Took it out of its case and handed it to her. She sat on a nearby chair and placed it on her lap, gently touching the pearl keys and rubbing her slender hands over the bell. First, she outlined the inscription with her thin finger and then read it aloud: *2 of 7, Adolphe Sax, 1846.*

"What an absolutely beautiful instrument, William. I'm so proud of you."

"It's an honour, alright. Not taking any risks. Carry it wherever I go."

"Hope you're careful."

"It's never out of my sight, don't worry. Shall we start meandering to The Forty-Three?"

As we entered Gerrard Street, I pointed out the 1917 Club housed in No. 4. Explained how its membership comprised of individuals without social standing but who shared liberal, even some socialist, views on political matters, especially foreign affairs. Founded during the war by a guy named Leonard Woolf. Comprised mainly of Labour Party and Liberal Party followers as well as a bevy of people in the arts, including a number of damn fine musicians. Several interesting speakers have presented papers on a variety of topics. The food's horrible but sharing conversations with like-minded individuals—men and women—had been stimulating.

"You've obviously attended more than a few events, then."

"Certainly have. Makes me understand that, no matter how others react to my cynical disillusionment, I'm not alone, at least politically.

We were greeted by a lengthy line outside The Forty-Three. As the doorman gazed at the crowd, he soon recognised me and ushered us forward.

"Go right in, Mr Travers. Mrs Meyrick wouldn't want you waiting."

As I helped Helena with her coat, Evie welcomed us both.

"Ah, see you've brought your horn. Plan on whetting our appetite?"

"No, no, Evie. Sorry to elevate your hopes. It's a special instrument that needs special treatment. Never leaves my side."

"I'll crack that hard shell of yours one day, you wait. Until then go downstairs and enjoy yourselves. Reserved your usual table. Oh, another thing: the Sabini gang—Darby and his four sons from Clerkenwell, who operate that racehorse protection racket—are in the house. They attract petty thieves by just being here, toughs who want to make an impression, 'make it big,' so to speak. Watch that horn of yours. Ripe for being nicked, I'd say."

"Thanks very much. Appreciate the dope. You're a Georgia peach, Evie, without the fuzz."

"Another Yank expression, I suppose. Where ... do ... you ... pull these from? Honestly."

"You must visit often, William. What fawning—but it's lovely to be known."

Had no more than got comfortable when Cobbie greeted us.

"Nice to see you again, Miss Bolton-Leigh."

"Well, I'm glad to be here, too. And very touched you remembered my name, Cobbie."

"Oh, that's no bother. You're the only thing this lad talks about."

Helena looked at me and smiled.

"How about a bottle of your best champagne, Cobbie?"

"My pleasure, Mr Travers. Back in a jiff."

"That was kind of her, William. Being part British, I'm not supposed say it but I'm, well, flattered you think about me so often."

"Ain't nothing to it, Helena. You're the easiest thing that's ever come my way. Speaking of 'easy', which I'm sure it wasn't, how and what did you tell your mother?"

"Explained how Sara and Gerald Murphy recommended we meet, that we got along, that I desired to continue seeing you, and hoped she'd offer her blessing and support. Shocked doesn't properly describe her reaction. Devastated is more accurate. *I will not countenance him visiting North Riding. It's taken much too long and too much effort to be accepted even mildly by the locals. You won't jeopardise our history here on a whim. We, Helena, yes, we, cannot afford to let this happen.* A few tense moments, for sure. Fixed her a martini, hoping to calm her."

"And …?"

"Worked, up to a point. She didn't understand how I could put her in such a difficult situation with Robbie's parents. If she hadn't known about us and if somehow the truth saw the light of day, she could feign ignorance; truthfully say she didn't know. But with my telling her, she couldn't."

"Sounds as if she's more concerned about embarrassing or shaming herself than about how you feel, about you having a meaningful life?"

"Perhaps, a bit. After her second martini she agreed. How did she phrase it? Oh, yes: *Go ahead, then, have a dalliance. A good, heartfelt dalliance and then purge it from your system. But it must remain in the south. And it will end when Robbie returns.*"

"Interesting. I've been recognised as an 'it'. Could be judged as progress, I suppose. Wonder how long it will take to become 'him' or, God forbid, 'William'?"

"Oh stop, this is serious. Mummy emphasised this couldn't have happened ten years ago. *I spent eighteen years developing you into a refined lady, to be educated and poised and confident, to be welcomed into Yorkshire society without strings, without conditions. Now it's gone. Eighteen years wasted.* She looked puzzled when I reminded her that I wasn't eighteen but almost twenty-six, an old maid, a spinster to her generation. Agreed with her this wouldn't have happened ten years ago but ... the war changed everything. Turned standards and expected behaviour on their head. Nothing's the same and never will be. The old mores don't apply. Tried to convince her I was still that educated, poised and confident woman that could be welcomed into Yorkshire society—even London society, God forbid—but the war had made me an unmarried, landholding businesswoman. *I wouldn't be such a person, Mummy, if the war hadn't come ... but it did, and like it or not, I have to live in the world it created. And so do you.* More than anything else, perhaps, that heartfelt plea made her understand my plight. Afterwards she began to cry sadly."

"If you remember, I suggested limiting our environs to London and further points south. Seems 'Mummy' agrees."

"That's why I wanted to surprise you. Why I'm here: let the dalliance go forth, my honourable sir!"

Whereupon she raised a determined right arm straight into the air as if announcing a royal edict. I laughed, but Cobbie thought we wanted something and came running over. Without hesitation, Helena smiled and ordered another bottle of champagne. Just part and parcel, I thought, of being a poised, smooth and confident woman.

"You realise don't you, William, our clandestine meetings in London are only temporary? I'm determined for you to see Yorkshire and be introduced to Mummy. Absolutely determined. We shall sit by the fire in Ure Manor House and drink martinis together. Promise?"

Not knowing how to respond, I skirted the issue.

"Does she know how I earn a living?"

"I told her, darling. You're not in the underworld or something. I'm not ashamed. And neither should you be!"

"I'm not embarrassed or ashamed, it's just people's initial impression of jazzmen is up there with their reaction to the sharp pong of a stinky French cheese like Époisses de Bourgogne."

"Love that cheese! Agree it's smelly, but the lingering aftertaste is so delightful. It was Napoleon's favourite, you know. Similar to jazz, I guess. People may not like hearing it initially, but after a couple doses, rhythm and syncopation consume their minds and bodies."

"Never appreciated the connection between smelly cheese and jazz."

"William, I'm trying to convince you it'll work."

"It's not me you have to convince—it's your mother. So, how'd she react?"

"You're not going to like it much. Said jazzmen are similar to magpies, always going after the brightest object. When I lose my lustre—whatever that refers to—you'll move on to someone else, someone shinier."

"Should be happy I'm a magpie, then … won't be around long. Gone before Robbie returns. Least I know finally how *'Mummy'* feels. I can relax now. Wonderful."

"Don't be angry. I'm hoping my 'lustre', as Mummy says, never fades in your eyes. You'll charm her as you've charmed Beatrice Joy and Evie. And you're forgetting something else: Mummy is American, one hundred percent. She may 'act' British, but the thoughts that lie deep within her soul are all American."

"Not worried about you becoming dull, Helena. Impossible, I'd say. As for the American bit, you know I harbour ambivalent feelings about the place. There's lots of beauty but there's also lots of crass vulgarity and, from what little I've read, the recent burgeoning mass commercialism will ruin it forever. I've remained in Europe for a reason. It wasn't by accident, you understand. It wasn't a post-war whim. So ...."

"So, being American won't clinch it. I understand. Then you'll win her over with your infectious personality. I'll liquor her up and you play a mournful tune. That should do it."

I wanted to continue the discussion but Evie approached the table.

"I always pay band members if they play beyond the time specified in their contract. Two musicians have prior engagements but the pianist and bass player will remain if, and only if I can persuade. you. So, what'll it be? Enough of an enticement? The floor's yours if you want it."

"Come on, William. It's half-four, no one from The Savoy's here or will be in the next ninety minutes or so. I'd love, absolutely love, to hear you."

The lure was immense. To relive my Paris days. To play hot jazz to an adoring audience. To make the music mine. Shouldn't have done it. The Savoy told me not to. But one rarely does what they're told, do they? Remembered camping in the Ohio Valley during the muggy summer with my father and became infected with poison ivy. The itch bordered on the unbearable but he insisted I not scratch it. To do so would only open the wound, he said, further spreading the poison. Didn't listen. Gave into temptation and scratched. The relief was instant. And, oh, it felt comforting. Had to stop eventually, of course. And when I looked at the infected area a bit later it had become even for virulent, the itch more intense, just as he said. So, I became more miserable. Playing at The Forty-Three would cause a slightly different itch but one that only could be satisfied by more playing at The Forty-Three. An immense, temporary pleasure that could jeopardise my employment. A Faustian bargain, for sure. Smiled at Helena, stood up, placed the case on the chair and unlocked it.

"Evie, will you introduce me to the boys?"

"My pleasure, Mr Travers. My *deepest* pleasure. Thank you."

Helena, giddy with anticipation, stood up and kissed me.

"I'll finally hear my jazzman the way he wants to be heard, where he wants to be heard. Thank you."

While I assembled my instrument, asked the pianist if he'd warm up the audience with 'Kitten on the Keys'. Didn't want guests hearing a void of silence. Being a fine jazz musician, he knew it. After hearing the first sharp ping of a single key I harkened back to Skeeter's solo performance at Sara and Gerald Murphy's house on the Right Bank. What times we had, I thought, what *damn good* times we had. What could have been, I thought. What could have been. The crowd didn't mind the songs I played were leftovers from Paris: 'Tiger Rag', 'Whispering' and 'Avalon'. Offered a few new ones too, like 'Sheik of Araby', which everyone particularly enjoyed. As I gazed toward the back wall I saw where Meyrick's Merry Maids had suspended their 'hostess' duties, deciding instead to dance together, to laugh together and make a grand time of it. Closed with two melancholy pieces I had relied on in Montparnasse: 'Poor Butterfly' and 'Meditation' from Massenet's *Thaïs*. Didn't know if the crowd had sore feet, were heavily pissed or painfully bored but throughout both numbers they stood still, they stared and they listened. The trio received a heartfelt round of applause when finished. Caught a glimpse of Helena, sitting alone at our table and beaming with pride. She smiled and blew a kiss. Didn't know for certain, but got the feeling I'd made her evening.

As I returned to my table to put away the sax it dawned on me how bored I'd become by the strict tempo, muted orchestrations and balanced instrumentation demanded by The Savoy. Had to cut short any further 'treasonous' thoughts as guests came over, shook my hand, patted me on the shoulder and asked where else I performed. Told them where they could 'see' me—and others—but we wouldn't be playing this kind of jazz. *Don't think they'd let me through the front door. Lack the accent, love. Sorry. Drop those posh surroundings and sign up here with Meyrick. Don't get none better, Yank.* Received encouragement also from the opposite end of the social spectrum—the rich, well born and the good— we've all experienced them, men with signet rings on their littlest finger and, of course, the sleek, slithering representatives of the Bright Young Things. *I say, are your services available for a private function at my country estate in Wiltshire? Could Mummy hire you for my coming out fete on Wilton Crescent in Belgravia?* I replied happily that I could but only on certain months of the year. I offered each my calling card and left it to fate.

"The Forty-Three and I need another dose of you and your jazz sooner rather than later, Mr Travers. Any chance of that happening?"

"Best I can promise is three weeks in August, Evie. That's the only time, except for January, when I'm not tethered to The Savoy. Will that suit?"

"Seven weeks out of fifty-two. Well, that's a little better than fifteen percent, isn't it? I'm buying it, then. Come around late afternoon one day soon, Mr Travers, and we'll put pen to paper."

Cobbie graciously had brought another bottle so I sat down to enjoy it. Helena smiled, took my hand and kissed it.

"Knew these fingers were special; didn't realise they're unique, too."

"Yeah, funny how special *and* unique they became after decades of practising hour after hour after hour."

"There's that wonderful cynicism shining through. What I want to ask, William, is why did you tell Evie you only could play three weeks in August, not four?"

"Ah … thinking about asking permission to spend a warm, luscious week with you in Yorkshire. Unless you object."

"You'd never have to ask my permission, darling. That will be lovely, absolutely lovely … and tense. I'll make all kinds of exciting plans—walking, picnicking— maybe even a few auto trips. But I must warn you: a warm summer in England, especially Yorkshire, is largely imaginary. You're in for a surprise."

"Not as surprised as when the matriarch of the Bolton-

Leigh family meets me, I assure you."

"You win on that score. We've got a few months to prepare her. Exactly how? Not sure It'll come to us."

Chapter Fifteen

A telegram arrived the evening before my departure. Helena recommended that instead of travelling to Askrigg under Scar as planned, I disembark a few stops earlier, at Redmire. She'd pick me up there, no problem. Didn't offer a reason.

The trip was uneventful. Slept most of the way. As the train entered the Dales, I realised I was seeing quintessential England. Something most Americans never experience. The black and white images in my high school geography textbook and junior year's 'Review of English History' had blossomed into full colour. Lush green fields full of grazing sheep divided by four-foot-high stone walls, lacking mortar or cement. Once the porter secured the coach door, I stepped onto the station platform and was hit with the pungent yet sweet smell of manure permeating the air. None of that mattered when I saw Helena standing on the other side of the exit gate, smiling and looking radiant.

"Welcome to North Riding, William. Let me show you *my* world."

I dropped my bags. Gave her a firm hug and a meaningful kiss.

"Hope no one recognises you in this village. Could be embarrassing. There'd be talk before I'd even met 'Mummy'."

"Been spared. She travelled to Edinburgh with friends. Said she can now comfortably deny ever knowing you visited. All gossipy talk will be directed toward me alone."

"If it wasn't so heartless I'd say it's almost canny."

"Simply beyond being concerned, William. I won't

blatantly flaunt us in front of the all-too-numerous 'upstanding people of Askrigg under Scar'—that's why I asked you to disembark here in Redmire—but I won't conceal it either. I'm an independent woman of the 1920s, not some Pollyanna heroine of a late Victorian novel."

Felt sorry for her after she'd finished. Could only imagine the admonishing words that had been used against her. Helena didn't deserve it. It's as if her mother, still filled with disappointment beyond grief, clung desperately to Helena—not to regain a sense of composure or a modicum of happiness, but to diminish Helena's expectations and opportunities for a fulfilling life.

"Well, I won't have her unexcused absence preoccupy me. Will ruin our time together. Just not willing to give into her; if I do, she wins, we lose."

After turning on the ignition she leaned over and kissed me. Her green eyes glistened over with moisture.

"Thank you, darling. You're a good man. A man that's good for me ... how novel."

"You make me better than I am, Helena. Believe me. Like your driving cap. Fetching. You wearing it, not the cap."

"Well, I'm impressed with your Yorkshire flat cap. How'd that come about?"

"Saw a newspaper article with a photo of the Prince of Wales wearing one. Thought it looked nifty. Asked around, learned it's somewhat unique to Yorkshire so I thought it perfect: *a wonderful way to impress you with my newly found sartorial elegance.* Happened by Lock & Co. on St James Street one afternoon and that was that. Hope I don't look rubbish wearing it."

"Rubbish? Not at all. Very natty. Suits you. And, coming from Lock & Co., that's simply the oldest hatter in all England. Leave it to you to find it!"

"Glad you like it. Cock it at a jaunty angle on purpose. Fits with the attitude of a jazzman, I think."

"Actually, you look like a local wearing it. Can't wait until someone hears you speak. That'll throw 'em. Americans seldom venture to the north."

Before putting the car in gear, Helena secured her cap and donned a pair of driving goggles. She caught me looking at her a bit oddly.

"We British have a saying: *make do and mend.* Probably didn't notice the driver's side lacks a windscreen. A pheasant flew into it a few months back and cracked it. So now you can appreciate that, while I excel at making do, I'm not too quick at mending."

"Reminds me of my days flying. Had a similar pair. Although I didn't look as attractive. Resembled more of a squashed fly, I'd say."

"Oh, William. Honestly."

The drive was short. Within fifteen minutes, Helena turned left onto a steep unpaved drive. To the right was Ure Manor House, a solidly crafted stone house covered in lush ivy. It dated from the late 1600s. Large—almost walk-through—bay windows, extending from the ground to the first floor, dominated the middle of the house. The main entrance was hidden on the right-hand side behind a row of ancient but well-tended boxwood plants. Perhaps ostentatious by rural Yorkshire standards, it was by no means attention seeking. Got the feeling that, at its heart, Ure Manor was the epicentre of a working farm. Fit the surrounding landscape beautifully. After getting out of the car I determined the house faced south, offering extended sunlight and a panoramic view of the River Ure five hundred yards or so away.

"The high, elongated fell beyond the river is Addlebrough. It's over 1,500 feet high, William. Ruins of two ancient settlements lie on the other side. Reached the summit a few times when younger. A bit challenging now, though."

"Another fine example of your British politeness. What you actually mean is: *too difficult for a guy with a gimp leg to attempt*."

"Suppose I am. Yes. Must be careful. You've become too perceptive of our subtle inferences. Let's get inside for tea and comfort. I'll take the suitcase, entrusting you with the horn."

"Sounds perfect."

"Just curious, why'd you bring the tenor sax?"

"Two reasons, actually. Thought I'd introduce your mother to a bit of calm jazz, and didn't want to leave in the flat for fear of it getting nicked. Mrs Joy's practically deaf. She'd couldn't hear if someone who doesn't belong found a way *to* belong in my apartment."

"Since Mummy's bailed, you can play for me then, if that's all right."

"Wouldn't mind at all, Helena. Not at all."

I was taken aback as I walked through the door. A short, wood-panelled hallway led to the drawing-room off to the left. A large, almost walk-in fireplace and marble mantelpiece dominated the room. Fine oil paintings of Yorkshire hunting scenes, pheasants, grouse, and various breeds of sheep hung on the walls. In the far corner was a burl walnut desk. Above it hung what appeared to be the depiction of a military campaign of some sort. I walked over for a closer look. Helena stood inquisitively by the mantel.

"An original 1845 lithograph titled *Surrender of Cornwallis*, which I'm sure any self-respecting Yank knows happened in Yorktown, Virginia in 1781. Printed by J Baillis of New York."

"Why in heaven's name does your family ... obviously something your mother brought over from the States?"

"No, it belonged to Father. See the profile of the British officer on the far right, on the edge of the print? That's Father's great-great-grandfather—Thomas Bolton-Leigh. Was a colonel in the 19th Regiment of Foot, which through time became the Green Howards, stationed in Richmond. Same regiment Robbie served with in Russia."

"I'm ... I'm impressed, to say the least. What a historical connection. And the irony ... your mother coming to Britain, and you being half American. Intertwining world history with family history amazes me."

"Of course, the biggest irony: Cornwallis wasn't present during the surrender to Washington. He delegated the job to his underlings. So the print, while interesting, is historically inaccurate."

"The ultimate in artistic licence. Suppose it's served its purpose, though, as long as Americans felt good about it."

"More idealistic cynicism?"

"Couldn't travel this far without firing off a few barbs, now, could I?"

"Let me show you the guest room so you can unpack. I'll have the fire going and some tea prepared when you return. How does that suit?"

"Suits perfectly."

She took the suitcase, leaving me the sax. Up the stairs we trotted. *She* trotted; I bobbled along. The master bedroom was on the left, positioned to absorb the sunlight offered by the bay windows. Further down the hall were the untouched rooms of her brothers. Eerily sad and depressing. The air in both rooms remained thick with the smell of death. The desk calendar in one room displayed October 1915, the last time, I suppose, one of her unfortunate brothers had visited on leave. At the far end on the right was Helena's room. Directly across the narrow hallway was the lone guest room—my room for the next six days. She encouraged me to relax and take my time unpacking and reorganising. I sat on a comfortable chair, absorbing the atmosphere as Helena glided through the room. She came over, sat on my lap and gave me a wonderfully slow kiss.

"Glad you're here, William. And I'm most happy we're alone. No one can touch us. No one can bother us. What'd I say in your flat several months ago: *To be alone, against the others. Left to ourselves. No rules. No intrusions.* So, for the next five or six days, the wider world doesn't exist. We're immune from outside invasion. See you downstairs soon. And please don't dally, darling."

"Time is tight. Not wasting any of it."

I sat in the chair, absorbing the room's décor, replete with arts and crafts desk and bookcases and William Morris wallpaper. The four-poster bed looked inviting. Atop a small but elegantly carved chest of drawers sat a black-and-white photograph housed in an Edwardian silver frame. I walked over, picked it up and stared at it for what seemed a long time. In the bottom right corner, someone—probably Mrs Bolton-Leigh—had handwritten: *August 1912, the day prior to Helena's departure for Bryn Mawr.* The image reflected confidence in the future, and pride of family, unaware that within four years death's shadow would claim three-fifths of the people depicted. Helena's face, radiant as ever, was a bit rounder and fuller, the chiselled cheekbones not having yet appeared. Her father looked dapper and content with his wife and progeny. The boys, George and Edward, were strapping young lads. Can easily visualise them in uniform, resembling in no small way my dead buddies from the Kicking Mule. And Helena's 'Mummy,' sitting comfortably on a large wicker chair appearing poised, proper and happy—a world far removed from her bitterness of today.

After changing my shirt and freshening up, I started down the hallway. Curiosity got the better of me as I approached Helena's room. Thought it rude to enter so I stood in the doorway, taking in whatever was easily visible. What a warm and feminine room, I thought. It smelled luscious. A white and blue silk canopy bed dominated the space, along with a dressing table complete with a low-lying seat and large mirror. Petite perfume bottles covered one side, while an ivory-coloured hairbrush and comb and a silver framed picture of a black cat occupied the other. To the right of the bed was her chest of drawers, home to several framed photographs. Artworks adorning the walls comprised pressed flowers, Pre-Raphaelite prints and a framed broadside from London's famous 1910 'Manet and the Post-Impressionists' exhibition.

I entered the drawing room to the sound of a crackling fire and the sight of Helena lounging comfortably on a small sofa.

"What'd you think of my room?"

"My room's most comfortable. Truly."

"No, William, *my* room. I know you and I know you took a quick gander, now, didn't you?"

"Yeah, you win. Sorry. Only peeked though. Didn't cross the threshold. Nosiness took over, I suppose. Looked nice. Reflects you and your interests perfectly. Look forward to you identifying the people in the photos."

"Come over, sit by me. I decided to forego tea. Poured you a double neat and a glass of, guess what? Champagne for me!"

"You read my mind. Had so much tea on the train I'm floating on the stuff."

"You realise, don't you, we have the house to ourselves? Totally to ourselves. Really. No one else. I gave our cook, Cora, the week off. She's the only one who knows about your visit, but she's a good lass. Won't say a word. Been with the family a long time, since I was an infant, actually. Felt concerned for us so she's left several game pies, an apple crumble, a bakewell tart and some biscuits. She's also visited the shops, so there's plenty of food we can prepare ourselves. Whatever and whenever, if ever we like."

"Sounds fine by me. You know I'm not too big an eater but certainly can prepare a hearty meal when needed. No problem."

"Oh, and our once-a-week cleaner, Mavis, who lives across the river in Worton, is up north on holiday—only by chance. So, she won't be bothering us either. She's unaware of your visit, thank goodness. Bit of a village gossip, if you know what I mean. No need of a telephone with Mavis around!"

"Good. We, and especially you after I leave, don't need her venomous words circulating about the village."

Took a sip of my drink and gazed around the room, absorbing its décor, its casualness and well-worn charm.

"Room's warm and comfortable, Helena, and *very* relaxing."

"It's in a state. Depressing actually. Everything's torn and tattered. Used to be fresh, full of life and uplifting conversation and laughter when George and Edward were around. All that remains is Mummy's maudlin comments on about everything—except the weather, surprisingly. Doesn't even discuss our horrible, rain-filled winter months. It's where I adjourn to have a drink with her after a long day's work—checking the fields and the sheep, answering various queries, inventorying storage barns, and finishing mounds of paperwork in my office. A tiring day, for sure. As I told you when we first met, Mummy's fine and jolly handling two martinis but after that— awful, simply awful."

"I empathise with her, actually, but only to a point. Everything and everybody that meant something in her world before 1914 is gone, except you, Helena. She should cherish and love you completely. You're all that's left. Baffles me why she can't appreciate that, to understand that."

"I've ceased caring or worrying about the whole damn mess. That's why I'm so elated you're here. In my house. In my world. Anyway, to talk about something more enjoyable. This usually is the time of day that Elgar visits."

"Elgar? Who's Elgar, the milkman? Thought they delivered before dawn."

"No, no, silly. Elgar's my little black cat. Named after the composer. Someone deposited him on our front step a few weeks before the war ended. Felt sorry for him so I took him in, against Mummy's wishes, I might add. Thought nurturing a new life would purge—however slight—my preoccupation with death and loss."

"Naming cats after well-known musicians and artists must be in vogue nowadays. After bumping into Sara and Gerald Murphy outside Le Meurice, before leaving Paris, I saw a black cat emerge from the Tuileries, cross Rue de Rivoli and sit patiently outside the hotel waiting for the doorman. When the door opened, I heard him welcome the adventuresome cat—whom he addressed as Monet, believe it or not."

"How cute … Monet. Bet the staff feeds him foie gras. Although Elgar spends most of his day outside, he loves visiting in late afternoon. Relaxes on a cushion by the desk in my office when the weather's wet and miserable. And, of course, late in the evening he finds his way to my bedroom. Something I hope you'll replicate."

"But I'm in the guest room."

"Oh, that, that's for appearances, for Mummy's sake. Since she went north to avoid implicating herself, I thought I'd extract a couple pages from her self-titled but unpublished manual, *Deception*. Your belongings will remain in the guest room while you enjoy the comforts and warmth of me in my room. That way, when Mummy asks whether you used the guest room, I can say 'yes' and not be telling a fib."

"What about the bed? Have to appear to have been slept in."

"I think we can manage *that* nicely, don't you? No problem."

"All fine with me, but how will Elgar treat an intruder?"

"You've seen the bed. Plenty of room for three, don't you think?"

"Hope he doesn't snore."

"Elgar and I should be concerned more about your thrashing to and fro. A genuine flipping kipper!"

"Residue from the war, I suppose. Doubt it ever will subside totally. By chance, did you hear an agreement was reached a few months back at the Washington Naval Conference to limit ...?"

"Stop! You're bringing the other world into ours, William. And I don't want it. Please?"

"Sorry."

After refilling our glasses and stoking the fire, Helena asked if I wanted to see her office, located a short distance down the hall from the drawing room and before the kitchen. I was struck, upon entering, by the imposing roll-top desk in the centre and the green, tufted armchair. Obvious relics from her father's era. Room was filled with leather-bound financial ledgers, perfectly aligned on fine oak shelves including correspondence files and agricultural publications dating from the 1870s. A plethora of blue ribbons, tarnished trophy cups, and framed photographs filled spaces where, I imagined, gaps had existed decades earlier.

It struck me that Helena was centre stage in most of the photos—well, she *and* sheep. The images covered her entire life, from when she was a small girl to recent images during the war years.

"That's father and me at my first market day in Hawes. I was only four years old. And I loved it. Suppose that's when sheep farming first entered my bloodstream,

William, and it's never left. Father often told his fellow farmers, probably only half-jokingly, *Helena's the best man I've got tending my sheep."*

"That independent ruggedness has never left you."

"Doubt it will, William. I doubt it ever will."

But it wasn't only seeing a four-year-old Helena that stood out. It was the manner in which the men dressed—tweed suits, ties and flat caps. The auctioneer was dapper as well. And the sheep, well, they looked spotless, well groomed, clean, and raring to go—wherever that may have been. Other photos included a grown-up Helena with her flowing red hair, winning a cup at the 1911 Wensleydale show. She beamed with pride, standing alongside her father and the prized animal.

"That was my last show with Father. Travelled to America the next summer to start at Bryn Mawr and, as you know, two years later he died and the war started. End of an era, I suppose. That's why I keep that photo and cup in such a conspicuous place. Reminds me of ..."

She stopped, came over and hugged me.

"But you're here now, William. We've begun something fresh. Something meaningful to both of us. We're happy. That's all that matters."

"Don't think I realised—in fact, I know I didn't—how much farming and the Yorkshire earth means to you, Helena. It *is* your life, isn't it? Defines you absolutely."

"Cheltenham and Bryn Mawr worked me over, rolled me about and polished me to a level so I could thrive in London and elsewhere, for which I'll be eternally grateful. Not intimidated at all, as you know, easily interacting with England's rich and well born, but my heart—my soul—belongs in Yorkshire. It's where I draw my sustenance."

Got up early the following morning. By the time I had pulled myself together and gone downstairs, Helena already had packed a picnic basket, selecting a few bits left by Cora—grouse and venison pies, a jar of gherkins and two bakewell tarts. Helena added two bottles of red wine, which she assured me were for digestive purposes only.

"I know how you *love* our full English breakfast, William, so I didn't make it. Fancy anything in particular?"

"No, black coffee and a slice of your wonderful bread with Yorkshire butter would suit me down to my ankles. Thank you."

"Last night was wonderful, William. And see, Elgar didn't mind at all."

"No, no, he didn't. Rather enjoyed it, too. He's a good lad. If my London garret wasn't so confining, I think I'd adopt a cat. Just wouldn't be fair, especially with the hours I keep."

"Make sure you bring your saxophone. Where I'm taking you lends itself to romantic playing. No one's around. We'll be on our own, surrounded by history. Got a small surprise before we reach our destination, though. So, if you're ready to go, we'd best get a wiggle on."

I hopped into the car, and off we went. It was a short but beautiful drive through rolling hills and green fields, with the occasional hare darting across the road and pheasants running harum-scarum. We descended a steep, unpaved road and to our immediate front was her surprise destination: Semer Water.

"It's one of only two natural lakes in the Yorkshire Dales, William. I visit often in the summer to swim."

"Swim? Swim? Which of my legs are you pulling,

Helena, the good one or the gimp one?"

"Neither of them. I'm wearing my swimming costume underneath! Don't worry, you can wear shorts."

"Oh, I'm not worried—because *I'm* not going in. Too cold for my tastes and my commonsense. What is it, sixty degrees?"

"No, this time of the year, it's about 13 degrees Celsius, or 55 degrees Fahrenheit. You guessed close."

"Five degrees cooler isn't close. Might be, if throwing hand grenades in combat—but not swimming. I'll sit on one of these huge rocks at the water's edge and watch you frolic about."

She approached the water wearing nothing but her woollen swimming costume. Made her way into the water until only her head remained visible. Then, suddenly, she started twisting and turning so much so she disappeared entirely. Became concerned. Thought I'd have to go in after her. But she resurfaced, gleefully holding her swimming costume in her right hand, high above her head.

"Here, catch!"

Whereupon she threw an almost perfect pitch, landing right in front of me. Had no idea she owned such a strong right arm.

"The girls and I loved playing baseball at Bryn Mawr. Enjoyed being the pitcher the most."

"I can tell. Excellent delivery. Gives new meaning to 'spitball'."

"Don't be rude."

Having had her fill after about ten minutes, Helena emerged from the water, making her way toward the shore. Although she was shivering, her arms remained firmly by her side, her cold body displaying all the natural signs of its ingratitude.

"I may be half-American genetically, William, but to be honest—and because right now there's nowhere else to go—I'm all Yorkshire."

"I can see you are. Definitely. And congratulations."

"Come on, *tout de suite*. Fetch my towel, please."

"Oh, I don't know. Viewing you in this peaceful setting, geese flying in a perfect wedge formation, fish jumping in the distance—magical, truly magical. Want to relish it a bit longer."

"William! Now! A warm towel. Please? I'll be yours forever."

"Promise?"

"Promise. Now … a towel, please?"

After drying and dressing herself and enjoying hot tea from a flask, Helena suggested we best get going. The landscape changed soon after leaving the quaint village of Hawes. The hills became steeper and rockier, the road more twisted. Fewer stone walls meant sheep grazed openly, ignoring autos on the road and making the trip somewhat dangerous. Most noticeable was the broad, wide-open horizon, void of trees and vegetation. Could see for miles. Helena manoeuvred the machine with aplomb. She wasn't fussed about not having a windscreen. Seemed to relish it, in fact, embracing the challenge. After an hour, Helena slowed the car and turned left. Facing us were the ruins of what appeared to be a castle in the middle of absolutely nowhere.

"This is Pendragon Castle, William. Legend says it was built in the fifth century by King Arthur's father, Uther Pendragon, but there's no pure evidence. Do know one famous owner, though—Sir Hugh de Morville who, with three others, murdered Thomas Becket. Isn't it romantic?"

"Becket's murder or the castle?"

"You're impossible. The castle silly, the castle. The perfect place for our picnic, for drinking wine, for playing your sax and for whatever enters our minds."

"Love the isolation. Heightens the imagination."

Although much of the surrounding walls had collapsed centuries earlier, we decided the castle's interior worked to our advantage. Could conceal ourselves amongst the dilapidated bits and not be bothered by the possibility of other encroaching romantics. Helena's woollen blanket and the plush grass offered the warmth and comfort I craved. Cora's venison pie was wonderful, thick with meat and oozing with spicy flavour. And my face expressed nothing but delight while devouring her bakewell tart, a pastry I'd never enjoyed before. The wine Helena brought was perfect: two bottles of an excellent and not too overpowering 1914 Bordeaux, Chateau Pichon-Longueville.

"I want to remember this day, William. What you're wearing. What you look like. Where we were. Want you to remember me in the same way."

"Should I grab a pencil and paper?"

Helena didn't reply, only walked to the car and opened the boot. Returned holding a Kodak camera.

"Brought something better."

She insisted one picture be me sitting on a large rock with the sax resting comfortably across my lap. The other—me standing with the instrument leaning comfortably against my right leg.

"It's the incongruity of it all, William. And besides, now that it's assembled it ensures you'll play something."

She took several snaps. I smiled sometimes and

looked contented—because I was. Other times I acted troubled and lost, the blank stare visible on the faces of veterans that roamed Paris and London. Then it was my turn. Leaned the instrument against its case and took the camera. Asked if she'd stand alongside the crumbling walls instead of sitting. Wanted the frame filled with as much of her as possible. Placed the camera up to my eye. She looked nice. Her brown herringbone skirt didn't conceal her figure, accentuating both the length of her legs and thin ankles. She unbuttoned her dark green tweed waistcoat and folded the right-hand side back underneath her lower arm, placing her hand on her hip, looking confidently into the camera. After I snapped a few, she moved her head alternatively to the left then right so I could capture her profile. Her final pose was meant as a joke. In actuality, it reflected a casual sophistication and a provocative sensuality. While facing left she took her right hand, gently pulled back her hair and raised her face slightly upward toward the camera. When I'd finished, she started laughing,

"See what you bring out in me? Acting like a thespian. Honestly. What would Mummy think?"

"She's not here and, from what you say, sounds as if she doesn't think much at all."

"Don't be rude. Now go and get your horn and play me something. Please?"

I started with Satie's 'Gnossienne No. 1'. Inspired by the myth of Theseus, Ariadne and the Minotaur at Knossos in Crete. Sent me adrift whenever I heard it. Had a similar effect on Helena. After hearing a few measures, she stretched out on the blanket, raised her arms up over her head and gazed into the sky. I followed with Satie's other alluring piece, 'Gymnopédie No. 1'. Don't know if it was the wine or the music but halfway through Helena got up, removed her waist-coat and started dancing in an ethereal, medieval-like manner; oblivious to my presence, consumed by reflective passion. When finished she stood pensively by an opening in the wall that faced the Eden Valley. I walked over, put my arms around her waist and kissed her cheek.

"You have a most expressive way of evoking the mood. Sent me away, far, far away, if you hadn't noticed.

"I noticed. Received a similar response when I played them in Montparnasse and in the brothel."

She turned and kissed me.

"Look at that view, William. Gorgeous, isn't it? There's yet another legend: Uther Pendragon wanted to divert the course of the River Eden to fill the castle's moat, but he failed. Father taught us a rhyme about it, something, I suppose, that's been passed down through generations of Yorkshire families: *Let Uther Pendragon do what he can, Eden will run where Eden ran.*"

Didn't say anything but wondered if this little ditty could be a harbinger. Human desire is a weak competitor against long-held expectations, especially in Yorkshire. I dismissed such thoughts after Helena led me to the blanket and began unbuttoning her blouse.

Our days together were wonderful—eclectic and filled with romance. Unbeknownst to me, Helena was an avid angler. She'd been fly fishing in the River Ure since she was eight. Because it was a mere five hundred yards or so from the house, I walked the distance with minimal pain. She lugged the picnic basket while I carried her array of fishing kit. When asked about my proficiency, I explained my skills and style mirrored that of Mark Twain's loveable character, Huckleberry Finn: trying a line to my big toe, lying quietly along the banks of Cincinnati's Mill Creek, pulling a straw hat over my eyes to block the sun and waiting for a gentle tug. I *was* rewarded using this method—but not often.

Her skill seemed unmatched to my untrained eye. After intensive back-and-forth wrist motion, she cast the line slightly above the waterline, tantalising any unsuspecting trout below. Seemed Helena was reeling in her catch seconds after the fly landed gently on the water's surface. Caught four trout in twenty minutes. Waded in water above her knees to catch the last one. Wanted to ask if this was necessary or whether she only trying to impress me, but I didn't.

The next day we travelled two hours by auto to the Royal Baths of Harrogate, a popular Turkish-style bath facility founded twenty-five years earlier. She thought I'd find the sauna's hot temperatures and surrounding environs relaxing.

"One small problem though: we can't enjoy it together. The sauna and steam rooms are segregated: assigned hours for men; assigned hours for women."

"So, what will the other one of us do, roam aimlessly through Harrogate's Valley View Gardens?"

"Don't be ridiculous. You know me, I wouldn't waste time like that. Scheduled a massage while the other is in the sauna."

"Sounds wonderful, except, you have any idea what men are like without women around? Sure as hell hope the sauna room isn't crowded with a gaggle of old men relaxing and farting."

"Oh, William, honestly. How crude. If there are, ignore them. Concentrate instead on the facility's beautiful Moorish design, the colourful arches, the glazed brickwork and the arabesque-decorated ceilings."

"I'll try, but that's a big ask."

"Are you, or will you feel, self-conscious about the leg?"

"Four years out, I've accepted its grotesqueness. Probably will bother others, though."

Helena was correct. Had a peaceful, relaxing day. The masseuse was a sympathetic young lady who treated my leg with a discreet tenderness of touch, which I appreciated. Said she wasn't taken aback in the slightest. In the first weeks of the war her fiancé lost his right arm up to and including bits of his shoulder, and two fingers on the left hand. Her revelation soothed my weary conscience. Also reaped the benefits of an underused sauna and steam room. Only three men, including myself, shared the ornately-designed space. No idle chit-chat, no gaseous noises or fumes, only intense heat surrounded by quiet.

When we met in the lobby, Helena suggested we re-energise at a newly opened tea room called Bettys.

"It's an easy walk up the hill to the town centre. Heard wonderful comments. The pastries are to die for, apparently. The founder's from Switzerland."

"Fine by me, but he'll have to go some to surpass Cora's bakewell tarts."

We crested the hill and approached the town centre. A sign was posted in the middle of a beautiful flower-filled garden: *Future Site of Harrogate's Memorial to the Fallen.* Scheduled to be dedicated sometime next year, in 1923, the artist's rendering depicted a stone obelisk on a square plinth. Names of the dead would be inscribed on two bronze plaques attached to the base so they could be viewed at eye level. We paused. I didn't say anything.

Had nothing to add about monuments of mourning. Earlier comments on the Cenotaph and Unknown Warrior had been enough, I thought. Helena didn't need to hear them again.

Bettys was a revelation. Rivalled any pastries, cakes or tarts in Montparnasse. Helena admitted, a bit sheepishly, the quality even surpassed Cora's sublime efforts.

"Wouldn't confess it to her, though. She'd be devastated."

"Oh, you can't. You can't. And being that you're in the middle of nowhere, Cora's delicacies are damn fine. She's talented. Lucky to have her."

"Oh, I am. Mummy adores her too. Cora won't hear a 'peep' from me. Don't worry. Promise."

Woke next morning, I thought at an early hour, but only Elgar and I remained in bed. A note lay on Helena's pillow: *Darling, I've left before dawn to make my rounds—checking the sheep, inventorying silage, overseeing the dipping—the basic joys of managing the business. Have issues with a few ewes so the vet is calling in before 10 am. You'll have the house all to yourself—well, Elgar will be there, too. Promise to return by 2 pm. Enjoy yourself. Loved last evening. Bloody marvellous. H.*

She's one dedicated woman, I thought. Serious-minded about her business. But then, she has to be. She must be. She's alone. Nobody else gives a damn. The burdens, the failures and whatever successes belong only to her. And, from what she's said, there's a line ten-deep of men hoping, waiting for failure. Admire her tenacity, her gumption. Rare even to find men possessing such attributes.

Occupied myself by doing as little as possible. Weather was lovely and warm, so I sat outside with a coffee, admiring the view. Elgar had taken to me for some reason, finding a welcoming spot on my lap. While I enjoyed a few sips of coffee he fell asleep, purring and shaking his paws in unison. Fifteen minutes later he woke, gazed at me, yawned, stretched and then toddled off for an adventure in adjacent woodland. Went into the drawing room, started a fire and found a book on the burl walnut desk that had been left open: *If Winter Comes* by ASM Hutchinson. Sounded a bit saucy so I gave it a go. After two hours I got the overall gist: a war veteran returns to an unhappy marriage, a divorce ensues and an unwed mother commits suicide. Didn't reflect my tastes but, if the back cover can be believed, it was a bestseller in England and America. Concluded that Mrs Bolton-Leigh had purchased the book. Couldn't imagine Helena surrendering to such melodrama.

Sheep issues took precedence, causing Helena to be later than expected. Wasn't bothered. Her dedication to work impressed me as much as her appreciation of me. Be selfish to accept one and not the other.

"Don't worry, Helena. Enjoyed the fire, a double neat and a casual read of *If Winter Comes*. An unexpected delight of yours?"

"Honestly. That's Mummy's tosh. Couldn't be bothered. But the returning veteran got me to think if Robbie ..."

She stopped herself midway. Lowered her head and apologised.

"How could I be so unkind? That's not like me at all. Forgive me, please?"

"Shall we have a double neat on it then?"

"Stayed away from Scotch since Bryn Mawr days. Bloody well time I get back on the saddle, don't you think? So, yes, a double, please."

On my last evening, Helena thought it'd be enjoyable to visit her favourite pub, The King's Head in Askrigg under Scar. Said the food was good and conversation convivial but the real draw, the reason she kept returning, was the owners: Douglas and Marlene Maria McClurg.

"Theirs is such a romantic story, William. Met when Douglas served with the 12th Battalion, Tank Corps, as part of the force occupying Germany along the Rhine. A newspaper clipping framed in the pub shows his tank on the embankment near Cologne's Hohenzollern Bridge. He's from Londonderry, and Marlene Maria, believe this or not, is from a small village outside Cologne, in Westphalia."

"How could that have happened?"

"Chocolate."

"They … like … chocolate?"

"Yes and no. She's from the village—Bergisch-Gladbach—something like that—famous for chocolate, supposedly. And Marlene Maria worked for a small chocolatier. A quaint shop Douglas and his fellow tankers visited a few times. Let me correct that: his buddies went twice. Douglas went whenever he could. His love of chocolate was a ruse. His interest was Marlene."

Arrived the village after a short drive. Helena parked in front of an impressive building, completed in 1678, called Old Hall. All I could think of when seeing the ancient parish church looming nearby was Helena's story about the vicar getting drunk after learning of his wife's infidelity. For some odd reason, we always remember pain and suffering more than happiness. At least I do.

The King's Head was homely and crowded. The village had two other pubs but Helena, and a majority of the village, it seemed, preferred this one. A large fireplace, alive with a crackling fire, dominated the bar area. To the right of the bar was the framed news clipping and photo of Douglas's tank alongside the Rhine. Oak-panelled walls in the dining area added warmth and a quiet formality. A chalkboard on the far wall served as the menu.

"They certainly like their lamb, don't they? Lamb stew, lamb pie, lamb pate, lamb shank, lamb chops, lamb rump, roast rack of lamb ..."

Before Helena could answer, a woman approached. Knew immediately it was Marlene She was thin, of medium height, had short, dark hair styled in a bob and owned a pleasant smile that exuded control and self-confidence. Non-locals, thinking they might get one over because of her attractiveness or foreignness, would fail and fail badly.

"Marlene Marie, I introduce my dear friend, William Travers, from London ... by way of America."

"Helena has high regard for you, your husband and the food here. Thoroughly enjoyed hearing how you met."

"Yes, yes, Helena likes repeating that story. The only good thing that happened during the war."

Could see Marlene was busy and couldn't spare time for idle chit-chat, so I didn't delve deeper.

"The only thing the war did for me was ensuring I wouldn't return to the States."

"Just before you came over, Marlene, William commented on your lamb dishes. It's the house speciality, isn't it?

"It is, yes, yes. Douglas can do more with a lamb bone than any man I've known."

"In that case, I'll try the rump and Helena will have

the roast rack of lamb, Triple M."

"What you mean, 'Triple M'?"

"Your name's Marlene Maria McClurg, correct? Three 'M's', so ... Triple M."

Face soured a bit, but after absorbing my friendly intent, she embraced it.

"I like it. Danke. Danke."

"Bitte schön, Triple M. Bitte schön."

Both looked at me. I shrugged my shoulders.

"Extent of my German. Sorry."

Didn't elaborate how in the barracks and on the flight line we'd alter the expressions to include loads of profanity. A juvenile way to lighten the burden of almost certain death.

"Should be ready in *zwanzig* ... Ah, excuse me, twenty minutes."

Smiled at Helena after Marlene left.

"Must be challenging for her. It is for me, at times, and it's *my* language. Some of it, anyway."

"Glad you clarified that. Lean forward, William. Don't want others to hear. Douglas's training and expertise is pastries. That's what he did in Londonderry before the war. About nine months after acquiring The King's Head, villagers, who had lost a son or spouse in the war, occasionally would find freshly baked bread or cakes or bakewell tarts or some mille-feuille on their doorstep. No explanation, only a note: *'We Shall Remember Them'*. To this day, no one knows who's doing it."

"And he's continued this, four years after the damn thing ended?"

"He has. He has—to those who remain in the area, at least. The Banks family lost their son, William, in the big push two months before the Armistice. Jane Ann Horn lost her husband, John, at the Battle of the Somme. Their daughter, Margaret, who's almost seven now, I guess, never met her father. The Millers lost their son, Thomas, at Armentieres in early 1918. I attended the memorial at St Oswald's a week after his parents received notification. James and Margaret Preston lost their son, Jim, at the Ypres Salient in autumn of 1917. He was a fine lad—schoolteacher at the local day school, sang in St Oswald's choir—he—even held the record for the five-mile run at his college in Leeds. Finished in less than thirty-three minutes or so. I can't remember them all, but there are about eleven others. All have benefited from Douglas's generosity, several times over."

"So, if it's a mystery how do you know about it?"

"Met Marlene one day while walking in the Bottoms. Got talking about the strangeness of our post-war lives—how, why and where we ended up. For some reason, she told me about Douglas's generosity. I promised never to tell. Until now, with you. No one knows, not even Mummy."

"Don't worry. Wouldn't spoil it. Nice of him … *both* of them, actually."

"He'd probably continue even if someone found out. He just doesn't like bringing attention upon himself. Has a tortoise shell exterior, but inside he's a softy. That's probably why Marlene married him."

"So, you and your mother benefit, too?"

"Yes, yes, we do, but I don't utter a word. I told Marlene only to deliver the bread or whatever twice a year to mark their birthdays. Mummy thinks it's sweet. Believes it's the vicar. We received a Victoria sponge cake last year on George's birthday and a Yorkshire curd tart on Edward's."

Halfway through our meal it became apparent that no one—except Marlene Maria, of course—had acknowledged Helena's presence. Not everyone would know her but a few certainly would. And those few were ignoring her.

"Think it's odd no one's spoken to you?"

"Ah, not much. They're nosy enough to want to know, too embarrassed to ask. Don't worry, we're providing them enough hard cheese and gristle to chew on for months."

She paused, put down her knife and fork, scoured the room and took a few sips of wine before returning to her food.

"I'd say there are fifteen or so here that know me. The woman in the distant back corner ... Edith Sparrow. And, let me say, there's no correlation between her surname and her physical size. Pardon my poor manners, William, but she's a pompous, gossipy old tit who's been watching our every move. She'd transcribe our conversations, if closer."

I dropped my napkin and turned my head to catch a glimpse of 'Sparrow Woman'. She *was* a hefty one: untidy, dishevelled and crooked-lipped. A dirt-under-the-fingernails type of person.

"What's the Bible verse from Matthew—*First cast out the beam out of thine own eye; and then shalt thou see clearly to cast out the mote out of thy brother's eye.*"

"Didn't know you were religious. I'm surprised and impressed."

"I'm not, so don't be. A favourite verse of my parents. One of many verses and quotes they made me memorise as a kid. This one stuck, for some reason."

Just then Marlene approached the table, sparing me the

embarrassment of reciting other memorised bits from my age of innocence.

"So, Herr Travers, enjoy dinner?"

"Your rump is gorgeous, Frau McClurg. Absolutely gorgeous."

Helena understood the double entendre. Doubted Marlene Maria did. She took my plate, smiled, turned slightly and slapped her bottom.

"It is nice, isn't it?"

She returned behind the bar. Felt my face turn pepper-red.

"Didn't think she'd be so clever with English, did you? That'll teach you."

The place began to clear while we enjoyed our second cognac. Three couples said hello on their way out. An old farmer—whom Helena said lived across the river in Worton—patted my shoulder: *Don't envy you, lad, but I wish you luck*. Didn't know what he meant exactly: good luck with the gimpy leg, or good luck canoeing in rough waters? Certain it was the latter.

Soon, no one remained but us. While Marlene cleaned the drink glasses and restocked the bar, Douglas sat down and introduced himself. Felt privileged, actually, that he joined us. Had thick black hair, dark blue eyes and was of medium height. His overall physical slightness, I thought, had probably worked to his advantage inside a tank. We shook hands.

"Understand you observed the abattoir from 800 feet. Lucky for you."

"Yes. Yes, I did. But could became part of it soon after being shot down, if I survived the crash."

"Know how to fly before the war?"

"Not at all. Uncle Sam decided—how, I don't know—

that I had an aptitude and, well, that was it. The only thing I'd experienced before the war was reading, analysing literary works, writing papers, playing saxophone and dating sorority girls. Never gave mechanics a thought. Wasn't my strength."

"My 'strength,' as you call it, was being a professional pastry chef. That's what I went to school for. Guess the British Army was full up on mess hall cooks and overweight chefs catering to brigadiers, so my arse went in a tank—Britannia's most expensive coffin."

"Come out whole? Any injuries?"

"None. Lot of bruises, bumps, welts and aching bones—but nothing lasting. Hearing's not the greatest. The boom of the guns and the continual clanking, droning noise of that damn machine could make you doolally. Got on with it, though—somehow, anyhow."

"It's beautiful here. Why the Dales?"

"Paying any attention to what's happening in Ireland since the partitioning?"

"Nope, just trying to live."

"So am I. That's why we're here—*just trying to live*. Too damn difficult in Londonderry. Saw enough killing for two lifetimes. Certain as hell didn't want to see or do any more of it, especially in my own damn city."

I'd either hit a nerve or he was a crusty veteran, tired of platitudes and bored with lies. He couldn't appreciate how much we had in common.

"With Marlene … any … any …"

"Few rat-turd issues, but nothing too negative. Nothing I couldn't handle. She's an only child. Father died years before the war, so it was only Marlene and her mother. And she died from the flu a month or so before the war ended. Came along at the right time, I guess. I took a risk … so did she. But it's been bloody good. Her country's suffering, and Londonderry … we've already discussed, so, yeah, overall, it's been fine. We're happy and, as you say, just trying to live."

"Got to make do with what's left us, I suppose."

"Don't know how far along the path you are with Helena—that you stayed a week says something, I guess—but there's no call for jazzmen. People are practical here, not artistic. You'll find it difficult if …"

He took another sip of cognac and gazed at the floor.

"Thanks for your reassuring words."

Lifted his head, cocked it slightly backwards and looked at me oddly. If he understood my sarcasm, he ignored it. Excused himself after shaking my hand. Had more cleaning in the kitchen to do. Helena took it in her stride.

"Told you his exterior was harder than a tortoise's shell. Don't give it any thought. I'm not. Come on. Let's get a wiggle on. I want our last night at Ure Manor House to be something I'll remember always!"

An 8:30 am train departure meant we got out of bed extra early. So early, in fact, that Elgar couldn't be bothered and remained hidden under a heavy woollen blanket. I kissed his forehead and told him he was a good lad. He rolled over, miaowed and shut his tired eyes. Helena, too, lacked her characteristic effervescence.

"I'm getting more out of life than I felt possible. And you, you alone, has made it so. I'm berry-black sad that you're returning to London. But we'll be together again soon. I promise."

"Holding you to that. Work at The Forty-Three most of the month. Don't return to The Savoy until the late August bank holiday, so any time before that, we could have a sporting good time."

"I'd be content just to lounge about in a room without windows and a room without doors."

"A fine offer."

I put the suitcase and sax in the back seat and closed the door. Glanced around, absorbing the views and the smells and the rural noise, in case I wanted to recall them at another time, at another place.

"Appears there aren't any repercussions from my visit. Your reputation remains intact."

"No, no, you don't understand Dalespeople. They won't comment now. They'll wait a few days, perhaps a week or so, and then—what's your expression, *blow a piston?* It'll ricochet off Ellerkin Scar, cross the river to Worton and bounce around Askrigg under Scar before permeating through the stone walls of Ure Manor House. Mummy will be privy before me. Probably hear it first from Mavis."

"How comforting."

It poured rain on the drive to Redmire. I remained dry, but Helena bore the brunt. Hair, face and chest became soaked. Said she was w*etter than an otter's pocket* but never complained, even when wiping rain from her goggles. Deluge stopped soon after we arrived. A brilliant sun parted the clouds. She took off her goggles and cap, brushed a hand through her wet hair and smiled. She was about to speak, but I interrupted.

"I realise I'm not the first owner of your heart, Helena. But … but … if you let me …"

"William, for most people today, life is nothing but vanity. And since death is inevitable, that means only love endures. Everything else is pointless. Everything. We found love. I won't lose it. *Contra mundum?*"

"Contra mundum."

Opened the car door and grabbed my baggage. Helena scooted across to the passenger's seat, rolled down the window and rested her chin on crossed arms. Her eyes glistened. After offering her a last kiss, I said goodbye and made my way to the platform. As an act of self-preservation, I didn't look back.

Chapter Sixteen

After finding my seat and getting comfortable, I reflected on the visit. Calmness and contentedness had taken hold. Helena rekindled what I once possessed—what had made me whole—before the war, before the disillusionment. Although broken, I had survived. And the broken parts seemed stronger now. No need to equivocate. Purpose and happiness and longevity would return to me, with Helena along. Our lives actually would mean something. Needed to begin planning.

A week or so later, I received a lengthy letter. She updated me on the business and other goings-on, but it largely concerned the hotly fuelled gossip burning through the village. Thought I'd enjoy a sampling of what had been bandied about. Said she hadn't heard such tripe since the Quaker minister ran off with a nubile parishioner years ago:

--*Helena took pity on a cripple visiting and assisted him.*

--*Helena's abandoned poor Robbie and all expected norms of decent behaviour, choosing to be mired in a relationship with a foreigner—Canadian—I heard.*

--*Aye. Mabel told me the bloke was from New Zealand. Met him in London at that government wool committee she supposedly works on.*

--*Fortunately, her mother was in Scotland and unaware. She'll find out right shortly, mind.*

--*I heard he's one of those jazzmen who believes in communism, fomenting revolution and destroying the monarchy. Our lovely lads didn't die for that!*

--Don't want those kinds of foreigners living in my Dale.

--Aye. Constance said they swam naked together in Semer Water. Imagine!

--Margaret said they also frolicked at Mill Gill Force.

Of course, what they should do, to use the local language, is keep their nebs out of our business. 'Neb' means nose, William, so you'll better understand.

The most biting criticism came from Mummy. That didn't surprise me, but I found its bitter, self-pitying tone shocking. Told Helena she *ruined everything, acted both underhandedly and disrespectfully* toward her and the memory of her husband. *Villagers pity me, Helena. Say you took advantage of my absence in committing such unsavoury acts.* No doubt these comments concerned Helena—especially replacing 'father' with 'husband'—but she thought the intensity would fall by the wayside over time. The more worrisome and disconcerting remark, one that potentially could have lasting effects, was her mother questioning whether their sheep would garner a competitive price at the market. *Doubt Dales folk will support someone who happily and publicly shuns, laughingly ignores, long-held convictions. I hope you appreciate your selfish actions can only be corrected when Robbie returns and you're reunited and married.*

Helena's curt response almost bordered on the dismissive: *why she thinks he's alive is beyond me.* May have said more to her mother, but that's all she related to me.

Couple evenings later, when playing at The Forty-Three, a stocky but dapper man approached. His cockney accent made for difficult going while his physical mannerisms—over-active hand gestures with back-and-forth, full-body swaying—bordered on the comical. When he'd finished, I'd deciphered the basic gist of his request. The man in the far corner wanted to speak with me. Had a personal issue. Never asked why he didn't come up and just ask me or another member of the quartet if we'd play a particular song. But, since I'm always willing 'to give 'em what they want,' I walked over. He stood as I approached. Looked about ten years older than me. Was wearing a starched, collarless shirt, a high-buttoned waistcoat where a gold watch chain ran from one side pocket across his expansive chest to the other side's pocket. A dark pinstripe suit completed the ensemble. Highly polished black shoes were offset by bright white leather spats. Gave a firm handshake and offered me a seat.

"Charles Sabini. Friends and associates call me Darby and, since I consider you my newest friend, I'll let you call me Darby too."

"Thank you, ah, Darby. So, what special request would you like to hear this evening?"

"Not want I want, see. Enjoy all your tunes, all of 'em. Especially the way you play that horn. Beautiful. Really beautiful."

Struck by the way he pronounced 'beautiful'. Hung onto the first syllable a long time; the 'ti' sounded like 'tee', followed by a hard sounding 'f' in 'ful' to finish. Clinched my teeth to keep from laughing.

"I'm having a gathering on the first Saturday in September at the Griffin, my office on Clerkenwell Road—family, friends, Father Gian Carlo, my mother. I want you to perform. I'll pay you, of course, handsomely. So handsomely you can't turn it down."

"I'm flattered, Darby. Glad you enjoy my music, but …"

"Now listen. I'm generous to women, to children and to the Catholic Church, *Praise, God … Mother Mary full of grace*. Also generous to people who please me, and you please me."

"I'm humbled by your admiration, but I work at The Savoy. Can't let down the band. Without me they'd be down two saxophones—an alto and this tenor. Truly sorry, Darby. Couldn't do it, regardless how much you pay."

"I'm peeved now, see. I'm offering good money, lots of money, for you to blow hot air through that cheap instrument of yours. And … and you're turning me down?"

"Again, I'm sorry. Can't break a contractual obligation. If I do, I'm out of a job. As a businessman you certainly understand."

"You're telling me, *no?* Is that what I'm hearing? What I'm understanding? Don't want that. Don't need that. Don't like that."

He'd increased the heat in the room considerably. Started getting nervous. So, I stood up, apologised and said it was nice meeting him. As he shook my hand, he pulled me close and whispered in my ear.

"Could have had a permanent gig with my operation, see. With you on my payroll you'd be farting through silk underwear instead of those tattered rags you're wearing."

He slapped me on the shoulder and dismissed me with the wave of his right hand. Knew then and there I was not in a good spot. My new 'friend' had become a concern.

After we'd finished for the evening, Evie came over to talk.

"Saw you with Sabini. What'd *he* want?"

Described what happened, as well as my concerns about possible reprisals.

"You didn't steal from him. You don't owe him money. You weren't disrespectful, so not to worry. Damaged his pride a little, I imagine. That's all. He thinks any musician worth his salt would leap at the chance to get on the Sabini payroll. He's got bigger legs to break and necks to slash than yours, Travers. But, to calm your nerves, I'll cue you in if I see his henchmen prowling about whenever you're here."

"Thanks much, Evie. That's very kind. In the old days I'd fight back. Wouldn't take crap from anyone, no matter who they 'thought' they were. But now, with a gimpy leg I'm about as intimidating as a butter knife."

"Doesn't pay to think like that. Be thankful you've got a bum leg. The way Sabini operates, if you threw a punch, he'd ruin your embouchure—punch out your front teeth, bust your jaw and mangle your lip. I must protect my investment. Can't have anything nefarious happening to my favourite saxophonist."

Returned to my flat about midnight. Knocked back a few double neats and pondered Evie's thoughts about Sabini. Concluded she was correct. His pride was hurt. Maybe felt embarrassed by me declining the offer within earshot of his henchmen. It'd soon blow over. Wouldn't bother his grubby hands over someone as insignificant as myself. Decided to bury my concerns. Had important personal issues: Helena's approaching visit.

During a brief afternoon practice, preparing for the band's return to The Savoy in two weeks, I received an unexpected telegram. Helena had to cancel her visit. Seems a horrific storm had spread through the Dales, causing serious damage to several silage storage facilities. Left in its wake was heavy flooding, meaning hundreds of sheep needed moving to higher ground or they'd drown. She felt terrible not coming, but didn't feel comfortable leaving everything to a few employees. She planned on travelling down later in the month if all went well. I was disappointed but not fussed. Won't have as much time alone together, but she could enjoy herself at The Savoy for a few nights. Remembered her saying the American Bar felt like home.

Upon reflection, it seemed the entire week was devoted to Helena. An unforgettable time. Five days after receiving the telegram, she sent a lengthy letter, including photos of herself at Pendragon Castle. My God, she looked nice. An absolute, beautiful doll. Took time looking at them. My favourite was where she had pulled back her hair and raised her face slightly upward toward the camera. Placed it on the mantel next to my buddies from the Kicking Mule. Settled into a comfortable chair—well, the only chair in the room—and began reading.

William, my darling

Hope you enjoy the pictures. Thought they were decent. I may have overacted but ... you brought it out in me! Something about you makes me a different girl. Yours are wonderful, too. I'll cherish them forever.

Something has happened. I blamed my earlier cancellation on a storm that never occurred. I made it up. Yes, I lied. You see ... Robbie's parents had received a telegram from the Foreign Office notifying them that after almost four years in captivity their son was coming home. I was packed for London, practically out the door, when they stopped to tell us. Unbeknownst to any of us, the Foreign Office had been negotiating with both Finland and the Soviet Union about releasing Robbie. When he went missing, the military thought he'd been killed and later eaten by animals but never admitted it officially. Actually, the communists (the Reds) had taken him prisoner. He remained in jail for over a year until suddenly he became a bargaining chip. The Finns had captured a Russian communist whom they charged with spying. The Soviets denied it but, for whatever reason, desperately wanted the man returned. And would offer anything to make it happen. Don't know how, but that's when our government became involved. And so, a lengthy negotiation process ensued. After eighteen months or so the Finns and the Soviets agreed to an exchange. While the Foreign Office was elated, they kept quiet until Robbie was safe inside the British Embassy in Helsinki. Few government officials were privy. Then the Finns became nervous. Began thinking the Soviets had tricked them. That Robbie _was_ a Soviet spy—a double agent—or something like that. And to release him to the British would be dangerous. He'd be free to walk the streets of any city in Finland, sending notes and communiques to Moscow to help spread revolution. So, Robbie was now sitting— rotting, I'd say—in a Finnish jail. Details remain sketchy but, because the British refused to give up—doing everything necessary to convince the Finns Robbie wasn't communist spy—he was finally released. Now he's on a British naval ship bound for Southampton.

If you think I'm being too matter-of-fact about the whole event and what it means, I'm not. Took several days to understand the ramifications. Endured conflicting bouts of elation and devastation. Elated his life has been spared and will return home. Devastated for ... for ... what it means for us, our future together. Spent endless working hours and sleepless nights sorting out my mind. Reviewing possible scenarios was truly a battle between the head and the heart. If I choose what my head says, my heart dies. If I choose what my heart says, my life in the Dales—Mother, self-respect, the farm—dies. Damned either way. The American in me wants to leave, to be with you and share in your unpredictable, unrehearsed life. The English in me wants to adhere to tradition, protect a legacy and live in assured comfort and ease.

And so, William—I'm—crying now so you know—I cannot be with you. Must remain here in the Dales with Robbie and Mother in Ure Manor House. It's the proper thing to do. You won't agree at all with my decision, I know that, but it's where I belong, where my family has lived for hundreds of years. I must remain faithful, to honour commitments and expectations, even those forced on me.

Please understand I shall cherish you and the memory of you forever and ever. Each time I hear a jazz tune, you'll be there. Each time I see a saxophone, you'll be there. Each time I drink a double neat, you'll be there. Each time I'm in London, you'll be there. And, each time I close my eyes at night to sleep, you'll be there. My love doesn't end because I can't see you, William. It shall endure to the end. Promise.

I know you're shocked and bewildered ... certainly angry. And I feel so, so sorry for you. My heart is aching. Truly aching. You probably grabbed a bottle of Famous Grouse a few sentences into the second paragraph. Please don't recede deeper into disillusionment. I wish you nothing but good things from life, William, and hope you'll be spared any senseless tragedy. I want you and your style of jazz to be vaulted to the top, ever onward, always upward until the world *embraces it as its own.*

*Please find happiness, darling ... if not for you, then for me.
Goodbye ...*
Love always,
Helena

Dropped the letter onto the floor. I'll be goddamned. All of us must eat a ton of shit in this life and, after twenty-six years, I've learned there's no declining a seat at that table. She'll miss me. The same way I'll miss her, that's for certain. Helena knew how and when to kiss me. When and how to stroke, to coax, to pour me a drink, to tumble and to ruffle me. That's gone. It's all gone. Truly alone now. There's no return. Being alone is good. It must be good. No one can hurt me now. And I can't hurt anyone. Safe at last, I suppose. Safe at last.

Pulled myself together the best I could. Had an evening gig at The Forty-Three. Couldn't disappoint the crowd. More importantly, couldn't disappoint myself.

Finishing at midnight, I critiqued my performance. It certainly wasn't my best. The jumpin' jazz numbers lacked intensity. And the melancholy songs sounded woefully sentimental. But the crowd, it seemed, was too pissed to care. Cobbie, surprisingly, noticed all was not right.

"What's cookin', Travers? Been tepid and a bit off all evening. Don't seem yourself. Missing Miss Bolton-Leigh, I bet?"

"Could say that, Cobbie. Will be missing her for, for …"

"Oh, God, something terrible has happened. I'm sorry. It's none of my … she didn't, didn't … die?"

"She's alive … dead to me."

Looked at me so inquisitively that, in between her serving drinks and me packing my horn, I told her what happened.

"Tragic. I feel sad for you, Travers. Each time you came in together we girls commented how good you looked together. Beaming, I'd say. Affectionate and respectful. Don't see no couples like them 'round here."

"Yeah, I'd agree. Didn't realise she was only a temporary elixir to deaden the pain of Paris. The grandest of illusions."

"Suppose I shouldn't say this so soon, but if you want to drop by sometime to talk or to drink or whatever you fancy, tell me. Happy to help. Always liked you."

"Thanks, Cobbie. That's kind. Very kind."

Returning to the flat, I decided not to accept defeat. Okay, my wings have been shot full of holes and I'm losing altitude—but the aircraft is in trim, ceiling's lowering, I've got fuel, and there's an abandoned airstrip ahead. Haven't bought it. Not yet. Decided to purchase a ticket first thing in the morning. Be in Askrigg under Scar no later than noon.

Changed my mind before arriving in York. Wasn't kidding anyone but myself, attempting such a farce. No matter how persuasive, whatever words were chosen, nothing could change Helena's mind. If she gallivanted around London's jazz clubs with me, she'd become the pariah of Wensleydale. Her mother would shun us both. She'd never be welcomed inside the ancestral home. So, I walked up the steps and crossed over the bridge and boarded the return train to London. My plan to win her, change her mind—to salvage *our* relationship—seemed eerily similar to Dr Confidence's philosophy during the war. Only God and Helena determined who'd marry her, no one else. Whatever influence I possessed vanished with her letter. Suppose, in the end, nothing tangible remained. It was all atmosphere, a mythical fantasy, fuelled by the froth of vanished happiness. Most disappointing was that despite her determination *not* to be constrained by rules and conventions or influenced by outside intrusions, she couldn't swallow the most difficult: ignoring the consequences. So, I loved her enough to let her go. Returned to the flat hours later and drank every emotion to the dregs. Promised myself not to think of her or what she was doing or how she was doing it or with whom she was doing it. Failed, usually. Thought of her plenty of times sober and whenever drunk.

Chapter Seventeen

Sounds pathetically similar to an old Victorian greeting card, but I had found myself in Helena. Since pain and loss weren't foreign to us, I *was* glad we followed Sara Murphy's prescriptive advice: *Might enjoy each other's occasional company. Perhaps a cocktail or two some afternoon.* We clicked at the first meeting in the Langham. We were better than good. And for ten months our emotions were bound together as tightly and perfectly as the movement of a fine Swiss clock. But it fell apart. Broken by the burden of past decisions.

If the loss of Helena wasn't weighing on me, my misery only became more acute in September 1922 while reading a headline in *The Times* about the Chanak Crisis. Britain, it seemed, had come near the brink of war with Turkey. But because Canada asserted its independence by refusing to follow Westminster's lead, the sabre-rattling factions pursued a negotiated settlement. Seemed the world, and certainly Britain, was full of over-zealous posturing, determined to shore up a disappearing empire, and hadn't learned from the recent past. It gave me pause. Filled me with disgust. Could humanity ever, ever stop this ridiculousness? Was it possible? Read somewhere years later that we can live completely—without issues, without concerns only when we accept the absurdity of life. Seemed there was nothing, absolutely nothing, we, as individuals, could alter.

Decided I'd continue at The Savoy. Had to, actually. There was nothing else at the moment. Not what I desired, but what I needed. Keeping with WF's earlier guidelines, I'd play The Forty-Three only during the off-season, January and August. So, I laboured on against the currents of personal desire.

After working so many nights at The Forty-Three, I found returning to The Savoy disappointing. It wasn't the boys in the band; wasn't the venue's formality. And, with so many new tunes such as 'A Kiss in the Dark', 'April Showers' and 'Dancing Time' it wasn't the music. In fact, WF had befriended an American composer, Isham Jones, and somehow persuaded him to allow The Savoy to perform a newly written but unreleased song, 'I'll See You in My Dreams'. Composed as a foxtrot, we slowed it down to a beautiful ballad—both a dance number and a pensive song about a lost love that stood on its own and could be listened to easily. What weighed on me, the core of my disappointment, were the guests. Except for the occasional act of frivolity by one of The Bright Young Things, bloated indifference reigned supreme. It's as if the war's brutality and the changes it wrought hadn't happened. Mentally, it seemed, these starched stiffs remained in 1913, relishing the last glorious summer before the war—night after night, month after month, again, again and again.

Ventured to The Forty-Three after a particularly boring and uneventful evening at The Savoy. At 2 am the place was humming. Before going downstairs for the jazz, I walked to the rear bar on the ground floor and ordered a double neat from the bartender—yet another Johnny. Although short and balding, he proved as affable and proficient as the other bartenders who shared his name. I also was back to drinking the old reliable. My champagne days belonged to the past. Placed the instrument upright on its end as to not trip another customer. Talked with Johnny a bit, paid the tab, grabbed the drink and bent down for my sax. Wasn't there. Gone.

Left my drink on the bar, did a quick canvassing of the area but nothing. No one looked suspicious. No instrument in sight. Started sweating. Hands shook. Left leg pain intensified. Approached Evie sitting at the front desk by the right of the door. Asked if she'd seen Darby Sabini or any of his henchmen.

"Not tonight, Mr Travers. The only thing odder than usual was a midget of a man in an ill-fitting suit wearing a flat cap that he never took off, as if he had no intention of staying. Watched him carefully as I didn't recognise him. Walked around both floors—looking for someone, I thought. Then I became distracted. Had to handle the throngs wanting to gain entry. Sorry."

"We don't know if he took it. Seems the type but in Soho, at this hour, could be any of these chaps—maybe even a flapper. But why? Why the hell take someone's instrument?"

Left in a panic. If gone, which it damn sure was, WF will bore me several new orifices. Make any army ass-chewing appear amateurish. Poured rain as I entered Regent Street. When I approached my building, noticed something leaning against the door, glistening in the rain. My God! *It's my horn.* As I got closer, I became enraged. Whoever took it had assembled it—mouthpiece, crook even the neck strap—and smashed the living hell out of it. Flattened it, as if an automobile had driven over it repeatedly. A note was tied around one of the keys. Sat on the step, took the horn and cradled it like a newborn. Then read the note: *See, Yank, you don't play for Mr Sabini, you don't play for nobody.* That damn midget. That fucking ferret of a human. Christ, it all had been planned in advance.

Arrived early next day at The Savoy. Needed to tell

WF what happened and prepare myself for everything thrown my way.

"You say, Travers, you weren't performing, only 'soaking up the jazz' after work?"

"That's correct, sir. Played The Forty-Three during August and am scheduled for January, in total accordance with your directive."

"Yes, yes. You didn't cross the line. Shows, however, there's danger patronising venues replete with crime, thugs, moneychangers, prostitutes, and God knows what else. Never drawn to it myself. Never saw the point, actually. And never encouraged members of the band to visit. Can't issue a blanket restriction on certain venues, I suppose, but damn, Travers, it's put *me* in a fix and *your* testicles in a vice, sad to say. Have to run it up the chain. Not my decision, unfortunately. Too many hands baked this pie. There you have it, I'm afraid. Now go out and play your alto like you've never played it before. Don't fret about this, old man."

Wasn't what I expected but then, as WF said, the decision was above his station. His calm reaction enabled me to play well. The boys in the band were shocked when I told them what happened. None had any idea what punishment, if any, would be handed me. The only example they offered was a trumpeter who had played in another hotel band managed by WF. The guy apparently spent all night after work at The Forty-Three and, when it closed, ventured to other clubs and pubs throughout the day. Came to work the following evening pissed beyond recognition, wearing a well-soiled dinner jacket and smelling like a cow stable. WF fired him on the spot.

Four days passed and still no decision. It was only after Sunday evening's stellar performance that I received a message to drop by WF's office.

"Travers, sit down please. May I offer a double neat?"

"Yes, certainly, sir. Thanks."

If I were about to get my ass kicked into the middle of next week, this was an interesting entr'acte. Took a healthy sip.

"Travers … difficult for me because well, goddammit, I liked you from the beginning. The Paris brothel, playing in Montparnasse and our meaningful conversation about the war at Les Deux Magots. Management is requiring me to compensate the tenor sax's owner because I had bragged that if the US Army trusted you with an expensive aircraft, The Savoy could trust you with its historic instrument. So that means …"

He poured another glass to the rim, gazed at the floor, took a lengthy sip and then looked me in the eye.

"You're no longer employed by The Savoy. The final cheque will be forwarded to the address on file. Know it's a shock. Damn shame, really, but there you have it, old man. Best of luck. You'll do fine. You're a damn fine sax player. And finish your drink, please. Least I can do."

Gulped it down, stood up and looked him in the eye, but he wouldn't reciprocate. Eyes remained fixated on the red leather desktop. Gathered my belongings and left, not saying a word.

Returned to the flat. Sat in my comfortable chair and submerged myself in the mire of human emotion. In the span of three weeks I lost Helena, lost my saxophone and lost my job. Ten hours later, around noon, I woke to the swooshing sound of something sliding beneath the door. Had thirty days to vacate my flat. Splashed water on my face, changed my shirt, walked to the ground floor and knocked on Mrs Joy's door.

"What the hell's this about? Haven't done anything wrong have I? Christ!"

"Come in lovey. Get comfortable, and I'll tell you. Give me a minute."

And with that she walked to the kitchen where I heard the clinking of glasses, some mumbling, even cursing. Although sparse, her flat was neat and tidy—immaculate, actually—a shrine to her two boys. Framed photographs through their years, childhood trinkets, a cricket bat, a pair of well-worn walking boots and two Memorial Plaques (better known as a Dead Man's Penny) with the corresponding message from George V. True to her word, ol' Beatrice returned within a minute, holding two glasses and a full bottle of Famous Grouse.

"Know you'd be upset and didn't know if you was home, so that's how come I slid it underneath the door. See, love, I don't own the building, only manage it. The owner told me two days ago, wants us *all* gone in thirty days, and Bob's your uncle. Plans to combine the six flats into three. Be mighty expensive ones too, I bet. Twenty-three years of loyal service to that git don't mean a lick to him. But you're not to worry now. I've got you fixed up, dressed up and ready to go if you want it."

"Don't worry about me! What are *you* going to do? Where're you moving to?"

"Sussex, love, back to Hurstpierpoint. Oh, it's lovely there! Should have moved after my boys were killed ... didn't. At sixes and sevens, I guess. But this is what I've planned for you, if you're interested."

She paused, allowing my mind to race. *Oh, God, she doesn't want me with her in Sussex, does she? That can't be right.* Actually, she was only waiting confirmation from me to hear her idea.

"Yes, yes, please, please go ahead, Mrs Joy."

"Dear friend of mine manages an exquisite building of flats on Cheyne Walk in Chelsea, next to the River Thames. Posh over there, you know. Said there's a smaller than small garret that's never used, seen no service since before the war. If interested, she can give you a good rate—cheaper than here—and nobody has to know, not even the owner. Lives in Scotland and only visits occasionally, mainly to blow smoke up his wealthy renters' arses. My friend, Violet Ashley, says you're welcome to have a nose. See what you think. Don't know your schedule but, if suitable, said you might call around noon tomorrow. Can you do it, lovey?"

Told her my tale of woe. And, bless her, she said all the right things trying to erase my pain. Helena didn't know what she gave up. The Savoy's too full of stuffed shirts to realise when they've got a better than excellent musician. And regarding Sabini, she'd heard some noise outside her window the other night but didn't get out of bed. *Don't know for certain, love, but may have been a bit tight, too much of The Grouse.* Whereupon she opened the bottle and poured us a triple neat.

"This'll take the sting out. Don't worry. You'll land on your feet, lovey. Got that certain something 'bout you. Oh, if I were twenty years younger."

She paused, winked at me, laughed and confessed.

"Blimey … thirty years younger, then."

We giggled and toasted our futures, no matter how dismal I thought mine would be. Taking a healthy sip, I laughed to myself, recalling Gabrielle's words in Paris: *memories of a life well led.* How far had I fallen?

Beatrice's assistance finding me new digs loosened the ground, encouraging further discussion. Told her an expression army aviators used that helped us understand the grim reality we faced. Thought it appropriate to the current situation: *Those who's got, get. Those who don't, won't.* Seemed obvious to me that all I'd got was a fat, up-my-bum nothing.

She lit the cigarette that had been dangling from her lower lip, refilled our Scotch glasses and encouraged me to continue.

Regardless of my plans and aspirations, outside events always interceded, making my life run afoul. The war, the return of Helena's fiancé, a destroyed saxophone, even being evicted from the flat. They just happened. Nothing I did. And the longer I thought about it, couldn't shake the absurdity of it all. Life—at least the life I had wanted to lead—simply had become incompatible with reality.

"Don't know how long I can keep up the pace, Mrs Joy. Doomed youth often has been considered romantic, hasn't it? Literature, music, poetry—even art—are replete with examples many embrace."

"Don't read none or listen to the phonograph and never been to an art show, so can't help you there. Sorry, love."

"As we age, seems failure and disappointment yield nothing but dread and angst. How long must we keep muddling through before it's over?"

"Don't have to keep muddling, lovey. Leave anytime, can't you? Your choice. Thought about it many times myself, especially after the boys were killed. Don't know why, just decided to stay on a bit. Can change me mind anytime, though. Probably will. Have the freedom. You have the freedom, too, young William. Up to you what you do with it, if anything."

Was taken aback by her frankness. Her comment

wasn't 'off-the-cuff,' so to speak. Something she'd thought about for a long, long time.

"See, lovey, my husband was walking by a construction site on Conduit Street, just off Regent Street. A hammer fell off a construction platform and hit him on the head. Fell to the pavement, cracking his skull wide open. Blood everywhere, covering the pavement. Before any police arrived, he was declared dead by a doctor who happened to be walking nearby. So, there I was—two boys, no job. Decided my life wouldn't be determined by the past. Had to face a new reality. And did so."

That's when I realised: she was a deeper thinker than I'd ever supposed. Only *she* could create her own reality. Her life, her choices—they weren't predetermined by the past. Angst and dread certainly would abound, but she had chosen to live without excuses.

"After losing Bernard, my husband, I decided I'd have to get more out of life than it contained. The loss of my boys only intensified the need. Might make a different decision when I've had enough. I'll let you know."

An authentic reflection of life, containing a full dose of British stoicism in eleven words. A philosophy to embrace. Prior to leaving Mrs Joy's, I reaffirmed my interest in visiting the Chelsea flat on Sunday.

Late morning the following day, I made my way to Cheyne Walk. What a gorgeous setting. Beautiful, reddish-coloured buildings ensconced by tall, shaded trees full of tweeting birds, and ladies owning cut-glass accents parading around in fancy frocks and smelling of Penhaligon perfume. If forced, I could become used to this. Had been instructed to wait on a bench in the back garden. Noticed a small black cat looking down from a nearby tree branch. Mrs Ashley arrived precisely at noon.

She was a spindly little thing. Thin as a whippet—if she turned sideways, you wouldn't see her—and—salt and pepper hair styled in a bob. Reading glasses hung from a chain dangling from her neck. She approached and confidently extended her hand.

"No doubt you're Mr Travers. Glad to make your acquaintance. Beatrice has told me so, so much about you that, well, I feel I know you already."

"That's kind of Mrs Joy. But you know her well enough to appreciate she tends to extend the truth occasionally."

"Oh, yes, she does. But never regarding people. She's spot on. Always. That's the only reason you're here. Shall I show you the flat?"

As we made our way to the fourth floor, I learned this garret-like flat could be accessed only by one door in the garden. The front door was, more or less, off-limits to me as much as the back door was to other tenants. Didn't bother me in the least. Seemed the little black cat also knew about the back door as she raced ahead, taking three steps to my gimpy one. Mrs Ashley also raced up the stairs and had opened the door and parted the curtains before I arrived. The place was small, very small, but quite intimate. A gas cooker, a single bed, and a more than adequate bath and sink. In-the-wall shelving dominated the wall nearest the bed. The sitting room window overlooked the Thames while the bathroom window overlooked the garden. On warm days, I could open both and share a delightful cross-breeze. Figured the only furniture I'd need was a writing desk or table and a soft chair or two. Seemed a comfortable place to protect that small remaining part of me, while pretending to be whole. The stairs would be challenging but could work to my advantage: either to keep me inside and safe, or outside and in trouble. The choice was mine. Being British, she didn't tell me I couldn't play my horn—but inferred it'd be best if I practised between ten and six, Monday through Saturday. Told her it wasn't a problem. I'd be out most evenings, often not returning until morning.

"Beatrice said you're one of the jazzmen. Keep odd hours, but a well-mannered lad who paid his rent on time and kept to himself."

"Now that, Mrs Ashley, is something Mrs Joy didn't exaggerate. Won't cause you or the other tenants any problems. When the owner arrives from Scotland for his occasional visit, I'll be as quiet as a church mouse or will have excused myself from the premises altogether. He'll never know."

"I like you already, Mr Travers Must ring Beatrice. She'll be over the moon. Here's the key. Move in anytime. Won't charge rent until the first of the month, which is what, another two weeks?"

"Is there an additional charge for felines?"

"Excuse me?"

I pointed to the black cat swinging wildly from one window curtain to the other.

"Oh, Gershwin, she's always around. Hope you don't mind. She's a wonderful companion. If you don't enjoy the company of cats, I can make the flat inaccessible to her. She's only two years old but settling in wonderfully."

"Please, don't do a thing. Adore cats, especially black ones. Have always found them personable and savvy. I'm sure we'll become best of friends. And besides, with a name like Gershwin, she's gotta love jazz."

"Honestly don't know, but you may have a point. Once she feels comfortable that your friendship is genuine, she'll confidently invite herself in. No problem. You'll never be lonely, Mr Travers. Of that, I'm sure."

"Then it's settled. Gershwin remains. And, if she accepts me, she and I will make this lovely garret our own."

Couldn't believe her generosity and my good fortune. Due entirely to ol'Beatrice Joy. Keen to move, I decided to pack and leave Langham Street within a few days. Didn't own much, so it was simple. Said goodbye to Mrs Joy, who also was in the throes of packing, leaving her home of twenty-three years. Presented her a bottle of Famous Grouse, which she insisted on opening. While sharing a few tipples, we promised to keep in touch. Sent several letters but all remained unanswered. Sadly, Beatrice became one of those 'ephemeral,' 'inconsequential' people who greatly influences one's life and then simply disappears. As the angst-filled thirties replaced the rollicking twenties, I accepted that I was essentially alone. And, whenever I thought seriously about it, I considered it a gift.

Chapter Eighteen

I stopped by The Forty-Three a few days after settling into my new garret. Wanted to discuss with Evie about the possibility of working regularly. She offered heartfelt sympathy for my situation—the Sabini incident *and* The Savoy. But I knew her well enough to know she also was cock-a-hoop at the turn of events. She was a businesswoman who understood how the club could capitalise on my misfortune. She'd be 'coining it in' with me and a few others jazzin' on stage. Agreed to a salary easily: £110 a week, £20 more than the other acts but £45 less than my intake at The Savoy. To compensate, she slotted me in at the busiest times on the best days, Wednesday to Sunday, 9 pm to 2 am. Thought I'd make up the difference by playing the smaller, grittier clubs springing to life in Soho. And those prime hours could also serve as the perfect introduction for wealthy, socially connected customers to hire me for posh parties in Mayfair and Chelsea. Hadn't figured out how I'd avoid encountering Sabini or how to deal with him or his ferret if we met face to face.

During the first few weeks, I performed with an on-call pianist whom Evie had contracted with for years. A proficient and likeable guy, he lacked that 'thing' which makes jazz hot and, makes people move. So, I explored the soft underbelly of London and sussed out jazz artists in hopes of forming my own band that I already had named: 'WT's 'Alley Cats'. Discovered the pianist at Lyon's Tea Room on Oxford Street. Said he'd be glad to join me. Tired of playing predictable dining music and of the 'Nippies' pestering him for fun and champagne after work at his expense. Learned a drummer had been sacked from the band of an upmarket hotel in Knightsbridge for promoting 'unsophisticated music'. Seemed exactly what WT's Alley Cats needed. A drummer with attitude. Through stealth and direct questioning of a few hotel staff, found him holed up in a flat close to where Cobbie lived. He jumped at the chance. Knew all about The Forty-Three and always had fancied performing there. Found two for the price of one: the trumpeter and a bass player, who also played guitar. Heard them one evening busking in Green Park, a shilling's throw from the Ritz Hotel. Returned a couple nights to hear more stellar performances. Helped underscore that their earlier playing wasn't a one-off, a fluke. Their panache attracted an attentive and adoring crowd. And they loved the idea of steady employment with a band full of promise. We were a motley crew—thus the name Alley Cats—but, damn, we were better than good. As a whole, the band was right up there, if not a tad above, the Paris boys. The goods were odd but the odds were good we'd do something fine together.

For almost ten years The Alley Cats worked The Forty-Three. Developed a loyal following and made decent seed. Evie loved us, and we loved Evie. But in spring 1927, the police raided the place, ostensibly for serving alcohol past 11 pm without a licence. Most considered it a minor infraction and took little notice. After closing a few nights and paying the fine, normalcy returned. But gradually, over time, the structure came tumbling down as the police tightened their investigative noose not only into The Forty-Three but into the sergeant responsible for ensuring Soho nightclubs operated in strict accordance with the law. Turns out the officer was corrupt; so was Evie. Throughout much of the decade, the officer had ignored the illegal activities within The Forty-Three in exchange for a hefty payout from Evie, so-called hush money. To cover his tracks with his superiors, and to create the illusion he was cracking down on illegal behaviour, the sergeant raided other clubs, bringing ample charges against their owners—but never touched The Forty-Three. After some delay, the case went to trial in 1929. Evie was found guilty of several breaches of the law, including money exchange, serving alcohol past hours and aiding prostitution. She was sentenced to fifteen months in Holloway Prison.

Her daughters operated the club during her absence, enabling us to continue playing to adoring crowds. Best of all, we still got paid. Evie was released in early 1930 and returned to The Forty-Three immediately. Employees threw her a swell party. Never forget it: champagne, caviar, shrimp, even crab legs. The best news was she hadn't lost her spunk. She remained cocked and loaded. Although lacking the protection of her 'police confidant'—who had also served time and was subsequently kicked out of the force—she unabashedly continued to flaunt the law. Almost relishing in it. Something I never got my head around. Her flamboyance was tantamount to inviting the police to raid the club. And they didn't disappoint. Raided the place several more times in the coming years, resulting in back-to-back incarcerations at Holloway in 1930 and 1931. She wasn't the same after returning from those two stays. She looked gaunt and unhealthy. She'd lost her spunkiness and toughness. Her inner fight was gone. After another conviction in 1932, her lawyer pleaded for, and won, a moderate sentence. In lieu of prison, she received a fifty-pound fine and a strict probation. But the cumulative damage had taken control on Evie and The Forty-Three. She died six months later in early '33 of influenza. Friends attributed it largely to the dampness and distress she suffered in Holloway. So, two eras ended that cold January day: The Forty-Three Club locked its doors forever, and WT's Alley Cats began walking the streets canvassing for work. As I had told Beatrice Joy a decade earlier, seemed outside events—which no one ever has control over—always interceded, making my life run afoul.

The financial roulette wheel operated by Americans throughout the 1920s stopped spinning in late October 1929. The impact wasn't immediate in England but soon arrived as demand for British products evaporated. Unemployment increased to over twenty percent in 1930, almost fourteen percent in London alone. Didn't begin to recover until late 1935, into 1936. So, the Alley Cats joined tens of thousands of others jockeying for work. Finding venues to play jazz, of course, wasn't the same as catching a hot shipbuilding rivet in Sunderland or pouring cement at a construction site in Birmingham. Took lots of selling, loads of convincing. But the boys and I persevered and eventually were rewarded with regular back-to-back gigs at some of Soho's newest and, some may say, off-colour clubs.

Played often at Frisco's on Frith Street which, like a can of sardines, was packed head to arse with intellectuals, authors, cultured Bohemians, cinema stars, and journalists. Found them attentive and courteous and, best of all, fluent in jazz-speak. Also played the Big Apple on Gerrard Street, not far from the old Forty-Three. Each evening, the Alley Cats walked by No. 43 on the way to another venue. We tipped our hat in appreciation, in memory of the old times. Jazzin' at these Soho clubs was hot and raw. The audiences responded to us and—perhaps only a sign of wishfulness—I thought the crowds doubled in size whenever we performed.

The boys and I enjoyed the varying atmospheres so much that during a rare night off, one, two or sometimes all of us would take seats as customers to hear our compatriots. The Shim Sham, located on Wardour Street, opened in 1935. Its clientele was different. Comprised the white, the rich, the well-born, and the good from Mayfair and Chelsea, theatre workers from Soho and an eclectic array of men who preferred men and women who preferred women. And none of it bothered anyone. Didn't give a 'hoot in hell' who they did or didn't pursue. I hadn't suddenly become a 'holy roller', preaching the gospel against sexual transgressions. I *had* played in a Paris brothel, after all. Made good seed and met some fine women. If they came to hear real jazz, hot jazz, the way it's supposed to be played, well, the Alley Cats delivered. Reminded me a lot of Montparnasse after the war. But, as the decade progressed and Europe became unsettled, the Shim Sham transitioned from a jazz haunt to a gathering place for anti-fascists, communists and supporters of pan-Africanism.

My room of choice, the place I enjoyed the most by myself, was Jig's Club. Its address was on Wardour Street but was entered from St Anne's Court around the corner. It was frightfully small but intimate, complete with nicotine-stained walls, smoky atmosphere and a smell unlike any other. The sign above the bar defined what the joint was about: *If you have nothing to do, don't do it here ... 'cause we're jazzin'*. Would play by myself or jam with whomever was there into the wee small hours, long after the regulars had left. Sometimes had the privilege of joining in with all or some of the Jig's Club band, comprising Cyril Blake—on trumpet, Freddy Grant—on clarinet, Lauderic Caton—on guitar, Brylo Ford—on bass, and Clinton Maxwell—on drums. Declined repeated invitations to join them. Couldn't abandon the Alley Cats and, to be honest, didn't want Jig's to become my place of employment. It was my refuge. Wanted it to remain so forever. The club's drink of choice was rum and peppermint. But, after the owners latched onto my jazz interpretations, I always found a bottle of Famous Grouse placed on the stool next to me. On the house, of course.

These clubs also attracted two formidable American guests: Louis 'Sachmo' Armstrong in July 1932 and Duke Ellington in June 1933. They made the scene after performing at the Palladium. Alley Cats were working the evening 'Sachmo' appeared at a rough-and-tumble place called The Nest, so we missed him. But, from what friends said, Louis enjoyed himself. Got out his horn and played a few numbers, 'Them There Eyes', 'You Rascal, You' and, of course, 'Tiger Rag'.

Got the surprise of my life when I walked into Jig's Club one evening. There was the Duke,—holding court behind the club's piano. The guy looked, smelled and acted with unadulterated class. Looked immaculate in his dinner jacket. Appreciating that many in the crowd didn't attend or couldn't afford seeing him at the Palladium, he reprised a few numbers. I remember if it were yesterday: 'Three Little Words', 'Ring Dem Bells', 'Rockin' in Rhythm' and the untouchable 'Mood Indigo'. Untouchable because it couldn't, and never will be, performed as exquisitely by any other band. Only

Ellington's. We talked a bit about jazz. Introduced him to Famous Grouse. Seemed curious as to how and why I remained in Europe after the war. Told him it was a tiresome tale for another day. Seemed to appreciate the candour. Hope I'd look him up if the Alley Cats ever played New York City. Whether sincere or only polite, I took it as the former and thanked him.

Unfortunately, throughout the 1930s, music critics, BBC decision-makers and the government threw darts— even a few javelins—at jazz music, ruining any chance of it infiltrating British culture to any great extent. Critics thought jazz endangered the personal reputations of those listeners interested in gentlemanly manners, good taste and knowledge. The BBC offered tepid support, believing it had only a minor place on British airwaves. The *coup de grâce*, of course, occurred in 1935, when the government effectively ended any chance of Britain experiencing American jazz bands. The Ministry of Labour declared it wouldn't issue permits for American musicians to perform until a reciprocal agreement could be arranged. That meant if Britain wanted to hear the latest from the States, it could only do so by purchasing records. Didn't know then, but my chance encounter with Duke in 1933 at Jig's Club would be my last.

Until it shut its doors in the mid-thirties, the club I enjoyed most outside the confines of Soho was the Bat Club. To older revellers it reminded them of Cave of the Golden Calf, a favourite pre-war haunt. Located on Albemarle Street, across from the Brown's Hotel and around corner from the Ritz on Piccadilly, The Bat Club was far racier than other clubs. Had a penchant for indiscreet cabaret acts and performers who had mastered the double entendre. Remaining open until early morning, it appealed strictly to the 'after hours' set. Fine dinner jackets for men and frocks that left little to the imagination for women were *de rigueur*. Except for the unique lighting of the bar, darkened intimacy dominated, replete with posh sofas and chairs, plush carpet and dimly lighted table lamps. But it was far from quiet. It was raucous. And the band culpable for this was Harry Roy & His Bat Club Boys. The band's suggestive 1931 hit, 'My Girl's Pussy'—just one of many—was a consistent crowd-pleaser. Don't think there ever was a time when guests didn't repeatedly shout out the suggestive refrain. The Bat Club was unlike any other venue I worked or patronised. Drawn to the place, I suppose, because it was one of the few places I could force my way through the hedgerows and rub arms with that segment of society inaccessible to people like me. Wanted to see for myself what Britain had gone to war in 1914 to preserve. While my frequent visits only reinforced long-held opinions, didn't want them to ruin the evening. Always understood, even if these wealthy revellers didn't, that unlike a fine wine the present never has legs.

While we had played gigs in Kent, Sussex and Surrey, venturing as far south as the Grand Hotel in Brighton, we hadn't travelled any further north than Oxford. That changed in 1940. The president of the Yorkshire Wool Association in Harrogate sent a letter of inquiry, asking if he could book us for three events in April: two at the Grand Opera House on Oxford Street followed by a special performance at the Association's annual meeting and formal dinner dance at the Hydro Hotel. He heard us in London some time ago, apparently, and was suitably impressed. Never keen to refuse a gig, the boys and I agreed to make the trip. Worked well logistically, too.

Each had an individual room at the host hotel and the hotel's manager also provided an adequate practice/warm-up room. Rare as hen's teeth to find such an accommodating establishment.

Felt odd returning to Harrogate. Hadn't been since Helena and I visited the spa and enjoyed a tart at a wonderful tea room that, I seem to recall, was named Bettys. Also provided the opportunity to view the completed war memorial dedicated over fifteen years earlier.

Our two nights at the Grand Opera House went swimmingly. Played to a full house both nights and, with a seating capacity of nearly 800, made us proud, gave us something to brag about whenever we felt the need. The boys and I adored the audience. Feeling a bit humbled, and in appreciation, we performed three encores: 'Deep Purple', 'Heart and Soul', and, our personal tour-de-force finale, 'Don't Be That Way'.

Afterward, as we cleaned and packed our instruments, heard a soft knock at the door. Thinking it a staff member bringing drinks, I shouted for him to come in.

"No worries. We're all decent, at least some are."

The door opened and a feminine voice responded, "I certainly hope so. Good evening, Alley Cats. Fab performance. Hello, William. Been some time."

Didn't know how to respond exactly. Figured some quick math.

"Almost eighteen years, Helena."

The boys recognised my past had entered the room and scurried off. The years had been kind to Helena. I could also discern they hadn't been easy. Her gorgeous red hair had lightened considerably, appearing almost honey-blonde-like. The bob was gone. Replaced by shoulder-length hair parted on the right side, resembling actress, Irene Dunne. Her emerald eyes lacked their characteristic sparkle and, similar to me and all our generation, the skin was loose and the middle soft. Reflecting, I suppose, on the times we had. But her smile, that infectious, incandescent smile remained.

"Can't believe you're here and that I'm playing Yorkshire. Aren't coincidences odd?"

"Not a coincidence, William. All was planned. You know me. I'm in charge of the annual meeting. All aspects, including entertainment at the dinner dance. Didn't know if you'd accept if I inquired so, after much cajoling, the president agreed to make contact."

"So, it was a ruse? The president—what's his name— George Eversharpe, never had seen the Alley Cats perform?"

"Of course not, silly. Do you think anyone in Yorkshire even has heard of WT's Alley Cats?"

"Thanks for the compliment."

"Didn't mean it like that. You remember their provincialism, their clannishness. If you're not Yorkshire, they're not interested. Took much convincing. Told him WT's Alley Cats would fit the bill better than any other band, certainly anything local."

"Should I be angry I got played or happy we sold out both performances?"

"Happy, I'd think."

"Then I am, and it is you that made it so. You took a risk hiring us, sight and sound unheard."

"Wrong again. Saw the Alley Cats a few years ago when visiting London on business. You were working at the Shimmy or …"

"The Shim Sham on Wardour Street."

"That's it, the Shim Sham. Jiving music and certainly an eclectic crowd. All kinds, I'd say. Those that do and those that don't."

Caught her humour immediately and belted out a good laugh.

"Your timing is spot on. You still got it, Helena. You've still got it."

"Yeah, I've got that but not much else."

Feeling she wanted to talk, asked if there was a bar or pub nearby. Naturally, she knew the landscape. Soon found ourselves in a dark, clubby-like bar called All That Heaven Allows. We were the only couple so privacy, since that's what we desired, was ours.

"Suppose it's a double neat of the Grouse?"

"Normally, yes. But this evening's special. I'm going for a double dry gin martini with a twist."

"Good. Fancy a dry martini myself. Abandoned champagne years ago."

"All's going well for you personally? Married with two grown-up, pheasant-hunting children?"

"No on both counts. Life with Robbie became, well, if I had done those things, I'd been forced to leave the Dales. Shunned. Forever. But with Robbie, everyone blamed it on his confinement in Russia and Finland. A convenient excuse, on which he often hung his hat. Enabled him to escape any responsibility concerning just about everything. Found someone else, eventually. Young, vulnerable, sympathetic—and so, I ended the marriage."

"So, it's only you and Mummy?"

"No, Mummy died ten years ago. Alcohol took over and destroyed her. She ended it herself. Drowned in the Ure on a bone-chilling winter's night. Authorities found the body days later, washed up in Ripon."

"Her drinking was a by-product of losing her boys, I suppose. The war never ended for her."

"Yes and no. She blamed herself for what happened between Robbie and me. And I'd have to agree with her. She felt responsible forcing me to honour the commitment, despite being dreadfully and totally in love with you. In 1922, she couldn't understand; in 1925, she accepted the pivotal role she'd played; in 1930, she was dead. And so, I remain at Ure Manor House managing the business, rejecting the pity people feel obligated to dole out. What about you, William? Surely, you've landed one of those cultured and moneyed West End girls?"

"Nope. Romance and affection flamed out with you. Not pining or carrying a torch. Only accepting. Like the old song from the last Great War, 'Pack Up Your Troubles in Your Old Kit Bag and Smile, Smile, Smile'. Sounds sophomoric, but I've learned it's best to use simplicity when facing difficulty."

"Suppose we're two orphans in the storm, then."

"The storm called life. Agree. Still cherish the photos at Pendragon Castle, though. My favourite is you with your hair pulled back, your head raised slightly upward toward the camera. Magical. It's framed, sitting on the mantel next to my Paris girls and Kicking Mule buddies. *Memories of a life well led*, to quote Gabrielle from the brothel."

"How I remember Pendragon Castle. Your sax playing. My dancing like a Greek goddess to, who was it, Satie?"

"'Gymnopédie No.1'. Never forget it. Never. Haven't played it in years. Don't know why, just haven't."

"From what I've read, the Alley Cats are doing fine.

Toast of the town, I'd say. Each time in London I see advertisements for you and the boys performing at one Soho club or another. You stuck at it and succeeded, William—well done, and congratulations!"

"Down to luck, good and bad, I'm afraid. Hell, in spring 1937 the American consulate contacted me. Thought first I'd done something wrong and was being deported. Actually, it was a letter from Sara Murphy and a contract proposal for WT's Alley Cats to perform for one month at Hotel du Cap on the French Riviera. After consulting the boys, we jumped and made a hell of a good time out of it. Enjoyed playing among the pines, jasmine and oleander. The guests were some of the wealthiest, most famous personalities I'd ever encountered. Friendly, solicitous in a condescending kind of way. The warm sun, the bright blue sea and the top-notch accommodations more than made up for mixing with the self-absorbed."

"Where the Murphy's there, too?"

"No, no. They were travelling to Switzerland to seek treatment for their son with tuberculosis. Nothing could be done, sadly, and he died. Their other son had died two years earlier from meningitis. Seems they're drowning in tragedy. Wrote a lengthy letter thanking her for referring the Alley Cats and for the fine experiences of the band at Hotel du Cap and, of course, my sympathies. That was in autumn 1937. Haven't heard anything since."

"I lost contact years ago. Partly my own doing, and because … already bored you with that woeful tale."

After finishing our second martini we made our way slowly back to the hotel.

"Sounds presumptuous, William, but can we share a few drinks tomorrow night after the dinner dance? Fellow

Alley Cats may not be appreciative, but ..."

"I think they'll understand. Look how they buggered out this evening."

"There is that. Thank you. Well, here we are at *your* war memorial, William. Any comments?"

"Better prepare to add more names. This Bore War, or Phony War as it's referred to in the States, won't last long. It will suddenly become real, hitting our shores and destroying our cities."

"It's all happening again. Don't know what to make of it myself."

"I do. How'd the world react after Abyssinia? After the Rhineland? After the Anschluss? After the Sudetenland? The strongest reaction was the agreement in Munich, *peace for our time* ... which ceded what remained of Czechoslovakia. The Nazi—Soviet Pact, of course, guaranteed the invasion of Poland. And here we are. The nation soon will be on fire."

"Glad I never had children."

"Thought about becoming reacquainted with the cockpit sometimes. Assisting in any way I can, and then ... and then other times—which is most of the time— bitterness takes over, dominates. Realise I'm still smouldering from the last one. No longer the naïve bastard that followed other sheep and signed on to American idealism in 1917. Never again, for America, for England, for France. I'm finished."

"You sound stateless."

"If I could be, I would. Don't know, Helena, how long I can tap my good foot until people understand how and why this war came about. Will I have to wait until the flags stop flying on Remembrance Day at every monument that immortalises 'the fallen'? Will I have to wait until the poor bastards from the war stop marching in the front ranks wearing their berets with chests adorned with rows of 'I was there medals,' but missing a leg or an arm? To remember, to recognise, what exactly? And the two-minute silence on one day of the year. Is that all their sacrifice meant?"

"William, honestly. Such pessimism."

"Perhaps, but I'm not naïve. Know I'm not doing anything for our current situation by accumulating indignation but that's how I feel."

The Alley Cats reached new heights of perfection the following evening. We impressed everyone attending, including ourselves. Helena's responsibilities overrode any chance of her enjoying herself. Saw her discussing issues with other members, engaging the hotel staff, ensuring every need was met and every question answered. Toward the end of the evening, I glanced out over the dance floor and saw her sitting alone at a table, drinking a martini. After finishing 'Begin the Beguine', I addressed the audience.

"Ladies and gentlefolk of the Yorkshire Wool Association, we have a unique request tonight, unique because it's not from you but from me, to a dear and special friend attending tonight."

And with that I started playing 'Gymnopédie No.1'. Once the boys got a handle on the rhythm, I was accompanied by the softness of the double bass and a drum brush. Helena remained at her table, wiping away tears as they streamed down her cheeks. When finished, the crowd, which had stopped dancing midway through to listen, broke out in rapturous applause. Helena stood up, raised her hands high over her head and clapped. As I bowed to the crowd to thank them, I overheard one of the boys say, *Fellas, look at the far back table. That's the woman occupying WT's mind of late. I'd be preoccupied too if she danced to my rhythms. Damn.*"

Met Helena in the lobby afterward to have drinks, as planned. She had other ideas.

"Didn't want to chance the risk of someone joining us, William, so all the necessaries for several ice-cold martinis are setup in my room. Hope you don't mind."

"Not at all. Not at all. After eighteen years, three would definitely make for an unwanted crowd. Thank you. Well planned."

So, we adjourned to her spacious room that overlooked Harrogate and Valley View Gardens. Larger and posher than my room, even my Chelsea garret. But then I *was* hired help.

"It's wonderful seeing you look so healthy, William."

"May look good but you're only being polite. Look at my shoulders, Helena, bent forward for being unbalanced for over twenty years. And my lower back hurts constantly, delivering pain and numbness to my supposedly healthy leg. Can't complain too much, though. Still have fingers and a good set of lungs. If the pain increases much more, I'll have to pull up a chair and perform sitting down."

"The audience wants to see and hear you. Won't care whether you're sitting or standing. Trust me."

"Still overwhelmed by your optimism. You never let go, do you?"

"Thought about what we discussed last evening. Thought about it all day, in fact. Didn't realise the impact of honouring my commitment to Robbie would have on your life, your mind-set. Assumed another woman would land effortlessly on your lap."

"As I said before, Helena, wasn't carrying a torch. My life had been rearranged by a series of events. Began with the war, not this one, the last 'great' war. Then my sorrowful relationship in Paris. Losing you was terrible, seemingly ushering in a series of non-stop events that I had no ability to control."

Told her everything: Sabini destroying the tenor sax, The Savoy sacking me, The Forty-Three closing, and being evicted from the Langham Street garret.

"How dreadful for you. How awful. I'm so sorry, William. Love didn't do right by us, or perhaps we didn't do right by love. Don't know the answer. I just don't know."

"One thing I'm sure of, Helena: we were nothing if not excellent actors in a brief, intense charade called 'being in love'. Enjoyed it, actually. Wish it hadn't ended so early. Would certainly have liked a longer run, but then you still remain part of my past that never will be severed. Never. So, in a sense, it's still going on in my head."

"I've never forgotten you either, William. Always reminiscing about our brief but exquisite time together. So, in keeping with your West End metaphor, any possibility of a second act, or perhaps a revival that could run for years?"

"Yesterday and today were formed by us remembering the past and anticipating the future. So, we'll have to wait. We'll just have to wait and see."

"Sounds a bit like ..."

"Despite personal plans, and aspirations and desires, outside events always impinge, forcing me to regroup, rethink and begin anew. It's April 1940, Helena. Last week, while walking around Westminster and St James's

Park, sandbags were stacked high on every government building. Windows tapped, to lessen injuries from blowing shards of glass. Directional signage to air-raid shelters were everywhere. Meanwhile, men sporting bowlers and pinstripes, women pushing prams, and the elderly struggling to get to their destination shared one commonality: all carried gas masks. Depressing, disconcerting, but truthful. Death and destruction will soon be delivered. Planning a future, any kind of future, with or without you, is near impossible, I'd say."

"I remember when my brothers left. Both said they'd be home soon. Christmas, I believe. Didn't, of course. Never made it home. And Robbie, all confident, all-knowing, all British, returned a broken and damaged—volatile, distant, and drunk most of the time."

"And yet the politicians' ineptitudes have enabled us to mount up and ride the merry-go-round yet again. Their so called 'good intentions' were simply inadequate. Wars don't begin nowadays because people want them, Helena, they start because the world has failed."

"Can't get my head around the absurdity of it all. And by all, I mean everything—war, peace, love, life. Just one absurd circus."

"Nothing absurd about absurdity that's for sure. Seems by only accepting it—which is different from liking it—can we even begin to live free, to live unencumbered, to make our own decisions. Unfortunately, it takes a lifetime, which is all we've got, to understand this."

"How should we leave it, then, between you and me? I'm here, enclosed within the stone walls of Yorkshire, whenever you want to escape the absurdity and the loneliness of life."

"Loneliness suits me. It's my one cherished

possession, perhaps my only one. Helps distil and define. How about if we leave it to when I crave truth, when I crave affection?"

"That'll do. Not what I asked for, but everything I hoped for."

"This isn't one-sided. It's open to you, if you'd like."

"I *would* like that. Like that very much indeed."

And then we kissed, for the memories and the longing of an earlier time and for the future, no matter how fraught, how unpredictable, how impossible.

The band's calendar was booked most of May and June at our usual Soho clubs. After the fall of France, however, demand lessened. July's bookings were slight. August amounted to nothing. Two Alley Cats left for government work in one capacity or another. Never knew the specifics. The pianist returned to Cornwall to assume civil defence duties. And the trumpeter enlisted in the Navy. Decided I had no interest in participating, preferring instead to watch how human inadequacy would deal with its newest creation.

To make some seed, returned to how I supported myself twenty-two years earlier—playing the street. The four corners at the intersection of Oxford and Regent streets didn't resemble the eclecticism of Montparnasse but passers-by never failed in showing their generosity and appreciation.

Also continued at Jig's Club, where I was rewarded regularly with a bottle of the Grouse. This charade of jazzin', of course, was to steel ourselves against the much-anticipated Battle of Britain. Wanted to enjoy our last bits of freedom, however and whenever we could. Whatever happened, whether in victory or defeat, I knew England would never be the same.

One evening in mid-August, while Gershwin slept on my lap, twitching and purring, I pondered what I'd do when the inevitable happened. I don't have children. No spouse. No responsibilities. Why, then, I asked myself, should I consume rationed food, avail myself of needed medicines and occupy a much-desired flat, when many have so little now—and will have less after the bombings? Even if it ends in our favour, all will be poorer. Then I harkened back to August 1918. Two of my buddies from the Kicking Mule had manoeuvred their aircrafts between several German aircraft, intent on shooting me down. This selfless act cost both their lives. It saved mine. Why shouldn't I act similarly? A sacrifice by other means. Only then could I deservedly say, *I had a life well led.*

Epilogue

In this the final chapter, the summing up—what I've labelled the epilogue—where I try my damnedest not to mimic contemporary authors who write confusingly, thinking their efforts sublime. As a novice author, I've judged the quality of my writing mainly by what I removed without losing anything. Instead of describing more personal events, I've taken several steps backward, proffering what I've learned and what's eluded me the past forty-five years.

Always been interested in human inadequacies—mine and others', but mine in particular, from both inside and outside a bottle. When we let ourselves down, no one knows but us. We regroup and trudge forward to something we think is just as good. It may be better, but not usually. We settle. We make do. We convince ourselves we've made the proper decision.

By virtue of not having lived in America for over twenty years, I've developed ideas and shared experiences with people of varying backgrounds and different nationalities. They taught me much. Knowledge I wouldn't have acquired had I remained cocooned in the States. The most important lesson was that mental poverty of interests is the worst kind of poverty anyone can have. Success or money doesn't remove it. An attractive woman by one's side compensates, but only slightly. She usually proves temporary. Those lacking mental curiosity don't travel because the depravity follows wherever they go. They won't experience anyone or anything unique because they can't. They won't question their life because they can't imagine it differently. And possessing few, if any, interests, they find it difficult to converse intelligently or comfortably with anyone unfamiliar. To compensate, they surround themselves with people like themselves, equally impoverished.

Relationship inadequacies between partners are complex, fraught with peril. Admitting personal vulnerabilities can deepen and solidify it, but that internal conflict—of offering too little or too much—persists. Stating opinions, expressing desires, questioning motivations brings initial praise but over time spawns concern and disinterest that descends toward disappointment, leading eventually to rejection. That golden euphoria of trusting another, of believing in another so completely, never happened for me. Got damn close a few times. Failed to break away to win the ribbon, I suppose. So did what I vowed never to do: settled wistfully into the past, my personal past, where events, friends, even places appeared more honest and more pleasant than they had before—but, if honest with myself, probably never were. Real or imagined, memories sustained me. Only with the briefest of hindsight can I appreciate that, because the present is so miserable and the future so bleak, there was nowhere really to turn except the past.

The Jazz Age, that mythical period in our recent collective history, while provocative, has been elevated unduly to heights difficult to justify. If a work of fiction, the era would fit nicely as a literary non sequitur. It's venerated today, I believe, not so much for what the era defined, but for what lay on either side—the catastrophe of world war on one side and worldwide economic collapse, followed by a more deadly conflagration, on the other. Senseless good times, hedonism and drink, folly and irresponsibility rose from the ashes, dominating our lives. The decade's purpose seemed twofold: blotting out the past, while serving as a foil for the future.

How politicians and nations deal with troubling issues within their country and the world isn't far removed from how individuals mismanage their affairs. The key difference is grandstanding politicians and roguish nations inevitably court disaster that's never dealt with until millions have died. Ineffective leaders serve far too long, running the world while bluffing all the while. Those in power after 1918 took us for granted and, by doing so, let down the entire world. Their uplifting ruminations about mankind's progress, a home fit for heroes, were mere canards. It's as if they knew the inevitable would inevitably happen but acted in a muffled kind of way that made us believe in a new world, a world of peace, a world without war. Cursory non-aggression treaties, tonnage limitations on warships, and a peace pact outlawing war outwardly signified stability and commitment to anyone who paid attention. Few of us did. But, in the end, these leaders failed because they either couldn't acknowledge, or ignored, their own fallibility. Their lives, so replete with unbroken successes, had left them arrogant and overconfident. Wasn't long before new imperialists on opposite sides of the globe abandoned signed agreements or ripped them up, causing the entire world to retrench. But nothing could be done to halt these juggernauts of aggression. The world had done nothing for far too long. Feeble attempts proved gutless. Politicians lacked the will to enforce and the stamina to lead. I've spent many late evenings the last five years sitting in my garret, nursing any number of double neats, asking the same question: where was the world, and where the hell was the League of Nations when Germany rearmed, igniting the long fuse to 1939? I doubt I'll learn the answer before the bombing and invasion of England gets underway.

Long before the war, perhaps before the last one, society was stumbling ever so slowly, perhaps reluctantly, toward stifling the instincts, passions and feelings of individuals. New indicators, pointing toward a meaningful life, replaced the old ones. Society substituted accumulating things for possessing a genuine sense of self and of life; substituted drugs for natural sensations; substituted mindless parties for intellectual conversation; substituted self-interest for friendship; and substituted competitive team sports for the fine arts. In the intervening years, these replacements worked their black magic, impoverishing the many while enriching a few. All are worse off because of it.

So, you may ask: *Why, then, Mr Travers, do you continue with the jazz you love and play so well?* Answer: selfishness. Playing is far less important for what it does and means to others than for how it enriches my life. It allows me to make things poignant. To make things different. To make things beautiful. To make things new. To make things free. To make things sensual. And to make *me* whole. Not doing so would render my life ordinary and second-rate. Never aspired to boredom.

Harkened back to my earliest days in Montparnasse to select the title for this writing effort. The young female dressed in a French aviator's uniform who seemed besotted with me for a month or so, made an impression. One that endured. She not only enjoyed the music, she often sat nearby wherever I ate dinner or nursed a drink. We talked only once. No, that's incorrect. She spurned my attempt, requesting I listen instead. Did what she asked: *Please remember my lovely jazzman, that the universal language isn't love but loneliness.*

At the time, I thought she was either a genuinely sad person recovering from a war loss or another Montparnasse philosopher anxious for attention. So, I didn't give her comment much credence. Wasn't germane to what I expected from life. Try as I might to forget, it kept returning to me in the intervening years. That simple declarative sentence achieved a level of importance I wouldn't have thought possible.

Loneliness really is something everyone shares. It *is* universal. A deep feeling that's never timid about making its presence known. Whether after the euphoria of success or in the agony of defeat, we sit alone, contemplating the how and the why. A celebratory toast and a slap on the back demand reflection as much as failure or rejection requires contemplation. Loneliness offered a kind of solitude where I could ask questions. Often come up empty, but I never regretted asking. Well-intentioned intrusions by others during difficult times never lessened the need to be alone. Loneliness, it seems, is the most effective way—and for me the only way—to mourn the death of friends, to reminisce about the past or to understand life. Many believe loneliness is unpleasant, a state of being that must be avoided if possible. If that's what a majority believe, and adhere to it faithfully, well, then fine, splendid. I never could. The aviator's prescience, her ability to appreciate how loneliness not only defines but assists in understanding the absurdity of our existence, has served me well.

If I sound bitter, I'm not. I participated in the jazz epoch. Present at the creation. A frivolous yet energised era full of over-indulgence that won't be repeated. Disrupting societal conventions, turning away from the past, and ignoring the future happened because the war happened. But the feeling of happiness ended too, collapsing under its own weight. My experiences are not unique. The good, the bad, the disillusioning, and the indifference didn't happen to me alone. I cannot be singled out for general misfortune. Only joined the ranks of many others in life, those who came before me, those of my own time, and, I dare say, certainly those of generations unborn. So, I'll try to continue on in a diminished world, struggling to make sense of it all.

CONCLUSION

It was after midnight when they finished. Fiona removed her glasses, rubbed her eyes and ran her fingers gently through her hair. Peter sat pensively at the opposite end of the sofa, taking a last sip of his martini and staring at the wall.

"I know we read the epilogue at Atkinson's, Fiona, but it makes sense now. Sadly, and a bit pathetically, it all makes sense."

"The title's appropriate. Bet many today are only steps away from Travers's experience."

"We should feel fortunate, then. Damn fortunate."

"Suppose I should, Peter. Suppose I should."

"You know, Fiona, a woman in Helena's situation today would have told her fiancé she was deeply in love with someone else. Though painful for Robbie, it would have worked to both their advantages. Wouldn't have endured a loveless marriage full of angst and deceit. Should have disregarded her mother's opinions entirely and married Travers. Yes, she may not have been as socially connected or even accepted, for that matter, but happier and more contented. Robbie would have found another woman—the colonel's daughter or the sister of a rich friend from Cambridge. Even in his dishevelled state years later, he found someone who took him in."

"Shows the stranglehold society's mores had on women back then. Robbie would have been forgiven if he ignored his commitment and turned away from Helena. Excuses would have been made: *It was the war ... The years of imprisonment ... He had made too rash a decision when a young man ....* The hypocrisy, sheer, utter hypocrisy."

"I'm also struck by the tragic similarities between Véronique and Helena: neither ever knew Travers's plans. Their actions unknowingly severed the possibility …."

"When they met in Harrogate by 'planned accident,' why didn't Travers tell her he'd boarded the train, planning to confront her mother and ask Helena to marry him? Do you think he remained crippled, emotionally, and couldn't—or, noting the passage of time, thought it irrelevant and meaningless?"

"We'll never know, Fiona. The reason for beginning, for nurturing, for ending or even resurrecting a relationship is problematic. Difficult to rationalise, more difficult to decipher. Hate to say it, but that's probably why the most important—and perhaps only—relationship you can have, is with yourself."

"I've never known you be so profound, Peter."

"What I understand about life so far is from what others have learned: *The brighter the smile, the darker the past.*"

"There's that idealistic cynicism. Was beginning to worry a bit. Thought you'd lost it. Still, I think you'll make great use of it one day."

"I thought his views on the Second World War were evocative. Got a full dose of his disgust and disillusionment."

"I agree, Peter. Definitely. The giddy foolishness of writers, artists and jazzmen between the wars—at their absolute worst—injured only themselves, their loves, or their families, didn't it? World statesmen let down everyone. Long in the tooth with power, yet ill-equipped to deal with what their appeasing ineptness wrought."

"Yeah. And their failure to prevent or, at a minimum,

cordon off aggression made world war inevitable. As Travers said: *Where was the world in 1935, when Germany's rearming ignited the long fuse to 1939?"*

As Peter opened the leather valise to return the neatly organised manuscript, he heard a crackling paper-like sound from what he thought came from inside the bottom cover. He looked closer, to discover the thick leather sleeve had a razor-thin, almost undetectable slice about eight inches long. He slid his two fingers underneath and removed a brittle, yellowed piece of paper, folded into thirds.

"Fiona, oh, my God, look at this! The auctioneer and Atchison probably never saw it. Didn't know it was there."

He read the content aloud.

26 August 1940

My Dear Mrs Ashley-

I want to first thank you for being an exquisite landlady, especially for the diplomatic manner in which you defended my lifestyle against the highfalutin affluence residing on Cheyne Walk. I've always appreciated your helpfulness. Your generosity, it seemed, knew no bounds. It is in this spirit that I am asking a final favour. The bombing of London becomes a certainty since the fall of France. I learned a valuable lesson during the last war, a philosophy I've followed every day since: prepare for the unexpected. Therefore, in this spirit, I'm requesting you to take charge and dispose of my meagre belongings to any family in need, should something happen. By belongings, I mean everything—furniture, clothes, kitchen utensils, artwork, typewriter, books, even music. In the large brown envelope is a substantial sum of cash; it's all I have, actually, except for what I carry for everyday use. Please take what's required to cover outstanding rent payments and preparing the garret for a possible tenant. I request any remaining money be given to the parents of young Thomas Kay in Flat 14. They can use the money as they see fit; however, my intention was to have it fund the young lad's education, including the purchase of a much-coveted trombone with corresponding music lessons at the Royal Academy.

I understand this may appear too personal a request, but you must understand, Mrs Ashley, I don't know anyone else I trust as much as you. Thank you again for your extended courtesies. And please, look after Gershwin should something happen. Unlike many Londoners who fear for their pets, I cannot euthanise the ol' girl. Never liked playing God. Believe she should have as much a fighting chance at life as the rest of us.

With my deepest respect,

William Travers

PS: The leather portfolio contains a manuscript concerning my early days in Paris and London. Spent days and months, that turned eventually into years, toiling over it. Cannot rewrite my life. All I can do is elucidate what happened and why. And, while I recognise it never will be published, it offers valuable insights into what history refers to as The Jazz Age. Most revealing, perhaps, is the paradox between the artificial hubbub of the Roaring Twenties, its aftermath, and the natural loneliness of life.

I request the entire manuscript be forwarded to a dear friend from long ago: Helena Bolton-Leigh, Ure Manor

House, Askrigg under Scar, North Riding.

"Well, I'm damned. That explains how it ended up in the Bolton-Leigh estate auction."

"And also opens a wide door to a bundle of questions."

"The first one being, what happened to Travers?"

Travers's fate continued to bother Peter. Why did the manuscript end in 1940? Did he and Helena ever meet again? When did the Bolton-Leigh family acquire the manuscript? His need for answers became an obsession in the weeks that followed. He began by reading *The Times* from its online archives. Starting in early May 1940 with what became known as the Fall of France, Peter read every issue twice—from beginning to end—desperate to find the slightest mention of Travers. Did advertisements from jazz gigs in Soho mention WT's Alley Cats? Besides busking, had he joined the band of another posh London hotel?

Never overly enthused about her husband's penchant for historical research, Fiona soon tired of his all-consuming thoroughness. Wasting too much time on an inconsequential matter. She thought the manuscript should be donated to an archive so they'd both be done with it. Let the archives staff research Travers if they felt inclined. That's why they're paid. Hours turned into days. Days into weeks. Weeks into months. Nothing. But all the while Fiona's frustrations grew, her patience thinned. When not working, she always found a way not to remain home.

Finally, a kernel of information. An article from early August 1940 summarised the findings of a local journalist. It seemed he had walked throughout the streets of London and asked people their thoughts on the impending attack and what, in particular, they were doing to prepare. A diverse group from various professions were included, from schoolteachers and retail clerks in Mayfair and Whitechapel to green-grocers and bankers in St John's Wood and the City. The journalist also included opinions from those in non-traditional vocations, such as street performers, buskers, and musicians. His survey didn't neglect the homeless either. Luckily for Peter, one of many street musicians interviewed was, in fact, William Travers. His comments offered a unique and personal perspective: *My AOE (area of entertainment) is on Albert Bridge, not by but on, in the middle. It's near my garret so it's also convenient. I've played for university cotillions, in army officer's clubs, in a Paris brothel, in a jazz band at exclusive clubs and private mansions, as well as with dance orchestras in London's grandest hotels and parties at sprawling country estates. Even had my own band, WT's Alley Cats. I've played for those with money. I've played for those without money. Performing during war will be different. Never done that before. And when I say during, I mean just that, while the bombs drop, buildings burn and the sky turns red. Not going to hide. Not going to panic. Jazzin' during the carnage may help a few. It certainly will comfort me. Keep me calm. Keep me focused. If I 'buy' it, so be it. My best friends and thousands of others 'bought it' over twenty years ago, on the first merry-go-round. Won't lose my place in line this time.*

Peter thought it provocative that, of all the people surveyed, the reporter editorialised about one person: *Upon reflection, it appears Mr Travers possesses either the fortitude of someone who lacks control, or a cynical idealism that's hardened since the last war and the passage of time. Whichever is the case, we wish him well and much luck.*

Thrilled with his discovery, Peter allotted any available time to re-reading and canvassing appropriate newspapers from the era. Three weeks later he landed another success. An article in the 16 September issue of a neighbourhood newsletter-type circular described what today would be termed a 'human interest story', amidst the unfolding horror of the Blitz. As people ran from damaged homes and businesses, looking for shelter, some reported seeing a well-dressed, middle-aged man standing in the middle of Albert Bridge playing a saxophone. He seemed undeterred by the air-raid sirens, searchlights, and falling bombs. The article also revealed a small piece of additional information: *As the smoke-filled skies over London competed with the yellow-orange flames rising high on the horizon in and around Fulham, Chelsea and Westminster, this either brave or mentally disturbed man continued playing, relishing in the rhythms of hot jazz from long ago.*

While many people could have seen fit to ignore the surrounding dangers and played an instrument, Peter thought few would be playing the sax. Fewer would be blowing jazz numbers from twenty years earlier. The article's ending revealed another important piece of information. Sometime after two or three in the morning, when weather forced *Luftwaffe* bombers to return to home airfields, a lady running across Albert Bridge reported to police a fully assembled saxophone was leaning against its opened case, sitting on the ground in the middle of the bridge. No one she encountered crossing to the other side knew to whom it belonged.

"Think the police took it as evidence? In case something untoward had happened?"

"Come on, Peter. You think the police bothered with something like this while London's burning and the nation's fighting for survival? I mean, really."

"Crimes occurred in wartime. You don't think once war is declared everyone becomes honest and forthright, living by the sentiments expressed in *Jerusalem, Rule Britannia* and *Pomp and Circumstance*? Don't think so."

"Okay, I see your point. So, what are you going to do?"

"I'll ring the Metropolitan Police—Scotland Yard. Can't hurt any. So, what if, after hanging up, the guy on the other end thinks I'm a nutter? He doesn't know me. Bet they receive inquiries like this lots of times. Some probably are more bizarre than mine."

After many false starts lasting several days, he finally reached someone at the Metropolitan Police who provided helpful information. He was advised to contact Westminster Coroner's Court. Part of that office's remit was to keep any evidence dealing with unexplained or sudden deaths. He sent an email but after five days hadn't received a reply. Tried calling but was 'greeted' with only a series of prompts—press one for this, press two for that. None of the five choices seemed appropriate. He decided to write a letter as a last resort. If he didn't receive a response, his only remaining option was to travel to London and visit in person. Fortunately, fifteen days later he received a written response. After reading it, felt he was playing the game, 'Where's Wally'. In 1989, to honour the fiftieth anniversary of the beginning of Second World War, all 'human interest' artefacts surrounding the Blitz were transferred to the Museum of

London, London Wall, Barbican.

Feeling a bit perturbed and admitting to himself it was a long shot Peter remained determined and rang up the museum. His first four attempts failed. He got through on the fifth. The head curator for three-dimensional objects told Peter he'd have to do some research, check the database, donation and transfer records, even the extensive collection backlog. He'd let Peter know what, if anything, he found. He cautioned Peter that it could take several days, perhaps weeks. True to his word, the curator called fifteen days later. Peter put down the receiver and looked at Fiona.

"Guess what? They have a saxophone and a man's washbag! Both were transferred from the Coroner's Court to the Museum thirty years ago. Not knowing anything about it, except that it was retrieved during the Blitz, the Museum staff placed it in the collection backlog. With no meaningful provenance and of questionable relevance, they've never done anything with it. In fact, the curator said he thought the Coroner's Court was having a cleanout and found the fiftieth anniversary offered the perfect excuse to unload what it considered useless clutter."

"If what we have relates to that instrument, it won't be 'useless clutter' any longer. What's next, then? Travel to London?"

"If you don't mind."

"The last eight months I've had to painstakingly listen to every kernel you found about Travers. Why would I abandon the cause now? It'd be similar to someone who announced they were no longer drinking alcohol right before their spouse surprised them with a vintage bottle of French champagne."

"You seem preoccupied with your phone today. Expecting a text from your investment advisor to liquidate everything?"

"Don't be daft. Just bored. Forgot my book. Tired of looking out the window. And those loud, obnoxious women from Hartlepool drinking Prosecco from plastic cups isn't helping. I wish you'd secured a quiet coach. Also wasn't counting on missing the train from Leeds, forcing us to leave from Northallerton. Just prolongs everything."

"Don't worry. Our appointment with the curator isn't until four. We'll have plenty of time after arriving. At least two hours, provided we're on time. We'll take the Hammersmith & City Line to Barbican and then it's a ten-minute walk to the Museum of London. Shouldn't be bad at all. To celebrate our hoped-for success, we'll have drinks at the Connaught and a romantic dinner at Andrew Edmunds. But I agree with you about the quiet coach. Sorry. Wasn't any room. Sold out. Other passengers must have received a warning and took pre-emptive measures.

After the curator obtained their signatures, he instructed them to walk down the hall to the third room on the left. The objects would be lying on the table. The only items Peter and Fiona were permitted to have in the room were loose sheets of paper, a pencil and a camera. Coats, handbags, briefcases, mobile phones, ink pens: all had to be checked at the front desk.

Excited, but filled with trepidation, Fiona and Peter walked down the hallway and entered the room. Sure enough, an instrument case and a badly preserved leather washbag were the only two items on the table. Peter walked over and opened the case. He felt the zeitgeist immediately. It was Travers's alto sax. The shine was gone, the finish badly tarnished, but the distinct smell of cork grease, lubrication oil and wooden reeds remained. Peter unsnapped the corner storage pocket to reveal a gold mouthpiece, a box of no. 2 reeds and a wrinkled, yellowed envelope with All Is Lost handwritten on the outside. Peter handed it to Fiona. She opened the envelope, unfolded the paper and began to read.

The passage of time determines which memories are kept. My memories, the ones I choose to remember, are stuffed with elation and sadness, honour and unfaithfulness, love and hate, truths and lies, and loneliness. The greatest of these is loneliness. I remember far, far back, as if the days of terror in the skies over France had been but fulsome nightmares. I thought their awfulness had been purged. I was wrong. They'd been there all the time: buried, hidden, waiting to illuminate my entire being. Absent only a catalyst. This new war brings the same carnage of old. The same hopelessness. The same futility. I had hoped Véronique and Helena would have been cures in the intervening years. The best they could be, the only thing they could be, were tonics, temporary elixirs. Betrayal from one and loyalty from another to another. They, too, had desires and obligations. A life that couldn't include me. The future offers nothing but what the past has bestowed already. I can't relive it. I won't relive it. All is lost. Sirens are sounding. Bombs are dropping. The noise is deafening. The sky's turning yellow-orange. The gig is up.

Out of a deep, abiding respect for Travers, Peter assembled the instrument and leaned it against the opened case. He and Fiona stepped back and stared at the ensemble, imagining the syncopated rhythms that had blown through that horn. Peter unzipped the leather washbag and emptied its contents on the table: a Cartier Tank watch, a Dunhill lighter, a silver Yard-O-Lead fountain pen, a much-yellowed silk scarf and two stunning black-and-white photographs. One identified as *Véronique, Paris (1921)* by Man Ray, the other was a simple but artistic photo of *Helena, Pendragon Castle (1922)*. Two alluring photos of women he'd loved. There was the proof. It was Travers's sax. They disassembled the instrument and returned it to the case but left the contents of the washbag on the table, believing the museum's staff probably would re-inventory its contents.

The couple retrieved their checked items from the front desk. Fiona needed the lavatory so she left her coat, hat and handbag with Peter in the lobby. Minutes later Fiona's phone, which she had left atop her handbag, pinged: a text. Peter read the message: *Champagne on ice. Waiting to launch your new life. Outside the building. How did he take it?*

Peter stood, motionless. Hurt confusion covered his face. He began pacing the room. Just then Fiona returned, refreshed and effervescent. Peter approached from the opposite end of the lobby.

"A text came while you were down the hall."

"Wonderful, darling. Anything important?"

"You tell me. Seems I don't know what I'm supposed to have known by now."

"Whatever are you talking about?"

Gave her the phone. His hand shaking, trembling

uncontrollably.

"Shouldn't have happened."

"That's how Travers began his manuscript. Expect a similar ending?"

"You're making this painful."

"Painful for whom? You? Me? Or the guy or *à la Véronique*, the woman in the car outside? There is a lot in life we don't want to happen, Fiona, but your integrity has been corrupted, made a mockery of my loyalty and showed you're an ugly person. You've made it impossible to go back, to return to the way we were. An utterly damnable situation."

"Stop it. I don't want to go back. Can't you understand? You're content with reading, studying and researching history, Peter—devouring bits and pieces from lives you admire but never will experience. That's as far as life's going to take you. Being a researcher at Sotheby's fits you. Reading *The Manuscript* made me yearn for what I've lost, what I haven't experienced being with you. If this is marriage, I don't think much of it."

"Reviewing the writings of a man who—we think—committed suicide over eighty years ago changed your life. Extreme, don't you think? Certainly reactionary."

"It solidified what had been percolating. Time is a thief. The lockdowns permitted reflection. Forced me to have silent conversations with myself. To find answers about my life. What I want. What I need."

"I see. Unfaithfulness helped you find the answers. Brilliant. So, your daily walks through Valley Gardens were a ruse. Guess he was one of the many after-work activities you seemed so cagey to discuss. You were actually flopping around in bed with another man. Also betting your 'conversation' with Dorothy Smithfield was a lie, too. Even your late night, the day before we bought Travers's manuscript, was another rendezvous. Wasn't it? Makes perfect sense now. Crystal clear. Should have known. Should have fucking known. Last nine months or more, you've been nitpicking me about things you used to like and respect about me. And I'm supposed to willingly accept your deception? Be grateful for it? I'm dumb, Fiona, not stupid."

"You could never be, not 'willingly'. Of that, I'm certain. But my, what you call 'deception,' was actually a way of protecting you. So, yes, it's a gift. Why prolong the pain? Our angst-filled discussions would escalate into arguments, into shouting matches. I knew an abrupt departure would be a hammer blow, but I also thought the sudden shock would wear off quicker than us meandering in concentric circles for weeks, perhaps months."

"Better get along, then. Shouldn't waste any more time. Whomever they are, they're eighty pence down on the meter. So, who is he—or she? Where'd they live?"

"I'm not telling you *his* name. He has a lovely fifteenth-century cottage in Rodmell, near Lewes."

"Try as you may, but the irony isn't lost on me. That's where Virginia Woolf lived and died. Ashes spread in the garden. How appropriate."

"See what I mean—the biting sarcasm? I was right. Though painful, the hammer blow was the correct strategy. I'll arrange a time to retrieve my clothes and other effects. We can talk then, when you're hopefully calmer. I already have my jewellery."

"Never doubted your expert planning skills, Fiona. A true wonderment. Congratulations. As for talking, seems you've made a decision already. So have I."

"Please wait, Peter. I want to tell you how much …"

To regain self-respect and an element of control, Peter ignored her. Simply opened the door and left, without uttering a word. Stunned by his quick and silent departure, Fiona sat down, lowered her face into cupped hands and cried.

"What have I done? What the *hell* have I done?"

Peter descended the steep steps but displayed no interest in scouring the horizon for Fiona's companion. He hailed an ecclesiastical-purple-coloured cab.

"Where to, guv'nor?"

"Albert Bridge, please."

The End

About the Author

Steve earned a BA and MA in history from the University of Cincinnati. After serving five years as a captain/attack helicopter pilot in the US Army's 9th Infantry Division (1980–1985), he worked as a professional archivist and historian for twenty-five years. He has published several articles in peer reviewed history journals in addition to three works of scholarly non-fiction including, *Britain's Battle to Go Modern: Confronting Architectural Modernisms, 1900-1925* published in 2018. His first novel, *Grey, Red, Blue . . . Gone* was published in 2021. He resides in the Yorkshire Dales National Park with wife, Suzanne, a studio potter, whom he met twenty years ago at a Chicago jazz club, and a three-year-old rescue cat named Vesper.

www.blossomspringpublishing.com